YVES BONNEFOY (1923–2
of the last fifty years, was the
poetic prose, and numerous
including studies of Baudela   ..cometti.
Between 1981 and 2016 he   ..ofessor (and then Emeritus
Professor) of Comparative Poetics at the Collège de France, a position
he inherited from Roland Barthes. His work has been translated into
scores of languages and he himself was a master translator of Shakespeare, Yeats, Keats, Leopardi, Seferis and others. He received a wide
variety of literary prizes.

ANTHONY RUDOLF is a poet and the translator of books of poetry
from French, Russian and other languages. He was associated with
Bonnefoy for more than half a century. He founded Menard Press
in 1969, now dormant after nearly 50 years and 170 titles. He is
Chevalier de l'Ordre des Arts et des Lettres (2004), Fellow of the
Royal Society of Literature (2005) and Fellow of the English Association (2010). His collected poems, *European Hours*, was published
by Carcanet in 2017.

JOHN NAUGHTON is Harrington and Shirley Drake Professor of the
Humanities at Colgate University. He has authored or edited seven
books in the area of modern French poetry, including *The Poetics of
Yves Bonnefoy* (1984) and *Shakespeare and the French Poet* (2004). His
translations have been honoured by the British Poetry Book Society
and by the Modern Language Association. He has received the medal
of the Collège de France in Paris for 'distinguished contributions to
the study of French literature'.

STEPHEN ROMER is a poet and the translator of Bonnefoy's
prose book *L'Arrière-pays* (1972/2012). He has served as Maître de
conférences at the University of Tours since 1991. His anthology of
twentieth-century French poems was published by Faber in 2002.
His poetry collections include *Tribute*, *Idols* and *Yellow Studio*. His
latest collection, *Set Thy Love in Order: New and Selected Poems*, was
published by Carcanet in 2017.

Fyfield*Books* aim to make available some of the great classics of British and European literature in clear, affordable formats, and to restore often neglected writers to their place in literary tradition.

Fyfield*Books* take their name from the Fyfield elm in Matthew Arnold's 'Scholar Gypsy' and 'Thyrsis'. The tree stood not far from the village where the series was originally devised in 1971.

> *Roam on! The light we sought is shining still.*
> *Dost thou ask proof? Our tree yet crowns the hill,*
> *Our Scholar travels yet the loved hill-side*
>
> from 'Thyrsis'

Poems
of
Yves Bonnefoy

edited & translated by
Anthony Rudolf, John Naughton & Stephen Romer

with other translations by
Galway Kinnell, Richard Pevear, Beverley Bie Brahic,
Emily Grosholz, Susanna Lang & Hoyt Rogers

FyfieldBooks

CARCANET

First published in Great Britain in 2017
by Carcanet Press Limited
Alliance House, 30 Cross Street
Manchester, M2 7AQ
www.carcanet.co.uk

Texts © The Estate of Yves Bonnefoy
Translations © their named translators, 2017. See page xlix.

The right of Yves Bonnefoy to be identified as the author of this work and of Anthony Rudolf, John Naughton & Stephen Romer to be identified as the book's editors and the authors of their respective translations and editorial texts has been asserted by them in accordance with the Copyright, Designs and Patents Act of 1988. The right of Beverley Bie Brahic, Emily Grosholz, Galway Kinnell, Susanna Lang, Richard Pevear & Hoyt Rogers to be identified as the authors of their respective translations has been asserted by them in accordance with the Copyright, Designs and Patents Act of 1988. All rights reserved.

'Le canot de Samuel Beckett' (Beckett's Dinghy), 'Ales Stenar' (Ales Stenar), 'Le tombeau de Giacomo Leopardi' (Leopardi's Tomb), 'Mahler, Le Chant de la terre' (Mahler, The Song of the Earth), 'Un souvenir d'enfance de Wordsworth' (A Childhood Memory of Wordsworth's): first published in Yves Bonnefoy, *Second Simplicity: New Poetry and Prose, 1991–2011*, selected, translated and with an introduction by Hoyt Rogers (Yale University Press, 2011), copyright © 2011 by Yale University. Printed here with permission.

A CIP catalogue record for this book is available from the
British Library: ISBN 9781784100759

Typeset by XL Publishing Services, Exmouth.
Printed & bound in England by SRP Ltd

The publisher acknowledges financial assistance from
Arts Council England.

Contents

Preface *by Anthony Rudolf*   ix
Introduction *by John Naughton*   xiii
Attributions   xlix

I. 1953–1967

from *L'Improbable* (1959)
  from Les Tombeaux de Ravenne / The Tombs of Ravenna
    (1953*)   3

from *Du Mouvement et de l'immobilité de Douve / On the Motion and Immobility of Douve* (1953)
  Théâtre / Theatre   8
  Aux arbres / To the Trees   20
  'Ainsi marcherons-nous' / 'So we will walk among
    the ruins'   22
  Chapelle Brancacci / Brancacci Chapel   22
  Lieu du combat / Place of Battle   22
  Lieu de la salamandre / Place of the Salamander   24

from *Hier régnant désert / Yesterday's Wilderness Kingdom* (1958)
  Le bel été / The Beautiful Summer   28
  'Souvent, dans le silence d'un ravin' / 'Often in the
    silence of a ravine'   28
  Le pont de fer / Iron Bridge   30
  Les guetteurs / The Watchers   30
  La beauté / Beauty   32
  L'imperfection est la cime / Imperfection Is the Summit   34
  Toute la nuit / All Night   34
  À la voix de Kathleen Ferrier / To the Voice of
    Kathleen Ferrier   34
  'Aube, fille des larmes, rétablis' / 'Dawn, daughter of tears,
    restore'   36
  Delphes du second jour / Delphi, the Second Day   38
  Ici, toujours ici / Here, Forever Here   38

from *L'Improbable* (1959)
   Devotions   40

from *Pierre écrite / Words in Stone* (1965)
   La lampe, le dormeur / The Lamp, the Sleeper   42
   Une pierre / A Stone ('He desired')   44
   Une pierre / A Stone ('I was quite beautiful')   44
   Une pierre / A Stone ('For two or three years')   46
   Une pierre / A Stone ('Your leg, deepest night')   46
   Une pierre / A Stone ('Fall but softly rain upon this face')   48
   Une pierre / A Stone ('Childhood was long by the grim wall …')   48
   La chambre / The Bedroom   48
   L'épaule / The Shoulder   50
   L'arbre, la lampe / The Tree, the Lamp   50
   Le myrte / Myrtle   52
   Le sang, la note si / Blood, the Note B   52
   L'abeille, la couleur / The Bee, the Colour   54
   Une pierre / A Stone ('A fire goes before us')   54
   La lumière, changée / The Light, Changed   56
   Une pierre / A Stone ('We used to cross these fields')   56
   Le livre, pour vieillir / The Book, for Growing Old   58

II. 1968–1977

from *L'Arrière-pays / The Arrière-pays* (1972)   63

from *Dans le leurre du seuil / The Lure of the Threshold* (1975)
   Le fleuve / The River   72
   Dans le leurre du seuil / The Lure of the Threshold   78
   Deux barques / Two Boats   98
   from L'épars, l'indivisible / The Scattered, the Indivisible   106

from *Récits en rêve / Dream Tales* (1987)
   Egypt (1977*)   116
   The Prague Discoveries (1977*)   120
   Rue Traversière (1977*)   129
   Second Rue Traversière (1977*)   130

III. 1978–1988

from *Récits en rêve* / *Dream Tales* (1987)
    The Origin of Utterance (1980*)   135
    The Decision to be a Painter (1982*)   135
    The Artist of the Last Day (1985*)   136
    On the Wings of Song (1985*)   139
    On Some Large Stone Circles (1985*)   142

from *Ce qui fut sans lumière* / *In the Shadow's Light* (1985)
    Le souvenir / The Memory   146
    L'adieu / The Farewell   154
    Le miroir courbe / The Convex Mirror   158
    Passant auprès du feu / Passing by the Fire   160
    Le puits / The Well   162
    L'orée du bois / The Edge of the Woods   164
    Dedham, vu de Langham / Dedham, Seen from Langham   166
    L'agitation du rêve / The Restlessness of the Dream   172

IV. 1989–2000

from *Début et fin de la neige* / *Beginning and End of the Snow* (1991)
    Hopkins Forest / Hopkins Forest   182
    La seule rose / The Only Rose   186

from *La Vie errante* / *The Wandering Life* (1993)
    Beckett's Dinghy   192
    De vent et de fumée / Wind and Smoke   196

V. 2001–2010

from *Les Planches courbes* / *The Curved Planks* (2001)
    The Curved Planks   209
    La maison natale / The House where I was Born   212

from *Goya: Les Peintures noires* / *Goya: The Black Paintings* (2006)
    Section VI, Chapter 3   230

from *La Longue chaîne de l'ancre* / *The Anchor's Long Chain* (2008)
    Ales Stenar   234
    Le tombeau de Giacomo Leopardi / Leopardi's Tomb   240
    Mahler, *Le Chant de la terre* / Mahler, *The Song of the Earth*   240
    Le tombeau de Stéphane Mallarmé / Tomb of Stéphane Mallarmé   242
    Sur trois tableaux de Poussin / On Three Paintings by Poussin   242
    Un souvenir d'enfance de Wordsworth / A Childhood Memory of Wordsworth's   244

VI. 2011–2016

from *L'Heure présente* / *The Present Hour* (2011)
    First Draft for a Production of *Hamlet*   249
    Hamlet in the Mountains   251
    L'Heure présente / The Present Hour   254

from *Le Digamma* / *The Digamma* (2012)
    God in *Hamlet*   276
    The Digamma   284
    The Digamma: A Final Note   287
    The Great Voice   288

from *Poèmes pour Truphémus* / *Poems for Truphémus* (2013)
    Un café / A Café   292
    Les tableaux / The Paintings   294
    D'autres tableaux / Other Paintings   294

Notes on the Contributors   299
Index of Titles   301
Index of First Lines   306

* Date of composition rather than of publication.

Preface

ANTHONY RUDOLF

Yves Bonnefoy's work for well over sixty years has been a two-track adventure in poetry and prose that has few equals since Baudelaire and Leopardi. Few poets have had a 'second' *oeuvre* in prose so intertwined with their poetry, so rich in signs and wonders, so complex and yet so trustful of readers. It was time to bring the two tracks together in one collection. Bonnefoy has observed that poetry, which, unlike prose, 'knows its own mendacity', is 'the memory of truth'. The phrase 'unlike prose' is thus tested in the present volume and might have to be reworded as 'unlike critical prose'. The reason is that this book, like the forthcoming French Pléiade edition of Bonnefoy's work, contains not only poetry as such but also what he himself calls the poetic prose he was writing around the time he composed various groups of poems. His comment has logically to refer to his critical prose, which will form a companion Carcanet volume in due course, containing some of his lengthy and remarkable essays on a wide range of topics including Rimbaud and Shakespeare, Yeats and Borges, Mozart and artists such as Piero della Francesca and Edward Hopper.

The six sections of this book have been created for the sake of convenience and manageability, although there is a certain logic to the ordering. The reader will notice that only the verse (and the alternate prose parts of 'Theatre') have the original French on the facing page. This was for reasons of space but it also implies a logical distinction between verse poetry and prose poetry or poetical prose. Nor is there any escape from the loss, even the violence, entailed in using extracts from poetry books conceived and structured as architectonic wholes. The books are artfully orchestrated ensembles that seek to contain and to reconcile opposing forces. Nonetheless, we hope that the reader will turn to the complete books already available in English translation, all of which contain the French originals.

Poets' prose has been essential to the life of literature in France for more than two hundred years because poetry became, in Bonnefoy's

words, 'a very calculated, self-conscious form, and thus at a far remove from everyday speech – from which it followed that a number of experiences that might have become poetry were left behind by verse and had to seek other means of expression, most notably in prose. And indeed they did. For example, the eminently poetic feeling for nature, which in England is active in the poetry of Wordsworth and Keats, has found its home in French in […] the prose of Rousseau, Joseph Joubert, de Guérin or Chateaubriand.' (from an essay written as a reply to an Oxford lecture, mainly about Bonnefoy, by Christopher Ricks).

Like Rilke's *Duino Elegies*, Bonnefoy's poetry names and celebrates the fundamental things, the simple things, of our world. Like that of Wordsworth, 'a man speaking to men', his poetry incarnates what it means to be a human being – one who thinks life, who thinks death, who thinks art, who thinks thought. At the same time, the extraordinary energy and potency of Bonnefoy's prose, 'sa gravité enflammée', in the fine phrase of Philippe Jaccottet's, are the result of a tension. This tension is, to simplify, between presence and concept: concepts are arrogant excarnations born of gnostic duality, denying presence, finitude and mortality. In *The Arrière-pays* (an excerpt is included in the present volume), the tension is brought to its most extreme, in that it impinges on the poet's own spiritual journey. Italy and its art generate a way of thinking about concept and presence, about abstraction and finitude. There is a kind of synthesis, Bonnefoy concludes, in Poussin (who lived in Rome for sixteen years) and his search for the key to a 'musique savante'.

Conceptual thought, which is 'the original sin of knowledge', always runs the risk of reductiveness to a single aspect (as in science and law), always runs the risk of abstraction or idealisation of what Rimbaud calls 'rough reality', the risk of alienating the gaze, in a word, the risk of dogma and fetishisation. Poetry guards against this by mirroring these dangers in a perpetual agon, for only thus can presence make itself felt in plenitude. 'Poetry is an unceasing battle between representation and presence', Bonnefoy writes in an essay where he confronts these issues and admits to having polemicised in earlier writings in a way which would be misunderstood by some readers. In his introduction to the present volume, John Naughton,

the most important Bonnefoy scholar outside France, explores the manifold implications of the poet's thinking in his poems and the way the poems and prose imbricate each other.

Bonnefoy has commented on the way the eminent translator Pierre Leyris would discuss translations 'word by word, with the patience which springs from the heart allied to the intelligence'. This was while they were both engaged in a major Shakespeare project involving several translators. In turn, the patience referred to is evident in the work of Bonnefoy translators loyal to him over many years, rewarding his support and generosity with their affection, gratitude and best work. Indeed, for this volume, unlike the forthcoming volume of critical prose, it has not been a question of soliciting new translations. We have often had the good fortune to select from several good versions of the same poem and have not hesitated to use the work of different translators even in sequences of poems. We hope that new and existing readers of Bonnefoy will explore the many-sided work of the senior figure who started out as a young surrealist at the end of the war and, for seventy years, continued to produce poetry and prose of such depth and richness. We experience 'The horizon of a voice where stars are falling, / Moon merging with the chaos of the dead'.

Yves Bonnefoy died on 1 July 2016, shortly after his ninety-third birthday. The selections for this volume (poetry and poetic prose) and, to some extent, for volume two (critical essays), were made by him in conjunction with the editors. He did not choose the translations, saying he had full confidence in our judgment. It is a great sadness that he did not live to see the publication of these two books in a language he loved and which he translated into French with such distinction and mastery. This essay and John Naughton's were written before Yves Bonnefoy died.

Introduction

JOHN NAUGHTON

Yves Bonnefoy is widely recognised as the most important French poet of the post-war era and as one of the most significant European writers of the last sixty years. His work is wide-ranging and diverse and includes poems in verse, poems in prose, fiction, literary and art criticism, and translations of Shakespeare, Donne, Keats, Leopardi, and Yeats. Bonnefoy is also the editor of the acclaimed *Dictionnaire des Mythologies et des religions des sociétés traditionnelles et du monde antique*. He has been a regular visitor to the United States, where he has been a guest professor at such places as the City University of New York, Harvard, Princeton, Yale, Wesleyan, Brandeis, Williams College, and the University of California. He has lectured in many places in Europe, as well as in Japan, Great Britain, and Ireland. He has won the Prix Montaigne, the Prix Goncourt, the Prix Balzan, and the *Hudson Review*'s Bennett Award among other prizes and has been the recipient of many distinctions, including honorary doctorates from Oxford, Trinity College (Dublin), the University of Chicago, the University of Edinburgh, and the University of Rome. In 2001, he was made a member of the American Academy of Arts and Letters.

Born in Tours in 1923 and educated there until the end of his teens, Bonnefoy lost his father, a railway foreman, when he was only thirteen. After his father's death his mother took a job as a teacher at a grade school outside Tours and looked after the education of her son. Bonnefoy eventually received an advanced degree in mathematics and philosophy before coming to occupied Paris in 1943. There he became involved in the surrealist circles, met and was admired by André Breton, and edited his own small review, called – with appropriate iconoclasm – *La Révolution la nuit*, after the painting by Max Ernst. He also married and taught mathematics and science for a time. The publication in 1953 of his first major book of poetry, *Du Mouvement et de l'immobilité de Douve* (*On the Motion and Immobility of Douve*), immediately placed him at the forefront of the new generation of French poets. Here was a voice, as even the somewhat

resistant Jean Grosjean admitted, to be listened to with 'the most serious attention'.

Inevitably the question was raised: who or what is Douve? A mysterious feminine presence, her death, physical decomposition, and resurrection put one in mind of the romantic notion enunciated by Edgar Allan Poe that 'the death [...] of a beautiful woman is, unquestionably, the most poetic topic in the world'. And her relation to the poetic narrator would seem also to support Poe's conviction that 'the lips best suited for such are those of a bereaved lover'.

On the other hand, she seems intimately related to the poetic process itself, to the nature of inspiration and to the impact of death on inspiration. Now, death is a category in this poem that involves recognition not only of the fate of flesh – the opening sequence, called 'Théâtre', deals with physical decomposition with a brutal frankness reminiscent of Villon – but also of the inertia and lifelessness of established representation. The constant resurrections of Douve, however, her almost Ovidian metamorphoses, are the poetic expression of the recurrent but ephemeral moment of epiphanous vision, which retreats from what would try to capture or express it: '... à chaque instant je te vois naître, Douve, / À chaque instant mourir'. ('each moment I see you born, Douve, / Each moment die'). Poetic utterance is not equal to the reality it seeks to articulate; what it touches dies from its touch, only to be resurrected as an unreachable domain, inexhaustible and eternally elusive. The French word *douve* means 'moat' or 'ditch'. But the word also contains the notion of opening (*d'ouverture*), 'tenté dans l'épaisseur du monde' ('attempted in the thickness of the world'), and poetry's refusal to resign itself to the impossible is the reminder that *Douve* is associated with the human spirit, with those spiritual aspirations suggested by the English word 'dove', traditional symbol of the Holy Spirit whose origins are mysterious (*d'où*: where from?). *Douve* seems also to be a reflection of Bonnefoy's idea of *présence*, which is the momentary apprehension of the fundamental unity of all being. This experience is always fleeting; it will, Bonnefoy tells us in his essay 'Les Tombeaux de Ravenne' ('The Tombs of Ravenna'), 'be lost a thousand times, but it has the glory of a god'.

> To the extent that it is present, the object never ceases disappearing. To the extent that it disappears, it imposes, it cries out its presence.

As readers of Bonnefoy, it is important for us to note that, however tempting it is to use his essays as keys to the poems, he has always insisted on 'the disparity [...] between the realm of the image and that of the formulation'.

Gaëtan Picon, writing of the new French poets who had emerged after the Second World War, said of them that they felt totally disinherited from all poetic tradition. Marked by war, by a history 'so monstrous that it denies all poetic possibility', the new generation of poets, in Picon's view, felt 'separated from the word it might be, from the universe it might name'. Appropriately, Picon placed the efforts of the new poets 'between the fact of ruin and the desire for reconstruction'. Some of these notions may be felt in certain of the poems of *Douve*.

> *Ainsi marcherons-nous sur les ruines d'un ciel immense,*
> *Le site au loin s'accomplira*
> *Comme un destin dans la vive lumière.*
>
> *Le pays le plus beau longtemps cherché*
> *S'étendra devant nous terre des salamandres.*
>
> *Regarde, diras-tu, cette pierre:*
> *Elle porte la présence de la mort.*
> *Lampe secrète c'est elle qui brûle sous nos gestes,*
> *Ainsi marchons-nous éclairés.*

> So we will walk among the ruins of a boundless sky,
> The horizon will unfold
> Like a destiny in the quickened light.
>
> The most beautiful country sought so long
> Will stretch before us, land of the salamanders.

> You will say, look at this stone:
> It carries the presence of death.
> Secret lamp, it burns beneath us
> As we move along, and so we walk in light.
>
> [translated by Anthony Rudolf]

The first line, on one level at least, seems to speak of a painful period of decline – the end of a certain idealist tradition, the repudiation of the now invalid images of romantic reveries. The heavens, which have collapsed with their images, represent precisely the infinite *imaginaire*, which is the extreme form of alienation. On the other hand, the 'ruins' of the first line of the poem already point to the guiding stone that will appear at the end of the text.

The future tense of the initial verbs is suggestive of the search or quest for meaning in an age of spiritual eclipse. The 'site' of which the poem speaks indicates the ground upon which the future dwelling will be established. This ground is the land of the salamander, spirit of resurrection, survivor of fire and flood, and symbol for Bonnefoy, through its silent, unpretentious adherence to earth, of 'all that is pure'. This land, which a misguided longing may have 'sought' unknowingly, is perhaps nothing so much as the simple evidence before us, its most common features – water, stone, tree – improbable and completely sustaining presences for the vision purified of an unbounded nostalgia, or, put another way, infused with the energy normally expended on transcendence and dream.

The exhortation of the last stanza is the poet's determination to convert the futurity of the projected quest of the first two parts of the poem into a present apprehension of both limitation and plenitude. This intuition is granted, as it so often is in Bonnefoy's work, by the stone, which he views as the 'exemplary form of the real'. Bonnefoy's stones are reminiscent of those sepulchres in Poussin's *Et in Arcadia Ego* paintings, which rise up as a reminder of death's presence even in Arcadia to control an absent-minded absorption in nature's splendours; they have something, too, of those skulls in Georges de la Tour that seem, more than the light from the nearby candle, to be the real source of the illumination on the penitent's face. Recognition of finitude is the 'secret' source of grounding and orientation

in the poem. It is what now illuminates the poetic effort, the act of 'knowing and naming'. The lamp of stone will accompany the poet through all his future wanderings, casting a dark but unmistakable light along his path. The poet will hold tight to this secret source in a kind of marriage with consciousness ('le mariage le plus bas').

> *Et si grand soit le froid qui monte de ton être,*
> *Si brûlant soit le gel de notre intimité,*
> *Douve, je parle en toi; et je t'enserre*
> *Dans l'acte de connaître et de nommer.*

> And however great the coldness rising from you,
> However searing the ice of our embrace,
> Douve, I do speak in you; and I hold you close
> In the act of knowing and of naming.
>
> [Galway Kinnell]

Douve works out a shattering death rite. But if it deals in destruction, if it seeks to shatter the safe enclosures provided by representation and idea, if it means to restore us to a primitive sense of mystery and awe in the presence of the simplest of things, and with death as its starting point, it does so in a largely mythic, a-temporal setting. In short, while the poem sets out to record the devastations of being and the travail of becoming, it does so without incorporating a sense of existential time, or of the poet's own specific place in it. The critic Jean Grosjean complained that *Douve* was primarily concerned with literary problems and that its heroine appeared to have passed through too many universities. Although the criticism is both harsh and misguided, it points to a judgment that will be levelled against Bonnefoy in varying forms throughout his career and to which I will return.

*

Bonnefoy's next book of poems, *Hier régnant désert* (*Yesterday's Wilderness Kingdom*), published in 1958, would in fact deal with the poet's own crisis in consciousness. 'What I accused in myself,' he would write in his autobiographical work *L'Arrière-pays* (1972),

'what I thought I could recognise and judge, was the pleasure of creating artistically, the preference given to created beauty over lived experience'. 'I saw correctly', he goes on to say, 'that such a choice, in devoting words to themselves, in making of them a private language, created a universe which guaranteed the poet *everything*; except that by withdrawing from the openness of days, by disregarding time and other people, he was in fact headed towards nothing except solitude.' This assessment in part explains the repeated attacks on formal beauty that are found in this work, as for instance in the poem 'L'imperfection est la cime' ('Imperfection is the Summit').

Il y avait qu'il fallait détruire et détruire et détruire,
Il y avait que le salut n'est qu'à ce prix.

Ruiner la face nue qui monte dans le marbre,
Marteler toute forme toute beauté.
Aimer la perfection parce qu'elle est le seuil,
Mais la nier sitôt connue, l'oublier morte,

L'imperfection est la cime.

There was this:
You had to destroy, destroy, destroy.
There was this:
Salvation is only found at such a price.

You had to
Ruin the naked face that rises in the marble,
Hammer at every beauty, every form.

Love perfection because it is the threshold,
But deny it once known, once dead forget it.

Imperfection is the summit.

[AR]

Hier régnant désert reflects more suffering and self-doubt than do any of Bonnefoy's other works. It is also the most painfully self-

conscious. Interrogation of methods, the effort to constitute a 'self', the struggle with the question of time, the search for artistic values, for new departure – the problems that pervade *Hier régnant désert* represent the difficult coming of age of the poet and translate his struggle to establish both a poetic and an ethical identity.

As is the case in all of Bonnefoy's poetic works – and their moral dimension resides in this – *Hier régnant désert* seeks to master the problems it presents and to balance one set of forces with another. The painful awareness of entrapment in a dark night of the soul ('I was lost in the silence I gave birth to'), the recognition of the nightmare-haunted child one has been, give way to a renewed sense of self-mastery, since these acknowledgements constitute responses and seek to convert, as Bonnefoy wrote a few years later in his study of Rimbaud, 'what one endures into what one takes on, suffering into being'. The entire movement of this work is to reconnect with that dawn which is 'the daughter of tears', and to restore 'the footstep to its true place'. The radiantly confident poems that end the book, inspired in part by a trip the poet made to Greece, are a sign of this renewal.

Ici l'inquiète voix consent d'aimer
La pierre simple,
Les dalles que le temps asservit et délivre,
L'olivier dont la force a goût de sèche pierre.

Here the unquiet voice agrees to love
Simple stone,
Flagstones time enslaves, delivers,
The olive tree whose strength tastes of dry stone.

[AR]

*

If Yves Bonnefoy's first two books of poetry are marked by a solitary and stoical vigilance, by an icy sleeplessness and constriction, his third book, *Pierre écrite* (*Words in Stone*, 1965), is striking precisely because of its contrasting expansiveness and trust, and because of

the sudden presence of a beloved other who appears in the opening poems of the book – 'smiling, pristine, sea-washed' – like some Venus from her shell, and whose 'frail earthly hands' untangle 'the sorrowful knot of dreams'. A new fullness and confidence pervade *Pierre écrite*, and the poet can exclaim:

> *Nous n'avons plus besoin*
> *D'images déchirantes pour aimer.*
> *Cet arbre nous suffit, là-bas [...]*
>
> We no longer need
> Harrowing images in order to love,
> That tree over there is enough [...]
>
> [Richard Pevear]

Why this confidence? Part of the explanation undoubtedly lies in the maturation upon which the poems repeatedly insist. Bonnefoy's translation of *Hamlet* appeared the same year as *Hier régnant désert*, surely Bonnefoy's 'greyest' book. Some years later (1978), Bonnefoy wrote an important essay called 'Readiness, Ripeness: *Hamlet, Lear*', in which he remarks that Hamlet confronts a world without meaning and hence feels that 'a single act still has some logic and is worthy of being carried out: and that is to take great pains to detach oneself from every illusion and to be ready to accept everything – everything, but first of all and especially death, essence of all life – with irony and indifference'. The 'ripeness' that is so often apparent in *King Lear* reflects 'the quintessence of the world's order, whose unity one seems to breathe', whereas the 'readiness' of Hamlet is 'the reverse side of this order, when one no longer sees anything in the greyness of the passing days but the incomprehensible weave'. One might characterise *Hier régnant désert* as a kind of Hamlet-phase, or Hamlet-crisis. The epigraph Bonnefoy chooses for *Pierre écrite*, on the other hand, is a quotation from *The Winter's Tale* – that play which Bonnefoy sees as 'in fact solar' and which he feels could be 'superimposed on *Hamlet* point for point': 'Thou mettest with things dying; I with things newborn.' Indeed, the new collection, with its rich and colourful evocations of nature and place, of languorous erotic experience, of the blessings of simple domestic life, does seem to constitute a fresh departure for the poet.

In the early 1960s, Bonnefoy and his second wife, American-born Lucille Vines, discovered an abandoned building in Provence, near the Vachère mountain, a building which at one time had been a monastery, and which, after the Revolution, had been converted into some kind of farmhouse. Bonnefoy's attachment to the place and to the surrounding countryside was instantaneous. It was here that he felt he must live:

> Wooded hills, a vast sky, narrow paths that run among the stones beneath red clouds, the eternity of the simple rural life, the few shepherds, the flocks of sheep, the silence everywhere: only Virgil or Poussin, whom I loved so much, had spoken to me seriously of these things. [...] This was the beginning of several years of profound attachment, despite great difficulties, and even a sense of contradiction that was painful to experience. We got rid of the hay and the partitions that the peasants had added after the Revolution to reduce the size of the rooms, and thus, thanks to our efforts, the religious character of what once had been the church was restored, but its authority scarcely lent itself to the daily life we had to lead, even though we tried – in vain of course – to bring this life as close as possible to the being of the snake beneath the stones of the entrance, or the buzzards and the owls and the hoopoes that built their nests in the walls or in the open barns. There was more of the real here than anywhere else, more immanence in the light on the angle of the walls or in the water from new storms, but there were also a thousand forms of impossibility – I won't go into all the turns this took – and so there was also more dreaming.
>
> [John Naughton]

This place is the central element both in *Pierre écrite* and in the later *Dans le leurre du seuil* (*The Lure of the Threshold*, 1975). Its memory haunts *Ce qui fut sans lumière* (*In the Shadow's Light*, 1987). And this is because Bonnefoy will have lived in this locale an experience of the profound oneness of being. This experience is promoted by Eros ('I was loving, I was standing in the eternal dream', one poem affirms). Love engenders a myriad of echoes and associations, and

assures entrance into what Georges Bataille has called 'the continuity of being'. A depth opens up behind things, as is reflected in the poem 'Le myrte'.

> *Parfois je te savais la terre, je buvais*
> *Sur tes lèvres l'angoisse des fontaines*
> *Quand elle sourd des pierres chaudes, et l'été*
> *Dominait haut la pierre heureuse et le buveur.*
>
> *Parfois je te disais de myrte et nous brûlions*
> *L'arbre de tous tes gestes tout un jour.*
> *C'étaient de grands feux brefs de lumière vestale,*
> *Ainsi je t'inventais parmi tes cheveux clairs.*
>
> *Tout un grand été nul avait séché nos rêves,*
> *Rouillé nos voix, accru nos corps, défait nos fers.*
> *Parfois le lit tournait comme une barque libre*
> *Qui gagne lentement le plus haut de la mer.*

> Sometimes I knew you as the earth, I drank
> Upon your lips the anguish of springs
> Welling among warm stones, and summer
> Loomed above the rapt stone and the drinker.
>
> Sometimes I called you myrtle and we burned
> The tree of all your gestures all day long.
> Those were the great brief fires of vestal light,
> Thus I invented you in your bright hair.
>
> A vast and empty summer scorched our dreams, rusted
> Our voices, increased our bodies, broke our chains.
> Sometimes the bed turned like a boat set free
> That slowly gains the high, the open sea.
>
> [Emily Grosholz]

The 'you' addressed in the poem assumes a variety of forms, and Bonnefoy organises the poem around the repetition of the initiatory

word 'sometimes' to suggest the intermittent manifestations of this beloved presence, represented by the elemental realities of earth, water, and fire which are evoked in succession. It is evident that Bonnefoy knows about the historical significance of myrtle – the fact that this evergreen shrub was sacred to Venus, the goddess of love, and that, while connected with resurrection and life-in-death, it is also closely associated with love, marriage and bounty. That the myrtle in Bonnefoy's poem keeps some of its traditional erotic symbolism is confirmed by the fact that the gestures – of bending to drink, of watching the flash of fire – are nicely ambiguous and could be read as suggesting the fundamental 'materiality' of the sexual act itself. But this is the richness of presence, that it leads from one thing to another, that it encourages the poet, as a part of his 'inventiveness', to see hair in fire, or fire in hair, or to feel lips in earth's water, water in lips.

One can identify several philosophical influences on Bonnefoy's poetics, and one of them comes from Plotinus. 'All Being is one', writes Plotinus in his *Enneads*. 'Being is bound up with the unity which is never apart from it; wheresoever Being appears, there appears its unity' (*Enneads*, 4.4.11). In his essays Bonnefoy has echoed this thought, which the poems express less explicitly. The simplest object – the salamander one sees on a wall, for instance – may suddenly become the gateway to an awareness of the unity of all being. 'Its essence', writes Bonnefoy, 'has spread into the essence of other beings, like the flowing of an analogy through which I perceive everything in the continuity and the sufficiency of a *place*, and in the transparency of *unity*.'

The love poems that make up the third section of *Pierre écrite* ('Un feu va devant nous') are among the most beautiful lyric poems of Bonnefoy's oeuvre. He has not, however, forgotten about human finitude, despite his feeling that he has 'reentered the garden / whose gates the angel closed forever' and that his lips have tasted an eternity dispelling all thought of death. A number of the poems that make up the second section of *Pierre écrite* (also titled 'Pierre écrite') are simply called 'A Stone', and they may be read as epitaphs on tombstones that recall the brevity or the futility of human existence. Still, what emerges predominantly in this work is the sense of affirmation

and peace, and the feeling of life being shared. Though death is ever present, even in the place that seems the pathway to unity and plenitude, it is made to share a place with 'the wisdom that chooses living'.

> *Nous vieillissions, lui le feuillage et moi la source,*
> *Lui le peu de soleil et moi la profondeur,*
> *Et lui la mort et moi la sagesse de vivre.*
>
> We grew old, he the leaves and I the pool,
> He a patch of sunlight and I the depths,
> He death and I the wisdom that chose life.
>
> [RP]

The emphasis on aging contributes to the sense of an ongoing and maturing relationship in which recognition of death and limitation is diffused through a tempered acceptance of life. The insistence upon gladness and love points to a change in vision, to that 'change in the light' of which another poem speaks.

> *Nous ne nous voyons plus dans la même lumière,*
> *Nous n'avons plus les mêmes yeux, les mêmes mains.*
> *L'arbre est plus proche, et la voix des sources plus vive,*
> *Nos pas sont plus profonds, parmi les morts.*
>
> We no longer see each other in the same light,
> We no longer have the same eyes, or the same hands.
> The tree is closer, and the water's voice more lively,
> Our steps go deeper now, among the dead.
>
> [JN]

In 1861, Baudelaire wrote a memorable letter to his mother in which he declared, 'with all my heart I want to believe (and with a sincerity I alone can know) that an outside and invisible being takes an interest in my destiny, but what can I do to believe it?' He could also affirm, however, that 'God is the only being who, in order to reign, does not even need to exist.' Bonnefoy's relation to divine transcendence also contains a paradoxical dimension. The poem 'La Lumière, changée', the first stanza of which was cited above, concludes in the following way:

Dieu qui n'es pas, pose ta main sur notre épaule,
Ébauche notre corps du poids de ton retour,
Achève de mêler à nos âmes ces astres,
Ces bois, ces cris d'oiseaux, ces ombres et ces jours.

Renonce-toi en nous comme un fruit se déchire,
Efface-nous en toi. Découvre-nous
Le sens mystérieux de ce qui n'est que simple
Et fût tombé sans feu dans des mots sans amour.

God, who are not, put your hand on our shoulder,
Rough cast our body with the weight of your return,
Finish blending our souls with these stars,
These woods, these bird cries, these shadows and these days.

Give yourself up in us the way fruit tears apart,
Have us disappear in you. Reveal to us
The mysterious meaning in what is merely simple
And would have fallen without fire in words without love.

[JN]

The poet speaks very directly and intimately to a force he seems convinced 'is not' ('Dieu qui n'es pas'). There is a significant difference in the way Bonnefoy experiences this paradox and the way Baudelaire does. Yes, the poem seems to say, 'God is not', but this 'absence' allows the reality that presents itself to the physical senses to assert itself, if not as a divine power, at least with enough certainty and significance as to completely sustain the person who adheres to it. In fact, the poem seems to place in opposition an immanence in which one can live fully and a transcendent order viewed as illusory and impracticable. 'Renouncing itself', this order, like a setting sun, gives its radiance to the real world, thus illuminating its rich and inexhaustible substantiality. The self merges with this simple immanence, refusing the lure of some ideal and imperishable world, governed by an invisible and all-powerful divinity.

Another of the major philosophical influences on Bonnefoy is the Russian thinker Lev Shestov (1866–1938). Shestov confirmed

Bonnefoy's intuition that the rational way in which we receive the world, largely through the mediation of conceptual thinking, in fact impoverishes us. 'Reason', wrote Shestov in his *Potestas Clavium*, which Bonnefoy read as a young man, 'with all its generalisations and its anticipations [...] does not enlarge but, on the contrary, infinitely restricts our already sufficiently impoverished experience.' There are some things, Shestov maintains, 'that it is better not to understand, not to explain. [...] Strange as it may be, it is often better to weep, curse, and laugh than to understand. [...] It does no harm not only for poetry but for prose as well to be, at times, not too intelligent and not to know everything.' And 'Men willingly accept every explanation, even the most absurd, provided that the universe no longer has a mysterious aspect.' The qualities that tradition has assigned to God – his omniscience, his omnipotence, his being always at rest – are qualities one would not wish on one's worst enemy. It would be tiresome to know everything in advance, and the deity 'who can do everything has no need of anything'.

A constant element in Bonnefoy's poetics, evident from the very outset of his career, is his critique of the concept and of the conceptual reception of the world. 'The concept, which is our unique way of philosophising,' he wrote in his essay 'Les Tombeaux de Ravenne' (1953), 'is a profound rejection of death, regardless of the subject it explores.'

> It is clearly always a means of escape. Because we die in this world and in order to deny our fate, man has constructed with concepts a dwelling place of logic, where the only worthwhile principles are those of permanence and identity. A dwelling made of words, but eternal. [... The concept] operates like opium. One can guess by this image the fundamentally moral critique I wish to make of concepts. [...] There is a lie in concepts in general, which allows thinking, thanks to the vast power of words, to abandon the world of things.

The concept is the veil that prevents full recognition of and participation in the world offered to our senses. 'Whoever crosses the space offered to the senses reconnects with a sacred water that flows

through each thing.' Shestov had also posed a fundamental and ironical question. 'Today sensible goods are accessible to all', he wrote:

> The crudest man, even the savage, sees the sun and the sky, hears the song of the nightingale, breathes the odour of lilac and lily of the valley, etc. Spiritual goods, on the contrary, are the lot only of the elect. But what if the opposite were the case: what if spiritual goods were accessible to all, what if everyone could assimilate geometry, logic, and the lofty ideas of morality, while sight, hearing, sense of smell were the portion of some only? How then would we establish our hierarchy? Would we continue, as before, to consider spiritual goods beautiful and sublime and declare sensible goods vile and base? Or would the arbiter elegantium (you know, of course, who he is and where he is to be sought) be obliged to proceed to a transmutation of values?

If one can see something of the sort of transmutation of values envisioned by Shestov in Bonnefoy's poem cited above, it is important to note that the attachment to the gifts offered to the senses is never permanently acquired. It often seems the object of a fervent wish, of an oft-repeated 'prayer', in which an effort of the will is fully engaged, and it is clear that the 'love' of which the last line of the poem speaks only exists precariously. This world of rich substantiality can all at once appear as devoid of all meaning. An abyss can suddenly open up, and 'the voices fall silent in the substance of the world', as Bonnefoy wrote in an essay on Giacometti. An unanswerable question – Why? – is raised with respect to all things, which can emerge not only in fragmented, but even in nightmarish form. Bonnefoy can be haunted by this kind of perception, and his poetry often vacillates between a precarious adherence and a sense of abandonment. A striking example of the kind of 'negative presence' I'm referring to can be found in the poem 'Les Guetteurs' ('The Watchers') in *Hier régnant désert*, where phenomena rise up in a terrifying groundlessness.

Il y avait un couloir au fond du jardin,
Je rêvais que j'allais dans ce couloir,

La mort venait avec ses fleurs hautes flétries,
Je rêvais que je lui prenais ce bouquet noir.

Il y avait une étagère dans ma chambre,
J'entrais au soir,
Et je voyais deux femmes racornies
Crier debout sur le bois peint de noir.

Il y avait un escalier, et je rêvais
Qu'au milieu de la nuit un chien hurlait
Dans cet espace de nul chien, et je voyais
Un horrible chien blanc sortir de l'ombre.

There was a passage at the far end of the garden,
I dreamed that I was walking down this passage.
Death approached with his tall withered flowers,
I dreamed I took the black bouquet from him.

In my bedroom were some shelves.
I entered at nightfall
And saw two shrivelled women standing
On the black painted wood, and crying out.

There was a staircase and I dreamed
A dog howled in the middle of the night
In that place of no dog and I saw
A dreadful white dog step out of the shadow.

[AR]

It is a hallmark of Bonnefoy's moral determination that he tirelessly seeks to convert these moments of frightening uncertainty and to reintegrate the disoriented self into the unity that was lost.

★

Pierre écrite ends on a note of provisional triumph: vision has been purified, changed, 'dredged from night', as the last poem of the collec-

tion puts it. Bonnefoy's next book of poems, *Dans le leurre du seuil* (*The Lure of the Threshold*, 1975), reflects this change, since the work is quite different from anything published earlier. The longest, densest, most complex of Bonnefoy's poetical works, *Dans le leurre du seuil* gives dramatic expression to the concerns of a lifetime: the search for place, the desire for transcendence, the meditation on death and the act of writing, on the role and status of the image. Divided into seven sections of varying length, the work has a continuous narrative flow that distinguishes it from the previous collections, although these too, it could be argued, have their own deeply buried narrative line. Once again, the poem is set in the house in Provence. The dwelling, with its gaping holes and missing stones, with its need for mending and restoration, becomes the symbol of a menaced but indomitable sacred order, the persistence of which the poet sees reflected in the simple, daily realities surrounding him.

The first section of the book begins during a sleepless, doubt-filled night. All the meaning the poet has seen gathered together suddenly collapses, 'avec un bruit / De sommeil jeté sur la pierre' ('with a sound / Of sleep thrown over stone'). But the poet remembers what he has heard about the strange death of his friend, the musicologist Boris de Schloezer. What had he seen at the moment of crossing the awesome threshold? What was he coming to understand, to accept?

Il écouta, longtemps,
Puis il se redressa, le feu
De cette oeuvre qui atteignait,
Qui sait, à une cime
De déliements, de retrouvailles, de joie
Illumina son visage.

He listened, long,
Then drew himself up, the fire
Of that work which reached,
Who knows, a summit
Of release, recovery, joy
Shone in his face.

[JN]

The transfigured vision reminds the poet of a painted image, doubtless of the Poussin painting on *The Finding of Moses*, which is now in the Louvre. The picture seems to evoke a world of peaceful harmony and even breathing, where mind and world are in perfect accord. It is as though longing had been dispersed in the real, and dreams dispelled to allow a simple evidence to emerge in the form of a child. The images in the painting – the boatman, the rescued infant, the Pharaoh's daughter – animate a whole network of verbal associations in Bonnefoy's poem.

The second section of the poem is a summons to the will to combat the seeming futility of the world. Then, in the following sections, the poet returns to the bed he has left and thus initiates the process by means of which he comes to participate in the kind of miraculously affirmative vision his friend has enjoyed and which he sees reflected both in Poussin's painting and in Shakespeare's *The Winter's Tale*, through the figure of Hermione, reanimated from the frozen immobility to which possessiveness and suspicion have reduced her. Parts 3 and 4 of the poem evoke the process of conception. But it is a characteristic of Bonnefoy's work to place erotic experience in the context of the vaster workings of nature and to present it as metaphorical for the search for marriage in writing between the word and the real. He therefore deals with the question of *generation* on both the biological and the spiritual level. The future child promises a new and joyful world, less tormented and rent, and is therefore both infant and sign – the force that 'carries the world'.

> *Oui, par l'enfant*
> *Et par ces quelques mots que j'ai sauvés*
> *Pour une bouche enfante. 'Vois, le serpent*
> *Du fond de ce jardin ne quitte guère*
> *L'ombre fade du buis. Tous ses désirs*
> *Sont de silence et de sommeil parmi les pierres.*
> *La douleur de nommer parmi les choses*
> *Finira.' C'est déjà musique dans l'épaule,*
> *Musique dans le bras qui la protège,*
> *Parole sur des lèvres reconciliées.*

Yes, by the child
And by these few words I saved
For a child's mouth. 'Look, the serpent
At the back of the garden hardly ever leaves
The lustreless shade of the box-tree. His only desire
Is for silence and sleep among the stones.
The painfulness of naming among things
Will cease.' There is already music in the shoulder,
Music in the arm that protects it,
Words on lips that have been reconciled.

[JN]

The last sections of the book, including extracts from 'L'épars, l'indivisible' ('The Scattered, the Indivisible'), published here, register a vigorous acceptance and affirmative certainty the poet had feared was lost.

*

Reading the last sections of *Dans le leurre du seuil*, one might have been tempted to think that Bonnefoy had arrived at a level of acceptance and serenity that made more writing unnecessary. And it is true that his first four books are a kind of theatre of self-knowing, in which the difficult struggle for self-mastery is played out, and to a certain extent achieved. His next book of poems, *Ce qui fut sans lumière*, published in 1987, twelve years after *Dans le leurre du seuil*, makes it clear, however, that the poet had yet another kind of drama to face: the moment of saying farewell to the house and countryside that had meant so much to him for so many years.

Adieu, dit-il,
Présence qui ne fut que pressentie
Bien que mystérieusement tant d'années si proche,
Adieu, image impénétrable qui nous leurra
D'être la vérité enfin presque dite,
Certitude, là où tout n'a été que doute, et bien que chimère
Parole si ardente que réelle.

Adieu, nous ne te verrons plus venir près de nous
Avec l'offrande du ciel et des feuilles sèches,
Nous ne te verrons pas rapprocher de l'âtre
Tout ton profil de servante divine.
Adieu, nous n'étions pas de même destin,
Tu as à prendre ce chemin et nous cet autre,
Et entre s'épaissit cette vallée
Que l'inconnu surplombe
Avec un cri rapide d'oiseau qui chasse.

      Farewell, he whispers,
Farewell, presence that was but dimly sensed
Though for so many years so mysteriously close.
Farewell, unfathomable image that beguiled us
All the more as it seemed the truth almost spoken,
Certainty, when all the rest was only doubt, and though
But a dream, speech so ardent it was real.
Farewell, no longer shall we see you come near us
With your offerings of sky and dry leaves,
No longer shall we see you bring toward the hearth
That profile of servant divine.
Farewell, our destinies were not the same,
You must take that path and we this other,
And between them grows deeper and denser
That valley which the unknown looms over
With the quick cry of the swooping bird of prey.

                [JN]

The sense of leaving this place, of turning toward the unknown, mingles with memories of other moments and other places in the past, particularly those of early childhood. The poet manages to translate the painful sense of loss into a confidence in the unforeseen, and to create from the strains of dispossession an autumnal register that is as haunting as anything he has ever written. Like all of Bonnefoy's work, this book is organised around the principle of death and resurrection, disappointment and resurgent hope, farewell and new departure.

Et ils se disent que peu importe si la vigne
En grandissant a dissipé le lieu
Où fut rêvé jadis, et non sans cris
D'allégresse, la plante qu'on appelle
Bâtir, avoir un nom, naître, mourir.

Car ils pressent leurs lèvres à la saveur,
Ils savent qu'elle sourd même des ombres,
Ils vont, ils sont aveugles comme Dieu
Quand il prend dans ses mains le petit corps
Criant, qui vient de naître, toute vie.

And they tell themselves it hardly matters
That the growing vines have scattered the place
Where once, and not without cries of joy,
They dreamed of the plant that people call
Building, having a name, coming to birth, dying.

For they press their lips to the savour of things,
They know that it wells up even from the shadows,
They go on, they are blind like God
When he takes in his hands the tiny, crying
Body that has just been born, all life.

[JN]

★

Shortly after the publication of *Ce qui fut sans lumière*, Bonnefoy was given the Prix Goncourt de la Poésie in France and the *Hudson Review*'s Bennett Award. In 1991, he published a short book of verse called *Début et fin de la neige* (*Beginning and End of the Snow*), which pursues memories of a winter spent in Massachusetts and of walks in Hopkins Forest. The richly evocative meditations on the snow are always suggestive of the poet's fascination with the possibilities and the limitations of the work he is doing with words.

Et parfois deux flocons
Se rencontrent, s'unissent,

Ou bien l'un se détourne, gracieusement
Dans son peu de mort.

D'où vient qu'il fasse clair
Dans quelques mots
Quand l'un n'est que la nuit,
L'autre, qu'un rêve?

And sometimes two flakes
Meet, unite,
Or else one turns away, gracefully,
Into its humble death.

How is it that daylight shines
In some words
When one is only night
The other, dream?

[JN]

The snow focuses the poet's attention on a quintessentially ephemeral material, an always newly configuring substance. It thus speaks of the precariousness of being and of the instability of every effort at inscription. But this is now a joyful recognition.

Flocons,
Bévues sans conséquence de la lumière.
L'une suit l'autre et d'autres encore, comme si
Comprendre ne comptait plus, rire davantage.

Snowflakes,
Harmless blunders of light.
One follows another, and still others,
As though understanding no longer mattered,
Only laughter.

[JN]

★

Introduction

If one were to try to summarise the central dimensions of Bonnefoy's conception of poetry's role and function during the period from the late 1940s through the end of the 1980s, it might be useful to refer to some of the interviews he gave during this period. In one of them (with John E. Jackson in 1976), Bonnefoy continues to affirm as principal pillars of his poetics the very elements of the criticisms that are sometimes levelled against him, for critics, especially among Anglo-American readers, but including some French ones as well, have been bothered by what they view as the abstract manner, the recourse to artistic and literary mediation, the feeling, as one put it, that in the poetry 'it's always about something other than him and me'.

> By the end of my surrealist phase, I had a sense of a poetry that would not seek to formulate our existential problems – this is the business of conceptual thinking – nor to have me appear in the guise of my own particular individuality, which is considered the standard for truthfulness. [...] in spite of how it seems, this would merely be a presence viewed from the outside, a kind of rhetoric – but rather would carry consciousness in action directly into the field of forces in play, those that determine as much as those that desire, the forces of the unconscious but also those of being, and would compose these forces by withdrawing, the self thereby expanding, deconditioning itself of its name, of its psychological past, by examining the effect of the finitude of fact on the infiniteness of language.

'Poetry', Bonnefoy has said more recently, in 1991, 'is first of all, if it is not exclusively, what frees itself from ordinary preoccupations.' Despite these pronouncements, many readers are struck by the astonishing degree to which Bonnefoy has allowed himself to appear more directly in his poetic work since the late 1980s. Already in *Ce qui fut sans lumière* (1987) there is an evocation of the garden of his youth.

> [...] *Et j'entre*
> *Dans le jardin de quand j'avais dix ans,*
> *Qui ne fut qu'une allée, bien courte, entre deux masses*
> *De terre mal remuée, où les averses*

Laissent longtemps des flaques où se prirent
Les premières lumières que j'ai aimées.
Mais c'est la nuit maintenant, je suis seul,
Les êtres que j'ai connus dans ces années
Parlent là-haut et rient, dans une salle
Dont tombe la lueur sur l'allée; et je sais
Que les mots que j'ai dits, décidant parfois
De ma vie, sont ce sol, cette terre noire.

[…] And I go into
The garden I knew as a child of ten,
Which was really just a short walkway
Between two patches of poorly toiled earth
Where the rainstorms left lingering puddles
That caught the first lights I loved.
But it is night now, I am alone,
The people I knew in those days
Are laughing and talking up there in a room
Whose feeble light gleams down on the walkway;
And I know that the words that I have spoken,
Sometimes determining the course of my life,
Are this very ground, this dark earth.

[JN]

The books that follow *Ce qui fut sans lumière* will give a clearer sense of who these beings are and will explore the birth of the words that determine a life's direction.

It is worth noting that in Bonnefoy's analyses of other poets and artists – and there have been a great many – his attention seems instinctively drawn to the artist's family of origin, and to the relations established there. This analysis, which often focuses on the mother, can be found in his studies of Nerval, Baudelaire, Rimbaud, Des Forêts, and Giacometti, and this scrutiny of his fellow artists has obviously inspired a similar reflection on his part regarding his own origins. This kind of approach appears to draw on psychoanalytic thinking and would therefore seem in contradiction with the declarations of 1976 cited earlier, the ones that insisted that poetry should

detach itself from problems of existence, that the poet should avoid trying to appear in the form of a specific individuality.

The section 'La Maison natale' ('The House Where I was Born') in *Les Planches courbes* (*The Curved Planks*, 2001) provides a striking example of the kind of change I'm suggesting. It is not, of course, as though Bonnefoy had never before allowed himself to appear in his own 'particular individuality'. Although this individuality is presented without sharply defined contours in much of the poetry, it is impossible not to sense it, and some earlier poems, such as 'Les Guetteurs' in *Hier régnant désert*, evoke very specifically the nightmare visions of the poet's youth. Still, 'La Maison natale' offers an extended glimpse of the poet's past, his family of origin, and the birth of a sense of poetic vocation, for the title suggests both the particular elements in a family structure and the genesis in the child of the determination to bring healing to that family, even through words 'that cannot say what they would'.

In an essay on Baudelaire written around the time of *Les Planches courbes*, Bonnefoy returned to the relation between the specifics of an existence and the act of poetry. 'A poetics', he writes 'is in fact involved in a specific existence', but, he adds, it is not 'simply as a text that would reflect it at its level, which is to say from the outside.' Poetry, while it aims at a truth that goes beyond the particular person, will have recourse to 'the everyday cares and dramas' of the poet, but this will be in order to 'disentangle [the poet] from his own limited form and thus accede to what is best in him'.

One can see this dialectic between specific psychic phenomena and its poetic overcoming at many points of *Les Planches courbes*, where early childhood experience is presented with unprecedented frankness. Certain poems, in fact, bear a resemblance to the narrative aspect of so much modern American verse. One of the most moving poems of the section evokes a moment between father and son. This is the second part of the poem:

(*Dans la salle à manger*
De l'après-midi d'un dimanche, c'est en été,
Les volets sont fermés contre la chaleur,
La table débarrassée, il a proposé

*Les cartes puisqu'il n'est pas d'autres images
Dans la maison natale pour recevoir
La demande du rêve, mais il sort
Et aussitôt l'enfant maladroit prend les cartes,
Il substitue à celle de l'autre jeu
Toutes les cartes gagnantes, puis il attend
Avec fièvre, que la partie reprenne, et que celui
Qui perdait gagne, et si glorieusement
Qu'il y voie comme un signe, et de quoi nourrir
Il ne sait, lui l'enfant, quelle espérance.
Après quoi deux voies se séparent, et l'une d'elles
Se perd, et presque tout de suite, et ce sera
Tout de même l'oubli, l'oubli avide.*

*J'aurai barré
Cent fois ces mots partout, en vers, en prose,
Mais je ne puis
Faire qu'ils ne remontent dans ma parole.)*

(In the dining room
on a Sunday afternoon; it's summer,
The shutters are closed against the heat.
The table cleared, he proposes a game of cards.
In the house where I was born
There are no other images to still
The demands of dream. Later he steps out,
And the awkward child takes up the cards;
He replaces the ones that had been dealt
With a winning hand, then waits with bated breath
For the game to begin again. Now the loser would win,
So gloriously that he sees it
As something of a sign, something that might nourish –
What, being just a child, he cannot know – some kind of hope.
But after this their paths diverge. One of them
Is lost, almost right away. And forgetfulness,
Forgetfulness devours all.

I've crossed these words out everywhere
A hundred times, in verse, in prose,
But I cannot: always they well up again,
And tell their truth.)

[Hoyt Rogers]

The poet admits to being haunted by his subject, and the fact that he has tried to treat it both in verse and in prose shows that the subject has an obvious narrative dimension. But the poem also has a connection to myth. The poet does not name himself or directly assume the role of the child. He becomes the speaking 'I' only at the end of the poem when he evokes his status as writer and the problems and choices he is obliged to confront. And if the text contains elements that bring forth a particular existence (the simple house; the remains of a Sunday meal; the game of cards), it tends toward something more universal: the child in his or her relation to a suffering parent. And the deepest concern of the poem is not the card game, but what this game represents, which is to say the child's desire to offer hope to the parent. In this, the poem, while clearly 'personal', attaches itself to a network of mythological allusions that run through the section.

The myth of Ceres is particularly present, especially in the form found in Ovid's *Metamorphoses*. Ceres is searching for her absent daughter, Proserpine, who has been abducted by Pluto. Weary and exhausted, she stops at a cottage to ask for water. An old woman, accompanied by 'a saucy, bold-faced boy', offers Ceres a barley-flavoured drink. When Ceres drinks greedily from the offering, the boy mocks her. In anger, she throws the drink in the boy's face, whereupon he is transformed into a 'starry-spotted newt'. Bonnefoy makes use of these figures, especially the goddess and the child, to suggest the human need to drink avidly from the 'cup of hope' and the response one might give to this need.

> *Et pitié pour Cérès et non moquerie,*
> *Rendez-vous à des carrefours dans la nuit profonde,*
> *Cris d'appels au travers des mots, même sans réponse,*
> *Parole même obscure mais qui puisse*
> *Aimer enfin Cérès qui cherche et souffre.*

> We must pity Ceres, not mock her – and so
> Must meet at crossroads in deepest night,
> Call out athwart words, even with no reply:
> And make our voice, no matter how obscure,
> Love Ceres at last, who suffers and seeks.
>
> [HR]

If, in *Les Planches courbes*, Bonnefoy continues to make use of mythological and artistic references, he does so in a way that makes much more explicit than in previous work his own personal investment in such material. He remembers his mother's 'evasive presence', as her eyes fill with tears and as she searches for 'a long-lost place in the here and now'. What he 'gleans' from her is 'the sense of exile', and it is her presence in his life that allows him to seize immediately the deep significance of Keats's Ruth, 'when, sick for home, / She stood in tears amid the alien corn'.

The father figure in *Les Planches courbes* is seen weighed down by fatigue, his 'only nimbus'. The child often sees him from afar, at the end of the garden, for instance, his gaze lifted 'toward the unachieved, or the impossible'. Bonnefoy has admitted that in choosing to write – and 'not gratuitously, but rather to indicate the values and the things needed in life' – he was 'giving a voice to his father'.

And in a later book, *Raturer outre* (*Beyond Erasure*, 2009), Bonnefoy returns to the father figure in a series of extremely moving evocations, as the father is seen as 'saying no to hope' and as 'wanting only fire for dead wood'.

> [...] *Déjà la mort*
> *Prenait sa main, lui disant de la suivre.*
>
> [...] Already death
> Was taking his hand, telling him to follow.

The book registers the painful feeling of frustration and powerlessness in the child (and later, poet) who wants desperately to 'hear some sound that might have changed life'.

Mais comment accepter de n'avoir pu
Répondre à qui avait désir sans espérance?

Qu'aurais-je dû offrir, qu'il pût aimer?
Qu'aurais-je pu lui dire, qui eût sens,
Le fleuve? Son eau cogne à des portes closes.

How unacceptable, not having known how
To respond to the one filled with hopeless longing.

What should I have offered that he might have loved?
What meaningful thing could I have said to him,
The river? Its waters beat against closed doors.

[JN]

Compassion, Bonnefoy has said in an essay on Baudelaire first published in 2000, is what we feel 'for the suffering of someone or, to put it better, for his deprivation, his defencelessness'.

There is, at the heart of the existence of every human being, a finitude, a relation to death, the drama of which everyone lives and in the face of which there is very little that other men or women can do, if not to be aware of this drama and of the person who lives it: the 'memory' that is preserved of this person, the vigil that is kept over him, the gift of that impalpable but absolute blessing, which is love.

It is compassion, Bonnefoy has said in his book on Goya (2006), that 'creates being' and founds 'an authentically human society'.

*

Raturer outre would eventually find a place in the volume *L'Heure présente* (*The Present Hour*, 2011). A bit earlier, in 2008, another important poetry collection appeared, called *La Longue chaîne de l'ancre* (*The Anchor's Long Chain*). Like the earlier *Les Planches courbes*, the book is made up of poems in verse, as well as of short

poetic texts in prose. One distinctive feature of the volume is the presence of sonnets composed as homages to a variety of fellow poets and artists, including Poussin, Wordsworth, Leopardi, and Mahler. This section of the book is called 'Presque Dix-Neuf Sonnets' ('Almost Nineteen Sonnets'). Some seem in imitation of Mallarmé's famous *Hommages et Tombeaux* poems, written in honour of Poe, Baudelaire, and Verlaine, among others. (Bonnefoy also has sonnets in this section on Baudelaire and Verlaine.) Bonnefoy's poems are a remarkable *tour de force*, but they also constitute celebrations of those figures who collectively form what he has called 'a community', and it is a community to which Bonnefoy feels himself allied, as in the *Inferno* Dante feels himself surrounded by the shades of Homer, Horace, Ovid, and Lucan, not to mention his guide, Virgil. What characterises the community of which Bonnefoy feels himself a part is a common determination to pursue an art exposed to limitations that are recognised and assumed. Of Leopardi, he writes:

Lui, c'est de consenter à tant de nuit
Qu'il dut de recueillir tant de lumière.

It is by consenting to so much night
That he was able to gather so much light.

And of Poussin:

Un vieil homme étonné, le soir venant,
Mais s'obstinant à dire la couleur,
Tard, sa main devenue pourtant chose mortelle.

An astonished old man, with evening coming on,
But insisting on expressing colour,
Late, his hand now become purely mortal.

[JN]

*

From the outset of his career, Bonnefoy has written in prose as well as verse. He spoke later of the existence of a kind of 'debate' in his

more recent writing between verse and a poetic prose – freed 'from the constraints of prosody' – that would allow him to re-establish contact with 'those other dimensions, which had not been able to find their place in the music of the verse' and to 'delve into their as yet unexplored depths'.

The poems of *Douve* (1953) emerged from early work in prose, but it was in 1977 that Bonnefoy's first work made up entirely of poems in prose appeared, entitled *Rue Traversière*. A number of these prose-poems are included in the present anthology, and they exist in a variety of resonances. There is, however, a common preoccupation in many that is explored at length in another prose work, *L'Arrière-pays* (1972). In this autobiographical work, which, unlike the poems in prose, is a book-length narrative, Bonnefoy describes his obsession with the idea of 'another land' – not, to be sure, essentially different from where we are, but some 'key' is missing here that obliges us to live 'on the surface of things', whereas in the other land we dream of 'thanks to a more nuanced language, or a tradition preserved, or to a feeling we don't have (I cannot and will not choose among these things), a people exists who – in a place that resembles them – have dominion over the world [...]' At moments when this 'idea of another land' takes hold of the poet, however, he can feel himself 'deprived of any happiness on earth'. This dream can therefore have a devastating effect on our full participation in the here and now, in the world actually before us, and what the book traces is the poet's effort to bring the world 'over there' into the world right here, for as Plotinus insists, 'there is nothing yonder that is not also here'.

The prose-poems that make up *Rue Traversière* are like the dreams we might have at night, the poet tells us in one of the texts. In 'Les Découvertes de Prague' ('The Prague Discoveries'), the poet develops a kind of discourse on the method to be pursued in the elaboration of a dream narrative. As opposed to the surrealist insistence on an automatic writing, which would supposedly give free expression to the unconscious, the poet insists on the importance of deleting or erasing (*raturer*), of letting conscious attention cooperate and collaborate with what emerges from the unconscious, thus allowing this material 'to grow, to breathe better, through the cautious exercise of deleting, which is only one more way of serving its needs'.

The dream narrative of 'Les Découvertes de Prague' is inserted between two blocks of commentary on method and concerns the discovery in a castle in Prague of unknown paintings from the Florentine School and of a major work by Rubens. A historian goes to the site where in a subterranean realm of the castle the paintings are to be found. He manages to descend into the room by means of a rope, and upon returning, is witness to the collapse of the walls and to the total destruction of the lost paintings. When asked to describe what he has seen by his female companion, he cannot find words other than to say that the paintings were 'different'. It turns out, however, that he cannot define their difference other than to say that there is something 'unexpected' about them, and it has to do with the fact that, having been lost, they have managed to 'remain with each other in the past', which is 'other'. The paintings we know and live with have become a part of our dream; 'they are [...] what we are'.

In the narrative 'Rue Traversière', the poet recalls a crossroads in the city of his youth where one direction leads to 'the ordinary world', while the other seems to go forth toward another world and the promise of a richer, fuller life. The 'Seconde Rue Traversière', however, complicates things in that the narrator recounts having met someone who has also lived in this place and who situates the Rue Traversière in another part of the city. The idea that he has remembered incorrectly enters into the narrator's consciousness and 'makes a place there'. 'Where is this street', he wonders, 'that I know with my whole being exists, and what is it called?' These doubts are the material that allows the Rue Traversière narrative to continue and develop. All the dubious memories of the narrator are the obscure material that he feels 'obligated' to tell to another child, for the writer 'owes meaning to his fellow human beings'.

The narrative called 'L'artiste du dernier jour' reflects on the proliferation of images in human history and fears that, since the number of images produced by humanity now outnumbers human beings themselves, the world is about to end. Unless, suggests the text, images can be 'washed clean' and 'delivered from the muddiness of our reveries and from the attraction for a puff of smoke, a shadow in appearance, and saved from all the work done by desire on some

aspect of things torn from their uniqueness, from their sacredness'. They must cease 'their illicit rivalry with what is' and rather than multiplying endlessly, seek to simply '*be*, the way the tree or the stone are, in the ignorance of their being'.

Images are obviously closely associated with language, and words for Bonnefoy, especially as they become conceptual constructs, fracture the unity of being. More often than not they are empty, attaching only to themselves and not to what they name. This conviction is made clear in the narrative called 'Sur de grands cercles de pierre', in which the poet gives expression to some of the most fundamental aspects of his poetics. God, he tells us in this text, is what is beyond signs. If named, we are left with nothing but 'an image that leads to falsehood'. But when signs withdraw, 'that light that language had taken from us, and that exists in all things, and that passes from thing to thing, shines forth'. The part becomes the whole, 'since the idea of the part is born with our signs'. And so the poet can associate God with pieces of simple, naked stone. Not a particular kind of stone, but an 'unformed mass', found at the bottom of a ravine 'in the unknown, in the night [...] where there is no specific place, no naming possible, not even any consciousness to desire giving a name'. And the simplest scrap of stone becomes 'the starry sky, the galaxies', and the poet recognises that with it and in it, he himself becomes 'everything, nothing, as soon as my own name disappears'. With this kind of 'perception' we can join more intimately with others, from whom language has separated us. It is through a relation to others freed from words that 'only say themselves' that the desire to build a common ground emerges, the need to give the names that create meaning. It is in 'what transcends the sign that the need for signs is born'. This is the mission of poetry, which 'remembers, and dreams, of an original, uncorrupted state of the word, when in the silence earthly things dwelt in before language, the word that came to birth reflected for a moment, outside time, the "unreflectable" dimension of the world'.

Similar ideas are treated in the later work *Le Digamma* (2012). In the narrative also entitled 'Le Digamma' there is a dialogue between two shadowy figures concerning a letter, the digamma, which disappeared from the Greek alphabet. Before its disappearance, there

was perhaps a 'perfect equivalency between speech and things', and when people spoke it was as if 'what was said was right against us, its warmth on our lips'. Could the digamma be brought back into our speech? Alas, one of the speakers says, 'first we would need to repair our minds, waken our hearts'.

In his poetry, and in the many texts that constitute his poetics, Bonnefoy makes clear that his aim is above all ontological, where words seek to elaborate a 'common speech', so that 'no longer being concerned with anything separated, closed off, they dissipate the last enchantments of the mythical self and speak of the simplest of human desires in the presence of the simplest of objects, which is being; they bring together the universal self'.

*

In the final section, we include some of Bonnefoy's playful fantasies about productions of *Hamlet*. In an interview that is included in a recently published book called *L'Hésitation d'Hamlet et la décision de Shakespeare* (2015), Bonnefoy notes: 'For me, it has always been about the words in Shakespeare; they drive the action by themselves with no need for scenery or even for actors.' And he adds, 'I would find it completely natural that a total obscurity envelop the stage and the whole theatre: nothing could be seen, but in the darkness one could better hear and better perceive the breathing of the words in the text.' He concludes by saying,

> If I were directing Shakespeare, I wouldn't be interested in how to stage the play in a theatre; rather I would want to transport the play, with its actors and its action, into crowds beaten by rain or into the mountains, places where his speech, smothered by the noise, carried off by the wind, would be all the more audible in its depths. I mentioned a *Hamlet* played entirely in the dark. Where the audience would be aware only of the voices, and where the actors wouldn't be able to see one another. It's another way of thinking of a vastly enlarged scene, since this darkness is the darkness that reigns between the stars, and it is this non-being upon which Hamlet ceaselessly meditates.

'I would like to unite, almost identify, poetry and hope', Bonnefoy wrote in 1959, in an important essay entitled 'L'Acte et le lieu de la poésie' (*The Act and the Place of Poetry*). This hope is anchored in a deep conviction that the world we are actually living in and the earth we all share offer us what Rimbaud called '*la vraie vie*', the true life. 'That this very world before us exists', Bonnefoy wrote at the very beginning of his career, 'is something of which I am certain: it is, in the ivy and everywhere, what offers us a substantial immortality.' It is in this world that we come in contact with the 'sacred water' that flows in each thing. And what is perceived by the senses is *presence*, a key notion in Bonnefoy's poetics, because through it he means to indicate that in the encounter with presence we experience the profound unity of being. Though ephemeral, these encounters are experiences of eternity, of indestructibility.

'The truly modern act', Bonnefoy affirmed in 1961, 'is to want to found a "divine" life without God.' Acutely aware of all the tendencies in Western consciousness that lure us away from this world, Bonnefoy sees even his own language as a closed, naturally 'Platonic' idiom, in which the physical, sensible world gets replaced by a world of intelligible essences, and in which 'the bewildering diversity of the real can be forgotten, and also the very existence of time, everyday life and death'. His poetry is a challenge to his language to 'celebrate presence [...] sing of its being [...] prepare us spiritually for encountering it', without, of course, being able in itself 'to allow us to achieve it'.

Supreme poet of the earth, Bonnefoy's poetry seeks to bring a world, smothered by abstraction, back to life. Few poets ask to be read with a fuller commitment of one's own sense of wonder, and few will reward more completely the act of serious and patient adherence.

Que ce monde demeure
Tel que ce soir,
Que d'autres que nous prennent
Au fruit sans fin

Let this world remain
As it is tonight:
Let others, beyond ourselves
Partake of the endless fruit.

[HR]

Attributions

This book contains individual translations by Anthony Rudolf (AR), Galway Kinnell (GK), John Naughton (JN), Stephen Romer (SR), Hoyt Rogers (HR), Beverly Bie Brahic (BBB), Richard Pevear (RP), Emily Grosholz (EG), and Susannah Lang (SL). The following list, organised by collection, attributes each translation to its author. For a list of attributions organised by poem title, refer to the Index of Titles.

From *On the Motion and Immobility of Douve*. AR: Theatre; 'So we will walk among the ruins'. GK: To the Trees; Brancacci Chapel; Place of Battle; Place of the Salamander.

From *Yesterday's Wilderness Kingdom*: all AR.

From *L'Improbable*: JN: 'The Tombs of Ravenna'; AR: 'Devotions'.

From *Words in Stone*. RP: The Lamp, the Sleeper; A Stone ('He desired'); A Stone ('I was quite beautiful'); A Stone ('For two or three years'); A Stone ('Your leg, deepest night'); A Stone ('Childhood was long by the grim wall…'); A Stone ('A fire goes before us'); The Shoulder; Blood, the Note B. AR: A Stone ('Fall but softly rain upon this face'). SL: The Bee, the Colour; A Stone ('We used to cross these fields'). EG: The Book, for Growing Old. JN: The Light, Changed. EG: The Bedroom; The Tree, the Lamp; Myrtle.

From *The Arrière-pays*: SR.

From *The Lure of the Threshold*. RP: The River; The Lure of the Threshold; Two Boats. JN: The Scattered, the Indivisible.

from *Dream Tales*. BBB: Egypt; The Prague Discoveries; Rue Traversière; Second Rue Traversière; On the Wings of Song; On Some Large Stone Circles. SR: The Origin of Utterance; The Decision to be a Painter; The Artist of the Last Day.

From *In the Shadow's Light*: all JN.

From *Beginning and End of the Snow*: all JN.

From *The Wandering Life*. JN: Wind and Smoke. HR: Beckett's Dinghy.

From *The Curved Planks*: AR: The Curved Planks. HR: The House where I was Born.

From *Goya: The Black Paintings*: SR.

From *The Anchor's Long Chain*. HR: Alés Stenar; Leopardi's Tomb; Mahler, *The Song of the Earth*; A Childhood Memory of Wordsworth's. BBB: Tomb of Stéphane Mallarmé; On Three Paintings by Poussin.

From *The Present Hour*: all BBB.

From *Digamma*: all HR.

From *Poèmes pour Truphémus*: all HR.

I 1953–1967

From *L'Improbable* (1959)

From LES TOMBEAUX DE RAVENNE / THE TOMBS OF RAVENNA (composed 1953)

The concept, which is our unique way of philosophising, is a profound rejection of death, regardless of the subject it explores. It is clearly always a means of escape. Because we die in this world and in order to deny our fate, man has constructed with concepts a dwelling place of logic, where the only worthwhile principles are those of permanence and identity. A dwelling made of words, but eternal.
[...]
Ever since the Greeks, to the extent that death is thought about at all, it is only as an idea in collusion with other ideas existing in an eternal realm where in fact nothing dies. What is true about us is this: we dare to define death, but we replace it with what is defined. And what is defined becomes incorruptible; it ensures a strange immortality in spite of death, provided we can forget brutal realities.

It's a provisional, but sufficient immortality.

It operates like opium. One can guess by this image the fundamentally moral critique I wish to make of concepts. Yes, there is truth in them, which I do not claim to judge. But there is a lie in concepts *in general*, which allows thinking, thanks to the vast power of words, to abandon the world of things. We know, ever since Hegel, the strength of sleep, the way a system can insinuate itself. Beyond coherent thought, I observe that the slightest concept is the architect of flight. Yes, idealism wins out the minute thinking becomes systematised. What is expressed obscurely is that it is better to remake the world than to live in it in danger.

Is there a concept for footsteps in the night, for a cry, for a stone rolling in the brushwood? For the feeling evoked by an empty house? No, nothing of the real has been kept except what suits our peace of mind.
[...]
I cannot study stone without recognising it as unfathomable, and this abyss of plenitude, this night covered by an eternal light, is for

me the exemplary form of the real. Pride that founds what is, dawn of the sensory world! What is traced in the stone *exists* in the fullest, most moving sense of this word. The ornamentation is in stone. If in the ornate world, form turns away from the physical life of beings, and soars away toward some heaven, the stone curbs the speech that is indifferent and sustains the archetype among us.
[…]

If conceptual thought has turned away from the tomb, let us at least take for granted that it has not been because of its knowledge of death. From what thing perceived by the senses, furthermore, from what stone anywhere in the world, has the concept not turned away? It is not only from death that it seeks to distance itself, it is from everything that has a face, from everything that has flesh, heartbeat, immanence, and as such, constitutes the most insidious danger for its secret avarice.
[…]

In conceptual man there is desertion of what is, an endless apostasy. And this abandonment means ennui, anguish, despair. But sometimes the world rises up, a spell is broken, and as if by some act of grace, everything that is alive and pure in being is given to us in an instant. These joys are a breach made by the spirit, an opening toward the difficult real.

These joys are like the ones felt at Ravenna, thanks to the tombs. And I go back in my mind toward Ravenna as to the source of a light that imposes in and by itself. In Ravenna, nothing tarnishes the purity of this great burst of light, without which, as I have learned, one cannot live; nothing distracts the genius of the tombs from its role as initiator in the destiny of the spirit.
[…]

I walk in this city. That mysterious distance that separates the echo from the cry is rediscovered between my presence and something absolute that precedes me … What is the world of the senses in fact? I said it was a city, because thinking fails to see that being is in appearance and that appearance is sumptuous and therefore an obsession, even with ruins, or with the humblest things, or with chaos. But what creates the distance between the world of the senses and the concept is not mere appearance.

What is perceived by the senses is presence. It is differentiated from the conceptual above all by an act, which is presence.

And by a shifting. It is here, it is now. And its place, since it is not the literal place, its time, since it is only a fragment of time, are the elements of a strange power, of a gift it makes, which is its presence. Oh presence, strengthened in its bursting apart on every side! To the extent that it is present, the object never ceases disappearing. To the extent that it disappears, it imposes, cries out its presence. If it remains present, it is as though a reign were established, an alliance beyond causes, an agreement beyond the word that exists between it and us. If it dies, it opens to that union in absence, which is its spiritual promise and in which it comes to fulfilment. In it, *losing itself*, hollowing out like a wave, it opposes the intensity of its being to the concept and says that this presence was for us. It was only a sign in being. But it was delegated for the good that saves me. Will I be understood? What is perceived by the senses is a presence, notion almost devoid of all meaning, notion forever impure for the conceptual mind: it is also our salvation.
[...]

I will say by allegory: it is this piece of the sombre tree, this torn leaf of ivy. The entire leaf, constructing its immutable essence with all its veins, would already be the concept. But this torn leaf, green and black, dirty, this leaf that shows in its wound all the depth of what is, this infinite leaf is pure presence, and hence my salvation. Who could tear from me the fact that it was mine, and in a contact, beyond destinies and sites, that binds me to the absolute? Moreover, who could destroy it, since it has already been destroyed? I hold it in my hand, I hold it tight as I would have loved to hold Ravenna, I hear its tireless voice. – What is presence? It seduces like a work of art; it is rudimentary like the wind or the earth. It is black like the abyss and yet it reassures. It seems a fragment of space among others, but it calls to us and contains us. And it is a moment that will be lost a thousand times, but it has the glory of a god. It resembles death ...
[...]

Is it death? In a word that should cast its fires over vague thought, a word rendered nonetheless contemptible and vain: it is immortality.
[...]

May I be pardoned for making clear that I do not in the least mean that immortality of the body or of the soul that the gods of former times guaranteed.

The immortality there is in the presence of the ivy, though it shatters time, is nonetheless in its flow. There is a coming together of an impossible immortality and an immortality that is felt; it is a taste of the eternal, but it is not a cure for death.

It's the cry of a bird I heard as a child, at the crest of a kind of cliff. I don't know where that valley is anymore, or why or when I was there. The light is the light of dawn or of evening, it doesn't matter. Through the brushwood runs the pungent smoke of a fire. The bird sang. Rather I should say, to be exact, it spoke, raucous on its misty height, for a moment of perfect solitude. Torn free from time and space, I keep the image of the tall grasses on the slope, which were immortal for that brief moment.

There is eternity in the wave. Fabulously, concretely, in the play of the foam at the top of the wave. Later I sought to build on general ideas. But I come back to the cry of the bird as to my absolute stone.

Whoever seeks to make his way through sensory space reconnects with a sacred water that runs through each thing. At the slightest contact with it, one feels immortal. What can be said afterwards? What proved? For a contact of this sort, Plato erected an entire other world, the world of the Forms. This world here exists, of that I am certain: it is, in the ivy and everywhere, the substantial immortality. [...]

There is no heaven. This immortality, the joy of which can be heard at times in Kierkegaard, has the freshness and echo of a dwelling place only for those who are passing by. For those who seek to possess it, it will be a lie, disappointment, night.

I was saying that the fear of death is the secret of the concept. In fact, it only is, it only begins with the concept. Death, at least its spiritual reality, which is fear in our soul, our existence cloistered in fear, only begins when we leave behind the world of the senses: with that movement toward the abandonment of the world of the senses, which is already the world of the concept.

But the concept flees death very badly. Doubtless it anguishes over its inevitability and seeks to vanquish it. But the vain and utterly false

immortality it invents is, in its very weakness, an acceptance. Fear, denied, but suffered – this is the power of death over the concept. And thus this strange game is made possible, that of fleeing death and yet taking pleasure in naming it.

The concept is an illusion. It's the concept that is the first veil of the old metaphysics. We need to be atheists and unbelievers with respect to it. For it is weak like a god. And let it not be said that in its absence, and in this tattered piece of ivy I held, and in the play of the sea foam, all truth becomes impossible, and every rule. To make a vow to immortality, this is the rule we can live by. There is plenty on this ground to build on.

[…]

One could throw the ashes of the dead to the winds, give in to nature's wishes, and complete the ruin of what once was. With the tomb and in this blatant display of death, the same act speaks of absence and yet maintains a life. It says that presence is indestructible, eternal. Such an assertion, twofold in its essence, is foreign to the concept. What concept could unite an ethical concern with freedom?

Here is the great stone, our servant, without which everything would have perished in misery and horror. Here is life that is not afraid of death (I'm echoing Hegel) and that recovers itself in death itself. To understand them, we need another language than that of the concept, another faith. The concept is silent before them, just as reason is silent in hope.

From *Du Mouvement et de l'immobilité de Douve* (1953)

THÉÂTRE

I

Je te voyais courir sur des terrasses,
Je te voyais lutter contre le vent,
Le froid saignait sur tes lèvres.

Et je t'ai vue te rompre et jouir d'être morte ô plus belle
Que la foudre, quand elle tache les vitres blanches de ton sang.

II

L'été vieillissant te gerçait d'un plaisir monotone, nous méprisions l'ivresse imparfaite de vivre.

« Plutôt le lierre, disais-tu, l'attachement du lierre aux pierres de sa nuit: présence sans issue, visage sans racine.

« Dernière vitre heureuse que l'ongle solaire déchire, plutôt dans la montagne ce village où mourir.

« Plutôt ce vent ... »

III

Il s'agissait d'un vent plus fort que nos mémoires,
Stupeur des robes et cris des rocs – et tu passais devant ces flammes
La tête quadrillée les mains fendues et toute

I. 1953–1967

From *On the Motion and Immobility of Douve*

THÉÂTRE

I

I saw you run along the terraces,
I saw you battle with the wind,
The cold bled on your lips.

And I have seen you break apart and take your pleasure in being
    dead – O you who are more beautiful
Than the lightning, when it stains the white window panes with
    your blood.

II

Summer coming to an end chapped you with monotonous pleasure,
we despised the imperfect ecstasy of living.

'Rather ivy', you would say, 'clinging to the stones of its night:
presence without issue, face without roots.

'Last joyous window pane the sun's claw rips, rather in the mountains
this village where one can die.

'Rather this wind ...'

III

It was a wind stronger than our memories,
Stupor of robes and cry of rocks – and you passed before those
    flames,
Your head square-ruled, your hands split open, and all

En quête de la mort sur les tambours exultants de tes gestes.

C'était jour de tes seins
Et tu régnais enfin absente de ma tête.

IV

Je me réveille, il pleut. Le vent te pénètre, Douve, lande résineuse endormie près de moi. Je suis sur une terrasse, dans un trou de la mort. De grands chiens de feuillages tremblent.

Le bras que tu soulèves, soudain, sur une porte, m'illumine à travers les âges. Village de braise, à chaque instant je te vois naître, Douve,

À chaque instant mourir.

V

Le bras que l'on soulève et le bras que l'on tourne
Ne sont d'un même instant que pour nos lourdes têtes,
Mais rejetés ces draps de verdure et de boue
Il ne reste qu'un feu du royaume de mort.

La jambe démeublée où le grand vent pénètre
Poussant devant lui des têtes de pluie
Ne vous éclairera qu'au seuil de ce royaume,
Gestes de Douve, gestes déjà plus lents, gestes noirs.

VI

Quelle pâleur te frappe, rivière souterraine, quelle artère en toi se rompt, où l'écho retentit de ta chute?

Ce bras que tu soulèves soudain s'ouvre, s'enflamme. Ton visage recule.

In quest of death on the exultant drums of your gestures.

It was day of your breasts:
And you reigned at last absent from my head.

IV

I wake up, it is raining. The wind goes through you, Douve, resinous heath sleeping close by me. I am on a terrace, in a pit of death. Great dogs of foliage are trembling.

The arm you raise, suddenly, in a doorway, lights me across the ages. Village of embers, each moment I see you born, Douve,

Each moment die.

V

The arm raised up, the arm that's turned away
Keep the same time only for our heavy heads,
But when these sheets of mud and verdure are thrown back,
Nothing remains but a fire out of death's kingdom.

The stripped down leg the great wind penetrates,
Driving heads of rain before it will
Light you only at the threshold of that kingdom,
Douve's gestures, gestures slower now, dark gestures.

VI

What pallor encompasses you, underground river, what artery in you breaks, echoing your fall?

This arm you raise up suddenly opens, catches fire. Your face shrinks

Quelle brume croissante m'arrache ton regard? Lente falaise d'ombre, frontière de la mort.

Des bras muets t'accueillent, arbres d'une autre rive.

VII

Blessée confuse dans les feuilles,
Mais prise par le sang de pistes qui se perdent,
Complice encor du vivre.

Je t'ai vue ensablée au terme de ta lutte
Hésiter aux confins du silence et de l'eau,
Et la bouche souillée des dernières étoiles
Rompre d'un cri l'horreur de veiller dans ta nuit.

Ô dressant dans l'air dur soudain comme une roche
Un beau geste de houille.

VIII

La musique saugrenue commence dans les mains, dans les genoux, puis c'est la tête qui craque, la musique s'affirme sous les lèvres, sa certitude pénètre le versant souterrain du visage.

À présent se disloquent les menuiseries faciales. À présent l'on procède à l'arrachement de la vue.

IX

Blanche sous un plafond d'insectes, mal éclairée, de profil
Et ta robe tachée du venin des lampes,
Je te découvre étendue,
Ta bouche plus haute qu'un fleuve se brisant au loin sur la terre.

back. What thickening mist wrests your gaze from me? Slow cliff of shadow, frontier of death.

Mute arms receive you, trees of another shore.

VII

Wounded one, blurred amidst the leaves,
But caught up in the blood of trails that vanish,
Party still to living.

I have seen you at your struggle's end, sunk in sand,
Falter at the edge of silence and of water,
Your mouth defiled by the final stars,
Break off your night-watch with a cry of horror.

O raising in the hard air sudden as a rock
A grand gesture of coal.

VIII

The crazy music starts in the hands, in the knees, then it is the head that cracks, the music intensifies under the lips, its certain knowledge penetrates the underside of the face.

Now the woodwork of the face is falling to bits, now the uprooting of sight can begin.

IX

White beneath a ceiling of insects, shadowy, in profile,
And your dress stained by the venom of lamps,
I find you stretched out,
Your mouth higher than a river bursting far away on the earth.

Être défait que l'être invincible rassemble,
Présence ressaisie dans la torche du froid,
Ô guetteuse toujours je te découvre morte,
Douve disant Phénix je veille dans ce froid.

X

Je vois Douve étendue. Au plus haut de l'espace charnel je l'entends bruire. Les princes-noirs hâtent leurs mandibules à travers cet espace où les mains de Douve se développent, os défaits de leur chair se muant toile grise que l'araignée massive éclaire.

XI

Couverte de l'humus silencieux du monde,
Parcourue des rayons d'une araignée vivante,
Déjà soumise au devenir du sable
Et tout écartelée secrète connaissance.

Parée pour une fête dans le vide
Et les dents découvertes comme pour l'amour,

Fontaine de ma mort présente insoutenable.

XII

Je vois Douve étendue. Dans la ville écarlate de l'air, où combattent les branches sur son visage, où des racines trouvent leur chemin dans son corps – elle rayonne une joie stridente d'insectes, une musique affreuse.

Au pas noir de la terre, Douve ravagée, exultante, rejoint la lampe noueuse des plateaux.

Undone being invincible being reassembles,
Presence restored in the torch of cold,
O watcher always I find you dead,
Douve saying Phoenix I keep watch in this cold.

X

I see Douve stretched out. In the very heights of carnal space I hear her rustle. Black-princes hurry their mandibles across that space where Douve's hands open out, bones without flesh becoming a grey web the massive spider lights up.

XI

Covered by the silent humus of the world,
Shot through by a living spider's rays,
Already yielding to the flux of sand,
And cut to pieces secret understanding.

Adorned for a feast in empty space
And teeth bared as if for love,

Fountain of my death, here and now, unbearable.

XII

I see Douve stretched out. In the scarlet city of air, where branches battle across her face, where roots find their way into her body – she radiates a shrill insect joy, a ghastly music.

With her black tread of earth, Douve, ravaged, exultant, returns to the gnarled lamp of the highlands.

XIII

Ton visage ce soir éclairé par la terre,
Mais je vois tes yeux se corrompre
Et le mot visage n'a plus de sens.

La mer intérieure éclairée d'aigles tournants,
Ceci est une image.
Je te détiens froide à une profondeur où les images ne prennent plus.

XIV

Je vois Douve étendue. Dans une pièce blanche, les yeux cernés de plâtre, bouche vertigineuse et les mains condamnées à l'herbe luxuriante qui l'envahit de toutes parts.

La porte s'ouvre. Un orchestre s'avance. Et des yeux à facettes, des thorax pelucheux, des têtes froides à becs, à mandibules, l'inondent.

XV

Ô douée d'un profil où s'acharne la terre,
Je te vois disparaître.

L'herbe nue sur tes lèvres et l'éclat du silex
Inventent ton dernier sourire,

Science profonde où se calcine
Le vieux bestiaire cérébral.

XIII

Your face tonight illumined by the earth,
But I see the spoiling of your eyes
And the word face has no meaning any more.

The inner sea alight with turning eagles,
This is an image.
I keep you cold, deep where images no longer take.

XIV

I see Douve stretched out. In a white room, her eyes pouched with plaster, her mouth vertiginous and her hands condemned to the lush grass invading her from all sides.

The door opens. An orchestra moves forward. And faceted coarse-haired thoraxes, cold heads with beaks and mandibles, flood over her.

XV

Oh you, gifted with a profile where earth never relents,
I see you disappear.

Bare grass on your lips and flintsparks
Invent your last smile,

Deep knowledge where brain's ancient
Bestiary burns to a cinder.

XVI

Demeure d'un feu sombre où convergent nos peintes! Sous ses voûtes je te vois luire, Douve immobile, prise dans le filet vertical de la mort.

Douve géniale, renversée: quand au pas des soleils dans l'espace funèbre, elle accède lentement aux étages inférieurs.

XVII

Le ravin pénètre dans la bouche maintenant,
Les cinq doigts se dispersent en hasards de forêt maintenant,
La tête première coule entre les herbes maintenant,
La gorge se farde de neige et de loups maintenant,
Les yeux ventent sur quels passagers de la mort et c'est nous dans ce vent
    dans cette eau dans ce froid maintenant.

XVIII

Présence exacte qu'aucune flamme désormais ne saurait restreindre; convoyeuse du froid secret; vivante, de ce sang qui renaît et s'accroît où se déchire le poème,

Il fallait qu'ainsi tu parusses aux limites sourdes, et d'un site funèbre où ta lumière empire, que tu subisses l'épreuve.

Ô plus belle et la mort infuse dans ton rire! J'ose à présent te rencontrer, je soutiens l'éclat de tes gestes.

XVI

Dwelling of a dark fire where our slopes converge! Beneath its vaults I see you glimmer, Douve, motionless, caught in the vertical net of death.

Douve inspired, thrown down: in step with the suns in funeral space, slowly she reaches the lower levels.

XVII

The ravine penetrates the mouth now,
The five fingers scatter amidst forest hazards now,
First the head flows through the grasses now,
The throat is painted with snow and wolves now,
The eyes blow on what passengers of death and we are in this wind
　　in this water in this cold now.

XVIII

Exact presence no flame could henceforth restrain; escort of secret cold; living, through that blood which revives and grows where the poem is torn apart,

It was necessary for you to appear, thus, at the dulled limits, and to undergo this ordeal in a land of death where your light worsens.

Oh you who are more beautiful, and your laughter steeped with death! I dare now to meet you, I can bear the flashing of your gestures.

XIX

Au premier jour du froid notre tête s'évade
Comme un prisonnier fuit dans l'ozone majeur,
Mais Douve d'un instant cette flèche retombe
Et brise sur le sol les palmes de sa tête.

Ainsi avions-nous cru réincarner nos gestes,
Mais la tête niée nous buvons une eau froide,
Et des liasses de mort pavoisent ton sourire,
Ouverture tentée dans l'épaisseur du monde.

AUX ARBRES

Vous qui vous êtes effacés sur son passage,
Qui avez refermé sur elle vos chemins,
Impassibles garants que Douve même morte
Sera lumière encore n'étant rien.

Vous fibreuse matière et densité,
Arbres, proches de moi quand elle s'est jetée
Dans la barque des morts et la bouche serrée
Sur l'obole de faim, de froid et de silence.

J'entends à travers vous quel dialogue elle tente
Avec les chiens, avec l'informe nautonier,
Et je vous appartiens par son cheminement
À travers tant de nuit et malgré tout ce fleuve.

Le tonnerre profond qui roule sur vos branches,
Les fêtes qu'il enflamme au sommet de l'été
Signifient qu'elle lie sa fortune à la mienne
Dans la médiation de votre austérité.

XIX

On the first day of cold our head escapes
Like a prisoner fleeing into the upper air,
But Douve this arrow for one moment falls
And breaks its crown of palms upon the ground.

So we had hopes again of reborn gestures
But with mind rejected, we drink a cold water,
Your smile is decked out with bundles of death,
Attempted breach in the thickness of the world.

TO THE TREES

You who stepped aside as she passed,
Who closed over your pathways behind her,
Stolid bondsmen for Douve: that even dead
She will again be light, being nothing,

You fibrous matter and density,
Trees, close to me when she leapt
Into the boat of the dead, mouth shut tight
On the obolus of hunger, of silence, of cold.

Through you I hear the dialogue she tries
With the dogs, with the misshapen oarsman,
And I become part of you as she travels
Through so much night in spite of all this river.

The deep thunder rolling on your branches,
The festivals it ignites at the peak of summer
Mean that she binds her destiny to mine
Through the mediation of your austerity.

(AINSI MARCHERONS-NOUS)

Ainsi marcherons-nous sur les ruines d'un ciel immense,
Le site au loin s'accomplira
Comme un destin dans la vive lumière.

Le pays le plus beau longtemps cherché
S'étendra devant nous terre des salamandres.

Regarde, diras-tu, cette pierre:
Elle porte la présence de la mort.
Lampe secrète c'est elle qui brûle sous nos gestes,
Ainsi marchons-nous éclairés.

CHAPELLE BRANCACCI

Veilleuse de la nuit de janvier sur les dalles,
Comme nous avions dit que tout ne mourrait pas!
J'entendais plus avant dans une ombre semblable
Un pas de chaque soir qui descend vers la mer.

Ce que je tiens serré n'est peut-être qu'une ombre,
Mais sache y distinguer un visage éternel.
Ainsi avions-nous pris vers des fresques obscures
Le vain chemin des rues impures de l'hiver.

LIEU DU COMBAT

I

Voici défait le chevalier de deuil.
Comme il gardait une source, voici
Que je m'éveille et c'est par la grâce des arbres
Et dans le bruit des eaux, songe qui se poursuit.

(SO WE WILL WALK AMONG THE RUINS)

So we will walk among the ruins of a boundless sky,
The horizon will unfold
Like a destiny in the quickened light.

The most beautiful country sought so long
Will stretch before us, land of the salamanders.

You will say, look at this stone:
It carries the presence of death.
Secret lamp, it burns beneath us
As we move along, and so we walk in light.

BRANCACCI CHAPEL

Candle of the January night on the flagstones,
When we had said not everything would die!
I could hear further off among like shadows
A step which each evening goes down to the sea.

What I cling to is perhaps but a shadow,
But see how it turns you an eternal face!
So had we taken toward darkened frescoes
The futile path of winter's muddy streets.

PLACE OF BATTLE

I

Here the knight of mourning is defeated.
As he guarded a spring, so now
I awaken, by the grace of trees
Amid the noise of waters, dream renewing itself.

Il se tait. Son visage est celui que je cherche
Sur toutes sources ou falaises, frère mort.
Visage d'une nuit vaincue, et qui se penche
Sur l'aube de l'épaule déchirée.

Il se tait. Que peut dire au terme du combat
Celui qui fut vaincu par probante parole?
Il tourne vers le sol sa face démunie,
Mourir est son seul cri, de vrai apaisement.

II

Mais pleure-t-il sur une source plus
Profonde et fleurit-il, dahlia des morts
Sur le parvis des eaux terreuses de novembre
Qui poussent jusqu'à nous le bruit du monde mort?

Il me semble, penché sur l'aube difficile
De ce jour qui m'est dû et que j'ai reconquis,
Que j'entends sangloter l'éternelle présence
De mon démon secret jamais enseveli.

Ô tu reparaitras, rivage de ma force!
Mais que ce soit malgré ce jour qui me conduit.
Ombres, vous n'êtes plus. Si l'ombre doit renaître
Ce sera dans la nuit et par la nuit.

LIEU DE LA SALAMANDRE

La salamandre surprise s'immobilise
Et feint la mort.
Tel est le premier pas de la conscience dans les pierres,
Le mythe le plus pur,
Un grand feu traversé, qui est esprit.

He says nothing. His is the face I look for
At every spring and cliffside, dead brother.
Face of a vanquished night bending
Over the daybreak of the torn shoulder.

He says nothing. What could he say now the battle is over,
He who was beaten by a word of truth?
He turns his helpless face to the ground,
To die is his one cry, of true repose.

II

But does he weep over a deeper
Spring and does he flower, dahlia of the dead,
At the gates of November's muddy waters
Which bear to us the sound of the dead world?

It seems, as I bend to the arduous dawn
Of this day which is owed me and which I won back,
That I hear sobbing the eternal presence
Of my secret demon who was never buried.

You shall surge up, shore of my strength!
But may it be despite this daylight leading me.
Shadows, you are no more. If the dark must be reborn
It will be in the night and by the night.

PLACE OF THE SALAMANDER

The startled salamander freezes
And feigns death.
This is the first step of consciousness among the stones,
The purest myth,
A great fire passed through, which is spirit.

*La salamandre était à mi-hauteur
Du mur, dans la clarté de nos fenêtres.
Son regard n'était qu'une pierre,
Mais je voyais son cœur battre éternel.*

*Ô ma complice et ma pensée, allégorie
De tout ce qui est pur,
Que j'aime qui resserre ainsi dans son silence
La seule force de joie.*

*Que j'aime qui s'accorde aux astres par l'inerte
Masse de tout son corps,
Que j'aime qui attend l'heure de sa victoire,
Et qui retient son souffle et tient au sol.*

The salamander was halfway up
The wall, in the light from our windows.
Its gaze was merely a stone,
But I saw its heart beat eternal.

O my accomplice and my thought, allegory
Of all that is pure,
How I love that which clasps to its silence thus
The single force of joy.

How I love that which gives itself to the stars by the inert
Mass of its whole body,
How I love that which awaits the hour of its victory
And holds its breath and clings to the ground.

From *Hier régnant désert* (1958)

LE BEL ÉTÉ

Le feu hantait nos jours et les accomplissait,
Son fer blessait le temps à chaque aube plus grise,
Le vent heurtait la mort sur le toit de nos chambres,
Le froid ne cessait pas d'environner nos cœurs.

Ce fut un bel été, fade, brisant et sombre,
Tu aimas la douceur de la pluie en été
Et tu aimas la mort qui dominait l'été
Du pavillon tremblant de ses ailes de cendre.

Cette année-là, tu vins à presque distinguer
Un signe toujours noir devant tes yeux porté
Par les pierres, les vents, les eaux et les feuillages.

Ainsi le soc déjà mordait la terre meuble
Et ton orgueil aima cette lumière neuve,
L'ivresse d'avoir peur sur la terre d'été.

(SOUVENT DANS LE SILENCE D'UN RAVIN)

Souvent dans le silence d'un ravin
J'entends (ou je désire entendre, je ne sais)
Un corps tomber parmi des branches. Longue et lente
Est cette chute aveugle; que nul cri
Ne vient jamais interrompre ou finir.

Je pense alors aux processions de la lumière
Dans le pays sans naître ni mourir.

From *Yesterday's Wilderness Kingdom* (1958)

THE BEAUTIFUL SUMMER

Fire haunted our days and completed them,
Its blade wounded time with each greyer dawn.
The wind clashed with death on the roof over our beds.
The cold surrounded our hearts unceasingly.

It was a beautiful summer, dull, rending, dark,
You loved the sweetness of the summer showers
And you loved death which dominated summer
From the trembling pavilion of its ashy wings.

That year you were almost able to discern
A sign still black and brought to your attention
By the stones, the wind, the water and the leaves.

And so the plough had started biting the loose earth.
And your pride loved this new light,
The ecstasy of fear upon the summer earth.

(OFTEN IN THE SILENCE)

Often in the silence of a ravine
I hear (or wish to hear, I do not know)
A body falling through the branches.
This blind fall that no cry ever
Interrupts or ends is long and slow.

Then I think how light traces a path through
The land where no one dies, no one is born.

LE PONT DE FER

Il y a sans doute toujours au bout d'une longue rue
Où je marchais enfant une mare d'huile,
Un rectangle de lourde mort sous le ciel noir.

Depuis la poésie
A séparé ses eaux des autres eaux,
Nulle beauté nulle couleur ne la retiennent,
Elle s'angoisse pour du fer et de la nuit.

Elle nourrit
Un long chagrin de rive morte, un pont de fer
Jeté vers l'autre rive encore plus nocturne
Est sa seule mémoire et son seul vrai amour.

LES GUETTEURS

I

Il y avait un couloir au fond du jardin,
Je rêvais que j'allais dans ce couloir,
La mort venait avec ses fleurs hautes flétries,
Je rêvais que je lui prenais ce bouquet noir.

Il y avait une étagère dans ma chambre,
J'entrais au soir,
Et je voyais deux femmes racornies
Crier debout sur le bois peint de noir.

Il y avait un escalier, et je rêvais
Qu'au milieu de la nuit un chien hurlait
Dans cet espace de nul chien, et je voyais
Un horrible chien blanc sortir de l'ombre.

IRON BRIDGE

No doubt there is still at the far end of a long street
Where I walked as a child a pool of oil,
Rectangle of heavy death under black sky.

Since then, poetry
Has kept its waters apart from other waters,
No beauty, no colour can retain it –
Iron and night
Cause it to suffer.

It nourishes
A dead shore's long grief, an iron bridge
Thrown towards the other even darker shore
Is its only real love, its only memory.

THE WATCHERS

I

There was a passage at the far end of the garden,
I dreamed that I was walking down this passage.
Death approached with his tall withered flowers,
I dreamed I took the black bouquet from him.

In my bedroom were some shelves.
I entered at nightfall
And saw two shrivelled women standing
On the black painted wood, and crying out.

There was a staircase and I dreamed
A dog howled in the middle of the night
In that place of no dog and I saw
A dreadful white dog step out of the shadow.

II

J'attendais, j'avais peur, je la guettais,
Peut-être enfin une porte s'ouvrait
(Ainsi parfois dans la salle durait
Dans le plein jour une lampe allumée,
Je n'ai jamais aimé que cette rive).

Était-elle la mort, elle ressemblait
À un port vaste et vide, et je savais
Que dans ses yeux avides le passé
Et l'avenir toujours se détruiraient
Comme le sable et la mer sur la rive.

Et qu'en elle pourtant j'établirais
Le lieu triste d'un chant que je portais
Comme l'ombre et la boue dont je faisais
Des images d'absence quand venait
L'eau effacer l'amertume des rives.

LA BEAUTÉ

Celle qui ruine l'être, la beauté,
Sera suppliciée, mise à la roue,
Déshonorée, dite coupable, faite sang
Et cri, et nuit, de toute joie dépossédée
— Ô déchirée sur toutes grilles d'avant l'aube,
Ô piétinée sur toute route et traversée,
Notre haut désespoir sera que tu vives,
Notre cœur que tu souffres, notre voix
De t'humilier parmi tes larmes, de te dire
La menteuse, la pourvoyeuse du ciel noir,
Notre désir pourtant étant ton corps infirme,
Notre pitié ce cœur menant à toute boue.

II

Frightened, I waited, I watched out for him.
Perhaps at last a door was open
(Thus sometimes in broad daylight
A lamp kept on burning in the room,
I have loved nothing but this shore).

Ah death, he was the very image
Of a great empty harbour, and I knew
Past and future in his greedy eyes
Would continue to destroy each other
Like the sea and the sand on the shore,

And all the same I would create in him
The sad place of a song I bore
Like the mud and shadows I made into
Images of absence when sea waters
Came to cleanse the shores of bitterness.

BEAUTY

The one who ruins being – beauty –
Shall be tortured, broken on the wheel,
Dishonoured, found guilty, made into cry
And blood, and night, of all joy dispossessed –
O you, torn apart on grates before the dawn,
O you, trampled on every road and pierced,
Our high despair shall be to see you live,
Our heart that you may suffer, and our voice
To humiliate you in your tears, to name you
Liar, procuress of the darkened sky,
Yet our desire being your frail body,
Our pity this heart that leads only to mire.

L'IMPERFECTION EST LA CIME

Il y avait qu'il fallait détruire et détruire et détruire,
Il y avait que le salut n'est qu'à ce prix.

Ruiner la face nue qui monte dans le marbre,
Marteler toute forme toute beauté.

Aimer la perfection parce qu'elle est le seuil,
Mais la nier sitôt connue, l'oublier morte,

L'imperfection est la cime.

TOUTE LA NUIT

Toute la nuit la bête a bougé dans la salle,
Qu'est-ce que ce chemin qui ne veut pas finir,
Toute la nuit la barque a cherché le rivage,
Qu'est-ce que ces absents qui veulent revenir,
Toute la nuit l'épée a connu la blessure,
Qu'est-ce que ce tourment qui ne sait rien saisir,
Toute la nuit la bête a gémi dans la salle,
Ensanglanté, nié la lumière des salles,
Qu'est-ce que cette mort qui ne va rien guérir?

À LA VOIX DE KATHLEEN FERRIER

Toute douceur toute ironie se rassemblaient
Pour un adieu de cristal et de brume,
Les coups profonds du fer faisaient presque silence,
La lumière du glaive s'était voilée.

IMPERFECTION IS THE SUMMIT

There was this:
You had to destroy, destroy, destroy.
There was this:
Salvation is only found at such a price.

You had to
Ruin the naked face that rises in the marble,
Hammer at every beauty every form,

Love perfection because it is the threshold
But deny it once known, once dead forget it,
Imperfection is the summit.

ALL NIGHT

All night the beast has moved about the room,
What is this road that does not want to end?
All night this boat has sought the river bank,
What are these absent wanting to come back?
All night the sword has coupled with the wound,
What is this pain that seizes on no thing?
All night the beast has groaned within the room,
Has stained with blood, denied the light of rooms,
What is this death that heals nothing at all?

TO THE VOICE OF KATHLEEN FERRIER

All softness and irony assembled
For a farewell of crystal and haze.
The deep thrusts of the sword were near-silent,
The light of the blade was obscured.

Je célèbre la voix mêlée de couleur grise
Qui hésite aux lointains du chant qui s'est perdu
Comme si au delà de toute forme pure
Tremblât un autre chant et le seul absolu.

Ô lumière et néant de la lumière, ô larmes
Souriantes plus haut que l'angoisse ou l'espoir,
Ô cygne, lieu réel dans l'irréelle eau sombre,
Ô source, quand ce fut profondément le soir!

Il semble que tu connaisses les deux rives,
L'extrême joie et l'extrême douleur.
Là-bas, parmi ces roseaux gris dans la lumière,
Il semble que tu puises de l'éternel.

(AUBE, FILLE DES LARMES, RÉTABLIS)

Aube, fille des larmes, rétablis
La chambre dans sa paix de chose grise
Et le cœur dans son ordre. Tant de nuit
Demandait à ce feu qu'il décline et s'achève,
Il nous faut bien veiller près du visage mort.
À peine a-t-il changé ... Le navire des lampes
Entrera-t-il au port qu'il avait demandé,
Sur les tables d'ici la flamme faite cendre
Grandira-t-elle ailleurs dans une autre clarté?
Aube, soulève, prends le visage sans ombre,
Colore peu à peu le temps recommencé.

I praise this voice mingled with grey,
Wavering in the distance of the song which died away
As if beyond pure form there trembled
Another song, alone and absolute.

O light and light's nothingness, O you tears
Smiling higher than anguish or hope,
O swan, real place in unreal dark waters,
O wellspring in the very deep of evening!

It seems you know well the two shores:
Highest joy, deepest sorrow.
Over there, in the light among the grey reeds
It seems that you soak up eternity.

(DAWN, DAUGHTER OF TEARS, RESTORE)

Dawn, daughter of tears, restore
The room to its grey thing's peaceful state,
The heart to its good order. So much night
Asked of this fire that it wane and die.
We must keep vigil over the dead face.
It has hardly changed… The ship of lamps,
Will it enter port as it required,
Turned to ashes on these tables, will the flame
Spread elsewhere into a different brightness?
Dawn, raise up, take the face without shadow,
Colour bit by bit time's new beginning.

DELPHES DU SECOND JOUR

*Ici l'inquiète voix consent d'aimer
La pierre simple,
Les dalles que le temps asservit et délivre,
L'olivier dont la force a goût de sèche pierre.*

*Le pas dans son vrai lieu. L'inquiète voix
Heureuse sous les roches du silence,
Et l'infini, l'indéfini répons
Des sonnailles, rivage ou mort. De nul effroi
Était ton gouffre clair, Delphes du second jour.*

ICI, TOUJOURS ICI

*Ici, dans le lieu clair. Ce n'est plus l'aube,
C'est déjà la journée aux dicibles désirs.
Des mirages d'un chant dans ton rêve il ne reste
Que ce scintillement de pierres à venir.*

*Ici, et jusqu'au soir. La rose d'ombres
Tournera sur les murs. La rose d'heures
Défleurira sans bruit. Les dalles claires
Mèneront à leur gré ces pas épris du jour.*

*Ici, toujours ici. Pierres sur pierres
Ont bâti le pays dit par le souvenir.
À peine si le bruit de fruits simples qui tombent
Enfièvre encore en toi le temps qui va guérir.*

* * *

DELPHI, THE SECOND DAY

Here the unquiet voice agrees to love
Simple stone,
Flagstones time enslaves, delivers,
The olive tree whose strength tastes of dry stone.

The footstep in its true place. The unquiet
Voice happy beneath the rocks of silence,
And the infinite, the undefined response
Of death, shore, cattle bells. Your bright abyss
Inspired no awe, Delphi on the second day.

HERE, FOREVER HERE

Here, in the bright place. It is no longer dawn
But day, now, with its speakable desires.
Of a song's mirages in your dream, there is
Only this flashing of stones to come.

Here, until evening. The rose of shadows
Will turn upon the walls. The rose of hours
Will shed its petals without sound. The bright flagstones
Will lead as they please our steps in love with day.

Here, forever here. Stones upon stones
Have built the land spoken by memory.
Hardly does the sound of simple falling fruit
Fire time once more in you, time which will heal.

★ ★ ★

From *L'Improbable* (1959)

DÉVOTION / DEVOTIONS

I

To nettles and stones.

To 'severe mathematics'. To dimly-lit trains every evening. To snowy streets beneath an immeasurable star.

I wandered about, I ended up lost. And words had trouble finding their way in the terrible silence. – To these words, patient and redemptive.

II

To the 'Madonna of the evening'. To the great stone table above the bountiful shorelines. To footsteps that came together and then separated.

To winter *oltr'Arno*. To the snow and so many footsteps. To Brancacci Chapel when night has fallen.

III

To island chapels.

To Galla Placidia. Narrow walls measuring out our shadows. To statues in the grass; and, like me perhaps, faceless.

To a door walled up with bricks the colour of blood on your grey façade, Valladolid Cathedral. To great stone circles. To a *paso* filled with dead black earth.

To Sainte-Marthe d'Agliè, in Canavese. Its red brick, grown old, expressing baroque joy. To a palace deserted and sealed up among the trees.
(To all palaces of this world, for the welcome they offer night.)

To my house in Urbino between number and night.

To Saint-Yves de la Sagesse.

To Delphi where one can die.

To the city of kites and great glass houses which reflect the sky.

To the painters of the Rimini school. Anxiously desiring your glory, I wanted to be a historian. Profoundly wishing that your absolute prevail, I would like to erase history.

IV

And always to quays at night, to bars, to a voice saying *I am the lamp, I am the oil*.

To that voice consumed by an essential fever. To a maple's grey trunk. To a dance. To these two ordinary rooms, for ensuring the gods remain in our midst.

From *Pierre écrite* (1965)

LA LAMPE, LE DORMEUR

I

Je ne savais dormir sans toi, je n'osais pas
Risquer sans toi les marches descendantes.
Plus tard, j'ai découvert que c'est un autre songe,
Cette terre aux chemins qui tombent dans la mort.

Alors je t'ai voulue au chevet de ma fièvre
D'inexister, d'être plus noir que tant de nuit,
Et quand je parlais haut dans le monde inutile,
Je t'avais sur les voies du trop vaste sommeil.

Le dieu pressant en moi, c'étaient ces rives
Que j'éclairais de l'huile errante, et tu sauvais
Nuit après nuit mes pas du gouffre qui m'obsède,
Nuit après nuit mon aube, inachevable amour.

II

— Je me penchais sur toi, vallée de tant de pierres,
J'écoutais les rumeurs de ton grave repos,
J'apercevais très bas dans l'ombre qui te couvre
Le lieu triste où blanchit l'écume du sommeil.

Je t'écoutais rêver. Ô monotone et sourde,
Et parfois par un roc invisible brisée,
Comme ta voix s'en va, ouvrant parmi ses ombres
Le gave d'une étroite attente murmurée!

From *Words in Stone* (1965)

THE LAMP, THE SLEEPER

I

I did not know how to sleep without you,
Did not dare risk the descending steps without you.
Later, I learned that this earth, whose paths
Fall into death, is another dream.

Then I wanted you at the bedside of my fever
Of not existing, of being blacker than such night,
And when I spoke aloud in the useless world,
I kept you with me on the vast ways of sleep.

The urgent god within me was these banks
Which I lit with vagrant oil, and you saved
My steps night after night from the pit that haunts me,
Night after night my dawn, unattainable love.

II

– I bent above you, valley full of stones,
I listened to the murmurs of your grave repose.
I could see far down in the darkness that covers you
The sad place where sleep's white foam glimmers.

I listened to you dreaming. O monotonous and hollow,
And sometimes broken by an unseen rock,
How your voice goes on, opening among its shadows
The narrow stream of a long-whispered hope.

Là-haut, dans les jardins de l'émail, il est vrai
Qu'un paon impie s'accroît des lumières mortelles.
Mais toi il te suffit de ma flamme qui bouge,
Tu habites la nuit d'une phrase courbée.

Qui es-tu? Je ne sais de toi que les alarmes,
Les hâtes dans ta voix d'un rite inachevé.
Tu partages l'obscur au sommet de la table,
Et que tes mains sont nues, ô seules éclairée!

UNE PIERRE

Il désirait, sans connaître,
Il a péri, sans avoir.
Arbres, fumées,
Toutes lignes de vent et de déception
Furent son gîte.
Infiniment
Il n'a étreint que sa mort.

UNE PIERRE

Je fus assez belle.
Il se peut qu'un jour comme celui-ci me ressemble.
Mais la ronce l'emporte sur mon visage,
La pierre accable mon corps.

Approche-toi,
Servante verticale rayée de noir,
Et ton visage court.

Répands le lait ténébreux, qui exalte
Ma force simple.
Sois-moi fidèle,
Nourrice encor, mais d'immortalité.

Up there, it's true, in enamel's gardens,
An impious peacock feeds on mortal lights.
But for you my shifting flame is enough,
You dwell in the night of a vaulted phrase.

Who are you? I only know your sudden fears,
The urgings of an uncompleted rite in your voice.
You divide the darkness at the summit of the table,
And how bare your hands are, alone in my light!

A STONE

He desired without knowing,
He died without having.
Trees, mists,
All lines of the wind and disappointment
Were his refuge.
He embraced
Nothing infinitely but his death.

A STONE

I was quite beautiful.
A day like this might resemble me.
But the thornbush triumphs over my face,
The stone weighs down my body.

Bend to me,
My vertical servant striped in black,
With your short face.

Pour out the shadowy milk that exalts
My simple strength.
Be faithful to me,
Still my nurse, but in immortality.

UNE PIERRE

Deux ans, ou trois,
Je me sentis suffisante. Les astres,
Les fleuves, les forêts ne m'égalaient pas.
La lune s'écaillait sur mes robes grises.
Mes yeux cernés
Illuminaient les mers sous leur voûtes d'ombre,
Et mes cheveux étaient plus amples que ce monde
Aux yeux vaincus, aux cris qui ne m'atteignaient pas.

Des bêtes de nuit hurlent, c'est mon chemin,
Des portes noires se ferment.

UNE PIERRE

Ta jambe, nuit très dense,
Tes seins, liés,
Si noirs, ai-je perdu mes yeux,
Mes nerfs d'atroce vue
Dans cette obscurité plus âpre que la pierre,
Ô mon amour?

Au centre de la lumière, j'abolis
D'abord ma tête crevassée par le gaz,
Mon nom ensuite avec tous pays,
Mes mains seules droites persistent.

En tête du cortège je suis tombé
Sans dieu, sans voix audible, sans péché,
Bête trinitaire criante.

A STONE

For two or three years
I was pleased with myself. Stars,
Rivers, forests, could not compare with me.
The moon sifted down on my grey robes.
From their dark arches
My deep-set eyes lit up the seas,
And my hair was more abundant than this world
with its downcast look, its cries that could not reach me.

Night creatures howl, this is my path now,
Black doors shut.

A STONE

Your leg, deepest night,
Your breasts, bound,
So black, have I lost my eyes,
My nerves of agonised seeing
In this darkness harsher than stone,
O my love?

At the centre of light, I abolish
First my head cracked by gas,
Then my name with all lands,
Only my straight hands persist.

At the head of the procession
I have fallen, godless, voiceless, sinless,
A crying trinitarian beast.

UNE PIERRE

Tombe, mais douce pluie, sur le visage.
Éteins, mais lentement, le très pauvre chaleil.

UNE PIERRE

Longtemps dura l'enfance au mur sombre et je fus
La conscience d'hiver; qui se pencha
Tristement, fortement, sur une image,
Amèrement, sur le reflet d'un autre jour.

N'ayant rien désiré
Plus que de contribuer à mêler deux lumières,
Ô mémoire, je fus
Dans son vaisseau de verre l'huile diurne
Criant son âme rouge au ciel des longues pluies.

Qu'aurai-je aimé? L'écume de la mer
Au-dessus de Trieste, quand le gris
De la mer de Trieste éblouissait
Les yeux du sphinx déchirable des rives.

LA CHAMBRE

Le miroir et le fleuve en crue, ce matin,
S'appelaient à travers la chambre, deux lumières
Se trouvent et s'unissent dans l'obscur
Des meubles de la chambre descellée.

Et nous étions deux pays de sommeil
Communiquant par leurs marches de pierre
Où se perdait l'eau non trouble d'un rêve
Toujours se reformant, toujours brisé.

A STONE

Fall but softly rain upon this face.
Put out the humble clay lamp slowly.

A STONE

Childhood was long by the grim wall and I was
The mind of winter, bending
Sadly, stubbornly, over an image,
Bitterly, over the reflection of another day.

Having desired nothing
So much as to help in the blending of two lights,
O memory, I was
Diurnal oil in its glass vessel
Crying its red soul to the long rains of the sky.

What will I have loved? The sea's foam
Above Trieste, when the grey
Of the sea of Trieste dazzled
The eyes of the erodible sphinx of the shores.

THE BEDROOM

The mirror and the river in flood, this morning,
Called to each other across the room, two lights
Appear and merge in the obscurity
Of furniture, within the unsealed room.

We were two realms of sleep, communicating
Through their courses of stone, where the untroubled
Water of a dream dispelled itself,
Forever recomposed, forever broken.

La main pure dormait près de la main soucieuse.
Un corps un peu parfois dans son rêve bougeait.
Et loin, sur l'eau plus noire d'une table,
La robe rouge éclairante dormait.

L'ÉPAULE

Ton épaule soit l'aube, ayant porté
Tout mon obscur déchirement de nuit
Et toute cette écume amère des images,
Tout ce haut rougeoiement d'un impossible été.

Ton corps voûte pour nous son heure respirante
Comme un pays plus clair sur nos ombres penché
— Longue soit la journée où glisse, miroitante,
L'eau d'un rêve à l'afflux rapide, irrévélé.

Ô dans le bruissement du feuillage de l'arbre
Soit le masque aux yeux clos du rêve déposé!
J'entends déjà grandir le bruit d'un autre gave
Qui s'apaise, ou se perd, dans notre éternité.

L'ARBRE, LA LAMPE

L'arbre vieillit dans l'arbre, c'est l'été.
L'oiseau franchit le chant de l'oiseau et s'évade.
Le rouge de la robe illumine et disperse
Loin, au ciel, le charroi de l'antique douleur.

Ô fragile pays,
Comme la flamme d'une lampe que l'on porte,
Proche étant le sommeil dans la sève du monde,
Simple le battement de l'âme partagée.

The pure hand slept beside the unquiet hand.
A body shifted slightly in its dream.
Far off, upon a table's blacker water,
Glittering, the red dress lay asleep.

THE SHOULDER

Let your shoulder be the dawn, for it has borne
All my dark harrowing by night
And all this bitter foam of images,
The high glowing of an impossible summer.

Let your body arch its breathing hour for us
Like a brighter country bent above our shadows
– Long be the day when the water of dreams
Runs shimmering, a quick flow, undisclosed.

O in the rustling leaves of the tree
Let the closed-eyed mask of the dream be hung!
Now I hear the sound of another stream rising,
to be stilled, or lost, in our eternity.

THE TREE, THE LAMP

The tree grows older in the tree, it's summer.
The bird traverses birdsong and escapes.
The red dress gleams and in the sky disperses,
Far off, the burden of an ancient pain.

O fragile country,
Like the flame within a lamp one carries,
When sleep approaches, closed in the world's veins,
Simple the pulse in the soul that's shared.

Toi aussi tu aimes l'instant où la lumière des lampes
Se décolore et rêve dans le jour.
Tu sais que c'est l'obscur de ton cœur qui guérit,
La barque qui rejoint le rivage et tombe.

LE MYRTE

Parfois je te savais la terre, je buvais
Sur tes lèvres l'angoisse des fontaines
Quand elle sourd des pierres chaudes, et l'été
Dominait haut la pierre heureuse et le buveur.

Parfois je te disais de myrte et nous brûlions
L'arbre de tous tes gestes tout un jour.
C'étaient de grands feux brefs de lumière vestale,
Ainsi je t'inventais parmi tes cheveux clairs.

Tout un grand été nul avait séché nos rêves,
Rouillé nos voix, accru nos corps, défait nos fers.
Parfois le lit tournait comme une barque libre
Qui gagne lentement le plus haut de la mer.

LE SANG, LA NOTE SI

Longues, longues journées.
Le sang inapaisé heurte le sang.
Le nageur est aveugle.
Il descend par étages pourpres dans le battement de ton cœur.

Quand la nuque se tend
Le cri toujours désert prend une bouche pure.

You also love the moment when the light of lamps
Begins to fade and dream in day.
You know it is the darkness of your heart that heals,
The boat that gains the shore and falls.

MYRTLE

Sometimes I knew you as the earth, I drank
Upon your lips the anguish of springs
Welling among warm stones, and summer
Loomed above the rapt stone and the drinker.

Sometimes I called you myrtle and we burned
The tree of all your gestures all day long.
Those were the great brief fires of vestal light,
Thus I invented you in your bright hair.

A vast and empty summer scorched our dreams, rusted
Our voices, increased our bodies, broke our chains.
Sometimes the bed turned like a boat set free
That slowly gains the high, the open sea.

BLOOD, THE NOTE B

Long, long days.
Blood hurls against blood, unappeased.
The swimmer is blind.
He drops by crimson stages into the beating of your heart.

When the neck is tensed
The always empty cry comes to a pure mouth.

Ainsi vieillit l'été. Ainsi la mort
Encercle le bonheur de la flamme qui bouge.
Et nous dormons un peu. La note si
Résonne très longtemps dans l'étoffe rouge.

L'ABEILLE, LA COULEUR

Cinq heures.
Le sommeil est léger, en taches sur les vitres.
Le jour puise là-bas dans la couleur l'eau fraîche,
Ruisselante, du soir.

Et c'est comme si l'âme se simplifie
Étant lumière davantage, et qui rassure,
Mais, l'Un se déchirant contre la jambe obscure,
Tu te perds, où la bouche a bu à l'âcre mort.

(La corne d'abondance avec le fruit
Rouge dans le soleil qui tourne. Et tout ce bruit
D'abeilles de l'impure et douce éternité
Sur le si proche pré si brûlant encore).

UNE PIERRE

Un feu va devant nous.
J'aperçois par instants ta nuque, ton visage,
Puis, rien que le flambeau,
Rien que le feu massif, le mascaret des morts.

Cendre qui te détaches de la flamme
Dans la lumière du soir,
Ô présence,
Sous ta voûte furtive accueille-nous
Pour une fête obscure.

So summer grows old. So death
Surrounds the gladness of a dancing flame.
And we sleep a little. The note B
Echoes for a long time in the red cloth.

THE BEE, THE COLOUR

Five o'clock.
A light sleep dapples the windows.
Day draws the fresh and rustling water of evening
From that well of colour.

And it is as if the soul is simpler,
Filled with a reassuring light;
But the One is torn on the dark leg
And you lose yourself where the mouth drank acrid death.

(The cornucopia with the red fruit
In the turning sun. And all this noise
Of bees swarming from the still flaming meadow,
As if a sweet impure eternity were near us.)

A STONE

A fire goes before us.
At moments I glimpse your neck, your face,
Then nothing but the torch,
Nothing but the massed fire, the flood-tide of death.

Ash fallen from the flame
in the evening light,
O presence,
take us for darkness and joy
under your furtive roof.

LA LUMIÈRE, CHANGÉE

Nous ne nous voyons plus dans la même lumière,
Nous n'avons plus les mêmes yeux, les mêmes mains.
L'arbre est plus proche et la voix des sources plus vive,
Nos pas sont plus profonds, parmi les morts.

Dieu qui n'es pas, pose ta main sur notre épaule,
Ébauche notre corps du poids de ton retour,
Achève de mêler à nos âmes ces astres,
Ces bois, ces cris d'oiseaux, ces ombres et ces jours.

Renonce-toi en nous comme un fruit se déchire,
Efface-nous en toi. Découvre-nous
Le sens mystérieux de ce qui n'est que simple
Et fût tombé sans feu dans des mots sans amour.

UNE PIERRE

Nous prenions par ces prés
Où parfois tout un dieu se détachait d'un arbre
(Et c'était notre preuve, vers le soir).

Je vous poussais sans bruit,
Je sentais votre poids contre nos mains pensives,
Ô vous, mes mots obscurs,
Barrières au travers des chemins du soir.

THE LIGHT, CHANGED

We no longer see each other in the same light,
We no longer have the same eyes, or the same hands.
The tree is closer, and the water's voice more lively,
Our steps go deeper now, among the dead.

God, who are not, put your hand on our shoulder,
Rough cast our body with the weight of your return,
Finish blending our souls with these stars,
These woods, these bird cries, these shadows and these days.

Give yourself up in us the way fruit tears apart,
Have us disappear in you. Reveal to us
The mysterious meaning in what is merely simple
And would have fallen without fire in words without love.

A STONE

We used to cross these fields
Where at times an entire god fell away from the tree
(And towards evening this was our proof).

I pushed you noiselessly,
I felt your weight against our pensive hands
— O you, my dark words,
Barriers across the evening roads.

LE LIVRE, POUR VIEILLIR

Étoiles transhumantes; et le berger
Voûté sur le bonheur terrestre; et tant de paix
Comme ce cri d'insecte, irrégulier,
Qu'un dieu pauvre façonne. Le silence
Est monté de ton livre vers ton cœur.
Un vent bouge sans bruit dans les bruits du monde.
Le temps sourit au loin, de cesser d'être.
Simples dans le verger sont les fruits mûrs.

Tu vieilliras
Et, te décolorant dans la couleur des arbres,
Faisant ombre plus lente sur le mur,
Étant, et d'âme enfin, la terre menacée,
Tu reprendras le livre à la page laissée,
Tu diras, C'étaient donc les derniers mots obscurs.

THE BOOK, FOR GROWING OLD

Stars moving from their summertime
To winter pastures; and the shepherd, arched
Over earthly happiness; and so much peace,
Like the cry of an insect, halt, irregular,
Shaped by an impoverished god. The silence
Rises from your book up to your heart.
A noiseless wind moves in the noisy world.
Time smiles in the distance, ceasing to be.
And in the grove the ripe fruit simply are.

You will grow old
And, fading into the colour of the trees,
Making a slower shadow on the wall,
Becoming, as soul at last, the threatened earth,
You will take up the book again, at the still open page,
And say, These were indeed the last dark words.

II 1968–1977

from *L'Arrière-pays* / *The Arrière-pays* (1972)

I have often experienced a feeling of anxiety, at crossroads. At such moments it seems to me that *here*, or close by, a couple of steps away on the path I didn't take and which is already receding – that just *over there* a more elevated kind of country would open up, where I might have gone to live and which I've already lost. And yet, at the moment of choice, there was nothing to indicate or even to suggest that I should take the other route. Often, I have been able to follow it with my eyes, and reassure myself that it didn't lead to a new earth. But that doesn't relieve my anxiety, since I also know that the other country wouldn't be remarkable for any novel aspects of its monuments or its soil. I have no taste for imagining unknown colours or forms, or a beauty superior to that of this world. I love the earth, and what I see delights me, and sometimes I even believe that the unbroken line of peaks, the majesty of the trees, the liveliness of water moving through the bottom of a ravine, the graceful facade of a church – because in some places and at certain hours they are so intense – must have been intended for our benefit. This harmony has a meaning, these landscapes, and these objects, while they are still fixed, or possibly enchanted, are almost like a language, as if the absolute would declare itself, if we could only look and listen intently, at the end of our wanderings. And it is here, within this promise, that the place is found.

And yet it is when I attain this kind of faith that the idea of the other country invades me most violently, depriving me of any happiness on earth. For the more convinced I am that it is all a phrase, or rather a music – both symbolic and material – the more cruelly I feel that there is one key missing among those that would let me hear it. We are at odds, within this unity, and what the intuition senses action can neither confirm nor resolve. And if one voice comes through clearly, for an instant, above the sound of the orchestra, well, then the century ends, the voice dies, the meaning of the words is lost. It is as if from the forces of life, from the syntax of colours and forms, from dense or iridescent words that nature perennially repeats, there is a single articulation we cannot grasp, even though it is one of the simplest; and our shining sun seems a blackness. Why can we

not dominate what is there, like looking out from a terrace? Why can we not exist other than at the surface of things, at chance turnings in the path; like a swimmer who would plunge into this process of becoming and come up wreathed in seaweed, broader in brow and shoulders – blind, laughing, divine? There are certain works that can, for all that, give us a fair idea of the impossible potential. The blue in Nicolas Poussin's *Bacchanalia with Guitar Player* has that stormy immediacy, that non-conceptual clear-sightedness for which our whole consciousness craves.

Thinking this, I turn again to the horizon. *Here*, we are afflicted by a curious unease of spirit, or else some snag in appearance, some fault in the manifest surface of the earth, which deprives us of the good it could do us. *Over there*, due to the clearer contour of a valley, or to lightning immobilised one day in the sky, or maybe thanks to a more nuanced language, or a tradition preserved, or to a feeling we don't have (I cannot and will not choose among these things), a people exists who – in a place that resembles them – have secret dominion over the world … Secretly, because I can conceive of nothing, even there, that might challenge our knowledge of the universe. This nation, or place of absolutes, is not so detached from our common condition that we should, in imagining it, surround it with walls of pure ozone. We lack so little here that the beings from over there have nothing to distinguish them from us, I suppose, except the unemphatic strangeness of a simple gesture, or of a remark that my friends, in commerce with them, never thought to question. But do we not tend to overlook the obvious? And yet – if ever the chance came my way – I might perhaps know what to look for.

So that is what I dream of, at these crossroads, or a little way beyond them – and I am haunted by everything that gives credence to the existence of this place, which is and remains *other*, and yet which suggests itself, with some insistence even. When a road climbs upwards, revealing, in the distance, other paths among the stones, and other villages; when the train travels into a narrow valley, at twilight, passing in front of houses where a window happens to light up; when the boat comes in fairly close to the shoreline, where the sun has caught a distant windowpane (and once it was Caraco,

where I was told that the paths were long since impassable, smothered by brambles), this very specific emotion seizes hold of me – I feel I'm getting close, and something tells me to be on the alert. What are the names of those villages over there? Why is there a light on that terrace, and who is greeting us, or calling us, as we come alongside? Of course, the moment I set foot in one of these places, this sense of 'getting warm' fades away. But not without it intensifying, sometimes for as much as an hour, because the sound of footsteps or a voice rose to my hotel room, reaching me through the closed shutters.

And then there was Capraia, so long the object of my hopes! Its form – a long modulation of peaks and plateaus – seemed to me perfect, and I could not tear my eyes away for minutes on end, especially at evening, since it had risen out of the mist on the second day of the first summer, and so much higher than where I imagined the horizon to be. Now, while the island of Capraia belonged to Italy, there was nothing to link Italy to the island I was on – it was supposedly almost deserted: so everything was set for this name – which reduced the island to a few shepherds, on their endless journey over the rocky table against the sky, in the jasmine and the asphodel (with a few olive and carob trees in the hollows) – to confer an archetypal quality upon it and make it, as I so wanted it to be, the true place. This went on for some seasons, then my life changed, I came nowhere near Capraia, almost forgot her, and several years went by. But then I happened to take a boat at Genoa one morning, departing for Greece; and suddenly, towards evening, something impelled me to go up on the bridge and look towards the west where, passing or about to pass very close on our right, were a few rocks and a shoreline. A sighting, an interior shock: a memory in me, deeper than consciousness, or more alert, had already grasped what thought had not ... Could it be possible, but yes, Capraia was in front of me, Capraia from the other side, the side I had never seen, the unimaginable! In its altered form, or rather in its formlessness (since we were passing so close, scarcely a hundred metres from the shore), the island approached, opened, declared itself – a brief coastline, some scrubland, and nothing else but a little jetty, a path leading off into the distance, a few houses

here and there, a sort of fortress on an outcrop – and almost as quickly disappeared.

And then I was seized with compassion. Capraia, you too belong, like us, to this world. You suffer finiteness, you are divested of your secret; recede then, back into the falling night. And keep watch there, having forged other links with me, about which I want to know nothing as yet, because I am importuned by hope still, and so lured onwards. Tomorrow I shall see Zante and Cephalonia, also lovely names, and larger islands, with their mysteries preserved by their depths. How well I understand the end of the Odyssey, when Ulysses reaches Ithaca, already in the knowledge he will have to set off again, an oar over his shoulder, and plunge on into the mountains of another land, until someone asks him about the bizarre object he is carrying, showing that he knows nothing of the sea! If shorelines attract me, the idea of the interior does still more, of a country protected by its gigantic mountains, sealed off like the unconscious. Walking at the water's edge, I watch the foam moving like a sign trying to form, but never doing so. The olive tree, the heat, the salt encrusting the skin – what more could one want – and yet the true path is over there, winding away, following rocky passes that get narrower and narrower. And the further inland I go, in a Mediterranean country, the more strongly the smell of old plaster in hallways, the sounds of evening, the rustling laurel, changing in intensity and pitch (as one says of a high note), combine to suggest, to the point of pain, traces that are enigmatic, and an invitation impossible to understand.

In the same way, I can never look at the system of little hills – easy walking, but part of an infinite interior – in Piero della Francesca's *Triumph of Battista*, without repeating to myself that this painter shares, among his other concerns, the one that haunts me. But by the same token I love the great plains where the horizon is so low as to be almost masked by the trees and even the grasses. At such moments invisible and tangible become confused, elsewhere is everywhere, the centre, perhaps, just close by. I have been on the trail for so long, there is just one more turning before I see the first walls, or speak to the first shadows ... And the sea favours this reverie of mine, because it guarantees distance, and

suggests such a vacant plenitude to my senses; but not only the sea, because I recognise that the great deserts, or the equally desolate road network crossing a continent, could fulfil the same function, providing the wanderer with space while indefinitely postponing the comprehensive view, which, grasping all, can renounce all. Yes, even the highways of America, and its slow trains that seem to have no destination, and the ravaged landscapes that go before them – but this, admittedly, is to follow my reverie too far into the fanciful. The same year, travelling through Western Pennsylvania by train, under snow, I suddenly saw the contradictory words 'Bethlehem Steel' on some dismal factory buildings in the middle of a massacred forest; and the same hope stirred in me again, but this time at the expense of truthfulness to the earth. Ceasing to look for excess of being in the intensity of its surfaces, I started imagining instead, in some side street, the most squalid of all, in some blackened yard, a door: and behind it mountains, birdsong and the sea, all smilingly resurrected. But this is the way we can unlearn the limits, but also the strength, of our being-in-the-world. And approaching Pittsburgh, I saw how the Gnostic denial of this world had little by little penetrated the Greek language, born of beauty though it was, and had risen to the notion of a cosmos.

I understood this even better in that my nostalgia itself constituted, in the blackest moments, a refusal of the world, even if nothing, as I have said before, touches me more than the words and accents of the earth. It is true, our lands are beautiful, I can imagine no other, I am at peace with my language, my distant god has only slightly withdrawn, his epiphany resides in the simple: and yet, supposing that the true life is over there, in that elsewhere I cannot situate, then what is here starts to look like a desert. I can tell this from how I act towards what I love, when this obsession grips me. I believe in the light, for example. Even to the point where I imagined the true country born of it, by chance, with the coming together of a season and a place where it would have been most intense. Night and day would be like everywhere else at any epoch. But at morning, noon and evening there would be a light so complete, and so pure, in its discovered modulation, that men, so dazzled they could only see against the light dark forms fringed

with fire, would have no use for psychology, with only the yes and no of presence inside them, and they would communicate as though by lightning, with an inspired violence rooted in untellable tenderness, the absolute revolution. But if I dream that, what is the light of the here and now to me, and what do I gather from it? Nothing but dissatisfaction; my desire constitutes its grandeur, and my exile is to dwell within it. How beautiful are these facades! How close to me Leon Battista Alberti feels when he constructs his music in Rimini and Florence! But by catching the sun here, he lights up the horizon; I look to where his intensity is gathered, what is he looking for, what does he know? And what of those Byzantine plates in silver and pewter? Their soft reflecting quality is so simple, so modest, and immaterial, they seem to speak from a special, luminous threshold. In a very old mirror (why did they use that fragile silvering, that soft silver leaf?) are fruits, piled high in abundance on the reflected table, as in 'inverted' perspective, and the face within it has also the indelible quality of a memory. Mysterious objects, that I come across sometimes, in a church or a museum, and stop in front of, like another crossroads. Beautiful and solemn they are, I invest them with all I have seen of the earth: but, every time, it is with an elan that dispossesses it … In fact, anything which touches me – however homely it be, a pewter teaspoon, a rusted iron box from another age, a garden glimpsed through a hedge, a rake leaning against a wall, a maid singing in the other room – can divide my being, and shut me out in exile from the light.

One night a long time ago, when I was still at school, I was turning the shortwave dial. Voices were replaced by others, swelling momentarily and then fading, and I remember I received an image of the starry sky, the empty sky. Men have language, ceaseless speech, but is it not as vain and repetitive as foam, sand, or those empty suns? How poor a thing is the sign! And yet with what certitude we seem at times to be progressing with it, on the prow of a ship, or in a bus moving through dunes, existing superior to it because we can see it forming, flowering and then dying away! Thinking this, I went on turning the dial. And then at one moment I felt I had just passed something that, through poor reception, still

awoke the fever in me and compelled me to turn back. I recovered what I had just heard, though the sound was still as precarious: what was it, exactly? A chant, but accompanied by the fifes and drums of a primitive society. The sound of raucous male voices came through, and then, intensely serious, a child's voice while the choir was silent, and then joined by the ensemble – quaverings and growlings in broken rhythms. And surrounding it all, I had an impression, whether or not this was subjective, of space. And then I saw. These beings live high up in a solitude of stones, at the mouth of an amphitheatre at the meeting point of mountain passes sealed by huge rocks. Above them are rock walls ravined by water and crumbled by saxifrage; a perch for the eagle who climbs still higher. On the horizon, on outcrops and in hollows, their villages stand with blind, heavy facades, often ruined beneath their towers. But where we are is more of a campsite, dotted with fires as night draws in; how to explain the nomadic – if circumscribed – life of these *awakened* societies? This country itself, these men and their music – are they from the Caucasus, or Circassia, from the mountains of Armenia or Central Asia? – but the very words have for me a kind of mythic value, a polar absolute not to be found on any modern map – in fact, the Mount Ararat to my ark, which ushers in the universe, is similarly surrounded by loud waters, the bare, black horizon, the vague, rapid current.

Soon the chant ended, and someone started talking in an incomprehensible tongue, and then the station was lost in static. The mysterious country had receded and I had invested the other side of the horizon with one of the riches of our own. But it was also from this moment on that I became sensitive to music. A richness, an alchemy from the other side had come to join with our experiences here, and had added to my limited powers ... And I should here point out that my gnosis, to which I confess, has two kinds of limits. First, even when my dream is at its most intense, our side is not simply or not always dispossessed in favour of the other. What departs with the spirit remains with the body; and the presence remaining is undermined, but intense, as if standing out from a desert, an excess of being in the heart of nothingness, as undeniable as it is paradoxical. Those in exile bearing witness against the country of their exile? But

as I've said, the slightest object can merge, at one time or another, into this ambiguous state and remain there, extending and illuminating its interrelations: finally, it is as though the whole world, loved initially like music and then dissolved as presence, *returns* as a second presence, restructured by the unknown but living a more inward relation with myself. From the other side we have learned the arts, poetry, techniques of negation, intensification, memory. This enables us to recognise and to love ourselves – but also, listening to that original music, to add our own chords, to which things nevertheless respond. Isn't being always an incompleteness, after all, the obscure song of the earth a draft less to be studied than to be recommenced, the missing key less a secret than a task? And what I dream of as an elsewhere must also be, in a profound sense, the future that one day – once the ingathering is complete, and men, beasts and things are called to the same place at the same hour – will show itself here, and absence throws off its mask of pastoral comedy, amid laughter and tears of joy, for the supreme reunion – world recently lost, world now saved?

But there is also this: I am only haunted by another world at those moments, in those places, at those crossroads, literal or figurative, within the experience of living. As if only part of the latter lent itself to this feverish volatilisation, while the other anchors me in the business of this world which absorbs me for periods of time, untroubled by the horizon; a part that is, in fact, sufficient. There is, finally, a hesitation, between gnosis and faith, between the hidden god and the incarnation, rather than irrevocable choice. There is a negation, but it feeds hungrily on what it deprecates. And to that must be added the fact that if the haunting remains, an evolution within it began long before. As I move, there is this long ridge of broken fire unfolding endlessly beside me; high and low, it crosses everything and drops away from everything when I approach, only to close up again behind me. And yet, how can I describe it: the point which caught my eye seems more remote in its spiritual space, while the moment the horizon closed behind me seems closer, and less rapid, as if my valley was lit up and widened. And I also feel the need to understand this double premise better, rather than, as I have done on occasion, merely to undergo it. Most of my memories of the *arrière-pays* are

early ones; this is because these are the only 'pure' evocations, more recent ones being over-intellectualised, more articulately sceptical, or at the very least somehow designed to supersede or reconcile the two dominions. Yes, there is a belated knowledge, which reasoned thought must aid even if the latter is limited and contradictory. Clarification can happen not so much through thought as within it, little by little, thanks to an evolution in one's whole being that is vaster and more conscious than words.

From *Dans le leurre du seuil* (1975)

LE FLEUVE

Mais non, toujours
D'un déploiement de l'aile de l'impossible
Tu t'éveilles, avec un cri,
Du lieu, qui n'est qu'un rêve. Ta voix, soudain,
Est rauque comme un torrent. Tout le sens, rassemblé,
Y tombe, avec un bruit
De sommeil jeté sur la pierre.

Et tu te lèves une éternelle fois
Dans cet été qui t'obsède.
À nouveau ce bruit d'un ailleurs, proche, lointain;
Tu vas à ce volet qui vibre ... Dehors, nul vent,
Les choses de la nuit sont immobiles
Comme une avancée d'eau dans la lumière.
Regarde,
L'arbre, le parapet de la terrasse,
L'aire, qui semble peinte sur le vide,
Les masses du safre clair dans le ravin,
À peine frémissent-ils, reflet peut-être
D'autres arbres et d'autres pierres sur un fleuve.
Regarde! De tout tes yeux regarde! Rien d'ici,
Que ce soit cette combe, cette lueur
Au faîte dans l'orage, ou le pain, le vin,
N'a plus cet à jamais de silencieuse
Respiration nocturne qui mariait
Dans l'antique sommeil
Les bêtes et les choses anuitées
À l'infini sous le manteau d'étoiles.
Regarde,
La main qui prend le sein,
En reconnaît la forme, en fait saillir
La douce aridité, la main s'élève,

From *The Lure of the Threshold* (1975)

THE RIVER

But no, once again
Unfolding the wing of the impossible
You awaken, with a cry,
From the place which is only a dream. Your voice
Abrupt, harsh as a flood. All the gathered
meaning falls into it, with a sound
Of sleep thrown over stone.

And you get up one eternal time
In this summer that haunts you.
Once more the sound of an elsewhere, near, far;
You go to the vibrating blinds ... Outside,
No wind, the things of night are still
As a thrust of water in the light.
Look,
The tree, the low terrace wall,
The field that seems painted on nothing,
The masses of light sandstone in the ravine,
Are barely trembling, perhaps the reflection
Of other trees and stones in a river.
Look! Look your eyes out! Nothing here,
Not this glen, not this flash
Of the storm at its crest, nor the bread nor the wine,
Has kept that forever of silent
Nocturnal breathing that wedded
Countless benighted beasts and things
In ancient sleep
Under the cloak of the stars.
Look,
The hand that touches the breast,
That recognises its form, that reveals
Its soft aridity, lifted away,

Médite son écart, son ignorance,
Et brûle retirée dans le cri désert.
Le ciel brille pourtant des mêmes signes,
Pourquoi le sens
A-t-il coagulé au flanc de l'Ourse,
Blessure inguérissable qui divise
Dans le fleuve de tout à travers tout
De son caillot, comme un chiffre de mort,
L'afflux étincelant des vies obscures?
Tu regardes couler le fleuve terrestre,
En amont, en aval la même nuit
Malgré tous ces reflets qui réunissent
Vainement les étoiles aux fruits mortels.

Et tu sais mieux, déjà, que tu rêvais
Qu'une barque chargée de terre noire
S'écartait d'une rive. Le nautonier
Pesait de tout son corps contre la perche
Qui avait pris appui, tu ignorais
Où, dans les boues sans nom du fond du fleuve.

Ô terre, terre,
Pourquoi la perfection du fruit, lorsque le sens
Comme une barque à peine pressentie
Se dérobe de la couleur et de la forme,
Et d'où ce souvenir qui serre le cœur
De la barque d'un autre été au ras des herbes?
D'où, oui, tant d'évidence à travers tant
D'énigme, et tant de certitude encore, et même
Tant de joie, préservée? Et pourquoi l'image
Qui n'est pas l'apparence, qui n'est pas
Même le rêve trouble, insiste-t-elle
En dépit du déni de l'être? Jours profonds,
Un dieu jeune passait à gué le fleuve,
Le berger s'éloignait dans la poussière,
Des enfants jouaient haut dans le feuillage,
Rires, batailles dans la paix, les bruits du soir,
Et l'esprit avait là son souffle, égal ...

Considers its own remoteness, its ignorance,
Withdrawn, it burns in the empty cry.
Yet the sky is lit by the same signs,
Why has meaning
Coagulated on the flank of the Bear,
An incurable wound, a clot
Like the cipher of death, that divides
The glittering rush of dark lives
In the river of all through all?
You watch the earthly river flow
Upstream, downstream in the same night
Despite all these reflections that join
The stars, in vain, with mortal fruit.

And you recall more clearly, now, that you dreamed
Of a boat loaded with black earth
Setting out from some shore. The pilot
Leaned his full weight on the pole
Which had touched bottom, you did not know
Where, in the nameless mud of the river-bed.

O earth, earth,
Why the perfection of fruit, if meaning,
Like a boat almost unguessed-at,
Eludes colour and form; and this memory
That grips the heart, of a boat
From another summer, level with the grass,
Where does it come from? And how,
Yes, how is such evidence through so much
Enigma, and so much certainty, even so much
Joy preserved? And why is the image
That is not appearance, that is not even
The mist of dreams, so insistent
Against the denial of being? Deep days,
A young god forded the river,
The shepherd went off into the dust,
Children played high in the leaves, laughter,
Quarrels in the stillness, the sounds of evening,
And there the mind breathed, easily …

*Aujourd'hui le passeur
N'a d'autre rive que bruyante, noire
Et Boris de Schloezer, quand il est mort
Entendant sur l'appontement une musique
Dont ses proches ne savaient rien (était-elle, déjà,
La flûte de la délivrance révélée
Ou un ultime bien de la terre perdue,
« Œuvre », transfigurée?) – derrière soi
N'a laissé que ces eaux brûlées d'énigme.
Ô terre,
Étoiles plus violentes n'ont jamais
Scellé l'orée du ciel de feux plus fixes,
Appel plus dévorant de berger dans l'arbre
N'a jamais ravagé été plus obscur.*

---

*Terre,
Qu'avait-il aperçu, que comprenait-il,
Qu'accepta-t-il?
Il écouta, longtemps,
Puis il se redressa, le feu
De cette œuvre qui atteignait,
Qui sait, à une cime
De déliements, de retrouvailles, de joie
Illumina son visage.*

*Bruit, clos,
De la perche qui heurte le flot boueux,
Nuit
De la chaîne qui glisse au fond du fleuve.
Ailleurs,
Là où j'ignorais tout, où j'écrivais,
Un chien peut-être empoisonné griffait
L'amère terre nocturne.*

Today the ferryman
Finds no shore that is not black, raging
And Boris de Schloezer, when he died
Hearing music from the landing
That his near ones could not hear (was it
The flute of revealed deliverance already,
Or a last gift from the lost earth,
A 'work', transfigured?) – left behind only
These waters burnt by the enigma.
O earth,
Never have more violent stars sealed the verge
Of the sky with such fixed fires, never
Has a more consuming call from the shepherd in the tree
Ravaged so dark a summer.

Earth,
What had he seen, understood,
Accepted?
He listened, long,
Then drew himself up, the fire
Of that work which reached,
Who knows, a summit
Of release, recovery, joy
Shone in his face.

Closed sound
Of the pole striking the muddy stream,
Darkness
Of the chain slipping to the bottom.
Elsewhere,
In the place of my ignorance, my writing,
A dog that may have been poisoned
Clawed at night's bitter earth.

DANS LE LEURRE DU SEUIL

Heurte,
Heurte à jamais.

Dans le leurre du seuil.

À la porte, scellée,
À la phrase, vide.
Dans le fer, n'éveillant
Que ces mots, le fer.

Dans le langage, noir.

Dans celui qui est là
Immobile, à veiller
À sa table, chargée
De signes, de lueurs. Et qui est appelé

Trois fois, mais ne se lève.

Dans le rassemblement, où a manqué
Le célébrable.

Dans le blé déformé
Et le vin qui sèche.

Dans la main qui retient
Une main absente.

Dans l'inutilité
De se souvenir.

Dans l'écriture, en hâte
Engrangée de nuit

THE LURE OF THE THRESHOLD

Knock,
Knock forever.

In the lure of the threshold.

At the sealed door,
At the empty phrase.
In iron, awakening
Only the word, iron.

In speech, blackness.

In he who sits
By night, motionless
At his table, laden
With signs, glimmers. And is called

Three times, but does not get up.

———————

In the gathering, that failed
Of celebration.

In the deformed wheat,
The parching wine.

In the hand that holds on
To an absent hand.

In the uselessness
Of recollection.

In writing, hastily
Garnered at night

Et dans les mots éteints
Avant même l'aube.

―――――――

Dans la bouche qui veut
D'une autre bouche
Le miel que nul été
Ne peut mûrir.

Dans la note qui, brusque,
S'intensifie
Jusqu'à être, glaciaire,
Presque la passe

Puis l'insistance de
La note tue
Qui désunit sa houle
Nue, sous l'étoile.

Dans un reflet d'étoile
Sur du fer.
Dans l'angoisse des corps
Qui ne se trouvent.

Heurte, tard.
Les lèvres désirant
Même quand le sang coule,

La main, heurtant majeure
Encore quand
Le bras n'est plus que cendre
Dispersée.

―――――――
―――――――

And in words that die out
Before dawn.

In the mouth that asks
Another mouth
For honey no summer
Can ripen.

In the abrupt note
That grows louder until,
Glacial, it almost
Becomes the crossing

Then the insistence
Of the hushed note
That releases its naked
Swell, under the star.

In the star's gleam
On iron.
In the anguish of bodies
Not finding each other.

Knock, late.
Lips wanting
Even as the blood flows,

The fist knocking
Most imperatively when
The arm is no more than
Scattered ashes.

---

*Plus avant que le chien
Dans la terre noire
Se jette en criant le passeur
Vers l'autre rive.
La bouche pleine de boue,
Les yeux mangés,
Pousse ta barque pour nous
Dans la matière.
Quel fond trouve ta perche, tu ne sais,
Quelle dérive,
Ni ce qu'éclaireront, saisis de noir,
Les mots du livre.*

*Plus avant que le chien
Qu'on recouvre mal
On t'enveloppe, passeur,
Du manteau des signes.
On te parle, on te donne
Une ou deux clefs, la vaine
Carte d'une autre terre.
Tu écoutes, les yeux déjà détournés
Vers l'eau obscure.
Tu écoutes, qui tombent,
Les quelques pelletées.*

*Plus avant que le chien
Qui est mort hier
On veut planter, passeur,
Ta phosphorescence.
Les mains des jeunes filles
Ont dégagé la terre
Sous la tige qui porte
L'or des grainées futures.
Tu pourrais distinguer encore leurs bras
Aux ombres lourdes,
Le gonflement des seins
Sous la tunique.*

Further than the dog
In the black earth
The ferryman rushes, crying
Toward the far shore.
Mouth filled with mud,
Devoured eyes,
Drive your boat for us
Into matter.
What bottom, what drift your pole may find,
You do not know,
Nor what, seized with blackness, the words
Of the book will light up.

Further than the dog
Under its thin cover,
They wrap you, ferryman,
In a cloak of signs.
They advise you, they give you
A key, two keys, the vain
Map of another earth.
You listen, your eyes already turned
To the dark water.
You listen, and the last few
Shovelfuls fall.

Further than the dog
That died yesterday,
Ferryman, they would plant
Your phosphorescence.
The hands of young girls
Have loosened the earth
From the stem that bears
The gold of future seed.
You can still see the heavy
Shadows of their arms,
The swelling of breasts
Under the tunic.

Rire s'enflamme là-haut
Mais tu t'éloignes.

Tu fus jeté sanglant
Dans la lumière,
Tu as ouvert les yeux, criant,
Pour nommer le jour,
Mais le jour n'est pas dit
Que déjà retombe
La draperie du sang, à grand bruit sourd,
Sur la lumière.
Rire s'enflamme là-haut,
Rougeoie dans l'épaisseur
Qui se désagrège.
Détourne-toi des feux
De notre rive.

Plus avant que le feu
Qui a mal pris
Est placé le témoin du feu, l'indéchiffré,
Sur un lit de feuilles.
Faces tournées vers nous,
Lecteurs de signes,
Quel vent de l'autre face, inentendu,
Les fera bruire?
Quelles mains hésitantes
Et comme découvrant
Prendront, feuilletteront
L'ombre des pages?
Quelles mains méditantes
Ayant comme trouvé?

Oh, penche-toi, rassure,
Nuée
Du sourire qui bouge
En visage clair.

Laughter flares above you
But you move away.

You were thrown bleeding
Into the light.
You opened your eyes, crying,
To name the day.
But the day was hardly uttered
When the curtain of blood
Fell again, with a huge dull sound
Over the light.
Laughter flares above you
Glowing in the thickness
That is breaking up.
Turn away
From the fires of our shore.

Further than the fire
That barely burns,
The witness of fire, the undeciphered,
Is laid on a bed of leaves.
Faces turned toward us,
Readers of signs,
What wind from the other face, unheard,
Will make them rustle?
What hesitant hands,
As if finding, grasping,
Leafing through the darkness
Of the pages? What hands
Meditating, as if
They had found what?

———————

Oh, bend down, comfort,
Cloud
Of a smile stirring
In a bright face.

*Sois pour qui a eu froid
Contre la rive
La fille de Pharaon
Et ses servantes,*

*Celles dont l'eau, encore
Avant le jour,
Reflète renversée
L'étoffe rouge.*

———————

*Et comme une main trie
Sur une table
Le grain presque germé
De l'ivraie obscure*

*Et sur l'eau du bois noir
Prenant se double
D'un reflet, où le sens
Soudain se forme,*

*Accueille, pour dormir
Dans ta parole,
Nos mots que le vent troue
De ses rafales.*

———————

*« Es-tu venu pour boire de ce vin,
Je ne te permets pas de le boire.
Es-tu venu pour apprendre ce pain
Sombre, brûlé du feu d'une promesse,
Je ne te permets pas d'y porter lumière.
Es-tu venu ne serait-ce que pour
Que l'eau t'apaise, un peu d'eau tiède, bue
Au milieu de la nuit après d'autres lèvres*

Be for him who shivered
Against the shore
Pharaoh's daughter
And her serving-girls

Whom the water, even
Before daybreak,
Reflects reversed
In their red dresses.

———————

And as a hand sorts
On a table
The nearly sprouted wheat
From the dark tares

And pausing on the water
Of black wood, is doubled,
A reflection where meaning
Suddenly forms,

Receive, to sleep
In your speech,
Our words riddled
By the wind's blast.

———————

'Though you come to drink of this wine,
I will not let you drink it.
Though you come wanting to understand
This dark bread, burnt by the fire of a promise,
I will not let you bring light to it.
Though you come only to quench your thirst
With water, a little warm water, drunk
After other lips in the middle of the night

Entre le lit défait et la terre simple,
Je ne te permets pas de toucher au verre.
Es-tu venu pour que brille l'enfant
Au-dessus de la flamme qui le scelle
Dans l'immortalité de l'heure d'avril
Où il peut rire, et toi, où l'oiseau se pose
Dans l'heure qui l'accueille et n'a pas de nom,
Je ne te permets pas d'élever tes mains au-dessus de l'âtre où je règne
    clair.

Es-tu venu,
Je ne te permets pas de paraître.
Demandes-tu,
Je ne te permets pas de savoir le nom formé par tes lèvres. »

———————

Plus avant que les pierres
Que l'ouvrier
Debout sur le mur arrache
Tard, dans la nuit.

Plus avant que le flanc du corbeau, qui marque
De sa rouille la brume
Et passe dans le rêve en poussant un cri
Comble de terre noire.

Plus avant que l'été
Que la pelle casse,
Plus avant que le cri
Dans un autre rêve,

Se jette en criant celui qui
Nous représente,
Ombre que fait l'espoir
Sur l'origine,

Between the unmade bed and the simple earth,
I will not let you touch the glass.
Though you come so that the child can shine
Above the fame that seals him
In the deathlessness of the April hour
When he may laugh, and you may, and the bird alights
In the nameless hour that welcomes it,
I will not let you lift your hands above the hearth of my bright
  kingship.

Though you come,
I will not let you appear.
Though you ask,
I will not let you know what name your lips form.'

———————

Further than the stones
That the workman, standing
On the wall, tears away
Late, in the night.

Further than the crow's flank, that marks
The mist with its rusty stain
And passes into the dream letting out a cry
Full of black earth.

Further than summer
Broken by the spade,
Further than the cry
Into another dream,

The one who stands for us
Rushes, crying,
A shadow that hope has thrown
Against origin,

Et la seule unité, ce mouvement
Du corps – quand, tout d'un coup,
De sa masse jetée contre la perche
Il nous oublie.

———————

Nous, la voix que refoule
Le vent des mots.
Nous, l'œuvre que déchire
Leur tourbillon.
Car si je viens vers toi, qui as parlé,
Gravats, ruissellements,
Échos, la salle est vide.
Est-ce « un autre », l'appel qui me répond,
Ou moi encore?
Et sous la voûte de l'écho, multiplié
Suis-je rien d'autre
Qu'une de ses flèches, lancée
Contre les choses?

Nous
Parmi les bruits,
Nous
L'un d'eux.

Se détachant
De la paroi qui s'éboule,
Se creusant, s'évasant,
Se vidant de soi,
S'empourprant,
Se gonflant d'une plénitude lointaine.

———————

Regarde ce torrent,
Il se jette en criant dans l'été désert

And the only oneness, this movement
Of the body when – now leaning
His full weight on the pole,
He forgets us.

We, the voice driven back
By the wind of words.
We, the work torn apart
By their whirling.
For if I come to you, who have spoken,
Rubble, streamings,
Echoes, the room is empty.
Is it 'another', this call that answers me,
Or, again, myself?
And, multiplied under the echo's arch,
Am I no more
Than one of its arrows
Shot into things?

We
Among the noises,
We
One of them.

Detached
From the crumbling wall,
Hollowed, splayed out,
Emptied,
Reddening,
Swelling with a distant fullness.

Look at this flooded stream,
It rushes howling into empty summer

Et pourtant, immobile,
C'est l'attelage cabré
Et la face aveugle.
Écoute.
L'écho n'est pas autour du bruit mais dans le bruit
Comme son gouffre.
Les falaises du bruit,
Les entonnoirs où se brisent ses eaux,
La saxifrage
S'arrachent de tes yeux avec un cri
D'aigle, final.
Où heurte le poitrail de la voix de l'eau,
Tu ne peux l'entendre,
Mais laisse-toi porter, œil ébloui,
Par l'aile rauque.

Nous
Au fusant du bruit,
Nous
Portés.

Nous, oui, quand le torrent
À mains brisées
Jette, roule, reprend
L'absolu des pierres.

Le prédateur
Au faîte de son vol,
Criant,
Se recourbe sur soi et se déchire.
De son sein divisé par le bec obscur
Jaillit le vide.
Au faîte de la parole encore le bruit,
Dans l'œuvre
La houle d'un bruit second.
Mais au faîte du bruit la lumière change.

And yet, motionless,
It is a harnessed team rearing
And a blind face.
Listen.
The echo is not around the noise but in the noise,
Its hollow depth.
The cliffs of noise,
The narrows where its waters break,
The saxifrage
Tear from your sight with a final
Eagle's cry.
Where the breast of the voice of water strikes,
You cannot hear it,
But be upborne, dazzled eye,
By the raucous wing.

We
In the burst of noise,
We
Upborne.

We, when the flood
With broken hands
Hurls, rolls, retrieves
The absolute of stones.

The predator
At the peak of its fight,
Crying out,
Bends back and tears itself.
From the breast cleft by the dark beak
The void spills out.
At the peak of speech there is still noise,
In the work
The swell of a second noise.
But at the peak of noise the light changes.

———————

*Tout le visible infirme
Se désécrit,
Braise où passe l'appel
D'autres campagnes*

*Et la foudre est en paix
Au-dessus des arbres,
Sein où bougent en rêve
Sommeil et mort,*

*Et brûle, une couleur,
La nuit du monde
Comme s'éploie dans l'eau
Noire, une étoffe peinte*

*Quand l'image divise
Soudain, le flux,
Criant son grain, le feu,
Contre une perche.*

———————

*Heure
Retranchée de la somme, maintenant.
Présence
Détrompée de la mort. Ampoule
Qui s'agenouille en silence
Et brûle
Déviée, secouée
Par la nuit qui n'a pas de cime.
Je t'écoute
Vibrer dans le rien de l'œuvre
Qui peine de par le monde.
Je perçois le piétinement
D'appels
Dont le pacage est l'ampoule qui brûle.
Je prends la terre à poignées*

All the wavering visible
Unwrites itself,
Embers through which the call
Of other fields passes

And the lightning is at peace
Above the trees,
Breast where sleep and death
Stir in their dreams,

And the night of the world,
A colour, burns
Like a painted cloth spreading
In black water

Now, when the image
Divides the flow,
Throwing its seed, fire,
Against a pole.

———————

Hour
Cut off from the sum, now.
Presence
Undeceived by death. Bulb
That kneels in silence
And burns
Defected, shaken
By the summitless night.
I hear you
Vibrate in the nullity of the work
That labours through the world.
I hear the trampling
Of calls
Whose pasture is the burning bulb.
I take up fistfuls of earth

Dans cet évasement aux parois lisses
Où il n'est pas de fond
Avant le jour.
Je t'écoute, je prends
Dans ton panier de corde
Toute la terre. Dehors,
C'est encore le temps de la douleur
Avant l'image.
Dans la main de dehors, fermée,
A commencé à germer
Le blé des choses du monde.

———————
———————

Le nautonier
Qui touche de sa perche, méditante,
À ton épaule
Et toi, déjà celui que la nuit recouvre
Quand ta perche recherche mais vainement
Le fond du fleuve,

Lequel se perdra,
Qui peut espérer, qui promettre?
Penché, vois poindre sur l'eau
Tout un visage

Comme prend un feu, au reflet
De ton épaule.

In this smooth-walled splaying out
Where there is no bottom
Before daybreak.
I hear you, I catch
The whole world
In your rope basket. Outside
It is still the time of suffering
Before the image.
In the closed hand of the outside
The wheat of things of the world
Has begun to sprout.

———————
———————

The pilot
Who touches your shoulder
With his meditative pole,
And you, already the one whom night covers
When your pole seeks, in vain,
The river's bottom,

He who is, he who will perish,
Who can hope, who promise?
Bending down, you see a face
Well up in the water

As a fire kindles, in the reflection
Of your shoulder.

DEUX BARQUES

L'orage qui s'attarde, le lit défait,
La fenêtre qui bat dans la chaleur
Et le sang dans sa fièvre: je reprends
La main proche à son rêve, la cheville
À son anneau de barque retenue
Contre un appontement, dans une écume,
Puis le regard, puis la bouche à l'absence
Et tout le brusque éveil dans l'été nocturne
Pour y porter l'orage et le finir.
– Où que tu sois quand je te prends obscure,
S'étant accru en nous ce bruit de mer,
Accepte d'être l'indifférence, que j'étreigne
À l'exemple de Dieu l'aveugle la matière
La plus déserte encore dans la nuit.
Accueille-moi intensément mais distraitement,
Fais que je n'aie pas de visage, pas de nom
Pour qu'étant le voleur je te donne plus
Et l'étranger l'exil, en toi, en moi
Se fasse l'origine … – Oh, je veux bien,
Toutefois, t'oubliant, je suis avec toi,
Desserres-tu mes doigts,
Formes-tu de mes paumes une coupe,
Je bois, près de ta soif,
Puis laisse l'eau couler sur tous nos membres.
Eau qui fait que nous sommes, n'étant pas,
Eau qui prend au travers des corps arides
Pour une joie éparse dans l'énigme,
Pressentiment pourtant! Te souviens-tu,
Nous allions par ces champs barrés de pierre,
Et soudain la citerne, et ces deux présences
Dans quel autre pays de l'été désert?
Regarde comme ils se penchent, eux comme nous,
Est-ce nous qu'ils écoutent, dont ils parlent,
Souriant sous les feuilles du premier arbre
Dans leur lumière heureuse un peu voilée?

TWO BOATS

The storm lingering, the unmade bed,
The window knocking in the heat,
Blood beating in its fever: I take back
This hand close to mine in its dream, this ankle
Secured to its ring
On the pier, in sleep's foam,
Take back from absence this glance, this mouth,
And the whole sudden waking in nocturnal summer
To bring the storm to it and make it end.
– Wherever you may be, so dark, when I take you,
The sea's sound having grown louder in us,
Consent to be indifference, that I may embrace
The most desert matter waiting by night,
As God the Blind would do. Receive me
Intensely but abstractedly,
Let me have no face or name for you,
So that being the thief I may give you more
And the stranger, exile, in you, in me,
May become the origin … – Oh, I would gladly,
And yet, forgetting you, I am with you,
Only unclench my fingers,
Form my hands into a cup,
I drink, close to your thirst,
Then I let water pour over all our limbs.
Water that gives us being, who are not,
Water that soaks through parched bodies
For a joy scattered among enigmas,
And yet we knew it! Do you remember,
We were walking over those stone-hedged fields,
And suddenly a cistern, and those two presences
In what other country of empty summer?
See how they bend down, just as we do,
Are they listening to us, talking about us,
Smiling under the leaves of the first tree
In their happy, slightly veiled light?

*Et ne dirait-on pas qu'une lueur
Autre, bouge dans cet accord de leurs visages
Et, riante, les mêle? Vois, l'eau se trouble
Mais les formes en sont plus pures, consumées.
Quel est le vrai de ces deux mondes, peu importe.
Invente-moi, redouble-moi peut-être
Sur ces confins de fable déchirée.*

*J'écoute, je consens,
Puis j'écarte le bras qui s'est replié,
Me dérobant la face lumineuse.
Je la touche à la bouche avec mes lèvres,
En désordre, brisée, toute une mer.
Comme Dieu le soleil levant je me suis voûté
Sur cette eau où fleurit notre ressemblance,
Je murmure: C'est donc ce que tu veux,
Puissance errante insatisfaite par les mondes,
Te ramasser, une vie, dans le vase
De terre nue de notre identité?
Et c'est vrai qu'un instant tout est silence,
On dirait que le temps va faire halte
Comme s'il hésitait sur le chemin,
Regardant par-dessus l'épaule terrestre
Ce que nous ne pouvons ou ne voulons voir.
Le tonnerre ne roule plus dans le ciel calme,
L'ondée ne passe plus sur notre toit,
Le volet, qui heurtait à notre rêve,
Se tait courbé sur son âme de fer.
J'écoute, je ne sais quel bruit, puis je me lève
Et je cherche, dans l'ombre encore, où je retrouve
Le verre d'hier soir, à demi plein.
Je le prends, qui respire à notre souffle,
Je te fais le toucher de ta soif obscure,
Et quand je bois l'eau tiède où furent tes lèvres,
C'est comme si le temps cessait sur les miennes
Et que mes yeux s'ouvraient, à enfin le jour.*

And doesn't it seem that another brightness
Wakes in the harmony of their faces
And mirthfully joins them? See, the water clouds
But the forms in it are purer, consumed.
Which of these two worlds is the true one
Does not matter. Invent me, increase me
At these limits of the torn fable.

I listen, I consent,
Then I push aside the folded arm
That hides the luminous face from me.
I touch the mouth with my lips –
All disorder, broken, a sea.
Like God the Rising Sun I bend down
Over the water where our likeness flowers,
I murmur: So this is what you want,
Wandering power that the worlds cannot satisfy,
To gather yourself, one life, in the bare
Earthen vessel of our identity?
And, true, for a moment all is silence,
You would think time was about to stop
As if pausing on its way,
Looking over the earthly shoulder
At what we cannot or will not see.
Thunder no longer rolls through the calm sky,
Rain no longer sweeps over our roof,
The blinds that knocked in our dream
Are quiet, turned in on their iron soul.
I hear I don't know what noise, get up
And search, still in the dark, and find
Last night's glass, half full, breathing
With us. I pick it up, I let you touch it
With your obscure thirst, and when I drink
The warm water where your lips were
It is as if time had ceased on mine
And my eyes were opened, to the day at last.

Donne-moi ta main sans retour, eau incertaine
Que j'ai désempierrée jour après jour
Des rêves qui s'attardent dans la lumière
Et du mauvais désir de l'infini.
Que le bien de la source ne cesse pas
À l'instant où la source est retrouvée,
Que les lointains ne se séparent pas
Une nouvelle fois du proche, sous la faux
De l'eau non plus tarie mais sans saveur.
Donne-moi ta main et précède-moi dans l'été mortel
Avec ce bruit de lumière changée,
Dissipe-toi me dissipant dans la lumière.

Les images, les mondes, les impatiences,
Les désirs qui ne savent pas bien qu'ils dénouent,
La beauté mystérieuse au sein obscur,
Aux mains frangées pourtant d'une lumière,
Les rires, les rencontres sur des chemins,

Et les appels, les dons, les consentements,
Les demandes sans fin, naître, insensé,
Les alliances éternelles et les hâtives,
Les promesses miraculeuses non tenues
Mais, tard, l'inespéré, soudain: que tout cela
La rose de l'eau qui passe le recueille
En se creusant ici, puis l'illumine
Au moyen immobile de la roue.

Paix, sur l'eau éclairée. On dirait qu'une barque
Passe, chargée de fruits; et qu'une vague
De suffisance, ou d'immobilité,
Soulève notre lieu et cette vie
Comme une barque à peine autre, liée encore.
Aie confiance, et laisse-toi prendre, épaule nue,

Give me your unreturning hand, fitful water
That I have disballasted day after day
Of dreams that linger in the light
And the bad longing for infinity.
May the gift of the source not cease
The moment the source is recovered,
May the distances not be cut off once more
From the near, by a scythe of water
Not dried up, then, but savourless.
Give me your hand, go ahead of me
Into mortal summer, with your sound of light changed,
Be scattered as you scatter me in the light.

Images, worlds, longings,
Ignorant desires that yet unbind,
Mysterious beauty with its dark breast
But with hands fringed with light,
Laughter, meetings on the roads,

And the appeals, the gifts, the assents,
The endless demands, this madness, birth,
The eternal and the hurried unions,
The miraculous promises that are not kept
But suddenly, late, the unexpected: that all
Should gather into the rose of flowing water
As it hollows out here, and be made light
At the still hub of the wheel.

Peace, on the bright water. You would think a boat
Was passing by, laden with fruit; that a wave
Of fullness, or of stillness,
Uplifted our place and this life
Almost like the same boat, still moored.
Trust, let yourself go, bare shoulder,

*Par l'onde qui s'élargit de l'été sans fin,
Dors, c'est le plein été; et une nuit
Par l'excès de lumière; et va se déchirer
Notre éternelle nuit; va se pencher
Souriante sur nous l'Egyptienne.*

*Paix, sur le flot qui va. Le temps scintille.
On dirait que la barque s'est arrêtée.
On n'entend plus que se jeter, se désunir,
Contre le flanc désert l'eau infinie.*

*Le feu, ses joies de sève déchirée.
La pluie, ou rien qu'un vent peut-être sur les tuiles.
Tu cherches ton manteau de l'autre année.
Tu prends les clefs, tu sors, une étoile brille.*

*Éloigne-toi
Dans les vignes, vers la montagne de Vachères.
À l'aube
Le ciel sera plus rapide.*

*Un cercle
Où tonne l'indifférence.
De la lumière
À la place de Dieu.*

*Presque du feu, vois-tu,
Dans le baquet de l'eau de la pluie nocturne.*

*Dans le rêve, pourtant,
Dans l'autre feu obscur qui avait repris,
Une servante allait avec une lampe
Loin devant nous. La lumière était rouge
Et ruisselait
Dans les plis de la robe contre la jambe
Jusqu'à la neige.*

On the swelling wave of endless summer,
Sleep, it is high summer; and one night
By an excess of light; and our eternal darkness
Will soon be broken; the Egyptian girl
Will bend down, smiling, over us.

Peace, on the flowing water. Time sparkles.
You would think the boat had landed.
All you hear now is the infinite water
Heaving and breaking against its bare side.

Fire, the joys of split sap.
Rain, or maybe just wind on the roof-tiles.
You look for your coat from last year.
You take the keys, you go out, a star shines.

Move off
Through the vineyards, towards the mountain
Of Vachères. At dawn
The sky will be quicker.

A circle
Where indifference thunders.
Light
In place of God.

Almost fire, you see,
In the trough of the nocturnal rain.

Yet in the dream,
In the other dark fire that flared up again,
A serving-girl went far ahead of us
With a lamp. Its light was red
And streamed
Down the folds of the dress against her thigh
Onto the snow.

Étoiles, répandues.
Le ciel, un lit défait, une naissance.

Et l'amandier, grossi
Après deux ans: le flot
Dans un bras plus obscur, du même fleuve.

———————

———————

Ô amandier en fleurs,
Ma nuit sans fin,
Aie confiance, appuie-toi enfant
À cette foudre.

Branche d'ici, brûlée d'absence, bois
De tes fleurs d'un instant au ciel qui change.

———————

Je suis sorti
Dans un autre univers. C'était
Avant le jour.
J'ai jeté du sel sur la neige.

From L'ÉPARS, L'INDIVISIBLE

Oui, par ce lieu
Perdu, non dégagé
Des ronces, puis des cendres d'un espoir.
Par ce désir vaincu, non, consumé

Car nous aurons vécu si profond les jours
Que nous a consentis cette lumière!
Il faisait beau toujours, beau à périr,
La campagne alentour était déserte,

Star-strewn sky,
An unmade bed, a birth.

And the almond tree, grown
Sturdier in two years: the flow
Of the same river in a darker arm.

———————
———————

O flowering almond tree,
My endless night,
Trust, child, lean
Against this lightning.

Branch here, burnt by absence, drink
With your brief flowers from the changing sky.

———————

I came out
Into another universe. It was
Before dawn.
I threw salt on the snow.

From THE SCATTERED, THE INDIVISIBLE

Yes, by this place
Now lost, never fully freed
From the brambles, nor from the ashes of hope.
By this desire, vanquished, no, consumed

For we will have lived so fully the moments
That were granted to us by the light!
The days were beautiful, beautiful beyond our dreams,
The countryside around us was deserted,

Nous n'entendions que respirer la terre
Et grincer la chaîne du puits, cause du temps
Qui retombait du seau comme trop de ciel.
Nous travaillions ici ou là, dans de grandes salles,
Nous ne parlions que peu, à voix rouillée
Comme on cache une clef sous une pierre.
Parfois la nuit venait, du bout des longes,
Parfaite femme voûtée de noir poussant muettes
Ses bêtes dans les eaux du soleil constant.

Et qu'elle dorme
Dans l'absolu que nous avons été
Cette maison qui fut comme un ravin
Où bruit le ciel, où vient l'oiseau qui rêve
Boire la paix nocturne ... Irrévélée,
Trop grande, trop mystérieuse pour nos pas,
Ne faisons qu'effleurer son épaule obscure,
Ne troublons pas celle qui puise d'un souffle égal
Aux réserves de songe de la terre.
Déposons simplement, la nuit venue, ces pierres
Où nous lisions le signe, à son flanc désert.

Que de tâches inachevables nous tentions,
Que de signes impénétrables nous touchions
De nos doigts ignorants et donc cruels!
Que d'errements et que de solitude!
La mémoire est lassée, certes, le temps étroit,
Le chemin infini encore ... Mais le ciel
A des pierres plus rougeoyantes du côté
Du soir, et dans nos vies qui font étape,
Lumière qui t'accrois parfois, tu prends et brûles.

We could only hear the breathing of the earth
And the creaking of the chain in the well, drawing up time
That spilled from the bucket like too much sky.
We would work here and there, in the vast rooms,
We spoke but little, in rusted voices,
As one might hide a key beneath a stone.
Sometimes night would come forward, from the end of the fields,
A perfect woman, dark, bending down, driving her silent
Beasts through the waters of the changeless sun.

And may it sleep
In the absolute that we have been,
That house which was like a ravine
Where the sky could rustle, where the dreaming bird
Could drink from night's peace ... Unrevealed,
Too grand, too mysterious for our steps,
Let us but graze her dark shoulder,
Let us not trouble her, for she draws with even breath
From earth's store of dreams.
When night comes, let us simply place by her naked flank
These stones on which we seemed to read signs.

How many unfinishable tasks we tried,
How many unfathomable signs we touched
With fingers that knew nothing, and so were cruel!
How misguided we were, and how alone!
Memory is weary, certainly, and time narrow,
The journey still infinite ... But the sky
Has stones that glow more brightly along the paths
Of evening, and at this stage our lives have reached,
Light that sometimes increases, you catch and burn.

———————

Oui, par l'après-midi
Où tout est silencieux, étant sans fin,
Le temps dort dans la cendre du feu d'hier
Et la guêpe qui heurte à la vitre a cousu
Beaucoup déjà de la déchirure du monde.
Nous dormons, dans la salle d'en haut, mais nous allons
Aussi, et à jamais, parmi les pierres.

———

Oui, par le corps
Dans la douceur qui est aveugle et ne veut rien
Mais parachève.

Et à ses vitres les feuillages sont plus proches
Dans des arbres plus clairs. Et reposent les fruits
Sous l'arche du miroir. Et le soleil
Est haut encore derrière la corbeille
De l'été sur la table et des quelques fleurs.

———

Oui, par naître qui fit
De rien la flamme,
Et confond apaisés
Nos deux visages.

(Nous nous penchions, et l'eau
Coulait rapide,
Mais nos mains, là brisées,
Prirent l'image.)

———

Yes, by the afternoon
When all is silent, being endless,
Time is sleeping in the ashes of yesterday's fire
And the wasp that knocks against the window has
Already sown up a great deal of the tear in the world.
We sleep, in the room upstairs, but we also
Walk, and forever, among the stones.

———

Yes, by the body
In the gentle sweetness that is blind and wants nothing,
And yet brings completion.

And at its windows the leaves are closer
In brighter trees. And the fruit is at rest
Beneath the mirror's arch. And the sun
Is still high, behind the summer
Basket on the table and the handful of flowers.

———

Yes, by birth that made
A flame from nothing,
And mingles
Our two faces, now at peace.

(We bent down, and the water
Was flowing fast,
But our hands, though broken,
Caught the image.)

———

Oui, par l'enfant

Et par ces quelques mots que j'ai sauvés
Pour une bouche enfante. « Vois, le serpent
Du fond de ce jardin ne quitte guère
L'ombre fade du buis. Tous ses désirs
Sont de silence et de sommeil parmi les pierres.
La douleur de nommer parmi les choses
Finira. » C'est déjà musique dans l'épaule,
Musique dans le bras qui la protège,
Parole sur des lèvres réconciliées.

———————

Oui, par les mots,
Quelques mots.

(Et d'une main,
Certes, lever le fouet, injurier le sens,
Précipiter
Tout le charroi d'images dans les pierres
– De l'autre, plus profonde, retenir.

Car celui qui ne sait
Le droit d'un rêve simple qui demande
À relever le sens, à apaiser
Le visage sanglant, à colorer
La parole blessée d'une lumière,
Celui-là, serait-il
Presque un dieu à créer presque une terre,
Manque de compassion, n'accède pas
Au vrai, qui n'est qu'une confiance, ne sent pas
Dans son désir crispé sur sa différence
La dérive majeure de la nuée.
Il veut bâtir! Ne serait-ce, exténuée,
Qu'une trace de foudre, pour préserver
Dans l'orgueil le néant de quelque forme,

Yes, by the child

And by these words I saved
For a child's mouth. 'Look, the serpent
At the back of the garden hardly ever leaves
The lustreless shade of the boxtree. His only desire
Is for silence and for sleep among the stones.
The painfulness of naming among things
Will cease.' There is already music in the shoulder,
Music in the arm that protects it,
Words on lips that have been reconciled.

Yes, by words,
A few simple words.

(And with one hand,
Of course, raise the whip, curse meaning,
Drive
The whole load of images against the stones
– But with the other, deeper hand, rein back.

For he who does not know
The right of a simple dream, that only asks
To raise up meaning, to soothe
The bleeding face, to colour
The wounded word with light,
This man, be he
Almost a god, creating almost an earth,
Lacks compassion, does not attain to
The true, which is only a trusting, does not sense
In his desire clenched over his difference
The major drifting of the cloud.
He wants to build! Be it only a feeble
Trace of lightning, to preserve
In pride the emptiness of some form,

*Et c'est rêver, cela encore, mais sans bonheur,
Sans avoir su atteindre à la terre brève.*

*Non, ne démembre pas
Mais délivre, et rassure. « Écrire », une violence
Mais pour la paix qui a saveur d'eau pure.
Que la beauté,
Car ce mot a un sens, malgré la mort,
Fasse œuvre de rassemblement de nos montagnes
Pour l'eau d'été, étroite,*

*Et l'appelle dans l'herbe,
Prenne la main de l'eau à travers les routes,
Conduise l'eau d'ici, minime, au fleuve clair.)*

———————

And this is dreaming too, but without joy,
Without having known how to reach the brief earth.

No, do not dismember
But deliver, and reassure. 'Writing', a violence
But for the peace that tastes of pure water.
May beauty,
For this word has a meaning, in spite of death,
Do the work of bringing together our mountains
For the scant waters of summer

And call them into the grasses,
And take the water's hand across the roads
And lead the water here, the narrow water, to the bright river.)

★ ★ ★

From *Récits en rêve* / *Dream Tales* (1987)

L'ÉGYPTE / EGYPT (composed 1977)

I

There were a lot of us on that ship, adrift for days, all its engines and lights off, but propelled, one felt, by a hidden force that kept those of us aboard from feeling alarmed, if not exactly carefree. 'One', 'we', the others, I, were a group of friends, with many events in our common past, then during the first period of the voyage or the dream, a thousand ups and downs, an abundance I still feel, that sense of a time truly lived. But this memory was being effaced, and it vanished completely with the final episode, right from the start, as if it were in its nature to unravel, without violence but for ever, something that the joys, preoccupations and lessons of a lifetime had brought to maturity.

A few certainties, all the same. It was summer, we were sailing the eastern Mediterranean, and although our voyage had no specific plan it began in Egypt, veered west, then pushed north towards shores I immediately felt would be mountainous.

One evening at nightfall, we arrived at a port whose houses, as it happened, staggered up the sides of a fairly high mountain, and even at times seemed to disappear in its folds. In this place, clearly, a major festival was drawing to a close; the streets were dotted with fires that mingled under the trees; the houses were open and glittered, and because of this it was easy to see that the higher-perched neighbourhoods were separated by stretches of woods or rock, bringing the hinterland down into the heart of the city almost. Here or there one made out among the roofs other dark spots, but these flickered phosphorescently – probably the site of churches. Another church, a sort of metropolis, sitting on a spur of land near the centre, its whole facade and the base of its great domes alight with a beautiful yellow light, looked down on the harbour in its entirety, and the whole of the bay – of all the places and monuments in this strange land the church was what one picked out from a distance. But it looked – was

it just an illusion? – deserted, silent.

I was at the ship's prow among the passengers gathered there, indistinct already, whispering – and I wondered, 'Is this Salonica? Is this Smyrna?' not excluding that it might be an entirely different city, one I might never have heard of. My only conviction, whence a preference, but slight, for Salonica, was that this port slowly looming up faced south and backed onto a vast, almost empty, region that vanished into Asia's depths. But the ship was coming alongside the quay, with the same slowness and gentleness it had had these past few days, and already we were disembarking among the men and women who lingered on the shore even if here and there the sea breeze had started to lift and scatter – sparks of brightness under others dying down – the wilted flowers and a debris of garlands.

And I question, gaily at first, some of the passers-by I meet, 'What city is this?'

It's strange, they don't understand. Heads turn towards me, they smile, they've caught the sense of my words, I can see, the lack of understanding hasn't to do with language, and yet, more deeply, nothing registers. Suddenly anxious, I attempt to rephrase my question. For example, 'What do you call this place you live in?' Or, 'If you were outside the town, and coming back (I vaguely perceive a track along the sea, under the cliffs, with a donkey, and the city in the distance against the sun, now setting), you would tell me: I'm going to …?' But none of these stratagems evokes the least response. It seems that even the notion of name, or of place, is utterly foreign to these people, at least as far as their city is concerned. Moreover, they are hardly listening to me, we move apart, politely, and in the meantime my friends have scattered in the crowd.

II

I wake, and all day I can't stop thinking about the brightly lit city, the quay, the total incomprehension, with immense sadness and a feeling of solitude.

Then, that evening, the telephone rang, and I learnt what had happened during the previous night. My mother, who lived alone in

the city where I was born, had had a stroke as she was going to bed; she'd spent the entire night and the following morning on the floor, almost unconscious – dreaming probably. I also learnt that she'd greeted her rescuers with the words of a diminished mind, the uncertain and whimsical perception of a child on the threshold of language, but with all her usual courtesy. She apologised for bothering so many people. She wanted, I believe, to offer them refreshments. I thought then, and not without sadness again, that always concealed beneath this courtesy, and even from herself, was the experience of a kind of distance: the people around her in this part of the country that she'd had to come to when she was young and spend her life in, remained foreign – cold, she used to say, distrustful, without the outgoingness and give-and-take she associated on the other hand, as its great virtue, with her place of birth, her father's native province.

Morning again, and I went to the station, early. A fine, crisp day, pale sunlight running across the surfaces of shadows that looked like water, shimmering. I saw a sort of little girl in jeans wandering along the quay, humming, her shadow falling on the pavement in two or three sharply curved lines that darted like birds; they seemed to me sentences, maybe rich with meaning. Sometimes, holding her right foot out gracefully in front of her in this game of black and white, she tested the ground as if it were thin ice, before putting her weight on it suddenly, laughing and tossing her head. Then she stopped, gazing off at I don't know what – nothing probably. And I understood – I too all of a sudden – that her name was *Egypt*. At this my spirits lifted, for I was no longer in the life where one feels sadness but back in the dream; and also because I understood perfectly that if the dream was starting up again now but in the places and situations of my waking life, in this country, here, where people and cities have names, it was closely related to this life, and it must therefore be a good dream. I boarded the train, once more in my life I looked at the quay; it was beginning to flow gently in the summer light, as if I were on a shore.

III

Once more in my life, and how many times! When I was a child, roughly the age of the little girl, I was in the other country, in the mountains, with the sun coming up behind on the left, the train that shot out from between the rocks on the right, rushed towards us with its brow unfurrowed, then was gone, splashing us with its shadow, scarcely broken between cars by the commas, the dots – or the words again? – of light. The whole village would go to the station early in the morning 'to watch the train go by'; would go back at the end of the afternoon to greet its return; my mother, my grandmother, my aunt, often traipsing along, in the idleness of summer, and sometimes we were the ones who climbed down the still-shuddering steps, with our holiday jumble of bags. Crushed by the long night spent in packed compartments and in two or three station buffets, brimming with unfinished dreams, flapping my wings like a dazzled owl, I saw clearly that they were all there together, the living and the dead! In the foreground, the held-out hands, the moustaches, the chignons with steel knitting needles stuck in them, sun glinting on a holy-dove brooch pinned to a bodice, but off in the distance, smiling, anxious as in a photograph in its oval frame, those aged faces of which they'd later say, 'No, you couldn't have known him. No, he was no longer around …' And always the *Promé té ché*, also known as the madwoman, on the quay going from group to group in her great bouffant – but tattered and dusty black dress – coiffed one might have said with a huge basket of fruit and flowers, long since fresh. She would go up to everyone, she would even lean over me, laughing, wagging her finger as if in warning, jokingly, or recalling an old promise. 'Oh, I promise you …' she'd say, and you told yourself, or I ended up believing, that a fiancé had once left her here in this station and hadn't come back. Everyone was talking very loudly, of course, exclaiming, laughing, no one paid her the least attention, any more than to the shadow that crossed her face when the last train door slammed shut. After which, with the last of the voyagers, humming, a little apart, she returned to the village and you'd see her there at night still, squatting in her dark doorway, busy stirring the embers under some cast-iron pots. I loved her; to me it seemed she was the earth itself, the earth that I sensed, in

the dying of villages, the last processions for good weather or rain, the last patois songs of the goose-girls in the meadows, was growing old aphasic. And I dreamt that one day I would – but how? – right the wrong done by the fiancé who had fled in the morning of the world.

LES DÉCOUVERTES DE PRAGUE / THE PRAGUE DISCOVERIES (composed 1977)

2 May 1975

As faithfully as possible, the moments of one of those reveries that now and then form within us, just as the other kind of dream, the night-time kind, form and dissolve.

  Brief prose texts I've been writing lately, also dreamlike, which must owe something of their intimacy to the unconscious, for I try not to let my reflections control whatever surprising, incomprehensible thing pops up. It seems to me that I am able to perceive what the secret parcel of life that appears under my pen already has of the organic and the specific; and that I can therefore help it grow and breathe by prudent pruning obedient only to the text's needs. Which amounts to thinking, let me say in passing, that André Breton was wrong to consider absolute automatism the condition of true speech. Everything one's most recent memories throw up, everything the eye catches or the ear is subjected to can enter unhindered, without the juxtapositions, measurement, careful weighings that any attempt at formulation, even without the mind's conscious approbation, entails. Crossing out, on the other hand, choosing while letting the other choose, facilitates an economy, encourages a deposit – who knows? incites the underlying thought to use this first rapid jotting down of one's thoughts as an opportunity for further composition by means of which, in certain works of poetry or in the arts, meaning brings peace, and music. Already in what we spontaneously call 'good dreams' this deeper work has taken place, thanks to which a form, heard in the élans of desire, can be freed and rise to the light, but to wait for it – this desire – to receive it, refresh it with its water, soothe it with its serious joy.

Les beaux rêves ... Just as surrealism was wrong to rush words' already impatient course, to prohibit stopping at what might be the crossroads, the short cut, the lost dwelling's threshold – yes, who knows? and why suppress the one big question – so psychoanalysis' understanding of desire would be impoverished if it didn't, in giving an 'aesthetic' dimension to its study of symbols, try to appreciate the elements of composition, rhythm, silence, rustlings in the margins – of *beauty* – which can put an unforgettable face on the scenes we traverse in our sleep.

But in what I mean to recount today, the reverie occurred unprompted, beyond the white page, beyond any project to experiment or to write, even rapidly, I'd say irresistibly until an interruption, without knowing whether this interruption was the end or an encounter with some obstacle. In the event I only listened, and I only want now, years later, to remember situations and questions engraved at that time in my memory. Of course, my writing is going to modify the details, whether for or against whatever was seeking itself there on a suddenly favourable occasion – believing myself faithful, I will not be *attentive* in the way I spoke of earlier. For the essential, however, I believe I am a serious witness, and merely a witness.

In the beginning, a brief newspaper item. In Prague Castle, I read, a room had been walled up and forgotten for centuries; one day someone detected its presence, opened it up and found it filled with paintings, including a good-sized Rubens collected in the seventeenth century by a prince who had himself perhaps hidden the paintings.

And immediately, this 'idea for a story', but so urgent, as I said, and so prompt to reveal itself that right away nothing else matters. A number of clues – I won't try to know which – made them think that there were some sixteenth- and seventeenth-century paintings very close by, in an underground room previously thought to be half filled with stones. They extract many of these huge blocks. They see another door, which they open and now there's a staircase whose steps are missing. A historian is charged with an initial reconnais-

sance. Still, if they give him the lamp and a rope, it's mostly due to his own impatience, which is beyond reason and astonishing – the stomping of a beast warned of some presence.

Down he goes, and spends half an hour or so in what one imagines to be a room or passageway. Then he tugs on the rope, they pull him up, and here he is, pale, while below him and thundering, at length, God! the roar of an avalanche, the falling, apparently, of countless other stones. What happened, what did he see? To begin with and for some time, he doesn't answer, then he states, his eyes wandering, or lowered, that nothing happened, he saw nothing. The paintings? No, there are no paintings. In any case, no one conceives of going back down, no, nor to look again for these canvases, for what just fell swept away and destroyed everything. This he is sure of. How can he be so sure? You might think he wanted this to happen, that he caused it! someone is already insinuating. Again he doesn't answer, his eyes elsewhere. Obviously the question was absurd.

So the day passes, and the historian goes home with a young woman, his friend, to his house off in the mountains, which overlooks a meadow dotted with flowers. She, still looking a little astonished, not saying much – this is her way of swimming through the water of days, sparkling, rapid – yes, she was there that morning, in front of the walled-up door, and since then she has been troubled. What happened is beyond any conceivable explanation, she feels – and yet she wants to know. All day long she has, therefore, with looks, invited him to confide in her but in vain. No denial on his part, no impatience, no, his face is closed, his eyes troubled. Now it is night, and despite the window open to the stars, and his nearness on the bed on which they have both lain down, she no longer sees his face, he can only sense her hand in the shadows, taking his – is this why? in any case, he speaks. Let's say he returns with a murmured allusion – what allusion I don't know – to the edge of the space that, since the morning, his silence has kept at bay, sealed off; and she, fast: 'Tell me? I feel sure you saw something.'

To which, equally fast, very low (the window is to his right, you can hear the breeze, the sky is calm): 'Yes, the paintings,' he answers.

'The paintings! But why on earth didn't you say something?'

'I was afraid.'

'Afraid, my friend? Afraid of what?'

'I don't know. Of the paintings ... no, not the paintings.' It's a strange voice he has now, as if broken, as if resigned, but also at times feverish and occasionally exalted, explaining, chaotically, he was afraid, and is still afraid, God knows! No, not of the paintings, with them, rather. Or with others, 'that we both know, my friend.' But afraid of the paintings too, yes, all the same. Afraid of them above all.

'But why?'

'Because they were ... different.'

A word that incites the avowal she alone could have provoked, because of how she looks straight ahead, her silences, and because of her voice, it too hesitant, stopping and starting up again. He is going to speak, he will even want to say everything, he will suffer not to be able to say everything, say all of it.

'Different? What do you mean? Unexpected?'

'Oh, yes!'

'How, unexpected? In what way?'

'I can't say.'

'And that's what's frightening? The unexpectedness?'

'Yes.'

'That's all?'

'No.'

'But in what way were they different? The paintings? Tell me. Was it the subjects?'

'Oh no, no.'

'The subjects were familiar? Which subjects?'

'I don't know. The usual. Some *Visitations*, some *Magi*. Mythological scenes. Portraits. As everywhere.'

'So was it the style? An unknown school?'

'No, oh no.'

'But what school was it? You must know, since it was familiar.'
'Yes. Some Florentines, especially. A lot of Florentine painting.'
'Which period?'
'The seventeenth century. Yes, above all. Some from before that. A lot of seventeenth-century work.'
'But don't you know that school of painting well?'
'Oh, God, yes!'
'So how could it be so surprising? Was it other painters? Ones you didn't know?'
'No.'
'You recognised them all?'
'Yes, no, I'm not sure. I didn't have time to see everything. Anyway that's not the question.'
'Give me names.'
'Cigoli, Giovanni da San Giovanni ... But others. Even some Venetians, I believe. And the Rubens. But mostly Florence. And again, let me tell you, this is not important. That's not ...'
'But what, what?' (Now she is pleading. She fears losing the contact.)

───────────────

'I told you, they were – how did I put it? – *different*. Other.'
'But how, please tell me, how? The details? The expressions?'
'Nothing in particular.'
'Go on. Was it the colour?'
'Oh, what an idea! The colour ... no.'
'Can you describe these canvases?'
'That would ... It wouldn't get us anywhere. The difference is not something you can describe. It's not a question of words.'
'Why?'
'Because words are going to be *our* words, don't you see?'

───────────────

'But you have something in mind right now, don't you? You see something?'

'Yes.'

'What? Say it fast, really fast!'

'Oh, nothing. An *Annunciation* perhaps.'

'Good. And then? Is it to do with the Virgin Mary? The angel?'

'It's the vase, too, and the flower.'

'What kind of flower? Unknown ...' (All of a sudden she shivers, she feels cold.)

'None of that. The usual flower. Different, yes, but not in the sense you are thinking. Understand. Understand. It was what you'd expect in the way of paintings. Not an unknown kind of Cigoli, or Rubens, an unfamiliar period of their painting, for instance. Everything there, believe me, I could have dated to within two years. And not another nature, no, it was the same flowers and the same trees, and not another theology, either. And not even other faces, other looks. But it was ... *other*.'

'Other – you mean, monstrous?'

'Not that, no. You're mistaken. No, not that.'

'So, more ... an excess of beauty? Of purity? Something terrible from too much beauty, too much purity?'

'No.'

'I'm so afraid!'

'Listen!' He's propped up on his elbow now, there in front of her, who sees the sky above him, around him, outside the big window on their right.

'Listen ... it's as if ... as if I had to understand suddenly that everything we have here in the way of painting, all these paintings from the past, and even from the recent past, yes, even Delacroix, even Cézanne – didn't exist, had never existed, were only an illusion.'

'But we have them, those paintings! Some of them are here in this house, close to us.'

'True. But they've always been under our eyes. So they are our dream. They are what we are. Whereas these others, their difference is that they've been lost, all of them together, because they've remained, how to put this, let me see, among themselves, in the past.

The past is *other*.' And again this feeling of not knowing how to be clear, to articulate.

'Listen. It's as if all of a sudden you realised that our languages … Yes, the words we use, the syntax, well, it wasn't even a language, it was … nothing, it was nothing, froth. Froth moving under the star.'

'And them?'

'Them? Us? The star. No, not the star. The stones.'

She weeps.

And he, bent over her, looking at her, sees her again at certain moments in the past, and yesterday; he recognises her. 'I tell you – it didn't surprise me.'

'God, who are you?'

'Let me tell you – there were days when I almost knew. As a child, yes, as an adolescent. Looking at landscapes, mythological scenes, questioning cloud, naked flesh glowing in the semi-dark. All evidence is an enigma! All plenitude is barred with a pale line, closed around itself, that we no longer see, but which, now and then, zigzags across the wheat of the image – yes, across the mountains, the bodies – and bleaches the colour from everything, my friend, like lightning. We stitch these tatters, these colours, these signs, back together. But underneath, in the abyss …'

'The sky? The stones?'

'I called that night.'

She weeps. The task is there, ahead of her. All the days of a whole life stretched out like a road through flowers, birdsong, shadows. The sound of water, dazzled, troubled, the sound of footsteps over stones. And through the window, which is open – why? – already all those stars wrapped in the haze of the Milky Way – and something like a form breathing in this mist. Dawn is going to appear soon, however, like the dispersal of the images.

4 May

To this 'transcription' I must add two remarks – for the moment. First, I haven't really done what I set out to do. In the dialogue

especially, I've added more than the few details I'd initially planned. Nothing that hinders the movement, I think – the sense, if there is one, shouldn't be affected. All the same, so many of the words, in the figure the story makes, point to simmerings where other figures are already pressing in. Who said the retelling of a dream is without value, inadmissible, because it replaces the multiple with the definite? Each sentence is a labyrinth, everywhere we see grottoes where water gleams on stones. And in fact, noting the same memory two or four years ago – as I said, it's very old – I might easily have used many of the same words already, like the 'meadows dotted with flowers', which come from the original dictation; still, I couldn't have ended up with the day before yesterday's text.

The other remark – since the whole of this piece of writing, despite the real difference in time, came into being very quickly, almost without any crossing out, I must consider these few pages, relative as they may be, a finished text, in which the reverie is for ever fixed. And what I must emphasise now is that I am not without regret for the possibilities thus abolished, whether they were variations or new themes: so much so that I wonder what would have happened if I'd used this 'idea of a story' to really write one, with all the surplus description and fictional developments that the initial givens perhaps required – and would in that case have furnished. After all, the writing clearly indicated that it was an 'idea', a point of departure – that could have led to more substance. And who knows whether, taking truth as a pretext, feigning to believe that the initial reverie was valid in itself, I wasn't trying to close a door as the 'historian' in Prague Castle did? How, for example, might the presence of the 'young woman' have been fleshed out? And the house in the mountains? Very often the writing is just a seal one affixes to a threshold – even if the seal has the radiant shape of an open threshold.

This act of closure I may, however, use as a threshold – all I need to do is break with its structure, align myself from the outset with the simmerings, or shimmerings I spoke of, and add the associations it awakes in me, like so many unsounded facts. So our friend, the reader of cards, lays other cards over the first card she turned up.

And it is in this spirit that I shall now evoke – in haste, I will come back – another 'idea for a story' that came to me two days ago while

I was writing, growing more and more insistent as I transcribed my phantasm and distanced myself from the point at which this idea could have been inserted. What brought it to mind, I think, was that scene with a group of men and women peering down into an underground passage. At that point, it crossed my mind that this room below them, buried in the bowels of the earth, might all the same receive some light from a bay – one among others, so many others, on one of the castle's outside walls. Specifically, I saw a high sun-splashed wall, with dozens of windows at various levels, opening, of course, into rooms or banal passageways: but one of these, forgotten by everyone, and impossible to situate, would have been that of the buried room – yes, despite the window's being located at this or that floor, up in the light. What a contradiction! And what glimpses, in this fearfulness, of the workings of thought, its matter, when one is brought face to face with this evidence! Perhaps one member of the group, as they were peering at the rope, ought to have voiced this hypothesis, if not reported the reasoning that invited them to do so.

A lit wall! Those closed-up windows – for many of the rooms, known or unknown, have been long deserted – on that castle wall which is turned towards God knows what horizon, what night, in the vast silent countryside. And perhaps me as a child, visiting some chateau of the Loire, and looking from the embrasure of one wing onto the alternating rows of stone and panes gently blazing back at the evening sky. In the vast salons, the bedrooms, the small wood-panelled rooms whose windows the guardian, who goes ahead of us, opens one after another endlessly – so noisily! and there are shutters in front of the panes, the light darts like a glance into the dusky rooms – figures, Leda, the Virgin, stir for a second in the dream, figures whose sky-blue August colours time has drowned, a sky riddled with a thousand swallow cries, under the shimmery water of brown varnish. Plunge, yes, plunge into the eddies and reflections of these layers of images, descend from level to level in the cool, fluid depths, now and then shot with sun, right to the bottom's push – and then rise again, o earth, transfigured, towards the pure sky, the leaves.

RUE TRAVERSIÈRE (composed 1977)

When I was a child I fretted a good deal about a certain cross-street whose name was Cross-street – Rue Traversière, rather. At one end, not too far from our house and the school, it was the everyday world while at the other end, over there ... Meanwhile the flashing lights of the street's name promised that it truly was the passage.

And I kept my eyes open whenever we walked down it, as occasionally happened, and we even went right to the far end of it, as if it were the same as any other street, but when I reached the far end I was tired, nodding off, and all of a sudden there was the bizarre space of the big botanical garden. – 'Is it here', I would ask myself, 'that over there begins? Here, at this house with its drawn shutters? Here, under this lilac? And this group of children playing with their hoops, and their marbles, on this pavement with weeds pushing up through the cracks, isn't one of them already on the far side, isn't he touching the hands of the little girls from over there with his shadowy fingers?' Notions of course contradictory, fleeting. All the more so as these modest houses, their vaulted backyards, in no way set themselves off from many others in our city; one sensed, one breathed right to the last painted metal door only the excess torpor of the suburbs and their kitchen gardens. How bland the face of what really matters! When we reached the botanical garden with its odour of otherness, where each tree wore a name tag, I raced off, jolted awake; I wanted to go far, enter elsewhere, but the paths must have turned in the shade of the boxwood and looped back to where they began, for I soon found myself yet again at the point of departure.

How good it was for me this name of Rue Traversière; and this garden of plant collections; and the vegetable Latin of the early evenings with their damp heat! Five years ago when my mother was in the hospital beside the botanical garden, I returned to the Rue Traversière two or three times in the early afternoon. All at once, after so many years away, I rediscovered the almost forgotten childhood city and this street which seemed to open onto another world.

Still the same prudence – or even peace; still the smell of wet lettuce in front of the doors, the old women in the windows, eternally

stitching at faded linens, the same Byzantine peacocks face to face in the lace of the dining-room curtains, one fluttering, perhaps, for a moment. And the chalky tuff still crumbling at the corners of walls. And the children, silent. No, Rue Traversière hadn't changed. And yet …

How to say this? It seemed to me that here, where I was, and there, where I was going, all together were what at one time I could only locate on the margins, in the invisible.

SECOND RUE TRAVERSIÈRE (composed 1977)

'Rue Traversière', someone says to me in an art gallery one afternoon – standing in front of the window I can see grey walls, passers-by on the Rue Jacob – 'Rue Traversière, oh, I recognised it in that piece you wrote, for – imagine – I too once lived in your city. How I loved its silence, and those big houses …'

'Big houses? No. It was a very poor street.'

'Not at all! I recall every detail. Gardens with walls, and trees. The archbishop's palace next door.'

'The archbishop's palace, no, absolutely not, it was the botanical garden.'

And so it goes; we evoke a part of town I, like him, know well, for I lived there as a teenager. Going to the *lycée* in those days I would sometimes cut through the archbishopric gardens, almost always deserted, coming out of them into empty streets. Shimmering, dangerous moments when I was tempted to shout, as loud as I could, to prove to myself that I existed in my own way, to verify that these rows of private houses and gardens in which nothing stirred, not a sound, save for the eternal far-off piano on which a scale was being picked out – to verify that this was, I would say, no, not even a décor, worse, the crystallisation of an unknown matter, with stainlike windows devoid of meaning, doors deaf as the surrounding stone. Shout, do something, anything, to make a curtain twitch, the piano stop, then race off, book-bag thumping on your back, towards the

little house of those days, near the canal, where my father had come to die. I know that neighbourhood well, and it's not Rue Traversière.

Unless ... I've known with such utter certainty, and for so many years, that Rue Traversière runs west, into the outskirts, the first farms, into the dampness of lilacs and the wheezing of pumps. I even walked along it a few years ago when the city of my childhood reappeared, then faded again. Yet the thought that I'm mistaken has just entered and taken up residence in me.

I return to my present home and I look for the map I've kept of the city, a very old map that has been much consulted in the past, but carefully, a map showing signs of wear, taped together on the underside with strips of brown paper. It still unfolds, the words and the streets meet up, again the dead language speaks at the crossings. And it's true, Rue Traversière is in the east, in the rich part of town. And over here, running out into the shapeless suburbs, what is the name of that street I took again only six or seven years ago, mulling over its importance in my life?

I peer closer, eyes blurring, and find nothing. Still, here are several streets that run west, long, zigzagging a little, like former country roads city planners have haphazardly straightened, but it seems to me that I know each of them by heart, and none of them is the street I see so clearly when I close my eyes. And as for others, elsewhere, there are one or two whose strange names could have conjured up the idea of a 'cross street' and merged with it later – as for the Rue de la Fuye, which comes back out of the blue, it's really too far from the garden of animals and plants – this Botanical, in sum, was a little Garden of Eden – Rue de la Fuye peters out in the south among the railway tracks. Where then is this street that I know with my whole being, which *is*, and what is it called? What is its real place in this network of places, equally real, which seem however to exclude it?

And asking myself these questions, here on the famous white page, repeating my astonishment to myself, nonetheless choosing my words, I know that this is still writing, I know that these new notations only continue *Rue Traversière,* the other account, and save a memory of being in nothing but error by complicating and giving weight to a poem. Still – please believe me – the enigma that I am articulating is in my life too, the astonishment will endure longer

than the words that express it. I can write and write, but I am also the person who looks at the map of the city of his childhood, and doesn't understand.

Which was the *other* Rue Traversière? How could I have lived so long with two distinct kinds of knowledge, two memories that never crossed? Who is the person in me who begins when the other – or an other, and which other? – goes into the little house along the canal where there's a clump of bamboo in the pocket-handkerchief garden – where we came to live two years ago, where the father is dying, which we will soon leave?

I move these figures with their vague, worn outlines about my table – these faces, these lost gazes that redden, these memories of the corners of halls, the wallpapers' faded flowers, the door to the laundry room out back with its slippery step; smells, including the smell of the chestnut trees on the boulevard at each spring's bright mystery, of swallows skimming the ground when the stormy sky tilts, sweeping the past away, outlining – might that not be the future, over there, those men and women in the cloud, the laughter of colour over shining water, that body like froth in Polynesia. Which card must I place on top of which other card; which one without faces, coloured crimson grey, unseeing, have I already laid over this other too significant one, unless the latter has resurfaced from the shuffled deck like – irresistible, final – not the meaning's annulment but the meaning? I have many uncertain memories still to decipher, I see. A whole long Rue Traversière to move far away among my first chance happenings, my first darkly seen places, my troubled affections, right to the at once absolute and indifferent origin, the origin which, though poor, was nonetheless – creatures and plants, and the smell of boxwood, and the dim figures of the man and woman – a whole world that I owe to another child. Chance, of which we are born, chance precariously, delicately, endlessly folded over us like the chrysalis' wing; you can only keep all of it in the colours of your ignorance as long as we are alone and as if asleep, turned to the shadows. To the other – be it the writing, the wing's unfolding, every now and then – one owes the sense.

III (1978–1988)

From *Récits en rêve* / *Dream Tales* (1987)

L'ORIGINE DE LA PAROLE / THE ORIGIN OF UTTERANCE (composed 1980)

The light was so intense! Reflected from everywhere, flashed off tiles and walls, off vaulting and palms, it discoloured people and things, and burned away their shadow: so that nothing which existed there, or perished there, might indicate substance beneath appearance, or that chance existed, in what seemed the endless present, space without a here or there, where essences alone survived in their expansive rustling of bright air which rises shimmering above a fire.

And I realised that *summer is language*. That words are born in summer as a snake sheds its fragile transparent skin. That it could only have been *in the south*, in the flashing of salt on rock – and among these burning bushes! these great wandering storms ... – that words were invented, and through them absence; that utterance was dreamed.

LA DÉCISION D'ÊTRE PEINTRE / THE DECISION TO BE A PAINTER (composed 1982)

He spoke. But the words he used were hollowed out by waves whitened with foam, and his thoughts took on a glassy flashing at the slightest thing named; people he didn't know would laugh at him from afar and make signs at him; others went up to congratulate or sympathise with him, but with words of broken glass, as unintelligible as his own would be. It was as though some events had happened, which he'd not been aware of, during the night; as though there were no more meaning in each word than in Siena's sandy earth which, in the evenings when he was a child, used to be carried in lumps, saturated in water and spangled with bubbles, down the gutters of the poorer streets. He didn't dare reply, still less ask questions. He would shake his head and quicken his step.

And suddenly, rounding a corner, he had the rising sun in his eyes like a great swathing cry, vaporous, blazing, in the incompleteness of the light.

L'ARTISTE DU DERNIER JOUR / THE ARTIST OF THE LAST DAY (composed 1985)

I

The world was going to end. Yes, the evil – for an evil it was, despite so many hopes – which had begun with the first idol crudely fashioned out of stone, or even before, with the first furtive gash made on a tree trunk, was about to come to fruition, ascending through the veins of nature into the rarest metals and into the tiniest particles. The world was going to end suddenly because – a voice seemed to prophesy – in a few weeks, in a few days, perhaps in a few hours, the number of images produced by humanity would have surpassed the number of living creatures. In that fatal second there would be more vague outlines of animals on the rock walls of caves, more Madonnas in red robes in the flaking frescoes, more landscapes, portraits, photographs, posters – not to mention undeveloped negatives in the archives and the debris – than ants, bees, monkeys, men. It followed from this that what upset the balance between life and illusion, in the scales ordained by God, was consciousness; the mind of a shepherd who one night rose to conceive, in the empty field of starlight, the idea of the sign. Perception is only natural; memory, which fades, runs where it will, in all places and upon all bodies, but quickly allows that impenetrable surface we call the manifest to reform and reclose upon itself; but the image, which adds, which modifies – what a novelty, in a world which until its appearance had been nothing but matter – and what a disturbing gleam it cast at the ground of things! God, who had dreamed of nothing other than of reproducing the Eternal, to admire himself in – and wasn't that the original error? –, God had not even foreseen this fire which for so long, it's true, had been slow to take, just a tiny muted sound

in the silence of Being. The artist of the first day had imagined that his creation alone would be adored, not these reflections of it, not these hasty variants. He hadn't accounted for the dream. And that's because he did not know he is only a dream himself.

11

The world was going to end. Life was going to crumble under the weight of the dream.

Unless, the voice had said – but did it say it clearly, it was very rapid, one evening, at the end of a field at the edge of a wood, a place where the earth was still as it had been on the first day, and a painter had come there, but what had he seen, or heard, – the sound seemed to emanate from a painting perhaps, from the heart of one more representation, that spring so soon dried up – unless an image, and this time a single one would suffice, were by some last-second alchemy, purified, cleansed, somehow – for here the voice was widely believed to have hesitated, looking for a word – purified, cleansed, of its being – of its difference – as an image.

Washed like the speck of gold in the stream; released, at its very birth in the artist's conception, from the mud of reverie, from its yearning for an insubstantial wisp, for a shadow in an appearance; freed from all desire directed at a mere fragment torn from the uniqueness, the sanctity of the original whole. That, all at once, this shape no longer show, express, suggest anything, no longer pose as an illicit rival of what exists – that it *be* itself quite simply, as images never were, which reproduce themselves endlessly, destroy each other and are born again, in their own enchainment; that it *be*, as a tree or a stone is, ignorant of itself. That fire consume fire, dispersing that great pile of ashes, the past, already stirring under apocalyptic winds : and then we would be reborn, my friends, we could look at each other with gladness in the dawn light.

But what could it possibly be, this second layer of flame? Pure chance, or supreme consciousness? A photograph of some trees on a ridge, but taken by accident, the camera going off by itself, an unintentional click, and then never developed, thrown away and

lost, really lost, returned to the dissolution and transmutation of matter under an avalanche of debris – the dampness destroying its salts, the star without size or colour rising in colour and form? Or else, and this was a thesis that had some currency, the work would have ripened in the studio of a great painter whose thought was both the most rigorous and the most urgent which art had ever had to produce in all its long history; a history at times so intoxicating, and even, so one would have thought, so enlightened, so clearly beneficent? But where would this keeper of life and death direct his researches? Would he think of the musician who has managed on occasion to produce forms which, in the aura above sounds, seem, without signifying anything, or uttering anything, to be the shining cloud – quite simply the light itself? But where the glory of sound becomes detached from memory, desire and the future, the most abstract mark is an image. Is that the sin of the eye? Nothing but two straight lines, at right angles, and a face emerges, covered with blood beneath a crown of thorns.

III

And what of him, under his sloping roof, who knows what he has to do, and the haste with which he must proceed while being infinitely cautious, and the decisiveness that will be required of him, faced with the blank canvas when the twelve fatal chimes begin to strike; the artist of the last day reflected in vain. Brush or pencil touching the sheet, nothing more. Should he suppress all the lighting? But the hand, the wrist, the eye itself have their own lamp in the memory. Should he bind his hand tightly, almost to the tips of his fingers, to a block of stone, obliging him to draw in pain and blood? Or would he allow himself to imitate, one more time, but with the face and the joy of a child, so much so that for an instant from his fingers the light of that joy, that inimitable light, which, as such, taking its mimesis from its central shadow, substituting its great wave-circles for the reflections and eddies of the imaginary world, would emerge, totally pure in the redeemed drawing.

He searched; and he knew moreover – which only increased

his anxiety – that he must search without being aware that he was searching, that he must forget the problem as much as the anguish, because anguish conjures what it most fears, and thought is memory. He searched, he sketched a mark in water-colour on the large clouded sheet and stopped, not knowing whether the earth was now in greater peril with the spreading of his black ink; meanwhile clouds were gathering in the sky, he could see them through his open door, massing on the horizon, on great red tripods, precursors of that mysterious hour when, because of the excess of images, consciousness would all at once cease.

SUR LES AILES DE LA MUSIQUE / ON THE WINGS OF SONG (composed 1985)

He would probably have said that the radio had been on for a while, only he wasn't paying attention what with all the comings-and-goings, the shouts, the conversations between levels as they packed to leave. But suddenly! A different music entirely! Two female voices responding to each other with a majesty and a simplicity he would never have thought possible. A dialogue, but a game of echoes too, of reflections in the way the second voice seems to retrace, from its vantage point, the shape of the first, though not without a shade of hesitation, at times akin to sorrow. – Will he come to think, he who is listening too now, and already with such fervour, that the music is like a mountain reflected in a lake whose water is so gently crumpled as to barely disturb the image? Or like a colour – a red nearly grenadine, haunted by blue – which has found in another colour, lying nearby, the consonance that does not detract from its solitude, its inwardness, its silence? But that would mean closing himself to the impression, also growing on him, of some change that the younger voice injects in the figure made by the other voice, which gradually modifies this sign, until perhaps, without one having noticed, it will have become completely different. No, this is not some dormant water, this response, it is an upland river, and the uplands are ending one morning, the water is going to pour down into the lowlands where the peak that yesterday still was reflected will be only that

distant red or blue shrouded in mist. The song speaks of the mystery of endless repetition, but it is also a kind of waiting, it knows the anguish of duration.

Even more than this accord of the timeless with time, what strikes him, now that he has edged closer to the radio, now he has dropped everything for the voices, is that, distant as they are – of this he is sure; also from time to time they fade and he fears losing the sound altogether – they are nonetheless perceptible, in this room, without anything having been recorded, over there, no intervention of any wave. The contralto voice, the other higher-pitched though not reedy, unfold, speak, perhaps struggle, in a place he knows nothing about, but – he would swear – this can only be happening in this moment that he himself is part of, and this is so obvious, so absolute, that the radio which has made a space for them has been as if consumed. The voices are here, they are here with him, in him, as the horizon is in us when our eyes seek it – in vain, but we think we see it smoking over there, under the earth's withdrawal. If they have this power to be heard from so much farther than all the world's other voices, it is simply because they are more real. What am I saying? Because they are what's real, the rest is mere shadow.

And he understands, all of a sudden – this is the second instant in any intuition, even the least violent. Yes, this song is here as much as over there, it fills, it can fill the whole space: and this is because it is happening, in this very moment, yes, but in the childhood house. 'Over there', yes, in effect: in the hamlet beside the big river whose coloured, dense, impenetrable flux he loved. What? The house? The house they closed up and sold fifty years ago? Can what no longer exists still be, can the unhoped-for happen, the miracle? If so one must drop everything on the spot and run towards the lost origin as the lamb runs into the pasture when dawn's barrier is pushed back. Arrive at the house of the first morning before the song ends.

Already, he has left his house, will he find a taxi, yes, here comes one from the shadows, and what luck, the car has a radio and it too vibrates with this immense song of unity, of duality, which he can listen to more calmly now that street yields to street, then to the highway. The voice, the lower one, is it his mother's? She almost never sang during her life, wouldn't have known how, all she had

learned were a few folk songs, not even all that old really, those tunes carelessly printed on folded sheets of paper which they once sold at fairs – would not have known how and would not have dared, yet it is her, he is sure, it all comes back, he loves it all again. And as for the other, that young and solemn presence, still a little childish, still so studious and yet so free in its decisions that come at times a little late, and so full of joy, undeniable sadness notwithstanding: yes, he knows it, he recognises it – he doesn't know it, he doesn't recognise it.

Hours while the car finds its way, finds its way, draws and effaces its fleeting places in the world's grisaille. Is the song pretty much the same? Or has the becoming that marks it already changed it so that days and days might have gone by in the house by the river, meaning that the exchange it has initiated has grown deeper, matured, and is closing in on a denouement, and will soon be interrupted? How long a trip this is, how difficult it is to end it on the small roads of past time in the desert of memory!

The journey is over now and the music goes on. The car is gone, here is the house in the shade of the tall limes and, first, the low door in its frame, ajar, then a few steps up to the threshold, and again, one side of the door is open and here at their source, in the downstairs room, are the voices. – He enters. His mother sits on a low chair beside the fireplace in which nothing is burning. She sings, her eyes on the fire dogs, the ashes, but what is she really looking at, as absorbed as her whole body appears to be by the movement of her fingers on the cords of the instrument, if that is an instrument – it looks almost like a piece of cloth, with a thread and needles? Beside her, the girl is sitting on the ground, no, on her knees, she has no instrument, she looks at the friend, the older sister, she muses, she sings. No one else. In the top of the room a little coloured steam; and all round, as far as the eyes can see, the silent countryside. He waits on the threshold. When the music stops, he is going to speak, he is going to say what he never knew how to say, it was forbidden, wasn't it, and now it is easy.

SUR DE GRANDS CERCLES DE PIERRE / ON SOME LARGE STONE CIRCLES (composed 1985)

Again, I look up and my eyes fall – above an arch this time – upon the figure that appears on so many walls in the West: a circle or oval whose rim, in relief on the wall, frames no mirror, no painted or sculpted image, just bare stone, rough and grey.

The circle is almost always quite large. One feels that the stone needs, within this well-defined space, room to be, to speak its truth, which is the expanse, the limitless, the desert. Sometimes two hands, a young woman's or a child's, hold the frame, present it to us.

God, through the stone.

God, not even by way of *this or that* stone that one perceives all of a sudden in its difference with another stone – slab of marble as opposed to menhir, gemstone against basalt – which is already a kind of language; and that one can locate in the sacred place or on a diadem among other realities, other signs, keeping it in the domain of meaning and among us. But by way of the rock fall, the formless mass, the other end of this landslide down there in the ravine, in the unknown, down there in the night – if this word still has any meaning – where there is no more place, no more denomination conceivable, no more consciousness even to want to give something a name.

God, in effect: what exceeds the sign. That which, signified, would be promptly extinguished, would be already as inconceivably absent from the embers as silence from noise, as line from point, as presence from the figure. God – that which, designated, though it be with the name of God, a word that contains the idea of the breakdown of meaning, has left us only an image, inducing us to lie.

But who, when the sign is effaced, begins to shine with this all-in-all and through-all light that language deprives us of.

'God'? Truly this is not our preoccupation today, this other of the notion, the remains of a conceptualisation that, endlessly displaced by the shifting nature of language, endlessly returns to prop up the new significance, the stay – indifferent, indulgent – that supports the weight, if not of the true – does such a thing exist? – at least of whatever justifies this ado about the signs. No, 'God' is the plenitude

that is wholly – peacefully – in the here-and-now of each earthly thing. Offering itself to the uninterpreted.

And in which the part is equal to the whole, for the idea of part comes into being along with the signs. This chunk, this lump of stone, is in itself the starry sky, the galaxy, the starry vapour that still trembles beyond. And it is that with which, in which, I myself am everything and nothing, for all that my name is effaced.

Others reappearing, at last, a particular other person whom one felt one could not reach; since we were divided by those words that know only how to say themselves, that only want to repeat, in each formulation, their absence. Other people inaccessible through speech, others of whom the very idea is lost or almost in the exercise of speech, other people are freed, un-immured by the gaze that engages with stone's absolute.

Hence it follows that it is from the experience of that which has no name, no place, that which cannot be made a sign, being, abyssally, only thing, that, in the presence of others, the need to build a place is born: the need to share it, to give names so that a place may be and become sense. From what forever transcends the sign the need of the sign comes into being.

A paradox? No, this is poetry.

For it must exist, it must somewhere be active in the quicksand of languages, this consciousness that remembers what is older and deeper than the sign: which remains a perception where any other gaze merely yields to conceptual thought's disorderly simplifications; but which, because of this, also knows what it is that justifies the sign, calling us back to it in those moments when all we can see is its lure. This act must be, it is impossible that it not be, contradictory as this may seem, the extreme point towards which all our use of words, haunted by our memory of the first presence, tends.

Wandering among the significations, poetry remembers, and dreams, of an original, forever virgin, state of the word: when in the silence of the earth of before language the word comes into being and for an instant reflects – but outside time – the irreflectable of the world.

With its plural, non-conceptual writing poetry wants to break apart the coordinated significations in order to revive, in each of its

great vocables, that surplus of perception that, were it sustainable, would constitute its utterance [*parole*].

And, as words lend themselves so easily to coordination, to the desire for power, so poetry tends to keep present among these puzzle pieces one piece which is just formless torn cardboard daubed with vague colours: a shape that fits none of the others and whose endlessly displaced insistence is going to blur the vain figure born of the signs' alliances. 'God' – this word could play this role, if dogmas were to give it back to language. Perhaps it does play this role in the great poems, whose effect is undimmed. But any plain word has the potential to be the totally open vocable that the word God, in sum, merely announces.

Poetry: to clear the brush away from this or that word to which one has had access, by chance: as one hears water trickling under stones and tall grass and comes back and discovers a spring. Dogmas inscribed their representations in this word, their values, their ends, hidden under other ends, their lures: clear away all that little by little (a lifetime), and let the water bubble free again! The poem that speaks of the absolute risks losing it; but there are works, long researches we term oeuvres, that speak *within the poem*, just as the worker has his hands in the water, already, as he pulls from the mud the stones and dry leaves.

And a metaphor for poetry, not just the poetic word, the metaphor sought perhaps obscurely throughout the centuries in the suffering, the hopes of numberless beings and forgotten societies is the dissemination of the Indo-European languages in which, with all their different names for the divine and for God, the group DV everywhere bubbles up.

One does not call God *by* his name, one calls him *in* his name, and this can therefore be in any name, it is in the name of love.

But I make a mistake spelling a name – as I write one letter takes the place of another; it – the name – grows obscure, unknown, at random I add another letter, many others – sadly I see a big word forming, bristling with erratic blocks, riddled with holes, deprived of sense: a field of rocks like the one where the place of the first furrow, of the first hearth, was cleared on the first day; or this rough slab, the

tomb, where the outline of the first name was traced and someone's existence for an instant survived.

Go to the tree, Basho says. In the swelling of the trunk find, in one particular place, in the twist of a branch, that which makes the tree itself and itself alone; and so relive the movement which from its own depths has led it to this form, this size and shape, this colour: to the unfolding of an essence which, though shared with the whole species, is still, inwardly, its own, the place that is its alone, in this moment which is the absolute, of its élan into space. What is this encounter with a presence that is already emptying itself of itself, its centre fleeing, pouring out like sand from an hourglass? Nothing that announces the mimesis, this discourse. No, this is the tracing of the stone circle.

Squeezing the child's hand, telling him 'It's nothing, don't worry': already the circle of stone.

The differentiated image, in sum, belongs to God: to the idea of God, to the idea that the word God is, even if it never completely effaces the proper name the word contains. And such simple forms on the wall, empty circles, rosettes, rinceaux – all ornament, in fact, in its relationship with stone, whence it exits history – this is the experience that might have barred the word God. The image is contradictory, it exhausts itself denying itself. But the naked line, lying beside itself there where it comes to life in the stone – this, perhaps, is the way.

From *Ce qui fut sans lumière* (1985)

LE SOUVENIR

Ce souvenir me hante, que le vent tourne
D'un coup, là-bas, sur la maison fermée.
C'est un grand bruit de toile par le monde,
On dirait que l'étoffe de la couleur
Vient de se déchirer jusqu'au fond des choses.
Le souvenir s'éloigne mais il revient,
C'est un homme et une femme masqués, on dirait qu'ils tentent
De mettre à flot une barque trop grande.
Le vent rabat la voile sur leurs gestes,
Le feu prend dans la voile, l'eau est noire,
Que faire de tes dons, ô souvenir,

Sinon recommencer le plus vieux rêve,
Croire que je m'éveille? La nuit est calme,
Sa lumière ruisselle sur les eaux,
La voile des étoiles frémit à peine
Dans la brise qui passe par les mondes.
La barque de chaque chose, de chaque vie
Dort, dans la masse de l'ombre de la terre,

Et la maison respire, presque sans bruit,
L'oiseau dont nous ne savions pas le nom dans la vallée
À peine a-t-il lancé, on dirait moqueuses
Mais non sans compassion, ce qui fait peur,
Ses deux notes presque indistinctes trop près de nous.
Je me lève, j'écoute ce silence,
Je vais à la fenêtre, une fois encore,
Qui domine la terre que j'ai aimée.
O joies, comme un rameur au loin, qui bouge peu
Sur la nappe brillante; et plus loin encore
Brûlent sans bruit terrestre les flambeaux
Des montagnes, des fleuves, des vallées.

From *In the Shadow's Light* (1985)

THE MEMORY

I am haunted by this memory, that the wind
All at once is swirling over the closed up house.
There is a mighty sound of flapping sail throughout the world,
As if the stuff that colour is made of
Had just been rent to the very depths of things.
The memory passes, then returns,
It is a man and a woman who are masked, they seem
To be trying to push a boat that is too big into water.
The wind thrashes the sail on their arms and hands,
Fire catches in the sail, the water is black,
What can I make of your gifts, O memory,

If not begin once more the oldest dream,
Believe that I am waking? The night is calm,
Its light is streaming on the waters,
The sail of the stars is scarcely stirring
In the breeze passing through the worlds.
The bark of each thing, of each life
Is sleeping in earth's heavy mass of shadow,

And the house is breathing, almost soundlessly,
The bird in the valley, the one we could not name,
Has faintly thrown out, too close to us,
Its two almost indistinct notes that seem mocking,
And yet not without compassion, which is frightening.
I get up: I listen to this silence,
Once again I go to the window
That looks out over the country I have loved.
O joys, like an oarsman in the distance, barely
Moving on the bright expanse; and further still
The torches of the mountains, the rivers, the valleys
Are burning, far from any earthly sound.

*Joies, et nous ne savions si c'était en nous
Comme vaine rumeur et lueur de rêve
Cette suite de salles et de tables
Chargées de fruits, de pierres et de fleurs,
Ou ce qu'un dieu voulait, pour une fête
Qu'il donnerait, puisque nous consentions,
Tout un été dans sa maison d'enfance.*

*Joies, et le temps qui vint au travers, comme un fleuve
En crue, de nuit, débouche dans le rêve
Et en blesse la rive, et en disperse
Les images les plus sereines dans la boue.
Je ne veux pas savoir la question qui monte
De cette terre en paix, je me détourne,
Je traverse les chambres de l'étage
Où dort toute une part de ce que je fus,
Je descends dans la nuit des arches d'en bas
Vers le feu qui végète dans l'église,
Je me penche sur lui, qui bouge d'un coup
Comme un dormeur que l'on touche à l'épaule
Et se redresse un peu, levant vers moi
L'épiphanie de sa face de braise.
Non, plutôt rendors-toi, feu éternel,
Tire sur toi la cape de tes cendres,
Réacquiesce à ton rêve, puisque tu bois
Toi aussi à la coupe de l'or rapide.
L'heure n'est pas venue de porter la flamme
Dans le miroir qui nous parle dans l'ombre,
J'ai à demeurer seul. J'ouvre la porte
Qui donne sur les amandiers dont rien ne bouge,
Si paisible est la nuit qui les vêt de lune.*

*Et j'avance, dans l'herbe froide. Ô terre, terre,
Présence si consentante, si donnée,
Est-il vrai que déjà nous ayons vécu
L'heure où l'on voit s'éteindre, de branche en branche,
Les guirlandes du soir de fête? Et on ne sait,*

Joys – and we never knew if it was in us,
Like idle murmurings and the glowing of dream,
This succession of rooms and of tables
Laden with fruit, with stones and with flowers,
Or if it was what some god, seeing how
Willing we were, had wanted to prepare
For a summer's celebration in his childhood home.

Joys, and time that passed through, like a river
Rising at night, flows into the dream
And wounds its shore and scatters
Its most peaceful images in the mud.
I do not want to know the question rising
From this tranquil earth, I turn away,
I cross the rooms of the upper floor
Where much of what I was is still asleep,
I go down into the night of the arches below
Toward the fire languishing in the church,
I lean over it, and it stirs suddenly,
Like someone sleeping who is touched on the shoulder,
Then rises a little, lifting towards me
The epiphany of its ember face.
No, rather return to sleep eternal fire,
Draw your cape of ashes over yourself
Go back to your dream, since you too
Drink from the cup of fast flowing gold.
The hour has not yet come to carry the flame
Into the mirror that speaks to us in shadow.
I must remain alone. I open the door that
Leads out to the almond trees, whose branches do not move,
So still is the night that clothes them in moon.

And I go forward, into the cold grasses. O earth, earth,
Presence so compliant, so fully offered,
Can it be that already we have lived
The moment when one sees, from branch to branch
The garlands of our joyful evenings die out?

Seuls à nouveau dans la nuit qui s'achève,
Si même on veut que reparaisse l'aube
Tant le cœur reste pris à ces voix qui chantent
Là-bas, encore, et se font indistinctes
En s'éloignant sur les chemins de sable.

Je vais
Le long de la maison vers le ravin, je vois
Vaguement miroiter les choses du simple
Comme un chemin qui s'ouvre, sous l'étoile
Qui prépare le jour. Terre, est-il vrai
Que tant de sève dans l'amandier au mois des fleurs,
Tant de feux dans le ciel, tant de rayons
Dès l'aube dans les vitres, dans le miroir,
Tant d'ignorances dans nos vies mais tant d'espoirs,
Tant de désir de toi, terre parfaite,
N'étaient pas faits pour mûrir comme un fruit
En son instant d'extase se détache
De la branche, da la matière, saveur pure?

Je vais,
Et il me semble que quelqu'un marche près de moi,
Ombre, qui sourirait bien que silencieuse
Comme une jeune fille, pieds nus dans l'herbe,
Accompagne un instant celui qui part.
Et celui-ci s'arrête, il la regarde,
Il prendrait volontiers dans ses mains ce visage
Qui est la terre même. Adieu, dit-il,
Présence qui ne fut que pressentie
Bien que mystérieusement tant d'années si proche,
Adieu, image impénétrable qui nous leurra
D'être la vérité enfin presque dite,
Certitude, là où tout n'a été que doute, et bien que chimère
Parole si ardente que réelle.
Adieu, nous ne te verrons plus venir près de nous
Avec l'offrande du ciel et des feuilles sèches,

And, alone once more in the night that draws to an end,
One wonders if one even wants dawn to reappear,
So strongly is the heart drawn to those voices
That are singing over there, still, and grow dim
As they fade away on the paths of sand.

I pass along
The side of the house toward the ravine, I can see
The simple earthly things shimmering faintly,
Like a road opening up, beneath the star
That prepares for day. Earth, can it be
That so much sap in the almond tree
The month of its flowering,
That so many fires in the sky, so much light at dawn
On the windowpanes, on the mirror,
That so much ignorance in our lives, but also so much hope,
So much desire for you, O perfect earth,
That all this was not made to ripen like the fruit,
In its moment of ecstasy, when it breaks away
From the branch, from matter, as pure savour?

I go on,
And it seems to me that someone is walking beside me,
A shade that seems to smile, and yet is silent,
Like a young girl, barefoot in the grass,
Who walks for a while with someone who is leaving.
He stops and looks at her,
He would gladly take this face in his hands,
This face that is the earth itself. Farewell, he whispers,
Farewell, presence that was but dimly sensed,
Although for so many years so mysteriously close,
Farewell, unfathomable image that beguiled us
All the more as it was the truth almost spoken,
Certainty, when everything else was only doubt, and though
But a dream, speech so ardent it was real.
Farewell, no longer shall we see you come near us
With your offerings of sky and dry leaves,

Nous ne te verrons pas rapprocher de l'âtre
Tout ton profil de servante divine.
Adieu, nous n'étions pas de même destin,
Tu as à prendre ce chemin et nous cet autre,
Et entre s'épaissit cette vallée
Que l'inconnu surplombe
Avec un cri rapide d'oiseau qui chasse.
Adieu, tu es déjà touchée par d'autres lèvres,
L'eau du fleuve n'appartient pas à son rivage
Sauf par le grand bruit clair.
J'envie le dieu du soir qui se penchera
Sur le vieillissement de ta lumière.
Terre, ce qu'on appelle la poésie
T'aura tant désirée en ce siècle, sans prendre
Jamais sur toi le bien du geste d'amour!

Il l'a touchée de ses mains, de ses lèvres,
Il la retient, qui sourit, par la nuque,
Il la regarde, en ces yeux qui s'effacent
Dans la phosphorescence de ce qui est.
Et maintenant, enfin, il se détourne
Je le vois qui s'éloigne dans la nuit.

Adieu? Non, ce n'est pas le mot que je sais dire.

Et mes rêves, serrés
L'un contre l'autre et l'autre encore ainsi
Là sortie des brebis dans le premier givre,
Reprennent piétinant leurs plus vieux chemins.
Je m'éveille nuit après nuit dans la maison vide,
Il me semble qu'un pas m'y précède encore.
Je sors
Et m'étonne que l'ampoule soit allumée
Dans ce lieu déserté de tous, devant l'étable.
Je cours derrière la maison, parce que l'appel
Du berger d'autrefois retentit encore.

No longer shall we see you bring toward the hearth
That profile of servant divine.
Farewell, our destinies were not the same,
You must take that path and we this other,
And between them grows deeper and denser
That valley which the unknown looms over
With the quick cry of the swooping bird of prey.
Farewell, already other lips are touching you,
The water of the river leaves to its banks
Only its great clear sound.
I envy the god of evening who will bend over
Your aging light.
Earth, what we call poetry
Will have felt, in this century, such desire for you,
Without ever taking upon you the blessings
Of the act of love!

He has touched her with his hands, his lips,
He holds her, she is smiling, by the neck,
He looks at her, in those eyes that disappear
Into the phosphorescence of what is.
And now, at last, he turns away.
I can see him going off into the night.

Farewell? No, this is not the word I can say.

And my dreams, pressed
One against another, and still another, like
Sheep that venture into the first frost,
Trample once more onto their old, familiar paths.
I wake up, night after night, in the empty house,
I still hear the sound of footsteps ahead of me.
I go out
And am surprised to see the light bulb burning
On the wall of the now deserted stable.
I run behind the house, because the shepherd's call
From times gone by is still resounding.

J'entends l'aboi qui précédait le jour,
Je vois l'étoile boire parmi les bêtes
Qui ne sont plus, à l'aube. Et résonne encore la flûte
Dans la fumée des choses transparentes.

L'ADIEU

Nous sommes revenus à notre origine.
Ce fut le lieu de l'évidence, mais déchirée.
Les fenêtres mêlaient trop de lumières,
Les escaliers gravissaient trop d'étoiles
Qui sont des arches qui s'effondrent, des gravats,
Le feu semblait brûler dans un autre monde.

Et maintenant des oiseaux volent de chambre en chambre,
Les volets sont tombés, le lit est couvert de pierres,
L'âtre plein de débris du ciel qui vont s'éteindre.
Là nous parlions, le soir, presque à voix basse
À cause des rumeurs des voûtes, là pourtant
Nous formions nos projets: mais une barque,
Chargée de pierres rouges, s'éloignait
Irrésistiblement d'une rive, et l'oubli
Posait déjà sa cendre sur les rêves
Que nous recommencions sans fin, peuplant d'images
Le feu qui a brûlé jusqu'au dernier jour.

Est-il vrai, mon amie,
Qu'il n'y a qu'un seul mot pour désigner
Dans la langue qu'on nomme la poésie
Le soleil du matin et celui du soir,
Un seul le cri de joie et le cri d'angoisse,
Un seul l'amont désert et les coups de haches,
Un seul le lit défait et le ciel d'orage,
Un seul l'enfant qui naît et le dieu mort?

I hear the barking that announced daybreak,
I can see the star drinking at dawn
Amid the flocks that are no longer.
And in the smoke of things transparent,
The sounds of the flute are still echoing.

THE FAREWELL

We have come back to our origin.
The place where all had been evident, now torn.
The windows mingled too many lights,
The stairs climbed too many stars
Which are collapsing arches, rubble;
The fire seemed to burn in another world.

And now birds fly from room to room,
The shutters have come down, the bed is covered with stones,
The fireplace full of the sky's dying debris.
It was here that we would talk at evening, almost in whispers,
Because of the echoing from the vaulted ceiling, here that
We would make our plans: but a boat,
Loaded with red stones, moved away,
Irresistibly, from a shore, and oblivion
Was already placing its ashes on the dreams
That we endlessly renewed, peopling with images
The fire that burned until the last morning.

Beloved, is it true
That in the language called poetry
There is only one word for designating
The morning and the evening sun,
One word for the cry of joy and the cry of anguish,
One for the woods upstream and the falling axe,
One for the unmade bed and the stormy sky,
One for the newborn child and the god who died?

Oui, je le crois, je veux le croire, mais quelles sont
Ces ombres qui emportent le miroir?
Et vois, la ronce prend parmi les pierres
Sur la voie d'herbe encore mal frayée
Où se portaient nos pas vers les jeunes arbres.
Il me semble aujourd'hui, ici, que la parole
Est cette auge à demi brisée, dont se répand
À chaque aube de pluie l'eau inutile.

L'herbe et dans l'herbe l'eau qui brille, comme un fleuve.
Tout est toujours à remailler du monde.
Le paradis est épars, je le sais,
C'est la tâche terrestre d'en reconnnaître
Les fleurs disséminées dans l'herbe pauvre,
Mais l'ange a disparu, une lumière
Qui ne fut plus soudain que soleil couchant.

Et comme Adam et Ève nous marcherons
Une dernière fois dans le jardin.
Comme Adam le premier regret, comme Ève le premier
Courage nous voudrons et ne voudrons pas
Franchir la porte basse qui s'entrouvre
Là-bas, à l'autre bout des longes, colorée
Comme auguralement d'un dernier rayon.
L'avenir se prend-il dans l'origine
Comme le ciel consent à un miroir courbe?
Pourrons-nous recueillir de cette lumière
Qui a été le miracle d'ici
La semence dans nos mains sombres, pour d'autres flaques
Au secret d'autres champs « barrés de pierres »?

Certes, le lieu pour vaincre, pour nous vaincre, c'est ici
Dont nous partons, ce soir. Ici sans fin
Comme cette eau qui s'échappe de l'auge.

Yes, I think so, I want to think so, but who are
These shades that are carrying off the mirror?
And look, thorns are springing up among the stones
Along the barely beaten path through the grasses
That took us out toward the young trees.
It seems to me today, here, that speech
Is that half-broken trough flowing
At every rainy dawn with useless water.

The grass, and in the grass the water shimmering,
Like a river.
The work of mending in this world never ends.
Paradise lies scattered, this I know,
It is our earthly task to recognise
Its flowers that are strewn in the humble grass;
But the angel has disappeared, a light
That suddenly was but a setting sun.

And like Adam and Eve we will walk
One last time in the garden.
Like Adam the first regret, like Eve the first
Courage, we will want and not want
To pass through the low, half-opened door
Down there, at the other end of the field, coloured
As though prophetically with a last ray of light.
Will the future spring from the origin
As the sky gives itself to a convex mirror?
From that light which has been the miracle
Of here and now, will we gather up
In darker hands the seeds for other pools of water
Hidden in other fields 'among the stones'?

Surely the place of victory, of victory over ourselves,
Is here in what we are leaving tonight. Endlessly here
Like that water overflowing from the trough.

LE MIROIR COURBE

I

Regarde-les là-bas, à ce carrefour,
Qui semblent hésiter puis qui repartent.
L'enfant court devant eux, ils ont cueilli
En de grandes brassées pour les quelques vases
Ces fleurs d'à travers champs qui n'ont pas de nom.

Et l'ange est au-dessus, qui les observe
Enveloppé du vent et de ses couleurs.
Un de ses bras est nu dans l'étoffe rouge,
On dirait qu'il tient un miroir, et que la terre
Se reflète dans l'eau de cette autre rive.

Et que désigne-t-il maintenant, du doigt
Qui pointe vers un lieu dans cette image?
Est-ce une autre maison ou un autre monde,
Est-ce même une porte, dans la lumière
Ici mêlée des choses et des signes?

II

Ils aiment rentrer tard, ainsi. Ils ne distinguent
Plus même le chemin parmi les pierres
D'où sourd encore une ombre d'ocre rouge.
Ils ont pourtant confiance. Près du seuil
L'herbe est facile et il n'est point de mort.

Et les voici maintenant sous des voûtes.
Il y fait noir dans la rumeur des feuilles
Sèches, qui fait bouger sur le dallage
Le vent qui ne sait pas, de salle en salle,
Ce qui a nom et ce qui n'est que chose.

THE CONVEX MIRROR

I

Look at them down there, at that crossroads,
They seem to hesitate, then go on.
The child runs before them, they have picked
By the armful, for their few vases,
Those field flowers that have no name.

And the angel is above, watching them,
Enveloped in the wind of his colours.
One arm bare in the red cloth,
He seems to be holding a mirror, the earth
Reflected in the water of this other shore.

And what is he showing now with his finger
That is pointing toward a place in the image?
Is it some other house or some other world,
Is it even a door
Among these things and signs now a single light?

II

They like to come in late like this. They cannot even
Make out the pathway that runs through the stones
Still welling with red and ochre shadow.
But they are not afraid. Near the doorway
The grass is easy and there is no death.

And here they are now beneath the vaulted ceilings.
It is pitch black and the dry leaves are stirring
On the flagstones, blown by the wind that never knows,
As it moves from room to room,
Which things have names and which are only things.

Ils vont, ils vont. Là-bas parmi les ruines,
C'est le pays où les rives sont calmes,
Les chemins immobiles. Dans les chambres
Ils placeront les fleurs, près du miroir
Qui peut-être consume, et peut-être sauve.

PASSANT AUPRÈS DU FEU

Je passais près du feu dans la salle vide
Aux volets clos, aux lumières éteintes,

Et je vis qu'il brûlait encore, et qu'il était même
En cet instant à ce point d'équilibre
Entre les forces de la cendre, de la braise
Où la flamme va pouvoir être, à son désir,
Soit violente soit douce dans l'étreinte
De qui elle a séduit sur cette couche
Des herbes odorantes et du bois mort.
Lui, c'est cet angle de la branche que j'ai rentrée
Hier, dans la pluie d'été soudain si vive,
Il ressemble à un dieu de l'Inde qui regarde
Avec la gravité d'un premier amour
Celle qui veut de lui que l'enveloppe
La foudre qui précède l'univers.

Demain je remuerai
La flamme presque froide, et ce sera
Sans doute un jour d'été comme le ciel
En a pour tous les fleuves, ceux du monde
Et ceux, sombres, du sang. L'homme, la femme,
Quand savent-ils, à temps,
Que leur ardeur se noue ou se dénoue?
Quelle sagesse en eux peut pressentir
Dans une hésitation de la lumière
Que le cri de bonheur se fait cri d'angoisse?

On, on they go. Down there among the ruins
Is the land where the shores are calm,
The paths motionless. They will put the flowers
In the rooms, near the mirror
That perhaps will consume, and perhaps save.

PASSING BY THE FIRE

In the empty room, with its shutters closed,
And its lights spent, I passed by the fire.

And I saw that it still burned, that it was even,
At that moment, poised between
The powers of ash and of ember,
When the flame can choose to be
Either raging or subdued in the arms
Of what it has seduced on its bed
Of fragrant grasses and dead wood.
He is the jagged piece of branch I brought in
Yesterday, in the summer rain falling suddenly so hard.
He seems one of the gods of India, watching
With all the gravity of a first love
The one who asks of him that she be wrapped
In the lightning from before the worlds.

Tomorrow I will stir
The nearly cold flame, and doubtless
It will be a summer day like those
The sky offers to all the rivers, those of earth
And those, darker ones, of blood. Man and woman,
When do they ever know
That their passion is binding or coming apart?
What wisdom in their hearts could ever sense
That, as the light flickers,
Their cry of joy becomes a cry of anguish?

Feu des matins,
Respiration de deux êtres qui dorment,
Le bras de l'un sur l'épaule de l'autre.

Et moi qui suis venu
Ouvrir la salle, accueillir la lumière,
Je m'arrête, je m'assieds là, je vous regarde,
Innocence des membres détendus,
Temps si riche de soi qu'il a cessé d'être.

LE PUITS

Tu écoutes la chaîne heurter la paroi
Quand le seau descend dans le puits qui est l'autre étoile,
Parfois l'étoile du soir, celle qui vient seule,
Parfois le feu sans rayons qui attend à l'aube
Que le berger et les bêtes sortent.

Mais toujours l'eau est close, au fond du puits,
Toujours l'étoile y demeure scellée.
On y perçoit des ombres, sous des branches,
Ce sont des voyageurs qui passent de nuit

Courbés, le dos chargé d'une masse noire,
Hésitant, dirait-on, à un carrefour.
Certains semblent attendre, d'autres s'effacent
Dans l'étincellement qui va sans lumière.

Le voyage de l'homme, de la femme est long, plus long que la vie,
C'est une étoile au bout du chemin, un ciel
Qu'on a cru voir briller entre deux arbres.
Quand le seau touche l'eau, qui le soulève,
C'est une joie puis la chaîne l'accable.

Morning fire,
The breathing of two people asleep,
The arm of one on the shoulder of the other.

And I who came
To open the room, let in the light,
I stop, I sit there, I watch you,
Innocence of the sprawling limbs,
Time so full it ceases to be.

THE WELL

You hear the chain striking the wall
When the bucket goes down into the well, that other star,
Sometimes the evening star, the one that comes alone,
Sometimes the fire without radiance that waits at dawn
For the shepherd and his flock to go out.

But the water at the bottom of the well is always closed,
And the star there remains forever sealed.
You can see shadows there, beneath branches,
That are travellers passing by night

Bowed down beneath a load of blackness they go
As if hesitating at a crossroads.
Some seem to wait, others withdraw
Into the glittering that flows without light.

Man's voyage, and woman's, is long, longer than life,
It is a star at the end of the road, a sky
That was shining, we thought, between two trees.
When the bucket touches the water that lifts it up,
There is joy, then the chain overwhelms it.

L'ORÉE DU BOIS

I

Tu me dis que tu aimes le mot ronce,
Et j'ai là l'occasion de te parler,
Sentant revivre en toi sans que tu le saches
Encore, cette ardeur qui fut toute ma vie.

Mais je ne puis rien te répondre: car les mots
Ont ceci de cruel qu'ils se refusent
À ceux qui les respectent et les aiment
Pour ce qu'ils pourraient être, non ce qu'ils sont.

Et ne me restent donc que des images,
Soit, presque, des énigmes, qui feraient
Que se détournerait, triste soudain,
Ton regard qui ne sait que l'évidence.

C'est comme quand il pleut le matin, vois-tu,
Et qu'on va soulever l'étoffe de l'eau
Pour se risquer plus loin que la couleur
Dans l'inconnu des flaques et des ombres.

II

Et pourtant, c'est bien l'aube, dans ce pays
Qui m'a bouleversé et que tu aimes.
La maison de ces quelques jours est endormie,
Nous nous sommes glissés dans l'éternel.

Et l'eau cachée dans l'herbe est encore noire,
Mais la rosée recommence le ciel.
L'orage de la nuit s'apaise, la nuée
A mis sa main de feu dans la main de cendre.

THE EDGE OF THE WOODS

I

You tell me you love the word *thorn*,
And this gives me a chance to talk to you,
Sensing the ardour that was my whole life
Well up again in you, even if you don't know it.

But there is no answer I can give, for words
Can be cruel: they will resist
Those who respect and love them
For what they could be and not for what they are.

And so all I have left are images,
Nothing but enigma, that is, and what
Would make you look away, suddenly sad,
Your eyes seeing only into what is.

Listen, it is the same with the morning rain
When you lift up the curtains of water
To venture out, and further than colour,
Into the unknown of puddles and shadows.

II

And yet, it really is dawn, in this country
That has stirred me so much and that you love.
The house of these last few days is sleeping,
And we have slipped into the eternal.

The water hidden in the grass is still in darkness,
But the dew has begun the sky once more.
The night storm has quieted, and the cloud
Has placed its fiery hand in the hand of ashes.

DEDHAM, VU DE LANGHAM

I

Dedham, vu de Langham. L'été est sombre
Où des nuages se rassemblent. On pourrait croire
Que tout cela, haies, villages au loin,
Rivière, va finir. Que la terre n'est pas
Même l'éternité des bêtes, des arbres,
Et que ce son de cloches, qui a quitté
La tour de cette église, se dissipe,
Bruit simplement parmi les bruits terrestres,
Comme l'espoir que l'on a quelquefois
D'avoir perçu des signes sur des pierres
Tombe, dès qu'on voit mieux ces traits en désordre,
Ces taches, ces sursauts de la chose nue.

Mais tu as su mêler à ta couleur
Une sorte de sable qui du ciel
Accueille l'étincellement dans la matière.
Là où c'était le hasard qui parlait
Dans les éboulements, dans les nuées,
Tu as vaincu, d'un début de musique,
La forme qui se clôt dans toute vie.
Tu écoutes le bruit d'abeilles des choses claires,
Son gonflement parfois, cet absolu
Qui vibre dans le pré parmi les ombres,
Et tu le laisses vivre en toi, et tu t'allèges
De n'être plus ainsi hâte ni peur.

Ô peintre,
Comme une main presse une grappe, main divine,
De toi dépend le vin; de toi, que la lumière
Ne soit pas cette griffe qui déchire
Toute forme, toute espérance, mais une joie
Dans les coupes même noircies du jour de fête.

DEDHAM, SEEN FROM LANGHAM

I

Dedham, seen from Langham. The summer is sombre,
Clouds are gathering. You might think that
The whole scene, the hedges, the distant villages,
The river, was about to vanish. That the earth
Was not even the eternity of the flocks and trees,
And that the chiming of bells, flung from
The church steeple, was also drifting away,
One more sound among the sounds of earth,
As the hope one sometimes has
Of having discovered signs written on stones
Falls when one examines more closely the tangle
Of markings: those shudders on the face of earth.

But you knew how to mix with your colour
A kind of sand which welcomes
The glitterings of the sky in matter.
Where it was chance that spoke
Among the rubble, in the clouds,
You vanquished
With the beginnings of a music
The form which is the dead face of all life.
You listen to the sound of bees in the things filled with light,
To the way the buzzing sometimes seems to swell
Into that absolute in the meadow's shadows,
And you let it live in you, more transparent,
Since now you know neither haste nor fear.

O painter,
The wine is your gift,
Your hand, your divine hand,
As if pressing the grape; and thanks to you
The light is no longer that claw
That tears apart every form, every hope,

Peintre de paysage, grâce à toi
Le ciel s'est arrêté au-dessus du monde
Comme l'ange au-dessus d'Agar quand elle allait,
Le cœur vide, dans le dédale da la pierre.

Et que de plénitude est dans le bruit,
Quand tu le veux, du ruisseau qui dans l'herbe
A recueilli le murmure des cloches,
Et que d'éternité se donne dans l'odeur
De la fleur la plus simple! C'est comme si
La terre voulait bien ce que l'esprit rêve.

Et la petite fille qui vient en rêve
Jouer dans la prairie de Langham, et regarde
Quelquefois ce Dedham au loin, et se demande
Si ce n'est pas là-bas qu'il faudrait vivre,
Cueille pour rien la fleur qu'elle respire
Puis la jette et l'oublie; mais ne se rident
Dans l'éternel été
Les eaux de cette vie ni de cette mort.

II

Peintre,
Dès que je t'ai connu je t'ai fait confiance,
Car tu as beau rêver tes yeux sont ouverts
Et risques-tu ta pensée dans l'image
Comme on trempe la main dans l'eau, tu prends le fruit
De la couleur, de la forme brisées,
Tu le poses réel parmi les choses dites.

Peintre,
J'honore tes journées, qui ne sont rien
Que la tâche terrestre, délivrée
Des hâtes qui l'aveuglent. Rien que la route
Mais plus lente là-bas dans la poussière.

But rather joy, flowing in festive cups, however dark.
Thanks to you, landscape painter,
The sky has paused above the world
As did the angel above Hagar when she went,
With empty heart, into the labyrinths of stone.

And when you wish it so, how much fullness
Dwells within the murmur of the brook in the grass
As it gathers up the distant sounds of the church bells,
And how much eternity is offered in the scent
Of the simplest flower! It is as though earth
Consented gladly to what the spirit dreams of.

And the little girl who comes in dream
To play in the fields of Langham, and who
Sometimes looks toward Dedham in the distance, wondering
If it is not over there that one should live,
Picks, aimlessly, the flower she is smelling,
Then throws it aside and thinks no more
About it – but the waters of life,
Or death, are not rippled at all,
In the eternal summer.

II

Painter,
As soon as I knew you, I trusted you,
For even when you are dreaming, your eyes are open,
And should you risk your vision in images,
As one might plunge a hand into water, you always seize
The fruit of broken form, of broken colour,
And you place it, real, among the names of things.

Painter,
I give praise to your days, which are nothing more
Than the earthly task, delivered

Rien que la cime
Des montagnes d'ici mais dégagée,
Un instant, de l'espace. Rien que le bleu
De l'eau prise du puits dans le vert de l'herbe
Mais pour la conjonction, la métamorphose
Et que monte la plante d'un autre monde,
Palmes, grappes de fruits serrées encore,
Dans l'accord de deux tons, notre unique vie.
Tu peins, il est cinq heures dans l'éternel
De la journée d'été. Et une flamme
Qui brûlait par le monde se détache
Des choses et des rêves, transmutée.
On dirait qu'il ne reste qu'une buée
Sur la paroi de verre.

Peintre,
L'étoile de tes tableaux est celle en plus
De l'infini qui peuple en vain les mondes.
Elle guide les choses vers leur vraie place,
Elle enveloppe là leur dos de lumière,
Plus tard
Quand la main du dehors déchire l'image,
Tache de sang l'image,
Elle sait rassembler leur troupe craintive
Pour le piétinement de nuit, sur un sol nu.

Et quelquefois,
Dans le miroir brouillé de la dernière heure,
Elle sait dégager, dit-on, comme une main
Essuie la vitre où a brillé la pluie,
Quelques figures simples, quelques signes
Qui brillent au-delà des mots, indéchiffrables
Dans l'immobilité du souvenir.
Formes redessinées, recolorées
À l'horizon qui ferme le langage,
C'est comme si la foudre qui frappait
Suspendait dans le même instant, presque éternel,

From the haste that blinds it. Nothing more
Than the road, the slower road, up there
In the dust. Nothing more
Than the mountaintops of our world, but freed
For a moment from space. Nothing but the blue
Of the water drawn from the well in the green of the grass,
But for conjunction and metamorphosis,
And so that the plant of another world may spring up,
Palms, clusters of fruit still pressed close together,
In the resolution of the two colours, our sole life.
You paint, it is five o'clock in the eternity
Of the summer day. And a flame
That burned throughout the world breaks free
From things, from dreams, transmuted.
It seems that nothing remains but a faint cloud
Of mist on the surface of the alembic.

Painter,
The star in your landscapes is the one missing
In the infinite that crowds in vain the worlds.
It guides things toward their true places,
Then throws a cloak of light around their shoulders,
And later,
When the hand from the outside tears apart the image,
And splatters it with blood,
The star brings their frightened flocks together again
For the hoofbeats at night, against the naked earth.

And sometimes,
In the blurred mirror of the last hour,
They say that the star knows how to draw forth,
As a hand wipes a window pane that shone with rain,
A few simple figures, a few signs
Gleaming beyond words, indecipherable
In the motionlessness of memory,
Forms that are drawn and coloured anew
On the horizon that closes our language;

Son geste d'épée nue, et comme surprise
Redécouvrait le pays de l'enfance,
Parcourant ses chemins; et pensive, touchait
Les objets oubliés, les vêtements
Dans de vieilles armoires, les deux ou trois
Jouets mystérieux de sa première
Allégresse divine. Elle, la mort,
Elle défait le temps qui va le monde,
Montre le mur qu'éclaire le couchant,
Et mène autour de la maison vers la tonnelle
Pour offrir, ô bonheur ici, dans l'heure brève,
Les fruits, les voix, les reflets, les rumeurs,
Le vin léger dans rien que la lumière.

L'AGITATION DU RÊVE

I

Dans ce rêve le fleuve encore: c'est l'amont,
Une eau serrée, violente, où des troncs d'arbres
S'entrechoquent, dévient; de toute part
Des rivages stériles m'environnent,
De grands oiseaux m'assaillent avec un cri
De douleur et d'étonnement – mais moi, j'avance
À la proue d'une barque, dans une aube.
J'y ai amoncelé des branches, me dit-on,
En tourbillons s'élève la fumée,
Puis le feu prend, d'un coup, deux colonnes torses,
Tout un porche de foudre. Je suis heureux
De ce ciel qui crépite, j'aime l'odeur
De la sève qui brûle dans la brume.

Et plus tard je remue des cendres, dans un âtre
De la maison où je viens chaque nuit,

It is as though the lightning, as it struck,
Held back its naked sword, and with surprise,
At that very instant, almost eternal,
Rediscovered the land of childhood,
Wandered along its paths; and touched once more,
With pensive hands, things long forgotten; the clothes
That languish in old closets, the two or three
Mysterious toys from the child's first moments
Of joyfulness divine. This light, this death
Undoes time as it roams throughout the world,
Shows us the wall all lit up at sunset
And leads us around the house and toward the arbour
To offer, for one brief moment, O blissfulness,
The fruit, the voices, the shadows, the sounds,
The gentle wine, in nothing but the light.

THE RESTLESSNESS OF THE DREAM

I

In this dream, the river again: upstream now,
A narrow, violent water, filled with tree trunks
That collide and glance off one another; I am
Surrounded on all sides by lifeless shores,
Giant birds assail me with a cry
Full of anguish and amazement – but I go on
At the prow of a boat, in a dawn light.
I have made, I am told, a pile of branches,
The smoke rises in swirls,
Then all at once the fire catches, two wreathed columns,
A sudden porch of lightning. I am happy with
This crackling sky, I love the smell
Of the sap burning in the mist.

And later I am stirring ashes in a fireplace
In the house I come to, every night,

Mais c'est déjà du blé, comme si l'âme
Des choses consumées, à leur dernier souffle,
Se détachait de l'épi de matière
Pour se faire le grain d'un nouvel espoir.
Je prends à pleines mains cette masse sombre
Mais ce sont des étoiles; je déplie
Les draps de ce silence, mais découvre
Très lointaine, très proche la forme nue
De deux êtres qui dorment, dans la lumière
Compassionnée de l'aube, qui hésite
À effleurer du doigt leurs paupières closes
Et fait que ce grenier, cette charpente,
Cette odeur du blé d'autrefois, qui se dissipe,
C'est encore leur lieu, et leur bonheur.

Je dois me délivrer de ces images.
Je m'éveille et me lève et marche. Et j'entre
Dans le jardin de quand j'avais dix ans,
Qui ne fut qu'une allée, bien courte, entre deux masses
De terre mal remuée, où les averses
Laissent longtemps des flaques où se prirent
Les premières lumières que j'aie aimées.
Mais c'est la nuit maintenant, je suis seul,
Les êtres que j'ai connus dans ces années
Parlent là-haut et rient, dans une salle
Dont tombe la lueur sur l'allée; et je sais
Que les mots que j'ai dits, décidant parfois
De ma vie, sont ce sol, cette terre noire.
Autour de moi le dédale, infini,
D'autres menus jardins avec leurs serres
Défaites, leurs tuyaux sur des plates-bandes
Derrière des barrières, leurs appentis
Où des meubles cassés, des portraits sans cadre,
Des brocs, et parfois des miroirs comme à l'aguet
Sous des bâches, prêts à s'ouvrir aux feux qui passent,
Furent aussi, hors du temps, ma première
Conscience de ce monde où l'on va seul.

But already they are wheat, as though
The soul of things past, at the moment of
Their last breath, broke free from the husk of matter
To become the seed of a new hope.
I take up by the handful this sombre heap,
But these are stars; I unfold
The sheets of this silence, but discover,
Very deep, very near, the naked form
Of two beings sleeping in the compassionate
Light of dawn, which hesitates to graze
Their closed eyelids with its finger
And ensures that this granary beneath its beams,
This smell of the wheat of years gone by
That slowly vanishes into the air,
That these remain a place for them, and happiness.

I must free myself from these images.
I awake, then get up and walk. I go into
The garden I knew as a child of ten,
Which was really just a short walkway
Between two patches of poorly toiled earth
Where the rainstorms left lingering puddles
That caught the first lights I loved.
But it is night now, I am alone,
The people I knew in those days
Are laughing and talking up there in a room
Whose feeble light gleams down on the walkway;
And I know that the words that I have spoken,
Sometimes determining the course of my life,
Are this very ground, this dark earth.
All around me the endless maze
Of other tiny gardens with their paltry
Greenhouses, their hoses lying on the flowerbeds
Behind fences, their sheds filled with
Broken furniture, pictures without frames,
Old pots, and sometimes mirrors that seem
Watchful beneath the sheets of canvas,

*Vais-je pouvoir reprendre à la glaise dure
Ces bouts de fer rouillés, ces éclats de verre,
Ces morceaux de charbon? Agenouillé,
Je détache de l'infini l'inexistence
Et j'en fais des figures, d'une main
Que je distingue mal, tant est la nuit
Précipitée, violente par les mondes.
Que lointaine est ici l'aube du signe!
J'ébauche une constellation mais tout se perd.*

II

*Et je lève les yeux, je l'ose enfin,
Et je vois devant moi, dans le ciel nu,
Passer la barque qui revint, parfois sans lumière,
Dans tant des rêves qui miroitent dans le sable
De la très longue rive de cette nuit.*

*Je regarde la barque, qui hésite.
Elle a tourné comme si des chemins
Se dessinaient pour elle sur la houle
Qui parcourt doucement, brisant l'écume,
L'immensité de l'ombre de l'étoile.*

*Et qui sont-ils, à bord? Un homme, une femme
Qui se détachent noirs de la fumée
D'un feu qu'ils entretiennent à la proue.
De l'homme, de la femme le désir
Est donc ce feu au dédale des mondes.*

Ready to give themselves to the passing fires;
These things, too, were my first awareness,
Outside time, of this world where we walk alone.
Will I be able to wrest from the hard clay
These pieces of rusted iron, these bits of glass,
These lumps of charcoal? Kneeling down,
I tear the inexistent from the infinite
And draw figures with it, my hand
Hardly visible, so rapid, violent,
Is the night that is drifting among the worlds.
How unlikely here the dawn of signs!
I sketch out a constellation, but everything fades away.

II

And I raise my eyes, at last I dare to,
And I see passing before me in the naked sky
The boat that reappeared, sometimes without light,
In so many of the dreams that shimmer in the sands
Of this night's long stretches of shore.

I look at the boat, as it hesitates.
It has turned, as though paths
Were traced for it across the rising swell
That gently runs, breaking the foam,
Through the immensity of the star's shadow.

And who is that on board? A man, a woman
Who stand out darkly from the smoke
Of a fire they are tending at the prow.
And thus man's desire, and woman's,
Is this fire that burns in the maze of the worlds.

III

Je referme les yeux. Et m'apparaît
Maintenant, dans le flux de la mémoire,
Une coupe de terre rouge, dont des flammes
Débordent sur la main qui la soulève
Au-dessus de la barque qui s'éloigne.

Et c'est là un enfant, qui me demande
De m'approcher, mais il est dans un arbre,
Les reflets s'enchevêtrent dans les branches.
Qui es-tu? dis-je. Et lui à moi, riant:
Qui es-tu? Puisque tu ne sais pas souffler la flamme.

Qui es-tu? Vois, moi je souffle le monde,
Il fera nuit, je ne te verrai plus,
Veux-tu que ne nous reste que la lumière?
— Mais je ne sais répondre, de par un charme
Qui m'a étreint, de plus loin que l'enfance.

IV

Et je m'éloigne et vais vers le rivage.
La barque, et d'autres barques, y sont venues.
Mais tout y est silence, même l'eau claire.
Les figures de proue ont les yeux encore
Clos, à l'avant de ces lumières closes.

Et les rameurs sont endormis, le front
Dans leurs bras repliés en dehors des siècles.
La marque sur leur épaule, rouge sang,
Tristement brille encore, dans la brume
Que ne dissipe pas le vent de l'aube.

III

I close my eyes again. And there appears
Before me now, in the flow of memory,
The image of a cup made of red earth, whose
Flames overflow onto the hand that lifts it up
Above the boat as it vanishes.

And the cup is a child, and he asks me
To draw near, but he is in a tree,
There are tangles of light in the branches.
Who are you? I say. And he, laughingly: Who are you?
Since you do not know how to blow out the flame.

Who are you? Look, I blow out the world,
It will be night, I will no longer see you,
Do you want only light?
– But I cannot answer, for I am seized
By a spell from further off than childhood.

IV

I leave and move off toward the shore.
The boat, with other boats, has landed, now.
But everything is silent, even the limpid waters.
The eyes of the figureheads are still
Shut, at the prow of these closed lights.

And the oarsmen have gone to sleep, their foreheads
Resting on arms folded outside time.
The mark on their shoulders, red as blood is,
Still gleams sadly in the mist
That the winds of dawn cannot dispel.

IV 1989–2000

From *Debut et fin de la neige* (1991)

HOPKINS FOREST

*J'étais sorti
Prendre de l'eau au puits, auprès des arbres,
Et je fus en présence d'un autre ciel.
Disparues les constellations d'il y a un instant encore,
Les trois quarts du firmament étaient vides,
Le noir le plus intense y régnait seul,
Mais à gauche, au-dessus de l'horizon,
Mêlé à la cime des chênes,
Il y avait un amas d'étoiles rougeoyantes
Comme un brasier, d'où montait même une fumée.*

*Je rentrai
Et je rouvris le livre sur la table.
Page après page,
Ce n'étaient que des signes indéchiffrables,
Des agrégats de formes d'aucun sens
Bien que vaguement récurrentes,
Et par-dessous une blancheur d'abîme
Comme si ce qu'on nomme l'esprit tombait là, sans bruit,
Comme une neige.
Je tournai cependant les pages.*

*Bien des années plus tôt,
Dans un train au moment où le jour se lève
Entre Princeton Junction et Newark,
C'est-à-dire deux lieux de hasard pour moi,
Deux retombées des flèches de nulle part,
Les voyageurs lisaient, silencieux
Dans la neige qui balayait les vitres grises,
Et soudain,
Dans un journal ouvert à deux pas de moi,
Une grande photographie de Baudelaire,*

From *Beginning and End of the Snow* (1991)

HOPKINS FOREST

I had gone out
To take water from the well, near the trees,
And then, the full presence of another sky.
Gone were the constellations from a moment before,
Three quarters of the firmament were empty,
Utter darkness reigned alone,
But on the left, above the horizon,
Blending with the tops of the oaks,
There was a pile of stars blazing
Like coals, and smoke was even rising from them.

I went back in
And reopened the book on the table,
Page after page,
Nothing but indecipherable signs,
Aggregates of meaningless forms
Though vaguely recurrent,
And beneath them the white of an abyss
As though what we call mind were falling there,
Soundlessly,
Like snow.
And yet, I turned the pages.

Many years earlier,
On a train as day was breaking
Between Princeton Junction and Newark,
That is, two random places for me,
The fall of two arrows from nowhere,
The passengers were reading in silence
As the snow swept the grey windows,
And all at once,
In a newspaper a few feet away,
A huge photograph of Baudelaire,

Toute une page
Comme le ciel se vide à la fin du monde
Pour consentir au désordre des mots.

J'ai rapproché ce rêve et ce souvenir
Quand j'ai marché, d'abord tout un automne
Dans des bois où bientôt ce fut la neige
Qui triompha, dans beaucoup de ces signes
Que l'on reçoit, contradictoirement,
Du monde dévastée par le langage.
Prenait fin le conflit de deux principes,
Me semblait-il, se mêlaient deux lumières,
Se refermaient les lèvres de la plaie.
La masse blanche du froid tombait par rafales
Sur la couleur, mais un toit au loin, une planche
Peinte, restée debout contre une grille,
C'était encore la couleur, et mystérieuse
Comme un qui sortirait du sépulcre et, riant:
« Non, ne me touche pas », dirait-il au monde.

Je dois vraiment beaucoup à Hopkins Forest,
Je la garde à mon horizon, dans sa partie
Qui quitte le visible pour l'invisible
Par le tressaillement du bleu des lointains.
Je l'écoute, à travers les bruits, et parfois même,
L'été, poussant du pied les feuilles mortes
D'autres années, claires dans la pénombre
Des chênes trop serrés parmi les pierres,
Je m'arrête, je crois que ce sol s'ouvre
À l'infini, que ces feuilles y tombent
Sans hâte, ou bien remontent, le haut, le bas
N'étant plus, ni le bruit, sauf le léger
Chuchotement des flocons qui bientôt
Se multiplient, se rapprochent, se nouent
— Et je revois alors tout l'autre ciel,
J'entre pour un instant dans la grande neige.

A whole page,
As the sky empties at the end of the world
To accept the disorder of words.

I brought together this dream and this memory
When I walked, at first all through autumn
In woods where snow was soon
To triumph in many of those signs
One receives, so often in contradiction,
From the world devastated by language.
It seemed that the conflict between two principles
Was coming to an end, two lights were mingling,
The lips of the wound were closing.
The white mass of the cold fell in gusts
Upon the colour, but a roof in the distance,
A painted board, resting against a gate,
This was still colour, and mysterious,
Like someone who would rise up from a sepulchre
And, smiling, say to the world:
'No, do not touch me.'

I really owe a lot to Hopkins Forest,
I keep it on my horizon, the part of it
That leaves the visible for the invisible
Through the quivering of the blue in the distant background.
I listen to it, through the sounds, and sometimes even,
In summer, my foot pushing the dead leaves
Of other years, bright in the half light
Of the oaks too tightly clustered among the stones,
I stop, I think that this ground is opening to
The infinite, that these leaves are falling there
Without haste, or else are rising upwards, down, up,
No longer existing, nor any sound, except the gentle
Whispering of the snowflakes that soon
Multiply, draw together, join to one another
– And then I see once more the whole other sky,
And enter for a moment the great heavy snow.

LA SEULE ROSE

I

Il neige, c'est revenir dans une ville
Où, et je le découvre en avançant
Au hasard dans des rues qui toutes sont vides,
J'aurais vécu heureux une autre enfance.
Sous les flocons j'aperçois des façades
Qui ont beauté plus que rien de ce monde.
Seuls parmi nous Alberti puis San Gallo
À San Biagio, dans la salle la plus intense
Qu'ait bâtie le désir, ont approché
De cette perfection, de cette absence.

Et je regarde donc, avidement,
Ces masses que la neige me dérobe.
Je recherche surtout, dans la blancheur
Errante, ces frontons que je vois qui montent
À un plus haut niveau de l'apparence.
Ils déchirent la brume, c'est comme si
D'une main délivrée de la pesanteur
L'architecte d'ici avait fait vivre
D'un seul grand trait floral
La forme que voulait de siècle en siècle
La douleur d'être né dans la matière.

II

Et là-haut je ne sais si c'est la vie
Encore, ou la joie seule, qui se détache
Sur ce ciel qui n'est plus de notre monde.
O bâtisseurs
Non tant d'un lieu que d'un regain de l'espérance,
Qu'y a-t-il au secret de ces parois
Qui devant moi s'écartent? Ce que je vois

THE ONLY ROSE

I

It's snowing, it's returning to a town
Where, as I discover as I go through
Empty streets I come upon by chance,
I might have happily lived some other childhood.
Beneath the snowflakes I notice façades
More beautiful than anything in this world.
Among us, only Alberti, then Sangallo,
At San Biagio, in the most intense room
That desire has ever built, have approached
This perfection, this absence.

And so I gaze avidly
At these masses the snow hides from me.
I seek, above all, in the wandering
Whiteness, those pediments that rise
To a higher level of appearance.
They tear apart the mist, it is as though,
With a hand freed from weight,
The mortal architect had brought to life,
In a single floral stroke,
The form sought for centuries by
The pain of being born into matter.

II

And up there I cannot tell if it is still
Life, or only joy, that stands out
Against this sky no longer of our world.
Oh you builders,
Not so much of place as of renewed hope,
What is there in the depths of these walls
That open before me? What I see

Le long des murs, ce sont des niches vides,
Des pleins et des déliés, d'où s'évapore
Par la grâce des nombres
Le poids de la naissance dans l'exil,
Mais de la neige s'y est mise et s'y entasse,
Je m'approche de l'une d'elles, la plus basse,
Je fais tomber un peu de sa lumière,
Et soudain c'est le pré de mes dix ans,
Les abeilles bourdonnent,
Ce que j'ai dans mes mains, ces fleurs, ces ombres,
Est-ce presque du miel, est-ce de la neige?

III

J'avance alors, jusque sous l'arche d'une porte.
Les flocons tourbillonnent, effaçant
La limite entre le dehors et cette salle
Où des lampes sont allumées: mais elles-mêmes
Une sorte de neige, qui hésite
Entre le haut, le bas, dans cette nuit.
C'est comme si j'étais sur un second seuil.

Et au-delà ce même bruit d'abeilles
Dans le bruit de la neige. Ce que disaient
Les abeilles sans nombre de l'été,
Semble le refléter l'infini des lampes.

Et je voudrais
Courir, comme du temps de l'abeille, cherchant
Du pied la balle souple, car peut-être
Je dors, et rêve, et vais par les chemins d'enfance.

Along the walls are only empty niches,
Partly stone, partly the absence of stone,
From which, thanks to symmetry,
The weight of being born into exile is lifted.
But snow has gathered there, has piled up,
I draw near to one of them, the lowest,
I bring down a bit of its light
And all at once it is the meadow I walked in at ten,
The bees are buzzing,
What I have in my hands, these flowers, these shadows,
Is it almost honey, is it snow?

III

And then I go on until I am beneath an archway,
The snowflakes are swirling, blotting out
The line between the outside and this room
Where lamps are lit: these, too,
A kind of snow, which hesitates
Between the high and the low, in this night.
It is as though I were at a second threshold.

And beyond, the same sound of bees
In the sound of the snow. What the countless
Summer bees were saying
Seems reflected in the infinite of the lamps.

And I would like
To run, as in the time of the bee, seeking
With my foot the supple ball, for perhaps
I am sleeping, and dreaming, and wandering along
The paths of childhood.

IV

*Mais ce que je regarde, c'est de la neige
Durcie, qui s'est glissée sur le dallage
Et s'accumule aux bases des colonnes
À gauche, à droite, et loin devant dans la pénombre.
Absurdement je n'ai d'yeux que pour l'arc
Que cette boue dessine sur la pierre.
J'attache ma pensée à ce qui n'a
Pas de nom, pas de sens. Ô mes amis,
Alberti, Brunelleschi, San Gallo,
Palladio qui fais signe de l'autre rive,
Je ne vous trahis pas, cependant, j'avance,
La forme la plus pure reste celle
Qu'a pénétrée la brume qui s'efface,
La neige piétinée est la seule rose.*

IV

But what I am looking at is hardened snow,
The flakes which have stolen onto the flagstones
And piled up at the base of the columns
Left and right, and far ahead in the dusk.
Absurdly, my eyes can only see the arc
That this mud draws on the stone.
My only thought is for what has
No name, no meaning. Oh my friends,
Alberti, Brunelleschi, Sangallo,
Palladio who beckons from the other shore,
I do not betray you, I still go forward,
The purest form is always the one
Pierced by the mist that fades away,
Trampled snow is the only rose.

From *La Vie errante* / *The Wandering Life* (1993)

LE CANOT DE SAMUEL BECKETT / BECKETT'S DINGHY

The island isn't far from the coast: it's a flat line hard to make out, topped by several trees, in the fog that hunkers down on the sea. All we know about the man who's taking us there in his boat is that he's kindly offered to show us around. It's raining when we push off, and we cross the narrow sound under a veil of inky shadows. We seem to be punching a hole in appearances, dreaming another world; and maybe we've almost reached it: a dim glimmer in the splotches of darkness. But after a few minutes, here's the shore. A tiny landing, where you disembark on three or four steps, hewn from glistening stone. Two little buildings, a light in one: the shut-up pub and the pub-keeper's house. He opens it on Sundays now and then, for the farmers from the other island, when they want to travel even farther west. But we don't approach the buildings; we go inland, to the right. The path is sodden – when there's a path at all – and we slog through a puddle-infested moor. We have to pick our way over barbed-wire fences – no easy feat. I scarcely understand our guide's rough, splendid accent, in a language foreign to me. Who knows where we're really headed: maybe to a stone cross from Celtic times, facing the surf; maybe just to the far side of the island. And in fact, now we've reached it. Here's the outer edge, with stout green waves in front of us; the rain has almost stopped.

We stay there for a while, at the tip of the island, admiring the ocean. We also look back at the path we've followed, or sidestepped – because of the holes, or for no reason at all. It's just a vague track that weaves through the scrubby grass, bordered here and there by low walls of stone. Then we set out on a wider trail that hugs the coast. Our guide, our friend, goes on talking. Since the surf's not as loud and the walking is easier, I understand him better now – perhaps because he's also turned to other thoughts. At any rate, tucked behind a tree, we come upon another house: so there's a third one on the island. It's only a couple of steps from the sea, but it has

a small enclosure. Lettuce, parsley, and potatoes used to grow there; some flowers as well, sheltered by a wedge of rock. 'Oh, the old lady who lived here!' the mariner says. He's a seaman, he just explained to us, and every year he carries a cargo around the world. 'When I was a child, she taught me in school; and later, for a long, long time, when I'd pass this way at night, I always knocked on her door. No matter if it was midnight, one or two in the morning, or almost dawn, I knew she'd be awake and dressed. She'd either be pottering around or sitting in her armchair next to the fire. And she'd open the door, laugh, and serve me some tea while she told me her stories. She had tons of them.'

He reminisces, but then falls silent, as though he's listening to a voice. 'She's no longer with us', he adds. We've circled back to the hamlet, the first pair of buildings. He insists we visit the pub. He knocks on the other door: a young woman with a child appears. He returns with the key, and jiggles it in the lock. We enter the pitch-black room, and he lights a lamp. Tables against the wall, the usual bar – though the bottles are empty, no doubt. The broad, bare floor seems worn, as though people had danced there thousands of times: in a past removed from our present, like water that's retreated far from shore. We're here to see the photographs on the wall; they're supposed to tell us about the former inhabitants of these two islands, before their community scattered and died out. Men and women dwell in another bank of fog: this paper that yellows and fades, like a metaphor of memory. Some of their faces stare back at us, distractedly reproachful, as though absorbed by a faraway vision – a knowledge, perhaps – that we can no longer share. Ireland from the forties and fifties, mysterious as a ship skirting the coast.

'And that one there, what a drinker he was!' the long-distance captain exclaims. The picture shows an old man seated in front of the ocean, pipe in hand: skinny, upright, stock-still. 'He'd cast off and catch lobsters for days on end, alone in his little dinghy. But he'd already be drunk before he left, and he'd stow flasks of whiskey with his nets and baskets. How on earth did he buck the worst of the weather and come back? Well, he always came back, so he must've been in God's own hand.'

I look at the beautiful face, which resembles Samuel Beckett's.

And I forget about the alcohol: merely a device of universal writing, this hand that seeks the hand of God. I think how the writer, too, has just vanished in the distance. He's slipped away into the throng of shadows, blackened by rain or fog; though here and there – and over there again – we glimpse a streak of yellow sun. Beckett, I tell myself, wrote the way that old man sailed, alone on the sea. Like him, he spent long days and nights beneath the clouds I've watched here, piling up as castles in the sky, or as cliffs, with dragons spitting fire from their ridges and crevasses. Suddenly, they shear apart before a sweeping beam, a 'spell of light', around three in the afternoon. From then until the evening swiftly falls, time slows to a halt, and gold seems to lie in the ocean's gentle hollows. Beckett is far from us now, though his boat is still dimly visible: maybe over there, where sunset ruffles a crest of sea. We should listen to his books only through the constant roll of waves, the intermittent drumming of the rain.

IV. 1989–2000

DE VENT ET DE FUMÉE

I

L'Idée, a-t-on pensé, est la mesure de tout,
D'où suit que « la sua bella Elena rapita », dit Bellori
D'une célèbre peinture de Guido Reni,
Peut être comparée à l'autre Hélène,
Celle qu'imagina, aima peut-être, Zeuxis.
Mais que sont des images auprès de la jeune femme
Que Pâris a tant désirée? La seule vigne,
N'est-ce pas le frémissement des mains réelles
Sous la fièvre des lèvres? Et que l'enfant
Demande avidement à la grappe, et boive
À même la lumière, en hâte, avant
Que le temps ne déferle sur ce qui est?

Mais non,
A pensé un commentateur de l'Iliade, anxieux
D'expliquer, d'excuser dix ans de guerre,
Et le vrai, c'est qu'Hélène ne fut pas
Assaillie, ne fut pas transportée de barque en vaisseau,
Ne fut pas retenue, criante, enchaînée
Sur des lits en désordre. Le ravisseur
N'emportait qu'une image: une statue
Que l'art d'un magicien avait faite des brises
Des soirées de l'été quand tout est calme,
Pour qu'elle eût la tiédeur du corps en vie
Et même sa respiration, et le regard
Qui se prête au desir. La feinte Hélène
Erre rêveusement sous les voûtes basses
Du navire qui fuit, il semble qu'elle écoute
Le bruit de l'autre mer dans ses veines bleues
Et qu'elle soit heureuse. D'autres scoliastes
Ont même cru à une œuvre de pierre.
Dans la cabine
Jour après jour secouée par le gros temps

WIND AND SMOKE

I

The idea, it was thought, is the measure of everything,
From which it follows that 'la sua bella Elena rapita',
As Bellori said of a famous painting by Guido Reni,
Might be compared to that other Helen,
The one imagined, loved perhaps, by Zeuxis.
But what are images next to the young woman
Who filled Paris with such desire? The only vine,
Is it not the trembling of real hands
Beneath the fever of ardent lips? Is it not the child
Who asks avidly of the grape and who drinks,
In haste, straight from the light
Before time surges back over what is?

That's not it,
A commentator on the *Iliad* maintained,
Anxious to explain, to justify, ten years of war,
The truth is that Helen was never sprung upon,
Was never transported from boat to ship,
Was never held captive, screaming, chained
On crumpled beds. Her abductor
Carried off only an image: a statue
That a magician's art had made of the breezes
Of summer evenings when all is calm,
So she would have the warmth of a living body
And even its breathing, and the look
That lends itself to desire. The pretend Helen
Wanders dreamily beneath the low arches
Of the fleeing ship, she seems to listen to
The sounds of the other sea in her blue veins
And to be happy. Other scholiasts
Have even believed in a work in stone.
In her cabin
Shaken day after day by rough weather

*Hélène est figurée, à demi levée
De ses draps, de ses rêves,
Elle sourit, ou presque. Son bras est reployé
Avec beaucoup de grâce sur son sein,
Les rayons du soleil, levant, couchant,
S'attardent puis s'effacent sur son flanc nu.
Et plus tard, sur la terrasse de Troie,
Elle a toujours ce sourire.
Qui pourtant, sauf Pâris peut-être, l'a jamais vue?
Les porteurs n'auront su que la grande pierre rougeâtre
Rugueuse, fissurée
Qu'il leur fallut monter, suant, jurant,
Jusque sur les remparts, devant la nuit.*

*Cette roche,
Ce sable de l'origine, qui se délite,
Est-ce Hélène? Ces nuages, ces lueurs rouges
On ne sait si dans l'âme ou dans le ciel?*

*La vérité peut-être, mais gardée tue,
Même Stésichorus ne l'avoue pas,
Voici: la semblance d'Hélène ne fut qu'un feu
Bâti contre le vent sur une plage.
C'est une masse de branches grises, de fumées
(Car le feu prenait mal) que Pâris a chargée
Au petit jour humide sur la barque.
C'est ce brasier, ravagé par les vagues,
Cerné par la clameur des oiseaux de mer,
Qu'il restitua au monde, sur les brisants
Du rivage natal, que ravagent et trouent
D'autres vagues encore. Le lit de pierre
Avait été dressé là-haut, de par le ciel,
Et quand Troie tomberait resterait le feu
Pour crier la beauté, la protestation de l'esprit
Contre la mort.*

Helen is represented half risen
From her sheets, from her dreams,
Smiling, or almost. Her arm is bent
With charming grace over her breast,
The rays of the sun, rising, setting,
Linger upon, then withdraw from her naked flank.
And later, on the terrace of Troy,
She still has this smile.
Who, though, aside from Paris perhaps, has ever seen her?
The slaves will only have known the reddish stone,
Rough, cracked,
That they had to carry up, sweating, cursing,
To the top of the ramparts, facing the night.

This rock,
This sand from the origin of Time, crumbling,
Is it Helen? These clouds, these gleams of red,
We don't know whether in the soul or in the sky?

The truth perhaps, though never spoken,
Not even Stesichorus admits it,
Is this: the semblance of Helen was only a fire
Built against the wind on a beach.
It is simply a mass of grey branches, of smoke
(For the fire was hard to start) that Paris loaded
Onto a boat at daybreak, when it was damp.
It is this brazier, ravaged by the waves,
Surrounded by the clamour of the sea birds,
That he restored to the world, on the shoals
Of the native shore, torn and pierced
By yet other waves. The bed of stone
Had been erected up there, near the sky,
And should Troy fall this fire would remain
To cry out beauty and the spirit's protest
Against death.

Nuées,
L'une qui prend à l'autre, qui défend
Mal, qui répand
Entre ces corps épris
La coupe étincelante de la foudre.

Et le ciel
S'est attardé, un peu,
Sur la couche terrestre. On dirait, apaisés,
L'homme, la femme: une montagne, une eau.
Entre eux
La coupe déjà vide, encore pleine.

II

Mais qui a dit
Que celle que Pâris a étreint, le feu,
Les branches rouges dans le feu, l'âcre fumée
Dans les orbites vides, ne fut pas même
Ce rêve, qui se fait œuvre pour calmer
Le désir de l'artiste, mais simplement
Un rêve de ce rêve? Le sourire d'Hélène:
Rien que ce glissement du drap de la nuit, qui montre,
Mais pour rien qu'un éclair,
La lumière endormie en bas du ciel.

Chaque fois qu'un poème,
Une statue, même une image peinte,
Se préfèrent figure, se dégagent
Des à-coups d'étincellement de la nuée,
Hélène se dissipe, qui ne fut
Que l'intuition qui fit se pencher Homère
Sur des sons de plus bas que ses cordes dans
La maladroite lyre des mots terrestres.

Mais à l'aube du sens

Clouds,
And one that takes from the other, that tries
To hold on, spilling
Between these bodies in love
The dazzling cup of the lightning.

Afterwards, the sky
Lingered for a moment
Over the earthly bed. You might say
A man and a woman, at peace: a mountain, water.
Between them
The cup already empty, still full.

11

But who has said
That the one embraced by Paris, the fire,
The red branches in the fire, the acrid smoke
In the empty sockets, was not even
That dream that wants to be a work of art to calm
The artist's longing, but rather, simply,
A dream of this dream? Helen's smile:
Nothing but that slipping of night's sheet, that reveals,
But only for a lightning flash,
The light sleeping at the base of the sky.

Every time that a poem,
A statue, even a painted image,
Prefers itself as form, breaks away
From the cloud's sudden jolts of sparkling light,
Helen vanishes, who was only
That intuition which led Homer to bend
Over sounds that come from lower than his strings
In the clumsy lyre of earthly words.

But at the dawn of meaning

Quand la pierre est encore obscure, la couleur
Boue, dans l'impatience du pinceau,
Pâris emporte Hélène,
Elle se debat, elle crie,
Elle accepte; et les vagues sont calmes, contre l'étrave,
Et l'aube est rayonnante sur la mer.

Bois, dit Pâris
Qui s'éveille, et étend le bras dans l'ombre étroite
De la chambre remuée par le peu de houle,
Bois,
Puis approche la coupe de mes lèvres
Pour que je puisse boire.

Je me penche, répond
Celle qui est, peut-être, ou dont il rêve.
Je me penche, je bois,
Je n'ai pas plus de nom que la nuée,
Je me déchire comme elle, lumière pure.

Et t'ayant donné joie je n'ai plus de soif
Lumière bue.

C'est un enfant
Nu sur la grande plage quand Troie brûlait
Qui le dernier vit Hélène
Dans les buissons de flammes du haut des murs.
Il errait, il chantait,
Il avait pris dans ses mains un peu d'eau,
Le feu venait y boire, mais l'eau s'échappe
De la coupe imparfaite, ainsi le temps
Ruine le rêve et pourtant le rédime.

When the stone is still in darkness, colour
Only mud, in the brush's impatience,
Paris carries off Helen,
She struggles, she cries out,
She surrenders; and the waves are calm, against the bow,
And dawn is radiant on the sea.

Drink, says Paris,
Who awakens, and stretches out his arm into the narrow
Shadow of the room rocked by the water's gentle swell,
Drink,
Then bring the cup to my lips
So that I can drink.

I bend down, answers
She who is, perhaps, or of whom he dreams.
I bend down, I drink,
I have no more name than the cloud does,
I tear apart as it does, pure light.

And having given you joy, I have no more thirst,
Light drunk.

It is a naked
Child on the great beach when Troy was burning
Who was the last to see Helen
In the thickets of flame at the height of the walls.
He was roaming, singing,
He had taken in his hands a little water,
The fire came to drink there, but the water
Leaked out from the imperfect cup, just as time
Ruins dreams and yet redeems them.

III

*Ces pages sont traduites. D'une langue
Qui hante la mémoire que je suis.
Les phrases de cette langue sont incertaines
Comme les tout premiers de nos souvenirs.
J'ai restitué le texte mot après mot,
Mais le mien n'en sera qu'une ombre, c'est à croire
Que l'origine est une Troie qui brûle,
La beauté un regret, l'œuvre ne prendre
À pleines mains qu'une eau qui se refuse.*

III

These pages are translated. From a language
That haunts the memory that I am.
The phrases of this language are uncertain
Like the very first of our recollections.
I have reconstructed the text one word after another,
But mine can only be a shadow of the first one.
Must we feel: origin is a burning Troy,
Beauty is regretting, art is gathering up
By the handful nothing but absent water?

V 2001–2010

From *Les Planches courbes* / *The Curved Planks* (2001)

THE CURVED PLANKS

The man standing on the bank, near the boat, was big, a giant of a man. Behind him the moonlight was reflected on the river. Hearing a faint noise, the child, who was approaching in complete silence, understood that the boat was stirring, brushing against the dock or a stone. He was clutching a small copper coin tightly in his hand.

'Good day, Sir', he said in a clear voice, clear but trembling for he was afraid he might draw too much attention to himself from the man, the giant, who stood there motionless. But the ferryman, who seemed distracted, had already noticed him, through the reeds. 'Good day, young fellow', he replied. 'Who are you?'

'Oh, I don't know', said the child.

'What do you mean, you don't know? Haven't you got a name?'

The child tried to take in what the man meant by a name. 'I don't know', he said again, quickly enough.

'You don't know! But you know very well what you hear when someone calls you or hails you.'

'Nobody calls me.'

'Nobody calls you when it's time to go home? When you've been playing outside and it's time for your meal, or for bed? Haven't you got a father, a mother? Where do you live? Tell me.'

And now the boy sought to understand what the man meant by a father, or a mother, or a place to live.

'Father', he said, 'what's that?'

The ferryman sat down on a stone near his boat. His voice came from less far away in the darkness. But at first he had chuckled a bit.

'A father? Well, that's someone who takes you on his knees when you cry, and sits down beside you in the evening when you're afraid to go to sleep, and tells you a story.'

The boy did not reply.

'It's quite true that often there is no father,' the giant continued, as if he had been giving some thought to the matter. 'But then, it is said, there are sweet young women who light the fire and sit you

down close by it, and sing you a song. If they move away, it's to cook some food, that's all; you can smell the oil which is heating up in the pot.'

'I don't remember that either', said the child in his light crystalline voice. He had drawn closer to the ferryman, who now fell silent; he could hear the man's regular slow breathing. 'I have to cross the river', said the child. 'I have enough money to pay you.'

The giant leaned over him, took him in his huge hands, placed him on his shoulders, straightened up and climbed into the boat, which gave way a little beneath his weight. 'Off we go,' he said, 'hold on tightly to my neck.' With one hand he gripped the child by a leg, with the other he stuck the pole in the water. With a sudden movement the boy clung on to the ferryman, and sighed. The ferryman was now able to grasp the pole with both hands. He steered the boat out of the mud, and it quit the shore, while the sound of the water grew stronger in the shadows, beneath the glimmers.

A moment later a finger touched his ear. 'Listen', said the child, 'would you like to be my father?' But he broke off at once, his voice choked by tears.

'Your father! But I'm only the ferryman! I never move far from the two riverbanks.'

'But I would stay with you, by the riverbank.'

'To be a father, you have to have a house, don't you understand? I don't have a house, I live in the rushes by the river.'

'I would be so happy to stay with you on the river.'

'No', said the ferryman, 'it isn't possible. Anyway, look!'

The child cannot fail to see that the boat seems to be sinking more and more beneath the man and himself, that their weight is increasing minute by minute. The ferryman has trouble moving forward; the water reaches the sides of the small boat, and then pours in, its currents filling the hull as they reach the top of the giant's legs, which are conscious that support from the curved planks is fading fast. All the same, the boat does not founder, rather it seems to vanish into the darkness, and the man is swimming now, with the little boy still holding fast to his neck. 'Don't be afraid', he says, 'the river isn't that wide, we'll soon reach the other side.'

'Oh please, be my father! Be my house!'

'You must put all that out of your mind', replies the giant in a low voice. 'Forget those words. Forget words.'

He takes the boy's small leg, which is already immense, in his hand again, and with his free arm he swims in the endless space of colliding currents, gaping chasms, stars.

LA MAISON NATALE

I

Je m'éveillai, c'était la maison natale,
L'écume s'abattait sur le rocher,
Pas un oiseau, le vent seul à ouvrir et fermer la vague,
L'odeur de l'horizon de toutes parts,
Cendre, comme si les collines cachaient un feu
Qui ailleurs consumait un univers.
Je passai dans la véranda, la table était mise,
L'eau frappait les pieds de la table, le buffet.
Il fallait qu'elle entrât pourtant, la sans-visage
Que je savais qui secouait la porte
Du couloir, du côté de l'escalier sombre, mais en vain,
Si haute était déjà l'eau dans la salle.
Je tournais la poignée, qui résistait,
J'entendais presque les rumeurs de l'autre rive,
Ces rires des enfants dans l'herbe haute.
Ces jeux des autres, à jamais les autres, dans leur joie.

II

Je m'éveillai, c'était la maison natale.
Il pleuvait doucement dans toutes les salles,
J'allais d'une à une autre, regardant
L'eau qui étincelait sur les miroirs
Amoncelés partout, certains brisés ou même
Poussés entre des meubles et les murs.
C'était de ces reflets que, parfois, un visage
Se dégageait, riant, d'une douceur
De plus et autrement que ce qu'est le monde.
Et je touchais, hésitant, dans l'image,
Les mèches désordonnées de la déesse,
Je découvrais sous le voile de l'eau
Son front triste et distrait de petite fille.

THE HOUSE WHERE I WAS BORN

I

I woke: the house where I was born.
Spume battered the rock. Not a bird;
Only wind, closing and opening the wave.
The horizon all around smelled of ash,
As though somewhere beyond the hills
A fire were devouring a universe. I went
Into the side room: the table had been set.
Water struck the sideboard, the table legs.
Yet she had to come in, the faceless one;
I knew she was rattling the hallway door,
There near the darkened stairs. But in vain:
Water was already flooding the room.
I turned the knob; the door wouldn't give.
I almost heard them on that far-off shore –
Children laughing in high grass. Others
Laughing, always others, in their joy.

II

I woke: the house where I was born.
Rain was falling softly in all the rooms.
I went from room to room, looking
At the water as it sparkled on the mirrors
Piled up everywhere – some shattered, others
Even tucked between the furniture and walls.
At times in those reflections I could see
A face appear, laughing with a sweetness
Other than the world's, beyond its ken.
And hesitant, in the image I touched
The dishevelled tresses of the goddess;
Through the veil of water I beheld
Her sad, distracted brow of a little girl.

Étonnement entre être et ne pas être,
Main qui hésite à toucher la buée,
Puis j'écoutais le rire s'éloigner
Dans les couloirs de la maison déserte.
Ici rien qu'à jamais le bien du rêve,
La main tendue qui ne traverse pas
L'eau rapide, où s'efface le souvenir.

III

Je m'éveillai, c'était la maison natale,
Il faisait nuit, des arbres se pressaient
De toutes parts autour de notre porte,
J'étais seul sur le seuil dans le vent froid,
Mais non, nullement seul, car deux grands êtres
Se parlaient au-dessus de moi, à travers moi.
L'un, derrière, une vieille femme, courbe, mauvaise,
L'autre debout dehors comme une lampe,
Belle, tenant la coupe qu'on lui offrait,
Buvant avidement de toute sa soif.
Ai-je voulu me moquer, certes non,
Plutôt ai-je poussé un cri d'amour
Mais avec la bizarrerie du désespoir,
Et le poison fut partout dans mes membres,
Cérès moquée brisa qui l'avait aimée.
Ainsi parle aujourd'hui la vie murée dans la vie.

IV

Une autre fois.
Il faisait nuit encore. De l'eau glissait
Silencieusement sur le sol noir,
Et je savais que je n'aurais pour tâche
Que de me souvenir, et je riais,
Je me penchais, je prenais dans la boue

Perplexity between what is and what
Is not, hand that hesitates on misted glass ...
Then I listened as the laughter trailed away
Down the corridors of the deserted house.
Here the only thing we ever own is dream:
Though we reach out, our hand can never cross
The rapid stream where memories recede.

III

I woke: the house where I was born.
In the night, on every side, trees
Crowded round our door. I stood there
On the threshold, alone in the freezing wind.
But no, not alone at all. Two large figures
Were speaking above me, speaking through me:
One was an old woman, evil and stooped;
The other stood outside, radiant as a lamp,
Raising the cup that had been offered her.
Eagerly she drank, with all her thirst.
Did I mean to mock her? Surely not.
The strangled sound I made was a cry of love,
But it rang with the strangeness of despair.
And then the poison seized me, head to toe.
Mocked, Ceres doomed the one who loved her:
So says today the life that's walled inside of life.

IV

Another time.
Night again. In silence
Water slid on the darkened ground.
I knew the only task I would have
Was to remember. And laughing,
Bending over in the mud, I gathered up

Une brassée de branches et de feuilles,
J'en soulevais la masse, qui ruisselait
Dans mes bras resserrés contre mon cœur.
Que faire de ce bois où de tant d'absence
Montait pourtant le bruit de la couleur,
Peu importe, j'allais en hâte, à la recherche
D'au moins quelque hangar, sous cette charge
De branches qui avaient de toute part
Des angles, des élancements, des pointes, des cris.

Et des voix, qui jetaient des ombres sur la route,
Ou m'appelaient, et je me retournais,
Le cœur précipité, sur la route vide.

v

Or, dans le même rêve
Je suis couché au plus creux d'une barque,
Le front, les yeux contre ses planches courbes
Où j'écoute cogner le bas du fleuve.
Et tout d'un coup cette proue se soulève,
J'imagine que là, déjà, c'est l'estuaire,
Mais je garde mes yeux contre le bois
Qui a odeur de goudron et de colle.
Trop vastes les images, trop lumineuses,
Que j'ai accumulées dans mon sommeil.
Pourquoi revoir, dehors,
Les choses dont les mots me parlent, mais sans convaincre,
Je désire plus haute ou moins sombre rive.

Et pourtant je renonce à ce sol qui bouge
Sous le corps qui se cherche, je me lève,
Je vais dans la maison de pièce en pièce,
Il y en a maintenant d'innombrables,
J'entends crier des voix derrière des portes,

An armful of branches and leaves.
I held them to my chest; they dripped
As I clutched them against my heart.
What should I do with this wood,
Where so much absence
Still rang with colour's sound?
It didn't matter. I hurried on,
Looking for a shed at least, reeling
Under branches that bristled with snags,
Throbbing hopes, points and cries.

And voices were casting their shadows
On the road, or calling me. And my heart raced
As I turned around, to face the empty road.

v

In the same dream
I lie in the hollow of a hull,
Eyes and forehead pressed to the curved planks
Where I can hear the river knocking.
Then suddenly the prow rides up. Already,
I imagine, this must be the river's mouth.
Even so I wedge my eyes against the wood
That smells of pitch and glue.
The images I've garnered in my sleep
Have been too vast, too luminous.
Why look outside again, why see the things
Words say to me, though unconvincingly,
When I desire a higher or less sombre shore.

But I renounce this floor that moves
Under my uncertain body. I get up,
I walk through the house from room to room,
And now the rooms are numberless.
I hear voices shouting behind the doors.

Je suis saisi par ces douleurs qui cognent
Aux chambranles qui se délabrent, je me hâte,
Trop lourde m'est la nuit qui dure, j'entre effrayé
Dans une salle encombrée de pupitres,
Vois, me dit-on, ce fut ta salle de classe,
Vois sur les murs tes premières images,
Vois, c'est l'arbre, vois, là, c'est le chien qui jappe,
Et cette carte de géographie, sur la paroi
Jaune, ce décolorement des noms et des formes,
Ce dessaisissement des montagnes, des fleuves,
Par la blancheur qui transit le langage,
Vois, ce fut ton seul livre. L'Isis du plâtre
Du mur de cette salle, qui s'écaille,
N'a jamais eu, elle n'aura rien d'autre
À entrouvrir pour toi, refermer sur toi.

VI

Je m'éveillai, mais c'était en voyage,
Le train avait roulé toute la nuit,
Il allait maintenant vers de grands nuages
Debout là-bas, serrés, aube que déchirait
À des instants le lacet de la foudre.
Je regardais l'avènement du monde
Dans les buissons du remblai; et soudain
Cet autre feu, en contrebas d'un champ
De pierres et de vignes. Le vent, la pluie
Rabattaient sa fumée contre le sol,
Mais une flamme rouge s'y redressait,
Prenant à pleines mains le bas du ciel.
Depuis quand brûlais-tu, feu des vignerons?
Qui t'avait voulu là et pour qui sur terre?

Après quoi il fit jour; et le soleil
Jeta de toutes parts ses milliers de flèches

I'm distressed by these torments that pound
At the decrepit doorjambs. I hurry by.
The night drags on. Fear weighs me down.
I enter a room crowded with desks.
Look, I am told. This classroom was yours.
Look at the wall. Those were your first images.
Look, there's the tree, and there's the yelping dog.
And this map that yellows on the wall,
This slow discolouring of names and shapes,
These rivers, these mountains that disappear
In the whiteness invading language:
This was your only book. Isis –
The plaster wall peeling in this room –
Has never had, will never have
Anything else to open up for you
Or close on you again.

VI

I woke up, but we were travelling.
The train had lumbered through the night.
Now it rolled toward massive clouds
That loomed in a cluster up ahead.
From time to time, lightning's whip tore the dawn.
I watched the advent of the world
Through the brush of the embankment; and suddenly
This other fire below, in a field
Of stones and vines. Rain and wind
Stamped its smoke down to the ground,
But the reddish flame stood up again,
Seizing the whole lower sky in its hands.
Grape-growers' fire, how long had you burned?
Who wanted you there? For whom on this earth?

Then daylight broke. The sun
Shot its thousand arrows everywhere

Dans le compartiment où des dormeurs
La tête dodelinait encore, sur la dentelle
Des coussins de lainage bleu. Je ne dormais pas,
J'avais trop l'âge encore de l'espérance,
Je dédiais mes mots aux montagnes basses,
Que je voyais venir à travers les vitres.

VII

Je me souviens, c'était un matin, l'été,
La fenêtre était entrouverte, je m'approchais,
J'apercevais mon père au fond du jardin.
Il était immobile, il regardait
Où, quoi, je ne savais, au dehors de tout,
Voûté comme il était déjà mais redressant
Son regard vers l'inaccompli ou l'impossible.
Il avait déposé la pioche, la bêche,
L'air était frais ce matin-là du monde,
Mais impénétrable est la fraîcheur même, et cruel
Le souvenir des matins de l'enfance.
Qui était-il, qui avait-il été dans la lumière,
Je ne le savais pas, je ne sais encore.

Mais je le vois aussi, sur le boulevard,
Avançant lentement, tant de fatigue
Alourdissant ses gestes d'autrefois,
Il repartait au travail, quant à moi
J'errais avec quelques-uns de ma classe
Au début de l'après-midi sans durée encore.
À ce passage-là, aperçu de loin,
Soient dédiés les mots qui ne savent dire.

(Dans la salle à manger
De l'après-midi d'un dimanche, c'est en été,
Les volets sont fermés contre la chaleur,
La table débarrassée, il a proposé

In that compartment where sleepers' heads
Still nodded, on the lace of blue wool cushions.
But I was not sleeping. I still
Lived too deep in the age of hope.
I devoted my words to low mountains
I saw coming through the windows.

VII

I remember, it was a summer morning.
The window was half-open. As I came closer,
I saw my father there in the garden.
He stood motionless. Where he was looking,
Or at what, I could not tell – outside everything.
Stooped as he already was, he lifted his gaze
Toward the unachieved, or the impossible.
He had laid down the pickaxe, the spade.
The air was cool on that morning of the world.
But coolness is impenetrable, and cruel
Are the memories of childhood mornings.
Who he was, who he had been in the light:
I did not know, I still do not know.

But I also see him on the boulevard
Slowly walking forward, so much tiredness
Weighing down his gestures of former days.
He was going back to work. As for me,
I was strolling with some classmates
In the early afternoon, timeless as yet.
To his passing by, observed from afar, let me
Dedicate these words that don't know how to say.

(In the dining room
on a Sunday afternoon; it's summer.
The shutters are closed against the heat.
The table cleared, he proposes a game of cards.

Les cartes puisqu'il n'est pas d'autres images
Dans la maison natale pour recevoir
La demande du rêve, puis il sort
Et aussitôt l'enfant maladroit prend les cartes,
Il substitue à celles de l'autre jeu
Toutes les cartes gagnantes, puis il attend
Avec fièvre, que la partie reprenne, et que celui
Qui perdait gagne, et si glorieusement
Qu'il y voie comme un signe, et de quoi nourrir
Il ne sait, lui l'enfant, quelle espérance.
Après quoi deux voies se séparent, et l'une d'elles
Se perd, et presque tout de suite, et ce sera
Tout de même l'oubli, l'oubli avide.

J'aurai barré
Cent fois ces mots partout, en vers, en prose,
Mais je ne puis
Faire qu'ils ne remontent dans ma parole.)

VIII

J'ouvre les yeux, c'est bien la maison natale,
Et même celle qui fut et rien de plus.
La même petite salle à manger dont la fenêtre
Donne sur un pêcher qui ne grandit pas.
Un homme et une femme se sont assis
Devant cette croisée, l'un face à l'autre,
Ils se parlent, pour une fois. L'enfant
Du fond de ce jardin les voit, les regarde.
Il sait que l'on peut naître de ces mots.
Derrière les parents la salle est sombre.
L'homme vient de rentrer du travail. La fatigue
Qui a été le seul nimbe des gestes
Qu'il fut donné à son fils d'entrevoir
Le détache déjà de cette rive.

In the house where I was born
There are no other images to still
The demands of dream. Later he steps out,
And the awkward child takes up the cards;
He replaces the ones that had been dealt
With a winning hand, then waits with bated breath
For the game to begin again. Now the loser would win,
So gloriously that he sees it
As something of a sign, something that might nourish –
What, being just a child, he cannot know – some kind of hope.
But after this their paths diverge. One of them
Is lost, almost right away. And forgetfulness,
Forgetfulness devours all.

I have crossed these words out everywhere
A hundred times, in verse, in prose,
But I cannot: always they well up again,
And tell their truth.)

VIII

I open my eyes:
This is the house where I was born,
Surely the one that was and nothing more.
The same small dining room looks out
On a peach tree that never grows.
A man and a woman have sat down
In front of the window, face to face.
They talk to each other, for once. The child
Sees them from the garden: he watches them,
Knowing that life can be born from these words.
Behind his parents the room is dark.
The man has just returned from work. Fatigue,
The only nimbus of his gestures
Ever granted his son to glimpse,
Detaches him already from this shore.

IX

*Et alors un jour vint
Où j'entendis ce vers extraordinaire de Keats,
L'évocation de Ruth « when, sick for home,
She stood in tears amid the alien corn ».*

*Or, de ces mots
Je n'avais pas à pénétrer le sens
Car il était en moi depuis l'enfance,
Je n'ai eu qu'à le reconnaître, et à l'aimer
Quand il est revenu du fond de ma vie.*

*Qu'avais-je eu, en effet, à recueillir
De l'évasive présence maternelle
Sinon le sentiment de l'exil et les larmes
Qui troublaient ce regard cherchant à voir
Dans les choses d'ici le lieu perdu?*

X

*La vie, alors; et ce fut à nouveau
Une maison natale. Autour de nous
Le grenier d'au-dessus l'église défaite,
Le jeu d'ombres léger des nuées de l'aube,
Et en nous cette odeur de la paille sèche
Restée à nous attendre, nous semblait-il,
Depuis le dernier sac monté, de blé ou seigle,
Dans l'autrefois sans fin de la lumière
Des étés tamisés par les tuiles chaudes.
Je pressentais que le jour allait poindre,
Je m'éveillais, et je me tourne encore
Vers celle qui rêva à côté de moi
Dans la maison perdue. À son silence
Soient dédiés, au soir,
Les mots qui semblent ne parler que d'autre chose.*

IX

Then came the day that I first heard
The extraordinary verse of Keats,
Evoking Ruth 'when, sick for home,
She stood in tears amid the alien corn.'

I did not have to grapple
With the meaning of these words,
Since it was in me from my childhood.
I only needed to recognise and love
What had returned from the depths of my life.

And truly, what could I have gleaned
From that evasive mother's presence
If not the sense of exile? Tears
Clouding her eyes that tried to see
A long-lost place in the here and now.

X

Life, then: and once again
A house where I was born. The granary
Above a ruined church enfolded us.
Pale clouds shadow-played at dawn.
It seemed this odour of dry straw
Had waited to pervade us – ever since
They stored the last sack of wheat or rye
In those unended days of bygone radiance,
Of summers filtering through sun-warmed tiles.
I sensed that dawn was going to break,
That soon I would wake up. And now I turn again
To her who dreamed beside me
In the house we have lost. This evening,
To her silence, let me dedicate these words
That only seem to speak of something else.

(Je m'éveillais,
J'aimais ces jours que nous avions, jours préservés
Comme va lentement un fleuve, bien que déjà
Pris dans le bruit de voûtes de la mer.
Ils avançaient, avec la majesté des choses simples,
Les grandes voiles de ce qui est voulaient bien prendre
L'humaine vie précaire sur le navire
Qu'étendait la montagne autour de nous.
Ô souvenir,
Elles couvraient des claquements de leur silence
Le bruit, d'eau sur les pierres, de nos voix,
Et en avant ce serait bien la mort,
Mais de cette couleur laiteuse du bout des plages
Le soir, quand les enfants
Ont pied, loin, et rient dans l'eau calme, et jouent encore).

XI

Et je repars, et c'est sur un chemin
Qui monte et tourne, bruyères, dunes
Au-dessus d'un bruit encore invisible, avec parfois
Le bien furtif du chardon bleu des sables.
Ici, le temps se creuse, c'est déjà
L'eau éternelle à bouger dans l'écume,
Je suis bientôt à deux pas du rivage.
Et je vois qu'un navire attend au large,
Noir, tel un candélabre à nombre de branches
Qu'enveloppent des flammes et des fumées.
Qu'allons-nous faire? crie-t-on de toutes parts,
Ne faut-il pas aider ceux qui là-bas
Nous demandent rivage? Oui, clame l'ombre,
Et je vois des nageurs qui, dans la nuit,
Se portent vers le navire, soutenant
D'une main au-dessus de l'eau agitée,
Des lampes, aux longues banderoles de couleur.
La beauté même, en son lieu de naissance,
Quand elle n'est encore que vérité.

(I was almost awake.
How I loved those days of ours, preserved
The way a river slows, already caught
In the resounding arches of the sea.
They moved with the majesty of simple things.
Vast sails, the sails of all that is, agreed to lift
Our fragile human life aboard the ship
That the mountains wrapped around us.
O memory,
Their luffing silence decked the sound
Our voices made, like water on stones.
No doubt on the horizon would be death:
But milky as that shade where beaches end,
At evening, when the children still touch bottom
Far into the sea, laughing in tranquil waters, and still play.)

XI

And I start out again, along a path
That climbs and turns. Moors and dunes,
Above a sound as yet invisible. In the sand,
Now and then, blue thistle's furtive gift.
Time goes hollow here, becomes
Eternal water surging in the foam.
And soon I stand two steps from the sea.
I discover that a ship waits offshore:
A black candelabra, all its boughs
Engulfed in flames and smoke.
What can we do? people cry out on every side.
Shouldn't we help the voyagers out there
Who're asking us for berth? Yes, darkness shouts.
And then I see how swimmers in the night
Race toward the ship with one hand raised
Above the stormy swells, holding lamps
That stream with coloured pennants.
Beauty itself in its place of birth,
When not yet anything but truth.

XII

*Beauté et vérité, mais ces hautes vagues
Sur ces cris qui s'obstinent. Comment garder
Audible l'espérance dans le tumulte,
Comment faire pour que vieillir, ce soit renaître,
Pour que la maison s'ouvre, de l'intérieur,
Pour que ce ne soit pas que la mort qui pousse
Dehors celui qui demandait un lieu natal?*

*Je comprends maintenant que ce fût Cérès
Qui me parut, de nuit, chercher refuge
Quand on frappait à la porte, et dehors,
C'était d'un coup sa beauté, sa lumière
Et son désir aussi, son besoin de boire
Avidement au bol de l'espérance
Parce qu'était perdu mais retrouvable
Peut-être, cet enfant qu'elle n'avait su,
Elle pourtant divine et riche de soi,
Soulever dans la flamme des jeunes blés
Pour qu'il ait rire, dans l'évidence qui fait vivre
Avant la convoitise du dieu des morts.*

*Et pitié pour Cérès et non moquerie,
Rendez-vous à des carrefours dans la nuit profonde,
Cris d'appels au travers des mots, même sans réponse,
Parole même obscure mais qui puisse
Aimer enfin Cérès qui cherche et souffre.*

XII

Beauty and truth. But tall waves crash
On cries that still persist. The voice of hope,
Above the din – how can we make it heard?
How can growing old become rebirth?
How can the house be opened from within,
So death will not turn out the child
Who asked for a native place?

Now I understand: it was Ceres
Who sought shelter on the night
Someone was knocking at the door.
Outside, her beauty suddenly flared –
Her light and her desire too, her need
To slake her thirst with the cup of hope:
She might still find that child again,
Even if lost. Though rich with herself,
Rich with her divinity, she had not known
How to lift her child in the young wheat's flame,
Laughing in the simple light that gives us life –
Before the god of the dead, and all his greed.

We must pity Ceres, not mock her – and so
We must meet at crossroads in deepest night,
Call out athwart our words, even with no reply:
And make our voice, no matter how obscure,
Love Ceres at last, who suffers and seeks.

From *Goya, les peintures noires* / *Goya: The Black Paintings* (2006)

SECTION VI, CHAPTER 3

But let us pause where that event has left its trace, I mean at the extraordinary painting of 1820, the date and meaning of which we owe to Goya himself, because he indicates as much in the lower foreground, that it is in gratitude to Doctor Arrieta, for the *acierto*, and the *esmero* – for the ingenious competence and the devotion – with which his friend cared for him during his brief but dangerous illness of a few months before.

The painting shows Goya in his bed, propped up by Arrieta, and his appearance is most alarming. His head lolls back, against Arrieta's shoulder. Although they are enfeebled, his hands clutch at the sheet, which he seems to want to draw over him in a farewell to the world. And if his eyes aren't closed, then they are upturned, in a semi-conscious state. Goya is saved from the abyss only by the intervention of the doctor seated on his bed, right up against him; one of his arms supports the nape as, his face tense with anxiety, he holds close to his mouth some medicine that the painter refuses. Clearly, the situation is very grave. It may be that the patient's very survival depends on his imbibing the potion. It is the critical moment in a crisis, a moment when man is in need of all his ingenuity, of all his *acierto*, to confront the danger.

But is it only the decisive action of the doctor, forcing his patient to drink, that Goya wished to commemorate in this painting? Especially as this crisis moment was also that in which he succumbed to hallucinations potentially fatal to him, for such surely are the three perfectly terrifying faces, which occupy the depths of the painting, while in the sombre alcove there is nothing and no one? Terrifying, chilling, these faces possess an almost ordinary human likeness, except in how they devastate it, and underneath the outer appearance, they possess some aspect, through which we understand, and with certainty, though we know not how, that they come from another world. To look at them reminds us of those infernal crea-

tures that would gather around the unrepentant sinner at the time of death – beyond choice, rather, through the fact of his own horror. And it is hard to doubt that Goya, with his eyes upturned, is similarly fascinated, rapt, and drawn towards these ghouls, that have put on a counterfeit humanity the better to undermine all faith in value and meaning.

It is not so much the health or illness of the body that are here in balance, nor even a question of being or not being, but rather whether we are still capable of investing the word being with meaning; it is to sink or not to sink into a darkness in whose dying lights the last faces perceived in the world of the living will be mere simulacra, stitched with madness, lust, and falsehood. And so it is that this image of a Goya on the brink of perdition, and the glass that Arrieta proffers with an almost desperate insistence, brings to mind, rather than the doctor, the priest, offering the eucharistic wafer, and the crucifix to be kissed: as if the gesture thus shown had the same salvific intention, which turns the painting, as indicated in the inscription, explicitly and deliberately into an ex-voto. A soul is at stake, at this potentially fatal instant, and salvation seems to be within reach, and as the painting shows the opportunity is seized. Goya shall soon open his eyes and see – possibly in a mirror that hangs before him, as the composition seems to suggest – Arrieta's anxious face, and his own in its extremity, and behind them nothing but the now half-dissolved reflection of the dreadful faces which seemed on the point of cancelling out all human hope.

But what happened, what exactly was the event that resembles religious salvation but which took place without any appeal to faith, or belief, and yet whose efficacy is not in doubt? The painting in fact reveals what happened, closing in on its invisible content with absolute clarity. As the painting presents him, Goya has his eyes turned away from what I would call external vision, and it is as if we too get a glimpse of the edge of the abyss from where he is looking out. Scarcely do we have the leisure to look at the things and the colours – few in number in any case – presented on the canvas, rather we are with him, as if actually within him. As such, we actually feel, almost palpably, from within his own body, the pressure Arrieta applies to his shoulders, in order to prop him up, and put him within

reach of the glass. We come to understand that Goya feeling his friend's arm, the last feeling that reaches him from the outside world – let us not forget that he is deaf, and that when his eyes are closed, little of anything gets through – is the only act happening within the ex-voto. The only one, but also the decisive event, that one that saves.

Why? Because the pressure exerted, so desirous to create some return to life in the patient, so designed to garner some remnant of energy in him that would confer on him the force, and especially the desire to drink the medicine, to turn back to the world, transmits something of the entirely disinterested affection that Arrieta has for Goya, which brings with it the proof that something else exists – has reality – other than the sharklike voracity that gulps down its prey, at every level of matter, before being itself torn to pieces and devoured in turn. Dr Arrieta's compassion, its intensity at the critical moment, is in no way destructible according to the melancholy laws of matter. It is not, unlike the religious illusion of centuries past, in denial of them, it has not lowered its eyes in the face of the claim of mere materiality to be the sinister end all of the world, but it climbs one rung, so to speak, on the ladder leading out of the darkness. And Arrieta's compassion is agency enough to surprise Goya, and to shake him, and chase out of his mind, out of his soul, to repeat that word, the demons of doubt and despair. He can live again. He can, as the painting suggests, re-open his eyes, and look once more.

We can formulate this differently. He might well have concluded, after the disasters of war, and in addition to these disasters, the privations of the peace, that there was no God, and no meaning or *raison d'être* to life as it is manifest in matter; that there was no particular value to blind and avid life when it took human form, and that nothing out there in the inky night picked out with stars can prove by its existence that there is a moral good to be followed, or a truth to be understood. To lead a 'moral' life – as the expression goes – and to strive for the good – nothing justifies or rewards such a position. The time is past, when one could expect some reward from a god of love; or when the just and charitable man, or at least he who imagined himself to be such, could legitimately look forward to the day when he would substitute his sufferings on earth for a state of blessedness in the other world. That is what had to be grasped, and it drove him

into retirement in the country, where he might be able to think of something else, as he awaited his end.

But it transpires that the same painter who appears to have wanted to decorate his final home with joyful landscapes, in part to counteract the horrible images that had too frequently assailed him, is also the painter who was never left unmoved by an impulse to compassion. Never, in his darkest approaches to cruelty and malice, did Goya feel any indulgence, or any shameful sympathy, for the evil act. Pity was the feeling that most often overwhelmed him, pity, as in the *Disasters of War*, pity, and an access of anger, that did not weaken the thought that it was vain. Beyond that, he never ceased to dream – in his drawings of faces, and their expressions – of something which in the heart of this unreality of meaning and value, would nevertheless have meaning and value, *lux* appearing *in desertis*. And it was this that prepared him to receive what was a grand example.

And what we must now grasp is that it is this example that decided Goya when, recovered from his sickness, he set to work with an energy and a capacity for invention that nothing could have predicted. The painter of *Doctor Arrieta* recovered being again, on the day celebrated by the ex-voto. And in terms of the spiritual conscience it is, literally, his resurrection. But he has also recovered his health, in the ordinary sense of the word, for a few seasons more at least, and then everything proceeds – and this is what I hope to establish – as if he had decided that the sudden awakening in him would work itself out in his painting, and be refracted in every level of his experimentation: this new energy was his personal contribution to a recovery of being that he could not have accomplished in any other way.

After his illness, Goya takes up his painting again, and we know with what intensity and greatness, because these late works are those on the walls of his house. Cured, Goya painted the 'Black Paintings' of the Quinta del Sordo. And it is impossible not to imagine a link of cause and effect between the 1820 painting, commemorating the day of grace, and these utterly astounding works. We need simply to understand this link, and the meaning it has for us.

From *La longue chaîne de l'ancre* (2008)

ALES STENAR

I

On dit
Que des barques paraissent dans le ciel,
Et que, de quelques-unes,
La longue chaîne de l'ancre peut descendre
Vers notre terre furtive.
L'ancre cherche sur nos prairies, parmi nos arbres,
Le lieu où s'arrimer,
Mais bientôt un désir de là-haut l'arrache,
Le navire d'ailleurs ne veut pas d'ici,
Il a son horizon dans un autre rêve.

Il advient, toutefois,
Que l'ancre soit, dirait-on, lourde, inusuellement,
Et traîne presque au sol et froisse les arbres.
On l'aurait vue se prendre à une porte d'église,
Sous le cintre où s'efface notre espoir,
Et quelqu'un de cet autre monde fût descendu,
Gauchement, le long de la chaîne tendue, violente,
Pour délivrer son ciel de notre nuit.
Ah, quelle angoisse, quand il travailla contre la voûte,
Prenant à pleines mains son étrange fer,
Pourquoi faut-il
Que quelque chose en nous leurre l'esprit
Dans cette traversée que la parole
Tente, sans rien savoir, vers son autre rive?

From *The Anchor's Long Chain* (2008)

ALES STENAR

I

They say
Boats appear in the sky;
And from some of them,
The anchor's long chain trails down
To our hidden, fleeting earth.
On our prairies, among our trees, the anchor hunts
A place to moor – but soon, a higher will
Wrenches it loose.
Elsewhere's ship does not want a here:
Its horizon opens in some other dream.

Even so, it can happen:
Maybe the anchor, heavier than usual,
Drags near the ground, rumpling the trees.
We almost see it catch on a church-door,
Under the arch where our hope fades away.
Awkwardly, someone from that other world
Clambers down the taut, lurching chain,
To deliver his sky from our night.
What anguish, as he works against the vault,
Grappling with his strange iron hook …
Why must something within us
Lure the mind, in this crossing
Our words attempt, unknowingly,
To reach their other shore?

II

Le prince de ce pays, que voulait-il
Quand il fit rassembler, sur la falaise,
Tant de pierres debout, pour imiter
La forme d'un navire, qui partirait
Un jour, sur cette mer entre ciel et monde,
Et, toujours hésitant, presque désemparé,
Peut-être rejoindrait enfin le port
Que d'aucuns cherchent dans la mort, imaginée
Vie plus intense, une ligne de feux
À l'horizon désert d'une longue côte?
La nef de son désir,
Cette proue dans le roc, ces beaux flancs courbes,
Va immobile. Et moi je cherche à lire
Dans l'immobilité le mouvement
Qu'il imprima au rêve, lui qui savait
Qu'il mourrait au combat, contre des hommes
Masqués et s'exclamant dans une autre langue
De ce monde d'ici où rien, jamais,
Ne dure que l'étonnement et la douleur.

Un inconnu parmi eux lui fait signe,
Un envoyé de là-bas sur la mer,
Il est tout de lumière blanche, dans la fumée,
Et lui, il rend les coups, il ahane, il crie,
Mais déjà, avec l'ange qui lui sourit,
Il se tait, il s'est établi dans cette cabine
À l'avant du navire, ils sont assis
Maintenant l'un auprès de l'autre, à une table
Où rien n'est plus des cartes, des portulans
De cette vie d'ici, ni des nourritures,
Ni même des images, que sa mémoire
Lui offrait, de ses mains faciles, la nuit venue
Dans l'étrange pays où l'on naît et meurt.
Mémoire d'autres heures que les combats,
Mémoire de paroles réprimées,

II

What did he want, the prince of this land,
When he had so many tall stones
Raised upright on a cliff, to rhyme
The form of a ship? Maybe to depart
One day, on this sea between world and sky –
Though still faltering, almost in distress –
And at last, maybe to enter that port
Some would seek in death, imagined
As a life more intense, a glimmer of lights
On the sweep of an empty coast.
The vessel, the nave of his desire,
This prow in rock, this beautiful curved hull,
Moves motionless. I try to read
In immobility the going forth
He printed on his dream, as one who knew
He'd die in combat with visored men –
Masks who'd shout in another tongue
From the world of here, where nothing
Ever lasts, but bewilderment and pain.

Among them, a stranger beckons to him now –
An envoy from out there, on the sea – his whiteness
Wholly luminous amid the smoke.
The prince gives blow for blow, he grunts and yells;
But falling silent at the angel's smile,
He takes his place forward on the ship.
There in the cabin, side by side, they sit
Together: at a table cleared of the meals,
The nautical charts, the playing cards of a life
Lived here. Even the pictures are gone:
His memory had dealt them with an easy-going hand,
When night would overtake
Our odd country of birth and death.
Memory of hours without war,
Memory of words held back,

*Mémoire de la douceur qui est obscure
Comme le vin qui alourdit la grappe,
Mémoire de l'aperçu mais incompris
Et de moments trop brefs d'affections gauches.*

*Il rêva, il partit. Mais aujourd'hui, ici,
Ce n'est rien devant nous et autour de nous
Que le ciel de ce monde, rayons, nuées,
Puis, sur les pierres qui noircissent et se confondent,
La flèche du tonnerre et soudain la pluie.
Toute une eau véhémente nous enveloppe,
Les stèles ne sont plus qu'une seule présence
Là ou là surgissante, disparaissante,
Bien qu'entre elles coure l'éclair. Et je veux croire
Que cette flamme, c'est une paix, et qu'elle embrasse,
Avec infiniment d'émotion, de joie,
Un qui lutte dans ce désordre, à gauche, à droite,
Contre trop d'assaillants, et va mourir.*

*Plus tard, me retournant
Vers le navire de pierre, sous le ciel
Redevenu celui des matins d'été
(Et que faire, sinon se retourner
Dans cette vie où rien n'est qui ne passe?),
Je vois que sur la pierre voulue la proue
Un grand oiseau de mer s'est posé: un instant
De l'immobilité mystérieuse dont est
Capable une vie simple, sans langage.
L'oiseau regarde au loin, écoute, espère,
Il mène le navire, et d'autres, d'autres,
Sont là, autour de lui, au-dessus de lui,
À crier et à s'effacer dans le sillage.*

Memory of sweetness dark
As wine clustered in grapes,
Memory of inklings misjudged,
And moments of clumsy affection,
All too brief.

He dreamed; he set sail. But here, today,
Before us and around us, there's nothing
But the sky of this world – clouds, rays of light;
Then, on the stones that blacken and merge,
The thunder's arrow; and suddenly, the rain.
Headlong, a downpour engulfs us, and now
The steles shape a single presence, bursting
Into view, there and there again – until it vanishes,
Even though the lightning still runs through them.
I want to believe
This flame is peace, bestowed with infinite joy
On the fighter who's outnumbered in the mayhem,
Left and right, and who will die.

Later, turning back
To the ship of rock, under skies
Of summer morning once again
(And what can we do but turn back,
In this life where nothing stands still?),
I see a big seabird alight
On the stone meant for a prow: an instant
Of the mystery, motionless and wordless,
A simple life can live. The bird looks off
Into the distance; he listens, and hopes.
He guides the ship on – and others, others
Surround him with their cries; around him,
Above him, they fade into the wake.

LE TOMBEAU DE GIACOMO LEOPARDI

*Dans le nid de Phénix combien se sont
Brûlé les doigts à remuer des cendres!
Lui, c'est de consentir à tant de nuit
Qu'il dut de recueillir tant de lumière.*

*Et ils ont élevé, ses mots confiants,
Non le quelconque onyx vers un ciel noir
Mais la coupe formée par leurs deux paumes
Pour un peu d'eau terrestre et ton reflet,*

*Ô lune, son amie. Il t'offre de cette eau,
Et toi penchée sur elle, tu veux bien
Boire de son désir, de son espérance.*

*Je te vois qui vas près de lui sur ces collines
Désertes, son pays. Parfois devant
Lui, et te retournant, riante; parfois son ombre.*

MAHLER, *LE CHANT DE LA TERRE*

*Elle sort, mais la nuit n'est pas tombée,
Ou bien c'est que la lune emplit le ciel,
Elle va, mais aussi elle se dissipe,
Plus rien de son visage, rien que son chant.*

*Désir d'être, sache te renoncer,
Les choses de la terre te le demandent,
Si assurées sont-elles, chacune en soi
Dans cette paix où miroite du rêve.*

*Qu'elle, qui va, et toi, qui vieillis, continuez
Votre avancée sous le couvert des arbres,
À des moments vous vous apercevrez.*

LEOPARDI'S TOMB

So many fingers have been singed,
Sifting ashes in the Phoenix-nest;
But he could harvest all this light
Only by assenting to all this night.

And his trusting words never raised
Some onyx chalice to a blackened sky.
Their palms joined to cup your face,
Mirrored in earthly water, O moon:

His friend. He offers you this cup,
And you lean down, you consent
To drink from his yearning hope.

I see you roam beside him on these lonely hills,
His native land. At times you move ahead; you turn
Around to him and laugh. At times, you're his shadow.

MAHLER, *THE SONG OF THE EARTH*

She comes out; but night hasn't fallen yet,
Or else it's the moon that fills the sky.
She walks, but also melts away: nothing
Is left of her face - nothing but her song.

Desire to be, you must renounce yourself:
This is what the things of earth demand –
So trustingly, that each of them reflects
The shimmering peace of this dream.

She moves forward, and you grow old.
Keep advancing, under interwoven trees,
And you'll glimpse each other, now and then.

Ô parole du son, musique des mots,
Tournez alors vos pas l'une vers l'autre
En signe de connivence, encore, et de regret.

LE TOMBEAU DE STÉPHANE MALLARMÉ

Sa voile soit sa tombe, puisque il n'y eut
Aucun souffle sur cette terre pour convaincre
La yole de sa voix de dire non
Au fleuve, qui l'appelait dans sa lumière.

De Hugo, disait-il, le plus beau vers :
« Le soleil s'est couché ce soir dans les nuées »,
L'eau à quoi rien n'ajoute ni ne prend
Se fait le feu, et ce feu le subjugue.

Nous le voyons là-bas, indistinct, agiter
À la proue de sa barque qui se dissipe
Ce que des yeux d'ici ne discernent pas.

Est-ce comme cela que l'on meurt ? Et à qui
Parle-t-il ? Et que reste-t-il de lui, la nuit tombée ?
Cette écharpe de deux couleurs, creusant le fleuve.

SUR TROIS TABLEAUX DE POUSSIN

Sa tombe, me dit-on ? Mais c'est ce creux
Qu'il a laissé, sombre, dans le feuillage
De l'arbre où Apollon vieilli médite
Sur qui est jeune et donc est plus qu'un dieu.

Et c'est aussi la trouée de lumière
Dans la Naissance de Bacchus, *quand le soleil*
Prend l'espérance encore inentamée
Dans ses mains, et en fait le ciel qui change.

O music of words, utterance of sound,
Bend your steps toward each other as a sign
Of complicity, at last ... and of regret.

TOMB OF STÉPHANE MALLARMÉ

Let his sail be his tomb, since no
Earthly breath could persuade the skiff
Of his voice to refuse
The river, summoning him to its light.

Hugo's most beautiful line, he would say:
'The sun set this evening in the clouds';
Add nothing, subtract nothing from water –
It turns to fire, and to that fire he is yoked.

We see him over there, a blur at the prow
As his boat fades from sight, waving
Something our eyes here can't make out.

Is this how one dies? Who is he speaking to?
And what will be left of him once night falls?
That dent in the river, his two-coloured scarf.

ON THREE PAINTINGS BY POUSSIN

His tomb, you ask? But it's this space
He left hollow, dark under the leaves
Of the tree where old Apollo meditates
On what's young, and so more than god.

It is also this chink of light
In the *Birth of Bacchus,* when the sun
Takes hope, not yet tarnished, in his hands
And with it paints the sky that changes.

Sa tombe? Ce que voit son regard sévère
*Se défaire, au profond de l'*Autoportrait
Dont le tain, qui aima son rêve, s'enténèbre:

Un vieil homme étonné, le soir venant,
Mais s'obstinant à dire la couleur,
Tard, sa main devenue pourtant chose mortelle.

UN SOUVENIR D'ENFANCE DE WORDSWORTH

Comme, dans le Prélude, *cet enfant*
Qui va dans l'inconscient de la lumière
Et avise une barque et, entre terre et ciel,
Y descend, pour ramer vers une autre rive,

Mais voit alors s'accroître, menaçante,
Une cime là-bas, noire, derrière d'autres,
Et prend peur et retourne à ces roseaux
Où de minimes vies murmurent l'éternel,

Ainsi ce grand poète aura poussé
Sa pensée sur une heure calme du langage,
Il se crut rédimé par sa parole.

Mais des courants prenaient, silencieux,
Ses mots vers plus avant que lui dans la conscience,
Il eût peur d'être plus que son désir.

His tomb? What this stern gaze sees
Unravelling, deep in the *Self-Portrait*
Whose silvering, that loved his dream, dulls –

An old man, at evening, astonished,
But still determined to say the colour,
Late, his hand become a mortal thing

A CHILDHOOD MEMORY OF WORDSWORTH'S

As in the *Prelude*, when the child sets forth,
Unconscious as the light, and spots a boat;
And pushes off, between the earth and sky,
To row toward another shore. But then,

Over there, he sees an ominous black crag,
Looming taller and taller behind the rest;
And in his dread, he hurries back into the reeds,
Where tiny lives eternally hum.

So this great poet must have launched
His thought on a tranquil hour of language,
And believed himself redeemed by speech.

But other currents, silent, drove his words
Ahead of what his mind could apprehend,
Till he feared he'd overtopped his desire.

VI 2011–2016

from *L'Heure présente* / *The Present Hour* (2011)

UNE MISE EN SCÈNE D'HAMLET / FIRST DRAFT FOR A PRODUCTION OF HAMLET

The production's only desire, they said, was to conform to the demands of the text.

For example, when the watchmen exchange their first words, the director wanted only to have night appear as the soldiers experience it on the ramparts, in the cold. A cold that pervades the theatre as well, if the place in which they are listening to this can be called a theatre. The spectators, when I arrive, huddle in their clothes, sometimes almost sprawled on the ground, and I have to pick my way through the narrow spaces between their bodies. I see lots of wool coats on the white sand, not so many silk dresses. In fact, it's as if these men, these women – very few children – had arrived days, or, rather, nights ago. Because they've built fires that glow red here and there through the endless darkness. And some of them sleep, I hear quiet, regular breathing, but I also encounter eyes on the lookout, sharp; they frighten me, I hurry on. Sometimes, in the distance, the kind of cries one utters in dreams. I stumble along, double back, keep my eyes on the stage.

The stage? It's vaguely lit, I can just make out some steep rocks, rain and four or five men or women busy round a table with a book on it. One of them picks up the book, looks at the page it is open at. 'I read,' he says, 'Who is there?' Muffled exclamations around him. The director's other great desire is, in fact, to understand the text. Yes, first of all, to take each word literally, but also to ferret out the whole meaning of what they say. How to do this, in this night? The director's assistants, these vague beings crowded round him, don't agree, with him or among themselves, it seems. 'Who is there?' Obviously, how to know who is there?

'And what does it say next?' someone calls. 'Friends to this ground,' answers another. At which a third person bends down, grasps a large stone lying on the ground, strains to lift it, waves his friends aside, tries to throw it, far. 'If the actor throws this stone,' he asks, 'does it

mean anything?' 'Careful,' responds a young woman. 'You are one of the actors, don't forget, and the show has already begun.' It has been underway for hours, days. Suddenly a commotion in the room, people are getting up, stretching, exclaiming, moving about because they've just realised that the play, in fact, is happening elsewhere too, elsewhere as here, for instance, at this very moment, in a chalet up in the mountain along a narrow path where it has snowed in places and puddles still lie on the ground. This chalet, one of those rickety Swiss cuckoo-clock constructions they used to install upstage in the days of *bel canto* and the grand old *fin-de-siècle* theatres. You have to push the door, glance into this lit room – a lamp on the table – see Hamlet insulting his mother. Gertrude? Yes, crumpled on a bed, shoulders bare, hair dishevelled. Her hand hides her face. 'Oh Hamlet, speak no more,' she groans. But who cares what happens to her? Now there's a rumour that higher up this same path the director has approached *Hamlet* from another angle. This time, an elegant facade in stone, with stairs leading up to columns, and at the top two indecipherable beings whom I – I, in any case – see silently battling, bare hands against bare hands. How long has this confrontation been going on, how many hours, how many nights will it go on for? Is this 'readiness', this, the sad wish that turns and turns and carves itself a hollow in the chasm of the word? Above this vain combat the rocky promontory, the cold wind.

So many other scenes! And the spectators aware that they must go in search of them, push deep into these sorts of moraines, under the firs crusted with snow, bravely pushing doors from behind which, at times, come rending cries. The theatre is big as the mountain. The theatre is the mountain. Ophelia traipses round, barefoot. We watch her go by, we make space, she is alone, she hums a little, how great her solitude!

What work, this production of *Hamlet*! So many temptations for the director, so many desires to eliminate, but to understand, first of all, to understand! For example, who's this child crying by the roadside? A wise man in travelling clothes, Basho, the benevolent, pauses alongside him, pats his shoulder, asks some questions, listens to him, nods, goes off. And who's this second girl, lightly dressed, feeding big black birds in a kind of stable, where we hear

horses stamp, the occasional neigh, in the shadows? They say that in *Hamlet*'s stage directions it's the playwright himself, an actor once more, who is supposed to come towards her, on a long road through the stones of time, the voices of space. He's coming, we don't know where he is exactly, perhaps he's going to turn up somewhere on the vast stage, holding a storm lamp, on his face the mask that is the words of poetry.

HAMLET *EN MONTAGNE* / *HAMLET* IN THE MOUNTAINS

They announced that *Hamlet* was being staged in the mountains.

Up there, one was acutely aware that in Shakespeare's mind the prince of Denmark is always surrounded by masses of rocks. Rocks that hang over or crowd round him, faults widening between them, whence it follows that his voice will only ever be heard in the distance, almost always muffled by the roar of water tearing down slopes under the shrieks of rooks from these other worlds.

And the spectators, once they get past the ticket office, a sort of sentry box at the trailhead near the base of a cliff, will have to keep changing place. Why? Is it because the play's scenes have been strewn about, with no regard for chronology, in as many mountain locations? They say some of the original directors expressed a preference for this concept. Some of them wanted Hamlet to insult his mother in a farmhouse up on one of the pastures. By the light of candles that servants would have borne here and there, in one of the rooms, making long shifting shadows on the walls, he would drag her by the hair, throw her on a bed, then collapse in tears at her knees that his frantic hands would have bared. And perhaps in some valley far away from anything, actors are acting, living, growing old in this dire manner in the inexhaustible world, with other scenes taking place elsewhere, ending and beginning again. But others said no, this is not what the mountain wants from Shakespeare.

And indeed! The spectators file across the theatre's narrow threshold, they press forward, all together, endlessly it seems, groping, stumbling, nearly falling into this black night; and over there, up

ahead, what is going on? 'Two people are fighting,' shouts a young man who, not without causing much confusion, is running towards me against the flow of the crowd. 'One of them grabbed the other by his collar, he's shaking him, he's shouting.' What does this mean, I want to know, I walk faster, I push through the backs that grudgingly part, under their umbrellas, because it's raining, the cold is also falling from the sky. But my efforts are useless. Upstream, the flux is compact, I am constantly blocked by the trampling and murmuring ahead, I am pushed off onto a side path where, to my astonishment, there is almost no one else.

A few steps on the bright sandy path, puddled with water, and suddenly, two men stride towards me, they go by me, they are talking. I even hear one say to the other, pensively, as they pass: 'What's Hecuba to him, or he to Hecuba?'

And I understand. The scenes of *Hamlet* are not dispersed about the mountain, the actors are dispersed in the crowd. And the scenes are broken up, the action has unravelled, but in the midst of the spectators who stream past, ever more numerous, the great scene nowhere to be found in the work in its simple text will perhaps come together, take shape, shout out its sense even without any of the play's characters nearby.

I can understand this way of thinking. And this desire, I approve of it: all the more in that for the action thus fragmented to have the same degree of density as this trampling which has no more origin and will go on without end, the director, in fact omnipresent, multiplies the number of actors as he sends them off, scattering among the shifting, turbulent flux of this astonished multitude many actors playing Hamlet, many playing Polonius or the startled Gertrude, many Laertes and many Ophelias as well. It follows that these are not just local men and women but as many examples of Hamlet, of Polonius, of Claudius, even as many figures of Rosencrantz and Guildenstern, who, henceforth real beings, more or less, because of the variations of their faces, faces beautiful sometimes, or of the wild gestures which they at times are given, will wander indefinitely in this haggard crowd on the grassy terraces of their immense Elsinore. All of them follow an idea of the self that their representatives serve, and with skill; but all too often they cannot find the words to express

this idea. Each is amazed to be what he is, each terrified of these looming rock faces which here allow only the narrowest of passages, but over there seem to open, majestically, on a beyond where torrents endlessly rumble in the bottom of a gorge.

I go on, on a side path, a little above the broadest part of the flood, which by a thousand different ways attempts to carve a path through the mountain, and which here has for the moment been reduced to a trickle of people.

A big man overtakes me laughing.

And now ahead of me, a dozen men, women, stopped. They form a circle, what are they looking at? I slip in among them. It's Ophelia. She's sitting on a stone, her umbrella at her side, bent over, distraught, groping in some sort of handbag. Scantily dressed, nearly naked, the girl, a poor holey black wool dress as if snatched at by chance upon waking in too big a dream. You can tell she's cold, that her hands shake. Will she draw from her squashed, crumpled bag the fennel, the rosemary, the columbine that the poet wanted her to offer to the world that doesn't listen and doesn't understand? But no, suddenly she gets up and with her head still a little bent, bag and umbrella clutched to her side, throws herself forward, lurching a little. Where is she going? What did she say? Where should I go next?

Hours, hours we are to spend climbing towards this summit which sometimes, at a switchback, lets itself be glimpsed, moonlit, indifferent. Roads fork, many of us have taken them already, others are still hesitating, the wind is still blowing, it won't stop, we know that, even life won't stop: being here is to have to not stop living. Besides, now someone on horseback frays a passage through the people around me, his horse neighs, a black horse, it rears; the actor, is that an actor astride it, is clad in armour, no doubt it's old Hamlet, the dead king. But why have they draped this red scarf over his coat of mail? True, the wind lifts it very prettily; round this hoary head, it's like the beautiful gestures of youthful writing. And how long it is, this banner, one could believe it endless and that it is already lost among the stars we can still see, God knows why, since it is blowing and raining harder than ever.

from *L'heure présente* (2011)

L'HEURE PRÉSENTE

I

Regarde!
Un éclair envahit le ciel, ce soir encore,
Il prend la terre dans ses mains, mais il hésite,
Presque il s'immobilise. S'est-il cru

Une phrase, une signature, non, il chancelle,
Nous le voyons qui tombe, illuminant,
Dans les bras l'un de l'autre,
Sommeil et mort.

L'éclair, une illusion,
Même l'éclair.

Une illusion, la forme
Qui se déploie, un rêve
Qui enlace la forme, et va tomber
Avec elle, brisée,
Dépossédée de soi, à ces confins,
Là-bas, de notre nuit d'ici,
L'heure présente.

Regarde, vois.

Regarde, théologien,
Ne crois-tu pas que Dieu
Se soit lassé d'être?

Tu imagines
Qu'il ne peut en finir, étant infini,
Avec soi.

THE PRESENT HOUR

I

Look! A flash
Of lightning invades the sky again tonight,
It takes the earth in its hands, but hesitates,
It stands almost still. Did it think

It was a sentence, a signature, no, it
    flickers,
We watch it fall, illuminating,
In each other's arms,
Sleep and death.

The lightning, an illusion,
Even the lightning.

An illusion, a form
Unfolding, a dream
That embraces form, and is falling
With it, broken,
Dispossessed of itself, over there
On the very edge of our night here,
The present hour.

Look, see.

Look, theologian,
Don't you think God
Has grown tired of being?

You imagine
That being infinite he cannot be done
With himself

*Mais tu sais qu'aucun sacrifice, à ses autels,
Ni même le sacrifice de son fils,
N'éveille plus son désir.*

*Se tourne-t-il
Vers celle qui dormait auprès de lui,
L'âme du monde,
Touchera-t-il son bras, sa hanche nue,
Il ne la réveillera pas.*

*Descendra-t-il
Dans ses jardins, de terrasse en terrasse,
S'arrêtant, quelquefois,
Comme ces bêtes
Qui s'immobilisent d'un coup
Pour un bruit, une ombre,
Il n'écoutera pas
Le bruissement du ciel. Ni davantage
Le cri du désespoir. Pas même
Le hurlement de la bête égorgée,
Pas même
Les notes hésitantes du pipeau
D'un berger attardé sous le dernier hêtre.*

*Se sont évaporés
Le bœuf et l'âne
Et cet agneau qui n'est qu'étonnement.
Les constellations, nous disait-on,
Auraient étincelé dans cette paille.*

*Et vois, là, c'est Vénus,
Penchée sur Adonis mourant. Et cette autre image,
C'est Niobé, all tears. Je vois Judith
Se redresser, sanglante. Je vois, dans la pluie d'or,
Danaé, ses cheveux épars. Mon amie, est-ce voir
Quand le peintre n'a eu entre ses mains
Que des corps dont les yeux se ferment? Je vous touche,*

But you know that no sacrifice, on his altars,
Not even the sacrifice of his son,
Now awakens any desire in him.

If he turns
Towards the one who slept beside him,
The soul of the world,
If he touches her shoulder, her naked hip,
He will not wake her.

If he goes down
Into his gardens, from terrace to terrace,
Stopping, now and now,
Like those animals
That stand stock-still
For a noise, a shadow,
He will not hear
The sky rustle. Nor the cry
Of despair. Not even
The howl of the slaughtered animal,
Not even
The hesitant piping of a shepherd
Lingering under the last beech tree.

Into thin air
The ox and the donkey
And that lamb, pure astonishment.
The constellations they used to tell us
Sparkled in that straw.

And see, up there, is Venus
Bent over the dying Adonis. And that other image
Is Niobe, *all tears*. I see Judith
Straighten up, bloody. I see, in the shower of gold,
Danae, her thinning hair. My friend, is it seeing
When the painter has had in his hands
Only bodies whose eyes are closed? I touch you,

Épaules nues, reflets dans la pénombre,
Fûtes-vous l'or que répandait un dieu?

Et te nommes-tu Ophélie,
Tu éclates de rire. Ta robe s'ouvre.
L'eau noire te pénètre, des courants
T'emportent. Tu te penches sur lui,
Le prince fou, écartant ses cheveux,
Que colle la sueur de sa fièvre, tu touches
Ses tempes de tes lèvres. L'eau rapide
Couvre ses quelques mots, disperse les tiens,
Ô trahie,
Te nommes-tu Desdémone?
Willows, willows...

Et te nomme-t-il J. G. F.,
Es-tu « son Électre lointaine »,
Écoute bien:
La maladie et la mort font des cendres
De tout ce feu qui jadis flamboya.
Et te nommes-tu...? Pas de nom
Pour toi, de tous les temps
Et de tous les pays, qui tombe,
Mains liées dans le dos, nuque brisée,
Voix bafouée, la bouche
Déjà pleine de terre. Pas de nom,
Pas de résurrection pour toi non plus.
Et pas même de mots, pas même les nôtres,
Puisque les mots se cabrent
Devant ce que celui qui cherche à dire
Ne saurait éprouver, ne peut revivre.

Ah, qu'est-ce que cela, sur le chemin?
C'est tombé d'un des arbres, je ramasse,
La matière est luisante, j'ai mon couteau,
Je déchire la bogue,

Bare shoulders, glimmers in the dark,
Were you the gold shower of a god?

And is your name Ophelia?
You burst out laughing. Your dress opens,
The black water penetrates you, currents
Carry you off. You bend over him,
The mad prince, combing his hair
Matted with fever's sweat, your lips
Brush his temples. The quick water
Muffles his few words, scatters yours.
O betrayed,
Is your name Desdemona?
Willows, willows …

And does he name you J. G. F.,
Are you 'his distant Electra'?
Listen carefully:
Illness and death make ashes
Of the fire that flamed for us.
And your name is …? No name
For you, of all times
And all places, who fall
With your hands roped in your back,
Your necks broken,
Voices jeered at, mouths
Crammed with earth. No name,
No resurrection for you either.
And no words, not even ours,
Since words baulk
At that which he who tries to say it
Has not experienced, cannot relive.

And what's that on the road there?
It fell from a tree, I pick it up,
The matter lustrous, I have my knife,
I cut into the husk,

Je tente d'entamer le bois du fruit
Mais la lame dérape. Ce qui est
À jamais se refuse. Dois-je jeter
L'amande impénétrée avec la bogue?

Lourde
Sous ses enluminures de ciel noir,
La page dans le livre. On veut en soulever
Ne serait-ce qu'un angle, voir au delà
Dans l'espace des autres pages. Mais la liasse
De ces autres fait masse. Elle semble collée
Par une eau de la fin du monde. De la tourbe
Pour rien qu'un dernier feu? Devons-nous croire
Que le signe qui prit au flanc des choses
Comme un éclair, et y étincela,
N'aura été que mains jointes en vain,
Rêves, enfièvrement de rien que des rêves,
Momie parée pour rien, sous sa chape de pierre?

Il fait nuit. Dans les chambres
Les corps sont nus. Parfois un mouvement
Pour rien, inachevé,
Prend un dormeur que tourmente son rêve.
Vais-je toucher cette épaule, cette autre,
Solliciter que des yeux s'ouvrent, s'élargissent,
Que des corps ressuscitent, comme on a cru
Que ce fut, une fois? Crier,
Reviens, Claude, reviens, Enzo, d'entre les morts?
Je crie des noms, personne ne se réveille.

Et si mêlés nos mots
Les uns aux autres! Ils ne se séparent pas.
Dorment–ils
Dans les bras l'un de l'autre? Rien ne semble
Battre dans cette artère que je touche
Au creux de leur épaule. Je pense au jour
Où, dans l'étonnement

I try to nick the woody fruit
But the blade slips. What is
Always refuses itself. Must I toss
Away the kernel with the husk?

Heavy
Under its illuminations of black sky,
The page of the book. One would like to pry
Even a corner up, see beyond
Into the space of other pages. But the pages
Are stuck, they wad. They seem glued
By a water of the end of the world. Peat
Good for one last fire? Must we think
The sign that caught the flank of things
Like lightning, and made a spark there
Was nothing but hands joined in vain,
Dreams, fitfulness of merely dreams,
A mummy all dolled up for nothing, under its stone lid?

Night falls. In the bedrooms
The bodies are naked. Now a movement
For no reason, incomplete,
Shakes a sleeper tormented by his dream.
Shall I touch this shoulder, this one,
Plead with eyes to open, open wide,
Bodies to resuscitate, as we once believed
Occurred? Shout,
Come back, Claude, come back, Enzo, from the dead?
I shout names, no one wakes.

And so entangled our words
With one another! Come apart – they don't.
Do they sleep
Folded in each other's arms? Nothing seems
To pulse in the arteries I touch
In the hollows of their shoulders. I think of the day
When, in the astonishment

Du ciel et de la terre s'approchant
L'un de l'autre, se confondant,
Devenant l'horizon puis le chemin,
Bois contre bois frotté se fit la flamme.

Et parfois l'un de nous tressaille, se retourne
Sur sa couche, il reprend
Ses yeux à sa chimère. Mais le miroir
Qui dormait près de lui ne s'éveille pas.
Reflète-t-il le cyprès, les étoiles,
Le beau visage de la jeune femme endormie
Sur la chaleur de son bras replié,
Non, si je le détache de la cloison
Et l'approche des choses du jour qui point,
Ce que je tiens, c'est un morceau de houille,
Les reflets n'y remuent que de la nuit.

II

J'ai ramassé le fruit, j'ouvre l'amande.
Dans la parole
La dérive rapide de la nuée.

Illusion,
L'âtre qui brûlait clair le soir, te souviens-tu,
Dans la maison que nous avons aimée.
Ce petit bois,
Ces boules du papier froissé, ce pique-feu,
Cette flamme soudaine, presque un éclair,
Un rêve, comme nous?

Et souviens-toi
Du chien empoisonné! Il griffait de ses cris
Le ciel, la terre. Mon amie,
Hier encore
Nous allions jusqu'à ces barrières, là-bas,

Of sky and earth approaching
each other, mingling,
Becoming the horizon, then the road,
Stick rubbed stick and turned to fire.

And now one of us shudders, rolls over
On his bed, he takes his eyes
Off his chimera. But the mirror
Sleeping at his side doesn't wake.
Does it reflect the cypress, the stars,
The lovely face of the young woman
Asleep on the warmth of her bent arm?
No, if I take the mirror from the wall
And hold it up to the things of dawn,
What I hold is a lump of coal,
The reflections stir in it only night.

11

I have gathered the fruit, I open its husk.
In our words
The quick drift of the cloud.

Illusion,
The hearth that burnt bright each evening, remember,
In the house we loved.
The kindling,
The paper crumpled up, the poker,
The sudden flame, almost like lightning,
A dream, like us?

And remember
The poisoned dog! Its yelps clawed
The sky, the earth. My friend,
Again yesterday
We walked all the way to those gates, over there,

Par ces creux où de l'eau brille dans l'herbe.
Hier, nous passions
Près de la grange vide. Une chevêche
S'envolait de dessous le toît. Je crie son nom,
Mais rien ne bouge sur ce mur que lune éclaire.
Pas d'yeux de bête effrayée.

Illusion l'amandier, toutes ses fleurs
Comme des feux parmi d'autres étoiles.
Rêve, fumée,
Ce ciel des nuits d'alors, de tant de grappes?
L'agneau? Rien qu'à jamais
Le couteau et le sang. Notre ravin,
Rien que le bruit d'une eau qui croît parfois
Puis presque cesse.
Personne
Dans le bruit du torrent. Personne
Dans la lumière. L'homme
Là-bas, à la cervelle d'or,
Qui titube sur le trottoir, ses doigts sanglants
Crispés sur des raclures de l'esprit,
Qu'offrait-il, quel bouquet? Je veux ces fleurs,
Les dégager du papier qui les couvre,
Cette page rougie, car j'aperçois,
Dans le don qu'il faisait, déjà mourant,
Les abîmes du ciel et de la terre,
Les images que forment les nuées
Et des corolles, l'homme, la femme,
Dont la couleur me semble restée vive,
Mais tout cela, c'est dans le caniveau,
Il a jeté l'offrande refusée,
Ne vais-je ramasser que du flétri,
De l'insensé, une odeur âcre, fade?
Roses, roses? N'existent
Que roses déchirées, pas de rose en soi,
Pas de corolle à soutenir un monde.

Through the dips where water shines in the grass.
Yesterday, we walked past
The empty barn. Tawny, an owlet
Flew from the eaves. I call its name,
Nothing moves on the moonlit wall.
No eyes of a frightened creature.

Illusion, the almond tree, all its bloom
Like fires among other stars.
Dream, smoke,
The skies of those nights, all those clusters?
The lamb? Only ever
The knife and the blood. Our ravine,
Nothing but water whose voice growls
At times, then dwindles to a thread.
No one
In the torrent's roar. No one
In the light. That man
There, with his brain of gold,
Who staggers along the sidewalk, his bloody fingers
Clawing at the mind's shreds,
What did he offer, which bouquet? I want those flowers,
To lift them from their wrapping,
The reddened page, for I perceive,
In the gift he, already dying, made
The abysses of sky and earth,
The images that clouds make
And corollas, the man, the woman,
Whose colour seems to stay bright,
But all of that – flung into the gutter,
He threw away the rejected offering,
Won't I be picking up only the wilted,
Senselessness, an acrid smell, insipid?
Roses, roses? Only torn
Roses exist, no rose in itself,
No corolla to build a world.

III

*Et pourtant, je puis dire
Le mot chevêche ou le mot safre ou le mot ciel
Ou le mot espérance,
Et voici que, levant les yeux, je vois ces arbres
Qu'embrase sur la route un soleil du soir.
C'est un feu de grande douceur, ses braises claires
Ont transmuté le feuillage en lumière,
Et ici, c'est le pré, là-bas des cimes
Et leurs mains se rejoignent, leurs corps se cherchent
Avec cette évidence, silencieuse,
Qu'il faut bien que l'on nomme de la beauté.
Je regarde ces arbres toute une heure,
Est-ce là du visible, à peine, puisque
La visibilité se fait or pur
Alors pourtant qu'alentour la nuit tombe.*

*J'écoute un mot, je cherche à voir ce qu'il désigne,
Et il me semble, irrépressiblement,
Que cette chose se recolore, que des yeux
Se rouvrent, étonnés,
Dans le rêve de pierre de l'esprit.
Les mots sont-ils porteurs de plus que nous,
En savent-ils plus que nous, cherchent-ils
Au bord d'une eau du fond de notre sommeil,
Noire autant que rapide, refusée,
Le gué d'une lumière? Et celle-ci
A-t-elle sens, sur une voie tout autre,
Certes, que l'espérance d'hier encore?
J'écoute un mot, le rapproche d'un autre,
Ce dormeur et cette dormeuse se réveillent
Dans un peu de soleil, leurs mains se touchent,
Est-ce que ce n'est là que du désir,
Le même rêve à changer de visage?
L'éclair qui troue en vain le ciel d'ici?*

III

And yet, I can say
The word *chevêche* or the word *safre* or the word *ciel*
Or the word *espérance*,
And glancing up I see those trees along the road
Set on fire by an evening sun.
It is a very gentle fire, its bright embers
Transmuting foliage into light,
And here, there's the field, over there some peaks,
And their hands meet, their bodies seek each other
With this silent evidence
That surely we must call beauty.
I look at the trees for a whole hour,
Is that the visible: barely, since
Visibility is changed to pure gold –
Yet all around us the night falls.

I listen to a word, I try to see what it designates,
And it seems to me, irrepressibly,
That this thing regains its colours, that eyes
Open once more, astonished,
In the mind's dream of stone.
Do the words hold more than we ourselves do,
Do they know more than we do, do they seek
At the edge of some water, black and rapid,
That we from the depths of our sleep refuse,
The stepping stone of a light? And this light,
Has it a sense, in a completely different way,
Of course, than yesterday's hope?
I listen to a word, set it beside another,
This sleeper and this other sleeper wake
In a patch of sun, their hands touch,
Is this merely desire,
The same dream despite its new visage?
The lightning that pierces in vain the sky of here?

Mais véridique est la peinture de paysage,
Véridique la fleur
Du genet, au désert,
Véridique la voix qui l'a nommée
Dans nos mots exterminateurs, sur des pentes tristes.
Et vois, sur le chemin,
Ces deux-là qui s'éloignent.
Ils s'arrêtent, soudain,
Se tournent l'un vers l'autre. S'affrontent-ils,
S'insultent-ils, vont-ils s'entredéchirer, par angoisse
D'être l'illusion qu'ils se savent être?
Mais non, ils semblent regarder le ciel du soir,
Où un soleil enfant paraît, sa tête immense
Haute déjà sur le vieil horizon.
Et c'est vrai que les arbres que j'ai vus
Se faire incandescence, continuent
Guère loin d'eux, à être ce rayon
D'on ne sait d'où venu, qui ne s'efface
Qu'en affinant, de son dernier instant,
Les grains d'un or qu'on dirait sans matière.

Regardez-moi,
Dit ce qui monte en eux du fond du langage,
Oubliez qui vous êtes pour que je sois,
Faites de moi ce que je cherche à être,
Renoncez votre rêve pour le mien,
Aimez-moi, donnez-moi forme, visage
De vos mains d'ombre et de lumière. Le ciel du soir
Est, peut-être, une rose. Rose à venir
Par vos travaux d'horticulteurs dans les nuées,
Rose d'arbres, de fleuves, de chemins,
De lits défaits, de mains simples, cherchant
D'autres mains, à l'aveugle. Rose des mots
Qu'une dit à une autre, par rien encore
Que le frémissement de la paume, des doigts.
Le ciel change. La rose sans pourquoi,

But veridical is the landscape painting,
Veridical the broom
Flowering in the desert,
Veridical the voice that named it
In our exterminating words, on some sad slopes.
And see, on the road,
Those two walking.
They stop, suddenly,
Turn towards each other. Do they argue,
Insult each other, will they tear into each other, out of anguish
At being the illusion they know they are?
No, they seem to be looking at the evening sky,
Where an infant sun appears, its huge head
Already high on the old horizon.

And it's true that the trees I saw
Become incandescence, continue,
Not far from them, to be that ray of light
Come from we know not where, effaced only
By refining, in its last moments,
The grains of a gold one would say immaterial.

Look at me,
Say what rises in them from language's depths,
Forget who you are so that I may be,
Make of me what I seek to be,
Renounce your dream for mine,
Love me, give me form, countenance
With your hands of shadow and light. The evening sky
Is, perhaps, a rose. Rose to come
Through your horticultural work in the clouds,
Rose of trees, of rivers, of roads,
Of unmade beds, of simple hands, seeking
Other hands, blindly. Rose of words
One person says to another, through nothing yet
But a tingling in the palm, in the fingers.
The sky changes. The rose without why

C'est vous, dans les jardins de sa couleur.
Regardez, écoutez! Le moindre mot
A dans sa profondeur une musique,
Le phonème est corolle, la voix, c'est l'être
Qui peut fleurir, dans même ce qui n'est pas.

Et tard, ayant pitié
Des images. Voyez que Danaé
Se dresse sur sa couche, même sachant
Qu'illusoire est le dieu. Et qu'Ophélie
Emporte dans ses yeux le ciel, la terre,
Comme une certitude, bien que se noie
Leur double feu dans sa totale nuit.
Devant nous, mes amis, est-ce le soir
Ou une sorte d'aube, informe? Du soleil
Tout de même, au profond de ces glaires rouges.

Tu regardes le ciel
Par la fenêtre ouverte, enfant
De ce siècle appauvri. Le monde,
Ces toîts de tôle grise, ces fumées,
Cette page souillée, déchirée? Non, tes mots
Refusent de s'effacer de l'univers,
De ce néant ils veulent faire des collines,
Des vallées, des chemins. N'est-ce que pierre
Et neiges ces montagnes, non, au sommet
De l'une, pas trop haute,
S'évase une prairie. Et de grande paix
Te semble, vu d'ici,
Le passage de l'ombre sur l'émeraude
De son herbe sans fin. Plus bas le fleuve
Rassemblant, éclairant. Vas-tu savoir
Espérer que cette évidence a quelque sens,
Qu'elle s'affermira dans ta parole,
Qu'elle sera l'aimant qui reprendra
L'esprit au désespoir, vas-tu penser
Qu'il n'est de l'être qu'en image mais que c'est là

Is you, in the gardens of its colours.
Look, listen! The least word
Has in its depths a music,
The phoneme is corolla, the voice – it is the being
That can flower, even in what is not.

And late, taking pity
On the images. See how Danae
Rises on her couch, though she knows
The god is illusory. And Ophelia
Bears away in her eyes, like a certitude,
Sky and earth, though their twin fires
Drown in her utter night.
Ahead of us, my friends, is that evening
Or a sort of dawn without form? Sun,
All the same, deep in those red glairs.

You look at the sky
Through the open window, a child
Of this impoverished century. The world,
These grey tin roofs, curls of smoke,
This soiled, torn page? No, your words
Refuse to be effaced from the universe;
Of this nothingness they want to make hills,
Roads, valleys. Aren't those mountains
Only stone and snow, no, at the summit
Of one, not too high,
A meadow lies. And utterly peaceful
Seems, from here,
The shadow that flits over the green
Of its endless grass. Further down, the river
Gathering, shining. Will you be able
To hope that this evidence has meaning,
That it will affirm itself in your words,
That it may be the magnet that will draw
Spirit back from despair; are you going to think
That there is being only in images but that this

*Suffisance mystérieuse, pour autant
Que ce néant consente à la lumière
Indifférente, incréée, par des gestes
De ses contours, des mouvements, du rire
Au profond de sa voix tragique se portant
Vers d'autres de ces ombres? Peut-être non.
Le ciel noircit d'un coup, la foudre tombe.*

*Mais tu te tournes
Vers ta chambre louée dans cette banlieue,
Elle est petite, mais ses murs sont presque blancs,
Et tu y as placé, en ce premier jour,
La* Diane et ses compagnes, *de Vermeer,
Une simple photographie mais d'un échange
De si grande douceur, à mains si pures
Que ces quelques figures se détachent
Du gris et noir de la couleur absente
Comme non le soleil mais mieux et plus.
Un rêve, c'est mensonge. Mais rêver, non.
Que se fassent tes rêves
Deux combattants, l'un masqué, mais parfois
Riche de son visage découvert.*

*Tu regardes vivre le soir. Le ciel, la terre
Nus, allongés sur leur couche commune.
Et lui, rien que nuées,
Il se penche sur elle, prend dans ses mains
Sa face respectée.
Dieu? Non, mieux que cela. La voix
Qui se porte, essoufflée, au devant d'une autre
Et riante désire son désir,
Anxieuse de donner bien plus que de prendre.
Ne vas-tu pas penser, ce soir encore,
Que puisse devenir un même souffle,
La matière, l'esprit? Que de leur étreinte
Apaisée, desserrée,
De la couleur, de l'or retomberait,*

Suffices as mystery, inasmuch as
This nothingness consents to the light –
Indifferent, uncreated – by the gestures
Of its contours, its shifts, of the laughter
In the depths of its tragic voice carrying
Towards others some of these shadows? Perhaps not.
All at once the sky darkens, lightning falls.

But you turn
Towards your rented room in this suburb,
It is small, but its walls are almost white,
And on them you've placed, this first day,
Diana and her Companions, by Vermeer,
Just a photograph but of an exchange
Of such mildness, with hands so pure
That the group of figures stands out
Against the grey and black of the absent colour
Not like the sun but better and more.
A dream is a falsehood. But dreaming, no.
Let your dreams be
Two fighters, one masked, but now and then
Rich in his discovered face.

You watch the evening live. The sky, the earth
Naked, reclining, on their common bed.
And he, clouds, simply clouds,
Leans over her, takes in his hands
Her respected face.
God? No, better than that. The voice
That goes, breathless, to greet another
And laughing desires her desire,
Anxious to give more than to take.
Aren't you going to think, this evening again,
That matter, spirit, can become
The same breath? That from their calm,
Restful embrace
Some colour, some gold may fall,

Quelque débris de verre, taché de boue,
Mais à briller, dans l'herbe?

Et la mort, comme d'habitude? Et n'avoir été
Qu'une image chacun pour l'autre, tisonnant
Un âtre, dans rien que nos mémoires, oui, je veux bien,
Mais souviens-toi
Des prairies de l'enfance: de tes pas
Pour t'allonger à regarder le ciel,
Si lourd, de tant de signes, mais se faisant
Immensément en toi cette bienveillance,
Les éclairs de chaleur des nuits d'été.
Heure présente, ne renonce pas,
Reprends tes mots des mains errantes de la foudre.
Écoute-les faire du rien parole,
Risque-toi
Dans même la confiance que rien ne prouve,

Lègue-nous de ne pas mourir désespérés.

Some shard of glass, mud-splashed,
But shining, in the grass?

And death, as usual? And having been
Only images each for the other, stirring up
Embers, in nothing but our memories, yes, I agree,
But remember
Childhood's meadows: remember walking
On the way to lie down and look at the sky
Charged with so many signs but immense
Within you this benevolence,
Flashes of heat lightning of summer nights.
Present hour, do not renounce,
Take back your words from the lightning's errant hands,
Listen to them making of nothing speech,
Risk, risk
Even the confidence that nothing can prove,

Will us not to die despairing.

from *Le Digamma* / *The Digamma* (2012)

GOD IN *HAMLET*

I

The rehearsals had started fairly well. But right away, puzzling events began to take place. First of all, the director felt a restless, overpowering urge to expand the stage: the usual space wasn't enough for him anymore. Already on the second day of our meetings, he wanted to knock down a wall left over from a former stage-set, and in his impatience he grabbed a hammer and banged at the painted boards. But they held firm; they wouldn't budge an inch. He had to give up, in a fit of tears.

We were amazed. But the desire to enlarge the scenic backdrop soon spread to the actors. They liked to keep their distances from each other. You might have said they wanted to leave the stage empty. The actor who played Polonius, a portly man with a slight limp, was always straying here and there, as if searching for cracks in an invisible wall: maybe those would provide him with the air he seemed to need. We kept having to call him back from wherever he was, and he only returned with regret. As for the young lady who had been chosen for Ophelia, somewhat by chance, she liked to sit off to one side, staring blankly ahead. One morning she let out a cry and jumped up, holding out her tremulous hands. Then it appeared she wanted to flee, but where? She collapsed a few steps further on – like the director, racked by tears. Hysteria? Come now, not a bit: she was always so thoughtful, so calm.

Soon the director decided we had to leave the theatre behind; he led us far, far away into the bleak landscape of that country. In a field, under the vast, lowering sky of this remote corner of the world, the actors would shout when they moved away from each other – shout to make themselves heard in the scene being studied at the time. With delays, their voices would double back as echoes from the nearby cliff, making them mingle. At such moments we came to love those harmonics, which clouded the sound and even the meaning of

the words.

We would meet early in the morning, on that expanse of grass riddled by sharp little stones; they were hard on Ophelia and Gertrude, who lurched along in their high heels. Polonius always arrived somewhat late, limping up with things he'd carried from home. He insisted on showing them to us, and even mixing them into the action. He would place them here or there, sometimes hiding them in a clump of brush. They were humble objects, since the actor was poor. One time he brought a long board, still bearing traces of reddish ochre. Another time it was a painted plate, with flowers and fruits closely intertwined. Two verses, written on the plate in a naive hand, said that 'the god of Cythera' loves 'mystery'. On a certain morning, when there was a storm, our Polonius showed up with a little girl: his daughter, who was patently furious. Though she resisted, he dragged her along. When he let go of her hand, she ran all the way to the big stone at the end of the field, and sat there sobbing.

11

I'll say nothing more about the other oddities of those first days. They amused us, they even disturbed us a bit; but they didn't make us uneasy, and so we tried to forget them. Still, it was something else again when undefined spasms swept over certain actors – to the point of choking them – who right before had been placidly endeavouring to master a scene. First it happened to Ophelia. We knew that Hamlet had entered her room a few days earlier, bearing all the marks of amorous frenzy: doublet undone, incoherent words, quaking hands. And she had been afraid. Wasn't he the heir to the throne, possessed of awesome power? And didn't she love him as well, without admitting it as yet to herself? Good reasons for being moved during this new encounter, especially since today the mad prince insulted her, with astonishing words.

But the actress playing this part had given no indication that she was the least bit impressionable. I have called her abstracted, even standoffish. We now saw her follow the director's bidding with

great care: he wanted her to portray a daughter who obeys her father without question, though he has set her an onerous task indeed. As we know, Polonius wishes to prove to the queen and king that her son, and his stepson, loves Ophelia. Her duty is to provoke Hamlet through her coyness into avowing his feelings for her once again. Meanwhile, the other three are concealed behind one of the tapestries that assume such a central role in the play. As to tapestries, we had none of those on this moor where puddles glistened after a recent rain. Claudius and Gertrude and Polonius simply kept quiet, a little to one side. And then the young prince appears – well, not so young anymore – muttering something or other about life and death, being and nothingness. He breaks up with Ophelia – and yes, he insults her – even if he tells her he had loved her all the same. Then she is supposed to murmur: 'Indeed, my lord, you made me believe so.' After that, Hamlet will reply: 'I loved you not' – though without convincing us. And Ophelia will say: 'I was the more deceived.'

While she managed to say the first words, when she came to the second line an immense flailing coursed through her body. Her throat stopped up, making her words unintelligible, and she was wrenched by sobs. Her arms flew up; they seemed to tear away from her, to float in space for an instant under the sky that had brightened again. Then she collapsed into the mud, prostrate and still trembling. She never looked at her companions, who fell over themselves to help her to her feet; she never even saw them. Was this a repetition of her bizarre outburst the other day? Merely the emotion of an actress, at the most climactic moment of a scene that was undoubtedly intense? No, her dazed eyes were rolling too wildly for that, when they managed to stand her up again, and her head was tossing back and forth. She had been assailed, but by what? By whom? The rehearsal had to be postponed – though could they ever take it up again?

After this there was a similar emotion, mysterious because excessive, which seized one of the actors – that is, the thespians Shakespeare included among the personae of his tragedy. It happened when he was declaiming a fragment from a work in his repertory: the story Aeneas recounts to Dido, already madly in love with him, about the final hours of Troy. Hamlet was listening raptly. The actor headed up a troupe newly arrived at Elsinore, and maybe the prince meant

to propose that on a later evening they should present this play, or poem, which he recalled for its clarity as well as its aplomb. The strange thing was that he knew entire passages of it by heart, and he had begun reciting his favourite, the death of Priam – speaking the verses with a flair all his own, at least in the opinion of Polonius. Even so, he soon broke off and deferred to the professional actor.

We listened along with Polonius, and all was going as well as might be wished: the players struck just the right tone of nonchalance and amusement, lending this conversation between actors and theatre-lovers the naturalness intended by Shakespeare. But when the actor caught up the words left hanging by the prince, he immediately struck me as struggling against an emotion that had pervaded him, a feeling that rapidly mushroomed. He continued his declamation, yet allowed the foolish Polonius to interrupt him; then he took it up again, and came to the death of Hecuba. By now his knees were wobbling, and his voice sounded strangled. This time once more, the author of the play wanted emotion, and he himself was clearly moved. The evocation of Priam overcome by blows, and of Hecuba in her distress, is as gripping as we can imagine. Saying these verses, superb in themselves, is more than enough to make you change colour, and to fill your eyes with tears.

But that scream! It was the howl of a mortally wounded animal – no, even worse. The actor bellowed it out, just as he was recalling the shriek Hecuba herself had flung at the face of the gods on the walls of Troy. That cry welled up from an abyss I cannot conceive within any human being. It engulfed the sob of the old woman, fused with it and shattered it – carried her shriek high into the sky, yet preserved it all the same. Undoubtedly, the shout of this tottering man was inherent to the text; but it was something far more – and something different as well, wholly different. It conveyed a terrible suffering, but also gave proof of an extraordinary sweetness – if I may put it so boldly – in that hoarse, enormous voice. As with Ophelia several days before, I had the impression (we all had the impression) that a power beyond all measure had slipped into a being of slighter size, and had ravaged it – though once again, more in order to identify itself with that lesser being than to destroy it. Besides, the actor soon recovered his spirits. He told us that he had seen, at the instant of his

scream – had seen, simply seen – the face of Hecuba, and her poor hands reaching toward Priam's bloody body. – But just as he was saying that, people shouted behind us. Someone had noticed that the actor playing Hamlet had fainted; he lay a couple of paces from our group, his forehead resting on tufts of grass.

We rather liked this man who played the title role; though his temperament was somewhat reserved, he was always affable and considerate. In this case, he stood up without saying a word, and commenced his work with the director again as soon as he was needed. Even so, it was he who soon afforded us the greatest of our surprises; I will try to recount it, but I know I will never succeed. This time it is night, and the drama devised by Hamlet, about a king murdered by his brother, has just been broken off. The actor portraying the prince must show the joy he has felt at the discomfiture of Claudius, who has also killed his brother. But on the emptied stage, Rosencrantz and Guildenstern now come forward – courtiers who are clearly spies. And Hamlet will mock them, will leave them confounded and abashed, in the well-known scene of the recorders. He has several of those instruments brought forth, and ironically bids Guildenstern to make music with them for him.

And so the actor who is Hamlet picks up one of the flutes; he holds it out, and he displays the holes the fingers need to cover. We watch him, the rest of us, as he prepares to grab a hand that pulls away, and to guide it with a laugh – he had mastered that little laugh – toward the slender wooden pipe, lit by the three or four lamps the director had requested. But suddenly our friend froze in place, as if struck by an unexpected thought.

He looked around him, right and left, in this night that enveloped us all. He looked at us – and with such uncanny eyes. He looked at the recorder: and then and there, he seemed to awaken. He pressed it to his lips and played it, though he had never done so before. And believe it or not, for some time a wondrous music poured forth, which I can only call divine. Like nimble shadows, his fingers danced along the glowing holes. Unbelievable sounds issued from this little object, normally employed for the teaching of birds. The world all around us – the darkness, the wind – stirred in its depths, as if it might disintegrate. This music from somewhere outside it

filled those humble, earthly forms with its violent beauty, both too perfect and too simply human ... Does what I am saying here make sense? I won't try to describe any further what was unsayable from the start. Then, too, perhaps we were dreaming. Maybe all we heard was an air from Shakespeare's time, pleasantly performed. All the same, for quite an interval our friend had mastered an art he knew nothing about. Right afterwards, emerging from his trance, he stared at the recorder, now silent once again. With stupefaction, he could not avoid recalling that it was foreign to him. He glanced at us with dread, then turned his back. As if he were lifting the curtain of the lamps, he headed off into the night, for almost an hour. As to us, we lost ourselves in conjectures: that was the evening we truly began to feel afraid.

And before long our fear turned to horror. The director had summoned us that morning, and the weather was beautiful, absolutely beautiful. As we tried to take up our work again, we spoke softly among ourselves. 'Where is Hamlet?' one of us exclaimed. Almost immediately, we heard a cry – a scream again, but this was the most frightening of all. We jumped to our feet. A hundred steps away from us, a flame rose from the ground straight to the sky; stark red, it was lined with a streak of black, but it had no sooner appeared than it vanished. Will you believe me? We ran over to look: and on the untouched grass, we could not help but recognise his body. Here was the actor chosen to play the role of a prince, supposedly mad. What a misfortune ... His corpse was more than half charred, but his head was still intact. It lay under his right arm. He had folded that arm sharply, since he must have tried to shield himself. From what, we could not grasp. Lightning? Impossible. The sky had been blue since daybreak, intensely blue and serene.

The director closed his actor's eyes, and then we carried the body to one of our vans. We abandoned that domain of grasses and large stones where we had tried to perform Shakespeare's tragedy.

III

Today, after so many years, I am still seeking the cause, or at least the meaning, of the events that thwarted our dream of staging *Hamlet*. Those cries, those tears, that music, those flames – was it merely a long series of chance occurrences? This is what I have always wanted to believe, though I have never succeeded. And as I grow older, I have resigned myself to an explanation which – unfortunately – answers all the questions we have always asked ourselves. Somewhere outside our world, there must be a god who is displeased with his own creation. He had undertaken it with confidence, and also with an idea of what we can well believe was beauty: the proof of this, still today, we find in the mountains here on earth, in the rivers amid their light. But he soon perceived that the beings he was moulding did not live up to his wishes. This is only natural, since what we name a creation, at whatever level it may be, is never anything other than writing – that is, it leaves a place, and possibly the main one, to the unconscious thoughts of him or her who is writing. This god had to admit to himself that there was a whole unknown and unknowable part within him, an unconscious. He had enjoyed designing the zebra's coat, with some amusement; but now he had to recognise, with a deep disquiet, that its meaning escaped him: there was a secret here, to which he would never find the key. And in the laugh of an adolescent girl, as she crossed the street with a boy, the anguish and hope that rose to the surface were equally opaque. God realised that someone within him, whom he did not know, troubled his intentions, darkened his thinking, disconcerted his intelligence. Someone? Perhaps even several wills, each contesting his power. He abandoned his unfinished schemes to the wind of that abyss.

But in his bafflement, it was only natural that he should take an interest in the theatre, where there are creatures, themselves plagued by disquiet, who imagine worlds in their own way – a new heaven, a new earth – and who feel as much as he does, in their ever-unravelling words, the disruptive force of an invisible presence. It was even more natural that he should become attached to *Hamlet*, where it is obvious that the unconscious – that great river, eternal and dark – suddenly overflows the mind from every side. In *Hamlet*, the prince

does not speak: no, his voice stumbles on the obscure thoughts he harbours. He gets a grip on himself, then leaves off again: you might deduce that he has fallen prey to a constraint nothing can ever unbind. Enough to give this sad god the idea that by listening to Shakespeare's work, he might burst through whatever locked doors he hid within himself. At least he might discover whether his failure was as foreordained, for example, as the movements of the stars in their spheres – that music created for nothing.

And so God begins haunting the places where people try to understand *Hamlet*. He observes their reactions to the text, and the hypotheses of actors who must reflect on their work. What emotion will he detect in Hamlet – in the actor taking the role of Hamlet – when this wholly ordinary man insults Ophelia, when he defies Laertes, when he forces Claudius to drink the poison he feels spreading through his own veins? Won't he need to penetrate that being, or others, so he can experience what is at play – such an odd word – from within? In grasping the potential of this, in that realm of the human he had left fallow before, won't he even press it into flower as an outlandish eventuality? That is why God wants to incarnate in several of the actors in turn, even at such and such a moment of their performances, out of the depths of a particular line with which, suddenly, the actor has become as one. With sympathy, with eagerness and hope, God is ready to flood their frail bodies with the energy and fire of his infinite power. Since he has remained walled-in by that power – mysteriously flawed though it may be – it is through them that he seeks to bore his tunnel of escape.

The series of events that beset and finally ruined our rehearsals of *Hamlet*, on that occasion which I have evoked, must reveal that he failed once again. We will never know with what a twilit anguish, with what a sadness, he must have cast his self-gutted gaze on life – in the distance, the clouds on fire, and on the ground, the infinity of stones – when he discovered he couldn't live the emotion that blasted Ophelia; couldn't even grasp the actor's impulse, wrenched by the thought of Hecuba; or why the music born in Hamlet, just as he believes himself free of his iron-clad constraints, was but a smattering of brilliant sparks, dispelled as soon as they formed. What did he feel? That an impediment rises up from the depths of matter, matter

which is his essence, to snatch from his eyes what he seeks in human beings, and which even in them has never managed to bloom. That an imperious constraint, as vast as the night, sends the words back down his throat, just when he assumed he had made a simple human pain into his own.

Is it absurd, my gloss on the strange events I witnessed? Of course: and first of all to my own reason, on which I must rely to discredit such tall tales. But when I write – and shortly after those days in the theatre, I knew that writing was my genuine need, an irrepressible urge woven of pain and of hope – I feel very strongly that an unquiet, jealous gaze weighs me down. I experience with great clarity that someone is there, prowling along the edges of language. I even understand to perfection that the words I am using desire more than what they express ... What a sensation steals over me at times! I stand up, I look around: nobody there. But all the same, I have to go out. In haste, I have to walk along the mountain path near the house where I've always lived. Here, at least, I am alone. At various distances, under the sky, huts of dry stone. Sometimes it's spring, and small flowers poke through the last patches of snow.

Walking on, I pick up one of the stones that are common in this region: grey, usually round and fairly flat, they are coloured here and there by tiny mosses. Stone, I look at you for quite a while. Under your lovely hues, I notice delicate, interlaced nicks that might be taken for signs. I try not to doubt what I know must be true: that these are not signs at all. And that it is better for us, stone of this world, to love you only for your gift of joining with others – which permits you for a time, now and then, to hold up an arch.

THE DIGAMMA

In the middle of the night, he told her excitedly about the digamma: no sooner had he learned of its existence – at thirteen, from his first professor of Greek, as the drum was already rolling for the ten o'clock recess – than he knew he was getting at the truth. In the first era of the alphabet that evolved into ours, there had been an additional letter; and the role of that letter must have been an enigma even

before its disappearance. This explained everything!

Ever since that day he had dreamed a great deal, he told her. The low, maternal, slightly muffled voice, faltering at times, which accompanied him in his sorrows and his joys, had taught him more and more clearly how he should frame the great problem, perhaps the only one. Yes, she murmured, the words of those early times, letter by letter, sound by sound, matched all the aspects of things. The earth, since language was unconstrained, without a pleat of its fabric out of place along her enormous body, was as naked then as those Korai would later be under their see-through tunics of bright marble. She could take us in her arms, and we dwelled within the truth. When we spoke, it was as if what we said were alive – holding us close, and with its warmth on our lips. When we tried to clarify an idea, with that added rigor – yet how easy-going – known as poetry, it was as if we walked amid the trickling of springs and the warbling of birds, our eyes open wide.

But one day, who knows why, we began to pronounce a certain letter badly – the digamma – and because of this, the simple reality of the world was veiled. Little by little, the correspondence between words and things came to an end. The desires that united verbal beings with each other fell out of tune. There was discord in the city, which up till then had been like music. And what we have named history began, that swollen flood on an earth which it was tearing from the shore ... Our disaster is the result of a faulty pronunciation. Can we introduce the digamma into our languages once again? Regrettably, first we would have to mend our minds, awaken our hearts.

– Our hearts?

– Maybe not ... And you're going to tell me that if another of the letters had vanished, not the digamma, the effect on being in the world would have been pretty much the same, with a similar rupture in the harmony of speech at its source. But that isn't what I believe, my friend. Have you ever seen the digamma's shape? A lumberman's axe. It rang in the remotest forests on the mountainsides of Thrace. The old woman squatting before her fire would pick it up to chop her kindling wood. At the same time, it was what broke things apart and gathered them together.

That's a lovely myth, she said. She turned toward him, in the half-light of a summer night. Through the open window near the bed, she can see the trees in the garden: two almond-trees, their leaves ruffled by a faint breeze. And the blue summits of low hills, a little further away.

A myth! he exclaims. Not at all. What do you think I'm doing here? I'm studying. You know that I'm a philologist. I've read Vendryès, Dupont-Sommer: they and all the others attest to the existence of the digamma. I'm told that in dialects which survive even today, on the mountains of Lucania, the digamma can still be heard. Meanwhile, all around, the age-old goats lurch down the slopes, nibbling at the leaves along the tree-trunks. Sometimes the herdsmen carry a reed-pipe they play, and their modest music fills the entire sky. I have a whole dossier of closely-written notes; I could fill up a book with them.

Nonetheless, he explains, he won't do this, since in his arguments he always comes across a sort of knot he can't untie. As if the disappearance of the digamma had also affected logic. Still, how tempted he is to set off to those disastrously forgotten regions of Southern Italy or Central Anatolia ...

– Among the goats, all alone? Let's go to sleep, she says. Or maybe not, since I feel as if I'm also having a dream.

She has sat up, and her voice has changed. Listen, listen! I was as beautiful then as I am today but – how can I tell you? – I was larger. Maybe I had the same eyes, but – will you understand? – they were wider open. I looked straight ahead of me. I was wearing a blue dress with a stole on top, of a colour that wavered between yellow and red. My sandals were so light that I went almost barefoot ... And what was that country where I walked down the paths, for longer than I could remember? Perhaps it was the one you are telling me about ... As it happens, I wasn't the only one who wandered like this, between earth and sky. Was he a shepherd, with his big staff in hand, the man who walked beside me? I could readily believe it, since a few steps further on we arrived at that tomb and its famous inscription. Two other young men were already there, and one of them had dropped to the ground on one knee. Leaning close, touching the stone with a finger, he was searching for a letter in one of the words.

And you as well, you who accompanied me, you lean close in turn. You want to show me that letter, but you haven't recognised it there. This bewilders you very much, and you look back at me when I place my hand on your shoulder. Oh yes, my friend, I see that question in your eyes, and I realise you know the answer. It's not a letter that's missing in the word, it's a word that's missing in the sentence, a certain word. And this word is a verb, a verb that must be read in the present tense, and – as you are well aware – in the first person. The verb that the painter, two of whose figures we are, wanted to be known as the crux of the world, but also as what always withdraws from the world.

She laughs. Her voice has already lost the solemnity that had gripped it for a moment. While speaking, she had almost sat on the edge of the bed, one leg dangling as her foot sought the coolness of the flagstones on the floor. But now she falls back again on the pillows; she stretches out and relaxes, a sensible and tender sister. Her eyes fill with the flickering reflections, coming from who knows where, on the low ceiling of the room.

And the water rises from every side. Those were not flagstones, cool or cold: this is the first flood-tide of the river, broad and eternal. Do not ask me my name, she cries, already so far away. Is it a letter that went missing in the alphabet? Is it a word that in language does not exist? Isn't it simply a name, just a name that you urgently need to say? Hold on to me, hold me with all your might. Don't let go of my hand. Other forces are pulling it away. Maybe this will be enough, even though the river is immense – is roaring and dark. It overwhelms me, it carries me away. But our room is narrow: here next to us is the credenza, the mirror. All is peaceful, and sleep steals over us. That isn't the lark we hear, is it my friend? Isn't that the nightingale?

THE DIGAMMA: A FINAL NOTE

The digamma's disappearance from the alphabet of the Greek language was probably not what one of my characters imagines – the cause of a later disjunction between things and the intellect in the

societies of the Western world. But when he learnt that the letter had vanished, adolescent that he was, it may well have caught his attention, since it leads us to think of other eclipses – for example, that of our knowledge of finitude, within the networks of conceptual meanings. A kind of defective pleat then arises between existence and its verbal clothing, a fold beneath speech that never stops shifting, without being reabsorbed into words. Owing to this, words will always be a fiction, despite the efforts – though in fact they are dreams – of what our own era has designated as writing: which bears witness, after all, to our need for poetry.

THE GREAT VOICE

I was in the land of Shakespeare, staying at the house of a friend – a professor, a poet. On Sunday morning, I found out he would be attending a church service, as he did each week; and I told him – without really thinking so – that I would enjoy going with him. The stark modesty of the chapel of grey stone seemed well suited to preserving a faith that is now rather shaky, perhaps; to an unbeliever, its plainness was appealing as well. We seated ourselves in the large room: it was still almost empty, though it quickly filled up behind us. These new arrivals inhabited the few houses nearby, a village not far from the university where my friend was teaching. Presently the celebrant appeared, and gave a sermon I considered boring. In the meantime, my eyes wandered over the sculptures on the walls and on the capitals, as a ray of winter sun slowly inched along them. At a certain point, the pastor stopped speaking, and the congregation began to sing. A simple tune carried by naïve voices, exactly as intended by the black, dog-eared books I had noticed, scattered along the pews, when we had chosen our seats. A music to make us consent to the insignificance of our lives – possibly with a remnant of expectation, or of childhood, in the unison that it required.

The singing had already lasted a minute or two when out of the blue, an unheralded voice arose: it soared gloriously through the light and shade of the chapel, taking possession of the hymn. A woman's voice, young and profound. A contralto voice, but of a range that

surpassed its tessitura, and with surges in volume that never distorted its timbre in the least: on the contrary, they deepened it, embellished it, transfigured it. Might I even dare to say they rendered it more human? Though isn't it true that the human, in ordinary circumstances, always falls short of its huge potential? The voice moved through the hymn with perfect ease, at once relaxed and intensely serious. It lifted the singing of the others on its wings with a gracious welcome, as well as with indifference, since it was entirely at the summit of itself, in that sphere of the spirit where the essence of the feminine could flower at long last ... Was I dreaming? Yes, no doubt; I made an effort to wake up, and succeeded, more or less. All the same, the voice there behind me, gliding above everything, was unusual and disconcerting. Once the observance came to an end, we rose from our seats amid the hubbub of footsteps and pews. People were already leaving the room when I saw a young woman cross the porch, pushing the wheelchair of an invalid.

'Who in the world are they?' I asked my friend, and he explained that the woman walking away from us, and the man she helped to go on living, were husband and wife. Though not so old, he had fallen victim to a sudden illness. She was a singer: to take care of him, she had abandoned a career that promised to be as exceptional as her voice – her great voice. The two of them kept to themselves, in a cottage set apart somewhat from the village; it may have been the childhood home of one of them. The only visitor they received was the doctor, people said. Of course, she didn't sing anymore, except at the Sunday service. That was all my friend knew. While he spoke, I watched the singer and the invalid, fairly far away from us by now: haltingly, they followed a path that climbed a bit. At times, to negotiate an uneven patch of ground, she had to shove the back of the wheelchair with both hands.

Several years have gone by since that morning, but I have never forgotten that hymn, that voice, and the young woman returning with her stricken husband – in silence, most likely – to their secluded house. There she grows old, and her voice may be declining. I tell myself that life has treated her unfairly; I feel the wrong she has suffered should be set right somehow, at least in part. And could I do something to that end? Her voice sang for no one in a church: could

I help make it known at any rate, if not heard, as a kind of testimonial? But how should I go about it? Writing is what I know how to do: my only resource is telling tales, and all in vain … When we write we stay locked inside ourselves, prey to the past that is ours, and to desires we cannot fathom. We have no inkling of others, except for the signs they may lend to this shadow of speech: we do not give, we take. Through words, I have tried in various ways to grant life to a remembrance that has never ceased to haunt me; but I have always done so by imagining, more or less, by devoting myself to fiction. And yet, as I could not forget, the singer had withdrawn from such a life: by being heard and acclaimed, she would have become a fiction for others, and probably for herself.

And I can say, as I do at present, that I reject such literature; however, even as I write that, I am still the one who is expressing himself. All the same, a thought has come to me: that is why today I have decided to evoke that morning from the past. A thought – the imagination once again, but with something added: that it will not mask the contradiction I have just pointed out. There may have been – 'once upon a time', as tales used to put it – a young man. Very young, let's say. That winter morning, he entered the chapel through its low-ceilinged porch, and found himself caught up in an observance. Behind him he heard that voice, both imaginary and real: redolent – to phrase it differently – of more than this base, always self-centred realm of words. But unlike me, he would have lingered in the village; he would even have lived there for days, going to loiter at times near the silent, thatch-roofed cottage. In front of it were clear hints of an ordinary existence: a car, two steps away; sometimes a basket on the threshold, with items inside; even a watering can, since small flowers had already sprung up along the wall; and also – so he notices – a plume of smoke above the chimney built of bricks.

A life. But the door and the windows are closed. Without a trill to break the silence unexpectedly, only to leave it stranger than before. The young man – but he may be an adolescent, or even a child, abashed as we are at that age by any kind of sheer amazement – clearly would not dare to knock at this front door that so enthrals him. Still, he constantly returns to the edge of the garden in front of the house. He even ventures into it one day, approaching the

threshold closer and closer.

And suddenly, he doesn't know how, here is the singer right before him, just a few paces away; watering-can in hand, she looks at him in astonishment. Up till now, he's only seen her from afar, with her back to him. Whom does she resemble? That is his question, right away. Is she beautiful? He couldn't say. What strikes him about these eyes that fix their gaze on him, these eyes of a faded blue, is that he has surely seen them before; and that they recognise him, too: something in his entire body tells him so. She looks at him. 'Who are you?' she asks. She may have felt a tremor of fear, but she has quickly recovered.

He doesn't know what to reply: those eyes, and their light, are dissolving the garden and the house; dissolving the figure who stands before him, in her quaint dress from another age, and even the face itself. 'Who are you?' Yes, who is he? And does he even exist? It's all too much for him. This is what takes hold of his inmost mind, his inmost anxiety, and expands them, flattens them, disperses them in the growing light. 'Who am I?' He knows very well he couldn't answer. It's as if he were waking up, as if his own eyes were flooded by dawn.

What is a voice when it has turned into song? When it rises above the others without relegating them to ordinary music, no matter how naïve and humble they may be? What is a fiction that seeks to mesh with the immaterial whorls of this balcony between earth and sky?

From *Poèmes pour Truphémus* (2013)

UN CAFÉ

Cet homme et cette femme,
Leur long silence inquiète la lumière,
Elle vient sur leurs mains, qui sont immobiles.
Peintre, anime leurs doigts
D'un peu de couleur claire. Que ce soit
Comme un reste de jour dans la nuit qui tombe.

Et l'une, alors,
Bougera, frémira. La table est d'angle,
Juste sous le vitrage à travers quoi
Sont visibles les hâtes du ciel du soir.

Des vitres? Non, un prisme. Et son rayon
Qui cherche, dans la pénombre de la salle.
Ici, rien que le monde. Là, dehors,
L'espérance qui rentre, avec fatigue,
De sa longue journée n'importe où en ville.

Ah, mes amis,
Passez, c'est tout un fleuve. Comment apprendre
À vivre, c'est-à-dire à mourir? Peu de temps
Pour cela quand déjà le café ferme.

Tant de malentendus! Mais sur la toile
Qui semble inachevée, ces verres vides
Mais à briller, un peu. C'est peut-être l'anneau
Unique de deux vies qui se confondent.

From *Poems for Truphémus* (2013)

A CAFÉ

This man and this woman …
Their long silence troubles the light:
It touches their motionless hands.
Painter, make their fingers come alive
With a bit of soft colour. Let it be
Like a remnant of day in the falling night.

And then, one of these hands
Will move, will quiver. The table stands in the corner,
Just below the window, where we see
The evening sky that hurries by.

Panes of glass? No, a prism. And its beam
Keeps searching, in the penumbra of the room.
Here, nothing but the world; there, outside,
Hope that returns, weary from its long
Day in the city, who knows where.

Ah, my friends,
Pass on: it's a river by now. How do we learn
To live – that is, to die? Not much time left
For that, when the café is about to close.

So many misunderstandings! But on the canvas
That seems unfinished, these empty glasses
Shine a little, even so. Perhaps it's the single
Ring of two lives that merge into one.

LES TABLEAUX

Mais oui, c'est vous, couleurs, c'est toi, lumière,
Vous êtes là quand il ouvre les yeux
Avant le jour. Vous étiez à veiller
Près de lui dans la nuit toute la nuit

Et remuiez vos mains dans cette eau, le rêve,
Ce qui était des ondes, qui étendaient
Les cercles d'un secret que vous, ses proches,
Vous pressentiez en lui et faisiez vôtre.

La terre n'est que le surcroît du rêve,
Un vêtement qui bouge sur le corps
De celle qui a beau périr jamais ne cesse.

Mystérieux ces plis. Ce qu'ils étaient,
C'est le soleil du soir derrière ses arbres,
C'est l'amande de l'invisible, qui s'ouvrait.

D'AUTRES TABLEAUX

Une dernière fois la chambre, le jardin.
Un peu de jour s'est glissé dans l'alcôve.
La couleur, ce courage des survivants,
Peut-elle ranimer ce qui n'est plus?

Ailleurs, dans des tableaux qui n'existent pas,
Un arbre croît au centre de deux corps
Que le peintre a voulus presque confondus.
Un arbre, non, plusieurs, toute une terre,

Et en eux ces couleurs: qui nous enseignent
Que la vie ne sait rien des mondes périssables.
Qu'elle plane au-dessus, qu'elle protège
Tout ce que nous aimons et qui nous aime.

THE PAINTINGS

Oh yes: it's you, colours; it's you, light.
You're there when he opens his eyes, before
Day breaks. Near him, you have kept watch
In the night, and throughout the night.

And with your hands you stirred this water,
Dream, forming waves that rippled outward:
The circles of a secret that you, his dear ones,
Sensed in him and made yours.

Earth is but the overflow of dream,
A garment that moves along the body
Of one who may perish, but never ends.

Mysterious, these folds. What they were
Is the evening sun behind the trees – is,
As it opened, the almond of the unseen.

OTHER PAINTINGS

For a final time, the room, the garden.
Into the alcove, a bit of light has slipped.
Can colour, this courage of survivors,
Grant new life to that which is no more?

Elsewhere, in paintings that don't exist,
A tree grows at the centre of two bodies
The painter wanted almost interfused.
A tree – no, several, an entire earth –

And in them, these colours: which teach us
That life knows nothing of perishable worlds.
That it hovers above, that it protects
Everything we love, and that loves us.

Bleu, dit le rouge sombre, viens près de moi.
Enlaçons-nous pour imiter la vie.
Non, pour qu'elle renaisse de nos cendres,
Et que lumière soit, fille de nous.

Blue, says dark red, come here, next to me.
Let us intertwine, so we imitate life.
No, so it rises, reborn from our ashes:
And let there be our daughter, the light.

Notes on the Contributors

GALWAY KINNELL (1927–2014) was a prominent and much admired American poet. He won the Pulitzer Prize for Poetry in 1982 for his *Selected Poems*. In 1968 he published *On the Motion and Immobility of Douve*, the first translation of a complete book by Yves Bonnefoy. Four of these translations are included in the present volume. Major influences on Kinnell were Yeats, Rilke and Walt Whitman. He taught creative writing for many years at New York University. Kinnell's updated *Selected Poems* and the Bonnefoy translation are available from Bloodaxe.

HOYT ROGERS has published a collection of verse, *Witnesses*, and a literary study, *The Poetics of Inconstancy*. His poems, stories, and essays have appeared in many periodicals. He translates from the French, German, Italian, and Spanish. His numerous translations include the *Selected Poems of Borges* and three books by Yves Bonnefoy: *The Curved Planks*, *Second Simplicity*, and *The Digamma*. With Paul Auster he published *Openwork*, an André du Bouchet reader, at Yale University Press (Margellos). He is now translating Bonnefoy's *Rome 1630* and his final poetry collection, *Together Still*, for Seagull Books. He lives in the Dominican Republic and Italy.

EMILY GROSHOLZ was born near Philadelphia and attended the University of Chicago and Yale University. Since 1979 she has taught philosophy at Pennsylvania State University, where she is Edwin Erle Sparks Professor. Her first book of poetry, *The River Painter*, appeared in 1984; *The Stars of Earth: New and Selected Poems*, forthcoming in 2017, will be her eighth. In 2012, Bucknell University Press published her translation from the French of Yves Bonnefoy's *Beginning and End of the Snow*. Many of her earlier translations of his poems appeared in the *Hudson Review*; she has translated his work for over forty years.

BEVERLEY BIE BRAHIC is a Canadian poet and translator who lives in Paris and the San Francisco Bay Area. Her translations include *The Little Auto* by Guillaume Apollinaire, which won the 2013 Scott

Moncrieff Prize; *Unfinished Ode to Mud* by Francis Ponge; books by Jacques Derrida, Julia Kristeva and Hélène Cixous; and several books by Yves Bonnefoy in the Seagull Books Bonnefoy project. Her second poetry collection, *White Sheets*, was a finalist for the 2012 Forward Prize. Her most recent poetry collection, *Hunting the Boar*, is a 2016 Poetry Book Society Recommendation.

RICHARD PEVEAR was born in Boston, grew up on Long Island, attended Allegheny College (BA 1964) and the University of Virginia (MA 1965). After a stint as a college teacher, he moved to the Maine coast and eventually to New York City, where he worked as a freelance writer, editor, and translator, and also as a cabinetmaker. He has published two collections of poetry, many essays and reviews, and some thirty books translated from French, Italian, and Russian.

SUSANNA LANG's most recent collection of poems, *Travel Notes from the River Styx*, is forthcoming from Terrapin Books. Her last collection was *Tracing the Lines* (Brick Road Poetry Press, 2013). A two-time Hambidge Fellow, her poems have appeared in journals including *Little Star*, *Prairie Schooner*, *december*, *Prime Number Magazine* and *Poetry East*. Her translations of poetry by Yves Bonnefoy include *Words in Stone* and *The Origin of Language*. Among her current projects is *Self-Portraits*, a chapbook collection of ekphrastic poems focused on women across the arts. She lives in Chicago, and teaches in the Chicago Public Schools.

Index of Titles

French titles are shown in *italic*. Initials refer to translators.
AR: Anthony Rudolf. BBB: Beverly Bie Brahic. EG: Emily Grosholz.
GK: Galway Kinnell. HR: Hoyt Rogers. JN: John Naughton.
RP: Richard Pevear. SL: Susannah Lang. SR: Stephen Romer.

À la voix de Kathleen Ferrier	AR	34
L'abeille, la couleur	SL	54
L'adieu	JN	154
L'agitation du rêve	JN	172
'Ainsi marcherons-nous'	AR	22
Ales Stenar	HR	234
Ales Stenar	HR	235
All Night	AR	35
L'arbre, la lampe	EG	50
L'Arrière-pays	SR	63
The Arrière-pays	SR	63
The Artist of the Last Day	SR	136
L'Artiste du Dernier Jour	SR	136
'Aube, fille des larmes, rétablis'	AR	36
Aux arbres	GK	20
La beauté	AR	32
The Beautiful Summer	AR	29
Beauty	AR	33
Beckett's Dinghy	HR	192
The Bedroom	EG	49
The Bee, the Colour	SL	55
Le bel été	AR	28
Blood, the Note B	RP	53
The Book, for Growing Old	EG	59
Brancacci Chapel	GK	23
Un café	HR	292
A Café	HR	293
Le canot de Samuel Beckett	HR	192
La chambre	EG	48
Chapelle Brancacci	GK	22
A Childhood Memory of Wordsworth's	HR	245

The Convex Mirror	JN	159
The Curved Planks	AR	209
D'autres tableaux	HR	294
Dans le leurre du seuil	RP	78
'Dawn, daughter of tears, restore'	AR	37
De vent et de fumée	JN	196
La Décision d'être Peintre	SR	135
The Decision to be a Painter	SR	135
Les Découvertes de Prague	BBB	120
Dedham, Seen from Langham	JN	167
Dedham, vu de Langham	JN	166
Delphes du second jour	AR	38
Delphi, the Second Day	AR	39
Deux barques	RP	98
Dévotion	AR	40
Devotions	AR	41
The Digamma	HR	284
The Digamma: A Final Note	HR	287
The Edge of the Woods	JN	165
Egypt	BBB	116
L'Égypte	BBB	116
L'épars, l'indivisible	JN	106
L'épaule	RP	50
The Farewell	JN	155
First Draft for a Production of *Hamlet*	BBB	249
Le fleuve	RP	72
God in *Hamlet*	HR	276
Goya: Les Peintures noires	SR	230
Goya: The Black Paintings	SR	230
The Great Voice	HR	288
Les guetteurs	AR	30
Hamlet en Montagne	BBB	251
Hamlet in the Mountains	BBB	251
Here, Forever Here	AR	39
L'Heure présente	BBB	254

Hopkins Forest	JN	182
Hopkins Forest	JN	183
The House where I was Born	HR	213
Ici, toujours ici	AR	38
L'imperfection est la cime	AR	34
Imperfection Is the Summit	AR	35
Iron Bridge	AR	31
The Lamp, the Sleeper	RP	43
La lampe, le dormeur	RP	42
Leopardi's Tomb	HR	241
Lieu de la salamandre	GK	24
Lieu du combat	GK	22
The Light, Changed	JN	57
Le livre, pour vieillir	EG	58
La lumière, changée	JN	56
The Lure of the Threshold	RP	79
Mahler, Le Chant de la terre	HR	240
Mahler, *The Song of the Earth*	HR	241
La maison natale	HR	212
The Memory	JN	147
Le miroir courbe	JN	158
*Une mise en scène d'*Hamlet	BBB	249
Le myrte	EG	52
Myrtle	EG	53
'Often in the silence of a ravine'	AR	29
On Some Large Stone Circles	BBB	142
On the Wings of Song	BBB	139
On Three Paintings by Poussin	BBB	243
The Only Rose	JN	187
L'orée du bois	JN	164
The Origin of Utterance	SR	135
L'Origine de la Parole	SR	135
Other Paintings	HR	295
The Paintings	HR	295
Passant auprès du feu	JN	160

Passing by the Fire	JN	161
Une pierre ('A fire goes before us')	RP	54
Une pierre ('Childhood was long by the grim wall …')	RP	48
Une pierre ('Fall but softly rain upon this face')	AR	48
Une pierre ('For two or three years')	RP	46
Une pierre ('He desired')	RP	44
Une pierre ('I was quite beautiful')	RP	44
Une pierre ('We used to cross these fields')	SL	56
Une pierre ('Your leg, deepest night')	RP	46
Place of Battle	GK	23
Place of the Salamander	GK	25
Les Planches courbes	AR	209
Le pont de fer	AR	30
The Prague Discoveries	BBB	120
The Present Hour	BBB	255
Le puits	JN	162
The Restlessness of the Dream	JN	173
The River	RP	73
Rue Traversière	BBB	129
Le sang, la note si	RP	52
The Scattered, the Indivisible	JN	107
Second Rue Traversière	BBB	130
La seule rose	JN	186
The Shoulder	RP	51
'So we will walk among the ruins'	AR	23
Le souvenir	JN	146
Un souvenir d'enfance de Wordsworth	HR	244
'Souvent, dans le silence d'un ravin'	AR	28
A Stone ('A fire goes before us')	RP	55
A Stone ('Childhood was long by the grim wall …')	RP	49
A Stone ('Fall but softly rain upon this face')	AR	49
A Stone ('For two or three years')	RP	47
A Stone ('He desired')	RP	45
A Stone ('I was quite beautiful')	RP	45
A Stone ('We used to cross these fields')	SL	57
A Stone ('Your leg, deepest night')	RP	47
Sur de Grands Cercles de Pierre	BBB	142
Sur les Ailes de la Musique	BBB	139

Index of Titles

Sur trois tableaux de Poussin	BBB	242
Les tableaux	HR	294
Theatre	AR	9
Théâtre	AR	8
To the Trees	GK	21
To the Voice of Kathleen Ferrier	AR	35
Tomb of Stéphane Mallarmé	BBB	243
Le tombeau de Giacomo Leopardi	HR	240
Le tombeau de Stéphane Mallarmé	BBB	242
Les Tombeaux de Ravenne	JN	3
The Tombs of Ravenna	JN	3
Toute la nuit	AR	34
The Tree, the Lamp	EG	51
Two Boats	RP	99
The Watchers	AR	31
The Well	JN	163
Wind and Smoke	JN	197

Index of First Lines

French first lines are shown in *italic*.

A fire goes before us	55
Again, I look up and my eyes fall	142
Ainsi marcherons-nous sur les ruines d'un ciel immense	22
All night the beast has moved about the room	35
All softness and irony assembled	35
As faithfully as possible, the moments	120
As in the *Prelude*, when the child sets forth	245
Aube, fille des larmes, rétablis	36
But let us pause where that event	230
But no, once again	73
Candle of the January night on the flagstones	23
Ce souvenir me hante, que le vent tourne	146
Celle qui ruine l'être, la beauté	32
Cet homme et cette femme	292
Childhood was long by the grim wall and I was	49
Cinq heures	54
Comme, dans le Prélude, *cet enfant*	244
Dans ce rêve le fleuve encore: c'est l'amont	172
Dans le nid de Phénix combien se sont	240
Dawn, daughter of tears, restore	37
Dedham, seen from Langham. The summer is sombre	167
Dedham, vu de Langham. L'été est sombre	166
Deux ans, ou trois	46
Elle sort, mais la nuit n'est pas tombée	240
Étoiles transhumantes; et le berger	58
Fall but softly rain upon this face	49
Fire haunted our days and completed them	29
Five o'clock	55
For a final time, the room, the garden	295
For two or three years	47

Index of First Lines

He desired without knowing	45
He spoke. But the words he used	135
He would probably have said that the radio	139
Here the knight of mourning is defeated	23
Here the unquiet voice agrees to love	39
Here, in the bright place. It is no longer dawn	39
Heurte	78
His tomb, you ask? But it's this space	243
I am haunted by this memory, that the wind	147
I did not know how to sleep without you	43
I had gone out	183
I have often experienced a feeling of anxiety	63
I saw you run along the terraces	9
I was in the land of Shakespeare, staying	288
I was quite beautiful	45
I woke: the house where I was born	213
Ici l'inquiète voix consent d'aimer	38
Ici, dans le lieu clair. Ce n'est plus l'aube	38
Il désirait, sans connaître	44
Il neige, c'est revenir dans une ville	186
Il y a sans doute toujours au bout d'une longue rue	30
Il y avait qu'il fallait détruire et détruire et détruire	34
Il y avait un couloir au fond du jardin	30
In the empty room, with its shutters closed	161
In the middle of the night, he told her	284
In this dream, the river again: upstream now	173
It's snowing, it's returning to a town	187
J'étais sorti	182
Je fus assez belle	44
Je m'éveillai, c'était la maison natale	212
Je ne savais dormir sans toi, je n'osais pas	42
Je passais près du feu dans la salle vide	160
Je te voyais courir sur des terrasses	8
Knock	79
L'arbre vieillit dans l'arbre, c'est l'été	50
L'Idée, a-t-on pensé, est la mesure de tout	196

L'orage qui s'attarde, le lit défait	98
La salamandre surprise s'immobilise	24
Le feu hantait nos jours et les accomplissait	28
Le miroir et le fleuve en crue, ce matin	48
Let his sail be his tomb, since no	243
Let your shoulder be the dawn, for it has borne	51
Long, long days	53
Longtemps dura l'enfance au mur sombre et je fus	48
Longues, longues journées	52
Look at them down there, at that crossroads	159
Look! A flash	255
Mais non, toujours	72
Mais oui, c'est vous, couleurs, c'est toi, lumière	294
No doubt there is still at the far end of a long street	31
Nous ne nous voyons plus dans la même lumière	56
Nous prenions par ces prés	56
Nous sommes revenus à notre origine	154
Often in the silence of a ravine	29
Oh yes: it's you, colours; it's you, light	295
On dit	234
Oui, par ce lieu	106
Parfois je te savais la terre, je buvais	52
Regarde-les là-bas, à ce carrefour	158
Regarde!	254
'Rue Traversière', someone says to me	130
Sa tombe, me dit-on? Mais c'est ce creux	242
Sa voile soit sa tombe, puisque il n'y eut	242
She comes out; but night hasn't fallen yet	241
So many fingers have been singed	241
So we will walk among the ruins of a boundless sky	23
Sometimes I knew you as the earth, I drank	53
Souvent dans le silence d'un ravin	28
Stars moving from their summertime	59
Ta jambe, nuit très dense	46

The concept, which is our unique way of philosophising	3
The digamma's disappearance from the alphabet	287
The idea, it was thought, is the measure of everything	197
The island isn't far from the coast	192
The light was so intense!	135
The man standing on the bank, near the boat	209
The mirror and the river in flood, this morning	49
The one who ruins being – beauty –	33
The production's only desire, they said	249
The rehearsals had started fairly well	276
The startled salamander freezes	25
The storm lingering, the unmade bed	99
The tree grows older in the tree, it's summer	51
The world was going to end. Yes	136
There was a passage at the far end of the garden	31
There was this	35
There were a lot of us on that ship	116
They announced that *Hamlet* was being staged	251
They say	235
This man and this woman	293
To nettles and stones	40
Tombe, mais douce pluie, sur le visage	48
Ton épaule soit l'aube, ayant porté	50
Toute douceur toute ironie se rassemblaient	34
Toute la nuit la bête a bougé dans la salle	34
Tu écoutes la chaîne heurter la paroi	162
Tu me dis que tu aimes le mot ronce	164
Un feu va devant nous	54
Une dernière fois la chambre, le jardin	294
Veilleuse de la nuit de janvier sur les dalles	22
Voici défait le chevalier de deuil	22
Vous qui vous êtes effacés sur son passage	20
We have come back to our origin	155
We no longer see each other in the same light	57
We used to cross these fields	57
When I was a child I fretted a good deal	129

Yes, by this place	107
You hear the chain striking the wall	163
You tell me you love the word *thorn*	165
You who stepped aside as she passed	21
Your leg, deepest night	47

Ruth Manning

Oliver's Branch

Black Bay Publishing 2015

Copyright © Ruth F. Manning 2015

Ruth F. Manning has asserted their right under the Copyright, Designs and Patents Act, 1988, to be identified as the author of this work.

This book is a work of fiction and no resemblance between the characters and actual persons, living or dead, is inferred. Any such resemblance is purely coincidental.

First published in Great Britain in 2015 by Black Bay Publishing

www.blackbaypublishing.com

Printed by Createspace Group in the UK and the USA

Oliver's Branch
By
Ruth F. Manning

Oliver's Branch

To Hannah ~ You're a woman now...
March 2010

Ruth Manning

Oliver's Branch

Acknowledgements

Oliver's Branch was conceived one wet and windy, wine inspired evening in England. The initial plan was to write a humorous novel about a couple moving to Crete, embracing 'The Good Life' by living off the land and also bringing up their young son in a totally different culture. Somehow it took on a whole life of its own. Thank you first and foremost to my partner Paul Ferguson, who was with me every step of the way. He was my sounding board and my most honest critic throughout the whole journey.

We came to live in Crete in 2008. By 2009 Oliver's Branch was finished, then put on a shelf, where it gathered dust, for the ensuing 5 years. It was a very private and often insular journey. Unlike so many completed works, with acknowledgements to an abundance of professional people and friends, there are very few people who were involved in the writing process of this novel. Maybe one day I will have many more people to thank for their input, but not this time.

Following a chance meeting with a retired proof reader about a year ago, the book was dusted off and passed on to him. It arrived back covered in red corrections. I was amazed at the amount of errors I managed to make. So thank you Eric for all your help and putting me back on the right path. Without your help I would never have got this far.

Thank you too Ian Yates, who has travelled down the path of self publishing with three novels to his name. You gave me the confidence, the encouragement and the help I needed. Without your support I would have given up and these words would just be dust in the wind.

I would like to mention friends and family who may read this and relate to characters and personalities on these pages. The story is a work of fiction, but people you know and love always leave their mark. So thank you all for providing me with the invisible threads of humour,satire,insight and love, which I have woven into the core of this story. Thank you for bringing life and heart to every page.

All errors and mistakes in this book are totally my own and I apologise.

Ruth F Manning

Crete – January 2015

Part 1
England

Ruth Manning

"Look backwards with gratitude"

One.

Looking through the window at a crisp late spring morning Jill rested her hands in the small of her back and put pressure on the now constant nagging pain there. How had things gone so wrong, when everything had been going so right? She was used to routine, work, and looking after her two children and somehow all of these things had disappeared. In their place was an eight-and-a-half-month-old 'bump', kicking and turning and giving her this constant back ache. She appreciated more by the day the life she had once had, but it was too late now to change the inevitable roller-coaster ride which was sweeping her along.

When did the total change and upheaval begin? Was it on the day she had taken her daughter to university with Jason and returned, almost a day later to an 'empty nest' where every room seemed to echo with memories of the last 22 years? Possibly - she'd think about this more at a later date.

The ring of the doorbell brought her back to the bleak present and wiping her hands on a now under-used tea-towel she went to answer it.

"You are getting slow in your old age." Jill's best friend Astrid was standing on the step. A tall, elegant woman she was everything Jill was not. Chic, confident and buzzing with joie de vie.
"Hi! What brings you here? I thought you had so much work to do I wasn't going to see you for another 5 years."
Astrid brushed past leaving her high heels on the mat and her coat over the banister.
"You know me. I'll do anything for a cup of tea and some chocolate! Anyway I wanted to see how things were and if there was the remotest chance of finding you back to your once bright, sociable and optimistic self."

Jill followed her, shuffling in the pink booty-slippers Jason had given her last Christmas as a joke (she hated pink!) They were a size

too big and if she tried to lift a foot off the floor a slipper would fall off, but Jill felt it was more than this which led to her almost elderly, rounded-backed gait. Was it really only last Christmas she had unwrapped the gift and laughed? It felt so much longer. Life was pressing heavily upon her and within her. Like Atlas she was stooped under the weight of the worries, concerns and changes she knew were only weeks away.

"Anyway I wanted to bring you this for the imminent arrival." Astrid dropped a small parcel on the sideboard, close to where Jill was filling the kettle. She noted the changes which had taken place in her friend's demeanour and made a silent promise to keep an eye on her far more closely. After all, Jill had been the big success career story, now it was her turn, but she wouldn't abandon her friend and mentor. If she hadn't had Jill as a teacher she would never be where she was today. Bless. Jill didn't look up from her task, as Astrid guiltily hid her thoughts away.

"You know I said that I don't want anything for this baby but thanks anyway. I'll make sure he gets it."

Astrid sat down and crossed her long elegant legs. Jill looked out of the window at the luxuriant garden of her next-door neighbour. Never having been very green-fingered she wasn't at all sure she understood the appeal of bending over doing whatever it was June did out there all day. Whatever it was though it worked. The garden had the air of an English country garden but with the sea as a backdrop. Myriads of flowers were in bloom and birds frequented her always copiously loaded bird table. Soon Jill too would have to start tending a garden, a very different type of garden but a place where plants and trees and weeds vied for equal attention. She pushed the thought out of her mind and poured the boiling water into the tea pot.

"Are you and Jason still on speaking terms? You still see each other don't you? With all the legal arrangements and paperwork you seem to have. By the way have you two chosen a name yet? I can't believe you opted to know what gender the baby would be. You certainly didn't want to know what sex your other two were."

Jill poured the tea and found an unopened bar of Cadbury milk chocolate. She put them both on the table in front of Astrid. She couldn't speak. She needed the anger to subside and be replaced by a modicum of calm, a semblance of normality. She wished the whole situation would just go away and she could resume her old life, but she knew this was not an option. She sat down with her cup and adjusted her bulk so the pain in her back would ease a little.

"Yes we're still talking to each other but the relationship has changed. I seem to be angry all the time and say things like – Why

Ruth Manning

ME? – on a regular basis. It's so stupid because I know *why me*. I had unprotected sex and got pregnant. End of story. But it isn't the end is it? It's just the beginning. The whole situation is stupid. I'm 48 years old with 2 grown-up children and now I'm about to have another one. My professional life is in ruins, which means I see more of my doctor than anyone else I know and I'm taking antidepressants to deal with post-traumatic stress disorder, whatever that is, which was caused by a complete annihilation of my professional status. I cry all the time, I can't sleep and I just want the whole thing to go away. God, I sound like a small child don't I? Stamping my foot and saying 'It's not fair, it's not my fault' but it is *my fault* and I have to deal with this." She put her head in her hands and began to cry, her tears cascading down her cheeks. Astrid thought the only way to describe her demeanour was as 'pitiful' and hated herself for the thought.

She went over to give her friend a hug. She knew no words of comfort to make her friend feel better and Astrid truly believed she would come through this, eventually. Privately she thought her friend's 'plan of action' was somewhat flawed (to put it mildly) but she also knew Jill was stubborn, and pig-headed and had once been strong and resilient. There was nothing she could do or say to change the events which would, very soon, take place. All she could do was be there.

Jill dried her eyes on the tea towel hanging across her shoulder. Looking at it brought back memories of her first months of motherhood all those years ago, when she always had a terry lined nappy in the same place, for the various mopping or wiping activities a new born baby seemed to require. How easy it had all seemed then. Each new day brought a new lesson to be learned and each night an endless round of feeding and changing. Her son had been a restless baby who could feed for what seemed to be hours and she had felt more like a milk factory than a human being, but she had loved it. She had been truly grateful for this little miracle. In fact with both her previous pregnancies she had flourished. Hair gleaming and thick, skin clear and without a blemish. She glanced at the large mirror on the opposite wall. The person looking back at her had neither of these qualities. Her hair was beginning to go grey and she hadn't coloured it or had it cut for months. It hung down in a limp and lifeless mess. She hadn't even brushed it this morning. Her eyes were bloodshot and swollen and the red maternity dress looked as if she had lived in it day and night for the last 2 weeks.

She turned to Astrid with an helpless shrug;

"I'm sorry, what a ridiculous sight I must be. Yes we are still talking, Jason and I, that is. All the legal side of things are almost completed. I think if this was the only problem I would probably deal with it better, but with the union issues over my job and the house not selling and with the likelihood the country is going into some kind of recession, I'm finding it increasingly difficult to be optimistic. Oh yes and I've got 'empty nest syndrome' by the way, everything keeps reminding me of the kids surely you can see why I'm such a pathetic excuse for a human being? I miss them both so much. I've no one to cook or clean for, no shoes in the hall to fall over, no dirty towels draped over every given surface. There's just no noise in the house at all. I don't even buy toilet rolls by the hundredweight. What do young people do with them? In my day 2 sheets was enough, now they seem to use a roll a pee. Do you realise this is the first time in over 20 years I've lived alone? I hate it and I hate myself."

Astrid was taken aback by this latest revelation. Both her children had also recently left home but unlike Jill, she had had no trouble at all coming to terms with the liberation of her own home and the new found freedom she too had discovered. Of all her friends, Jill was the one she had least expected to hear this from.

"I know things are really bad at the moment for you, Jill, but you have to stop beating yourself up like this. Yes, things do seem to be in a dreadful mess, but they will get better and one day you'll look back on this as a distant memory. If the house won't sell without an enormous drop in price, why not remortgage it and then rent it out? I'm not particularly hot on what it involves but I have a friend who is married to one of those people who manage properties. At least then you could pay off your debts and move on."

Jill looked at her in amazement. This idea hadn't even crossed her mind and she had no idea how she would go about it. She hadn't had a mortgage for years and wasn't sure she wanted to be an absent landlord but this could financially solve a lot of problems. This would enable her to pay off Jason for the house on Crete, which they had bought jointly and also some final adjustments to the financial settlement of her divorce. A seed was planted in that moment and she was determined to look into it in more detail. She thought, not for the first time, how Astrid always seemed to have the solution to a problem tucked neatly up her sleeve.

"You know, that sounds worth investigating. Give me your friend's phone number and I'll look into it today. First though I need a bath and a bit of 'me time.' I look a wreck."

Ruth Manning

Astrid folded the foil over the half-eaten bar of chocolate (family size at that) and finished her tea. They walked to the door together and held each other close. Astrid prepared herself for the coolness of the spring day and after promising she would be in touch went to leave.

Jill touched her on the shoulder and looked into her eyes.

"By the way" she said. "We have chosen a name for the baby. He's going to be called Oliver."

Oliver's Branch

Two.

Lying in a warm relaxing bath less than an hour later. Jill tried to focus on the near future and how it might possibly turn out. To do this she needed to go over the recent past (for about the hundredth time) and put events into some sort of perspective.

Up until eight and a half months ago things had been going well. Nothing amazing, just ticking comfortably along. Then her youngest child, Grace, had gone to university. In fact she had been driven there by Jason with Jill map reading. Grace sat in the back seat surrounded by virtually all her earthly possessions, somewhat scrunched up among the flotsam and jetsam of an average 18 year-old's life in this materialistic, high- tech society.

As they were travelling mainly by motorways map reading was reasonably straightforward, which was lucky as Jill's map-reading skills were somewhat limited.I t was only a few hours before the scenic Sussex fields and greenery gave way to the industrial North and within 6 hours they arrived outside the hall of residence which was to be Grace's home for the next year.

After finding her flat, on the third floor of a modern, characterless block, countless journeys were made up and down the stairs (the lift was out of order – no surprise there then!) transferring all the gear. Grace at last stood amidst her various boxes, bags, suitcases and personal memorabilia, looking excited and yet so vulnerable. Jill remembered how Grace's bedroom at home now looked; empty, sad and rejected, and far too tidy. After a brief look around the kitchen and living area, and with the arrival of one of her new flatmates, Jason and Jill suggested they go and find a hotel and come back later. Amidst the banter of the two new friends they were dismissed with a quick kiss on the cheek and "Yeah OK. See ya soon."

An hour later, having driven around Manchester's one way system about five times, they managed to find a reasonable hotel and settled down for a few hours before returning to pick Grace up for a meal. Jason went to lie down and was snoring peacefully as soon as his head touched the pillow. She regarded him with so much love and affection she thought her heart would burst. Thank God he would still be there over the coming days, months, years, forever......

Having always hated goodbyes Jill had known tomorrow was going to be one of the most difficult separations of her whole life. She knew too there could be no tears in front of Grace, as she wanted it to be a

positive separation but she knew she would cry. It was just a matter of when.

Grace had been the most wonderful child and even the teenage years did not bring the angst and rebellion she had experienced a few years earlier with her son, Nick. She and Grace had laughed and cried together and Jill felt her daughter was far more emotionally stable and mature than she was! Now she was going to have to let her make her own life and her own mistakes. Jill was dreading it. At home there was a picture of two babies sitting on a cloud with the inscription 'There are 2 things you can give your children in life, one is roots – the other is wings'. Now her little girl was set to fly and Jill hoped she would soar, but she was worried because she may not be there to support her and the home Grace had known all her life would, hopefully, soon be sold.

In the following hours she reflected on the many happy times she had experienced with her two children. She had a feeling; in the years to come she would be reflecting and remembering a great deal more.

She had woken Jason at just before seven in the evening, and after the usual ablutions and donning of glad rags, a thing that she rarely did now-a-days, they made their way back to her daughter's new flat and new life.

They had decided to eat at an Italian Restaurant which it turned out was staffed by Chinese waiters and cooks and where countless other parents were going through the same last-supper ritual with their offspring. There was a pleasant atmosphere, the food was good and the conversation flowed as freely as the wine. All three of them enjoyed each others' company. Even though Jason was not Grace's father they had a good relationship and he too was feeling the hugeness of tomorrow's parting.

Well after midnight they caught a cab and escorted Grace back to her flat. She had made friends with the girl she met earlier and as the keys she had picked up from the estate agent on their arrival didn't open any of the doors, they had agreed Grace would phone her when she arrived back and so get into the flat.

Grace leapt nimbly out of the taxi and with another quick peck on the cheek to each of them, plus "Thanks for the meal it was great, see you tomorrow," she was gone. The journey back was filled with an unspoken tension but no tears. Luckily the taxi driver, a bubbly

Oliver's Branch

Rastafarian with a broad Mancunian accent kept them amused with stories about student pranks and life in the big M! Just as they reached the hotel Jill's mobile phone rang. The gist of the call from Grace was there was no one in the flat and she was stuck outside. The taxi driver was already doing a U turn as Jill hung up and 20 minutes later all three of them were on their way back to the hotel.

Poor Jason ended up on the floor while Jill and Grace shared the bed. As Jill lay close to her sleeping daughter she cherished the moment and stayed awake well into the early hours, savouring the warmth of her daughter's body and the quiet, even breathing as she slept. Jill knew it would be a long time before they were this close again.

The morning saw a trip back to the flat having been to the estate agent for the correct set of keys. By this point Grace was itching to make her mark on the small room which was now her own. Jill and Jason went for a walk around the local area and on impulse bought a small TV as a goodbye gift. They had arranged to have lunch with her and then leave, but Jill was having second thoughts.

"I don't think we should do lunch with Grace, it'll be too final, too tense, too contrived. I want to give her the TV and then go. Is that OK with you?" she asked as they walked back to the halls.
Always ahead of her and knowing how she often worked, Jason had given a small shrug and grinned.
"I thought you might say that. Yes of course it's fine and means we'll get home in daylight." Thank goodness Jason was with her, he really did know her so very well.
They walked back in silence, holding hands. It was time to say goodbye.

When they arrived the flat was busy and noisy. Two more of the flatmates had arrived and they all seemed to be talking to each other at once. Jill was often amazed how, as soon as Grace was with her peers, her language appeared to change and she was lucky if she caught one word in every ten her daughter spoke. Picking up a full conversation was a total impossibility. She managed to draw Grace to one side and explained her decision.
"Listen, sweetheart, we're going to make a move. I know we said we'd have lunch first but you seem to have loads to do and need to get to know your flatmates. Is that OK?"

Grace had looked at her, almost with relief. "That's fine mum, and at least you'll get to travel in daylight. Thanks for everything, I couldn't have done it without you."

Ruth Manning

As they hugged and kissed goodbye, Jill had felt the strength of their love. Jason hugged Grace too and slipped a twenty-pound note into her hand, and within a few minutes they were back in the car waving goodbye and then heading south.

Jason had glanced over at Jill with a knowing look. She was sitting bolt upright and was poker-faced, unable to speak.

"You can cry now, poppet" he had said, turning off one faceless motorway onto the next. "Well done!"

Jill had sobbed loudly and uncontrollably for a while, then silently for the next fifty miles.

Three.

Jill looked at her fingers which were prune-like from too much soaking. The water was decidedly tepid now. Reluctantly she eased herself out of the bath, knowing and yet dreading having to face another day. Walking into the large bedroom she had shared with Jason until just under a month ago. Memories of their night together on the return from Manchester came vividly in to her mind. They had enjoyed a fillet steak with a good red wine in the candle-lit dining room. Jason had tried to keep the conversation light but she had felt bereft and empty. Even he could not make her smile. In bed he had held her in his arms while she cried and then they had made love tenderly and slowly. This was the night, she was sure, Oliver had been conceived. It had been a night when the emptiness had been replaced by love and the agony replaced by ecstasy, at least for a short while.

She surveyed the room. It was immaculate, as was the rest of the house. Having put the property on the market a few months earlier with the decision having been made to live on Crete, she had diligently followed all the rules of those awful make-over programmes she always made fun of and laughed at. Now, silk covers and matching cushions covered the beds in all 4 bedrooms. Window sills and door frames had been painted and not a thing was out of place. Both the bathroom and kitchen gleamed and fluffy, fresh towels were neatly folded and strategically placed. Even the linen cupboard was a show-piece for God's sake. Yet still there had been very few viewings and no offers. There were rumours house prices were falling and some sort of slump was on the way, but she took little notice of all this doom and gloom, she had enough of her own to try and cope with.

Finding a fresh, only slightly-creased maternity smock in the wardrobe, she dressed and made a mental note to put a wash on sometime in the near future. The dowdy, red smock she had worn earlier needed a rinse through. She glanced briefly in the dressing-table mirror and as always was amazed at the stranger who stared back at her. She looked old, grey and totally defeated. What a difference 6 months could make.

Walking slowly down the flight of stairs to the middle floor she glanced briefly in her daughter's 'old room'. Only now it was nothing more than a sterile, clean and well-aired place. Even the floor was clean and totally visible with not a dirty towel or random shoe in sight. Opposite, her son's old room was the same, no dirty socks or

mountains of T-shirts and jeans cluttered the pristine, gleaming, laminate covering.

Grace had come home for Christmas and found it hard to accept this order and showiness. She said it was like living in a 'house not a home,' so had quickly remedied this situation by spreading her belongings and clothes all over the place. Having brought back the biggest suitcase she could find she had managed to pack 12 pairs of shoes along with enough clothes to last her for at least 6 weeks. As she was only home for two, Jill had thought this a bit over the top, but said nothing. Instead she had diligently washed and ironed everything so her daughter would return to university with a clean and well-packed suitcase.

Christmas had been both a happy and a sad time for Jill and her two children. For Jason it was a time of 'bah humbug' with a sigh of relief when it was all over and some semblance of normality and routine returned. For Jill, Nick and Grace Christmas had always been full of laughter and fun. Jill always went totally over the top with gifts and food. Traditions had been maintained right up until last Christmas when Nick had drawn the line about writing a wish list to send to Santa. He had explained the new e-mail provision, recently installed at the North Pole which he would use instead. He had reminded her he was 21 years old and not a small child any more. Jill had visualised millions of small children, many as young as six or seven, logging on and e-mailing their wish lists to the North Pole. This she found very depressing. It was as if all the innocence and naivety of Christmas was being eroded away by modern technology. (Grace wrote a lovely letter, which Jill filed away for the future.)

All the same, the tree was decorated; the Santa sacks were hung at the ends of their beds and Christmas morning saw both children sitting on her bed opening their 'presents from Santa'.

As she watched them she felt a slight, gentle stirring in her body. Amidst the laughter of her two almost-grown children she suddenly realised that her youngest child was making himself a part of their lives, by stirring for the first time within her swelling belly. It was an almost surrealistic moment, a few seconds at most but it was like an imprint into her soul. She was nurturing a living, breathing human being who one day would experience Christmas through the eyes of a child. She felt humility and fear for the days ahead and the emotions she would feel. This was one roller-coaster ride she didn't want to take, yet, at the same time it was as if her unborn child was

giving her strength and support for the trauma and upheaval she knew lay ahead. Soon, far too soon, she would have to tell her children about the tiny entity lying within her womb and she had no idea how she was going do this. The caress and movement ceased and the present returned. Jill felt as if she had just been in some kind of other dimension which had given her a strength she had been unaware she possessed. It had been, she was convinced, a gift from Oliver, to see her through the news she was soon to break to her children about her pregnancy and the uncertainty of the coming months.

It was a happy day and yet there had been an undercurrent of sadness which all three of them had sensed. Both children knew their mother was putting the house up for sale in January. This was to be their last Christmas in the home they had grown up in and where they had celebrated every Christmas since they were born.

On Boxing Day, Jill had sat and told them not only about the pregnancy but also the plans she and Jason had discussed in regards to the unborn child. Both of them had been shocked and bewildered by her cataclysmic news. Although they knew, at some point, she and Jason were moving to Crete, the full implications of their mum, Jason and now a *baby* was a new scenario. They had to clarify with her the fact that she was apparently leaving them behind and moving so far away. They both found it totally daunting. They felt she was deserting them and her priorities were 'all wrong'. It had probably been the most devastating interaction she had ever had with her children. In fact 'interaction' was too optimistic a view of the scene that had ensued. It had been like a battlefield where only the casualties or dead were left behind and all three of them were casualties of this particular war. Every emotion possible played itself out and in the end there was just exhaustion and complete disbelief.

The plan she explained to them would in fact change in the next few months, but at this point none of them knew this. Life has a way of knocking you back, just as you feel you are getting on your feet. The ensuing months would knock Jill back again and again and again.

She had been dreading the moment ever since she had found out she was pregnant and discussed it with Jason. Their relationship seemed less robust and she knew she was mentally very fragile. The reaction of her children was one of unified disbelief and anger. How could their mother have got into this mess and why was she now willing to take a course of action which, in real life, could not possibly happen?

Ruth Manning

"You have to be kidding, Mum?" Nick had said. "That is just utter rubbish. You've been reading too many books or something and have lost sight of reality. I know things haven't been easy, what with the job situation and everything but you seriously need to think this through. How the hell did you get pregnant anyway?"

Grace raised one eyebrow, and then added her reaction to the situation.

"This is a joke, right Mum? I know you look a bit rounder but for someone who rammed the importance of using contraceptives and all that 'safe sex' stuff down our throats from a very early age, this is all a bit ironic. You reckon it'll be a May baby then? If you want to know what I think, I think you must be having one of those phantom things like dogs have, when they imagine they're having puppies and walk around with a cuddly toy substitute in their mouth, moping. You may also have noticed neither of us is laughing?" Things had become very heated and they had both made it quite plain they thought she should be committed to an asylum. This was not how they expected her to behave and having a baby at her age was disgusting. She was far too *old*.

Trying to block any further memory of the scenes which ensued and returning to the present, she walked slowly downstairs. It was time to face the world.

Loading the washing machine, she heard her mobile ringing in the kitchen. She hoped this wasn't the union representative as she was in no mood for the complications these calls added to her life. Luckily the caller ID told her it was Astrid.

"Hello you," she said with very little enthusiasm in her voice.
"Hiya, only me. I've got the name and number of the property management chap for you. Shall I text it you or have you got a pen and paper handy?"

Jill smiled to herself. As always Astrid's efficient manner meant she had forgotten how Jill had once been as efficient and on the ball as she was. Yes, she may have lost her edge but there was rarely a time when she didn't have a Post-it block and pen close by.
"Thanks. Go ahead I've got a pen poised and ready."
She scribbled down the name and number and Astrid wished her luck, explaining she had to dash; she was "SO busy."

Oliver's Branch

William Slowstern. Jill looked at the name. She imagined he was probably quite officious and brusque, she was sure if she wasn't careful she was going to get ripped off, her vulnerability shone through like a beacon. She stuck the paper on the rather chaotic memo board in the kitchen and decided she would deal with it another day.

She looked out of the window. A light shower had just begun. June, her neighbour, was hunched over a clump of some sort of bush, wearing a yellow sou'wester and a big yellow rain-hat, looking more like Paddington Bear than Paddington Bear. She looked togged up for a Force 9 gale as opposed to a spring shower! She may have sensed she was being watched because she looked over and waved. Within the blink of an eye she dashed over to the fence and started beckoning to Jill. It was grey, cold and miserable but Jill knew if she didn't go and find out what her neighbour wanted, June would be round in a flash and the morning would be gone before she knew it.

"I thought you might like some of this" June said, holding out a bunch of green leaves. She must have seen the bewildered look on her neighbours face and added; "It's wild mint. Makes a fantastic cuppa and is a real pick-me-up and YOU certainly look as if you could do with that. Pour boiling water on about six stems and add three spoons of sugar. Take the stems out after about two minutes. Stir well and drink. Pure nectar of the gods. How are things going on the house front?"

Taking the clump of leaves and about to reply she was cut off by June's next remark. "By the way, I've got a friend who has a friend who knows someone in Essex who is looking to move into the area. A civil servant, well something like that, with a young family. I've given him your house details and she may contact you. See you later, work to do." Then she was off and Jill walked back into her kitchen. Strangely, June had never asked her about her pregnancy, even though she had told her about it in late November. June all over, she thought. Totally self-absorbed and living in her own world. Glancing in the mirror she realised the irony of this thought and mentally slapped herself. "What about you then you stupid bitch?" she mumbled. Her reflection simply mimicked her words and features back at her.

Looking at the clock she was amazed at the time. Where had the last 2 hours gone? She had a doctor's appointment in 45 minutes and parking was a nightmare near the surgery. Placing the 'pick-me-up' leaves by the sink, she put on her coat, found her car keys and headed towards the front door.

Ruth Manning

It was only as she was parking, she remembered – she hadn't turned on the washing machine.

Oliver's Branch

Four.

The doctor's surgery was full, as always. Small children were huddled in their mothers' arms, looking decidedly sorry for themselves, the old and infirm glaring at them if they so much as sniffed. Jill hated these appointments. In November it had been about the pregnancy. Being a 'geriatric mother' meant that she would be closely monitored on a regular basis. Was she sure she would not abort? Did she want the Down's syndrome test? How would she cope with a baby at nearly fifty? Would she try to breast feed? All the questions and the intrusive prodding and 'monitoring' made her feel like a piece of meat. Refusal to attend prenatal classes at the hospital on a weekly basis had met with a lot of tut-tuttting and head shaking. Her doctor was a 'no nonsense' young woman who always wore a black suit but varied the shirts. Over the last six months, Jill had never seen her in the same shirt twice. She imagined her wardrobe full of identical black suits which she also changed on a regular basis.

Yes, all of the intrusiveness from November onwards had been bad enough, but then at the beginning of December the unimaginable happened; she was informed she did not 'fit in' at her place of work and was to be 'moved' immediately. This decision, she was told, had not been taken lightly, but it would be best for all concerned. Having worked as a counsellor in a school for the past 2 years and having never received any complaints, she could not understand what was happening. Apparently she was to go to another school in a direct swap with the counsellor there. This had left her feeling professionally manipulated and discarded. Her career had fallen apart and part of her life with it. Having given up teaching to follow this route – losing out financially through the choice, this was a double whammy. She had tried to put things in to perspective, to see it as a new start, but the last thing she wanted, at her age, was a new start. She had also felt she was letting her clients down and that was heartbreaking.

Oh she had talked about it to friends and colleagues and they had all been very sympathetic. She had tried the other school feeling ashamed and dejected. She wondered if the staff there saw her as an oddity they had been 'lumbered with.' Day by day it became more difficult to go to work as if nothing was wrong. She felt sick and shaky all the time. After the second week she started having panic attacks ..... then the tears had come.

In one way it had been a blessing as it forced her to go to the doctor for help. Trying to describe the situation had left her sobbing and

Ruth Manning

shaking so badly, in the end she had given up trying to speak at all and just sobbed instead. Her doctor had been sympathetic and understanding. A sick note for 3 months was issued and mild antidepressants were prescribed (which, the doctor explained, would not affect her baby). Her manager sent letters and, later, absence procedure documents but nothing else. She even had to go to a clinical psychologist – or something like that – who diagnosed her 'sane' but believed her to be suffering from post-traumatic stress. She would be able to resume her work 'in due course'. Seeing her career fizzle out and her confidence ebb away, Jill had realised it was, in fact, time to take another path.

This path had been laid 2 years earlier when she and Jason had bought a lovely little house in a small village on Crete. They had spent most of their holidays there ever since. It needed some love and basic work, but it was totally inhabitable. After a great deal of discussion about the job situation and also the arrival of Oliver in late May, she and Jason had agreed they would move there as soon as it was humanly possible. Over the next month she began sorting her home out and packing what she would be taking. Juggling her pregnancy, her depression, packing, and putting her house on the market as well as getting ready for Christmas, meant the self-pity she had wallowed in lessened, slightly. Unfortunately she had also become more self-absorbed and less sensitive to other people. In particular this applied to her relationship with Jason. It had deteriorated and become fragmented, broken. The closeness became a vast expanse of misunderstanding and trivial arguments. Much as they both tried to see light at the end of the tunnel it seemed to become darker and darker. Then, in late April, everything came to a head. Following yet another row, Jason had told her calmly and factually he was no longer going to go with her to live on Crete. Instead he was moving back to his own home and would work things out from there -BUT- he wanted equal custody of the baby. He told her he had been unhappy for a while. He felt completely superfluous to her and, or so it seemed, to the baby. She had made it clear she would do things alone, in her own way. She had blocked him out and left him isolated and very unhappy. He was aware she did not see this, but things had changed and they no longer, as far as he could see, had a future together .He wanted her to buy his share of the house on Crete *and go without him.* Suddenly she had hated him; she hated this baby, his baby. Obviously not noticing the look of complete horror on her face he had continued, explaining to her how he had worked out his own affairs and now she must do the same. He would arrange for them to see a solicitor to sort out the legal implications regarding 'their son'. He would not shirk his

Oliver's Branch

responsibilities as the child's father and obviously he would support them all he could financially.

Jill could not understand how their relationship had gone so wrong, without her realising there was an enormous problem. She had thought back, fleetingly, to the early days of their relationship, over 6 years ago, when sex had been far more regular and active than it was in the later years. When they had joked about the possibility of a pregnancy and Jill had said it was an impossibility, she had gone through the change! If she did get pregnant, which she couldn't, then there was no question about it; she would have a termination. Had she been more on the ball she may have noticed the monthly twinges and sometimes the small specks of blood which accompanied these, but she had not. It was only in November her body started telling her things had changed. Sore breasts, and a sickness in the morning she couldn't put down to food poisoning, led her to the chemist where she bought a pregnancy-test kit.

She remembered how Jason had actually said he would like another child. He had 3 by his previous marriage, which had ended in divorce before he met Jill. They were all grown up and reasonably settled. She thought briefly about the day she had seen the result of the first test and she gave an involuntary shudder at the memory. The woman beside her in the surgery gave her a questioning look before returning to her newspaper. The doctor was running late, the flashing neon message board read. Nothing new there then.

The argument between her and Jason came back into her mind. When she had registered exactly what he was saying and the implications of it all she had, suddenly, inexplicably, felt something within her 'give' and a red mist seemed to cloud her vision. She could still hear herself screaming at Jason...screaming and shouting words in a deluge of self-pity and anger. She could not remember the exact words she had used, but this outburst changed both their lives forever and, following it, plans were made which seemed to snowball into a bizarre and complex farce. There was no going back, even though she had wanted to on so many occasions. Why had she not had a termination?

Jill changed position to ease the pain in her back and found her thoughts once again settling on the past. She noted how they followed a confusing pattern, skipping backwards and forwards over past events, almost randomly.

She knew why she had not had a termination. After the fourth home pregnancy test had read positive, she had gone to the doctor and waited for the telephone call with a result which would prove her

totally wrong. When it came of course it proved the tests were all totally right. Jason had been ecstatic and somehow had managed to pull her along with his infectious joy and excitement.

"Think about it, Jill" he had said with a broad smile on his face. "We'll get things sorted here and go and live on Crete. It may take a few years but we can do this. The baby can grow up in the sunshine and we can enjoy OUR child together. We've been saying we'd like to make the move sometime next year, so now we will."

So it had been decided, sometime in the not-too-distant future they would leave. Jill would put the house in England on the market and nearer the time Jason would sort out his own property. How easy and straight forward it had all seemed. Yet somewhere deep down she had continued to feel a nagging guilt, she did not want another child and all the responsibilities she knew it would bring. She did not want this baby. All this had been before the job ordeal though. It was this which had made them decide to leave as soon as possible. Then the argument had changed everything, forever.

How ironic the whole thing was. The tapestry of memories had fluttered around and sequentially things were blurred. The lines were fuzzy. Times, places, incidents, had darted about in her mind for the last 35 minutes. She wondered, not for the first time, if her inability to put things in the right order in her head, meant she was also unable to put things in some kind of order in her life. It certainly felt like that, most of the time.

"Mrs Slater," came the doctor's voice over the speaker, "please come through."

Jill got up and slowly made her way through to the consultation room.

Oliver's Branch

Five.

Returning home, Jill put on the washing machine. Dyson, her daughter's 9-year-old Labrador, looked up at her mournfully and then went back to sleep.

The doctor had issued another 3-month sick note but suggested that the antidepressants should be changed to a smaller dosage, as the pregnancy was so near to full term. Having battled her way through hoards of people in the pharmacy (there appeared to be some kind of epidemic, hopefully not the dreaded bird flu,) she now had the new tablets, although she was in two minds about taking them. She had been sporadic with the last batch and did not in any way want to affect the baby.

Taking off her coat and scarf she sat down to write a list of what she needed to do. Until recently she had hated lists and in the past had often laughed at her ex-husband, who was an avid exponent of them. Now though, she felt there was just too much to sort out to rely on her befuddled brain.

The main thing she knew she must do was to start packing in earnest. She had made a weak attempt over the months and things looked far less cluttered but there was still a massive amount to do. Admittedly the time-line was not totally settled yet and a great deal depended on selling the house, but there was still 22 years of accumulated 'stuff' to organise. This was going to be tough for her. She was a seasoned hoarder. Although a regular supplier to the many charity shops in the area over the past few months, the sentimental items were proving hard to dispatch. Her son's Brio, her daughter's soft toys, their memory boxes packed with so much love by each of them over the years, her own very large dolls house which she had had since her father had brought it home for her on her 3rd Christmas. He had felt sorry for the man who was selling it, he said. Apparently the old man had spent over 3 years making it and all the furniture for his granddaughter but in November of that year the family had been forced to move to a bungalow and the dolls house was just too big. He hoped it would be played with and loved by some other little girl, and it was. Grace had never taken to the hobby, but Jill had bought miniatures all her life and every room had a sense of individuality and reality about it, to her. How could she 'get rid of it'?

Buy plastic boxes and tissue was the only thing written at the top of fresh piece of A4 paper when her mobile signalled a received text and she went in search of it. After a short search she located it under

the wild mint, which was looking decidedly droopy. The message from Jason read "Hiya, is it OK to pop over after work?" Short and sweet, as always. Funnily enough although they were no longer living together their relationship was much improved. She no longer felt angry at Jason, more at herself and the world in general, and they were able to laugh a little now though not in the same way as during the early years of their relationship. There had been a lot to sort out and when the house was sold she would be buying his share of Paparooni (meaning poppies), the Greek house. There had been a massive amount of paperwork to sign and many discussions but, as she had said to Astrid, this was virtually complete. They had even talked about Jason coming over to visit at some point. He had hated letting go of the 'Greek dream' but realised it was impractical as things stood. She sent a text back saying of course it was fine, she'd see him later.

A ring at the door brought her back to the present and, somewhat reluctantly she went to answer it. There stood June with a small very oriental-looking kitten.
"I thought it would be a good idea to introduce Archy to your two cats," she said, as she pushed past Jill and bustled into the front room.
"His real name is Archilles, because he can run like the devil, but we've shortened it to Archy. Much more down to earth, don't you think?"
Jill sidled past her and managed to put the wilting mint into the cupboard without being seen, then went to sit at the table with June.
"Good idea I suppose, although Brightey may have a bit of a problem with a kitten, he's getting very antisocial in his old age. Aspro will probably run a mile". Jill's 2 cats had been named by the children 14 years ago. Brightey belonged to her son and was so-named because he had always been a cunning and clever minx. Her daughter had used the Greek word for white, thinking this was far more cultured. The cats were pure white and twins although easy to tell apart as Brightey had a blue eye and a brown eye.
"He'll be fine. I just thought they could get to know him a bit. We won't let him out without a lead for a month or two anyway, so he'll be a lot bigger. How was the tea by the way? You certainly look perkier."
"It was lovely," Jill lied as she went to fetch the cats from the conservatory.

On her return, with one under each arm, June put Archy on the floor. Jill did the same with her two. Aspro disappeared under the

Oliver's Branch

sofa while Brightey gave the kitten a disdainful look and walked back into the conservatory.

"That went well then" muttered Jill, but her neighbour clapped her hands in glee.

"See they're friends already. I feel much better about things now. Is there a cuppa in that pot?" Jill resigned herself to the fact that she would now have at least another hour before she could go into 'packing mode', and put on the kettle.

As she saw June out an hour and a half later she glanced up at the clock. It was now well into the afternoon. Much as she enjoyed making tuna and mayo sandwiches and sharing them with her neighbour, who always had the same thing for lunch, she felt annoyed that she hadn't been more constructive. Still at least she had eaten.

Closing the door, she was aware that the pain in her back had worsened. It was a strange pregnancy this. With her other two there had been no back pain, just raging heartburn in the later stages. There were still technically two weeks to go and she hoped that it would ease off a little. The pregnancy had gone amazingly well, especially as she was a 'geriatric mother'. How she hated the term. To her geriatric meant being eighty-something and hobbling around with a stick, talking about bowel movements or other bodily functions, and she certainly wasn't doing that yet. Admittedly she felt more drained of energy than she had before but other factors had entered the equation making her feel less buoyant. Also she was not looking forward to this birth the way she had the other two. She had had so many hopes and dreams for her son and daughter, sadly and guiltily, she had none for Oliver.

Jason had been over the moon about everything to do with the baby. Before 'The Quarrel' he had been interested in every doctor's appointment and the initial 3-month scan. There was nothing he wouldn't do for Jill and he spoilt her all the time. Gifts, flowers, foot massages and countless other small, thoughtful gestures became the norm and she felt very loved. After the quarrel the onus shifted to the welfare of the baby. At times Jill felt almost invisible and totally unloved. They were still friends though, and maybe things would get better, but she was not sure they could ever completely heal the chasm between them. Too much had been said and decisions taken, making it almost impossible to imagine they would ever be as close as they had been in the past. The wounds felt too deep to ever completely heal.

Ruth Manning

She heard a car approaching the front door and looked out of the window. Jason was parking up. He must have got off work early. She walked through the living room to let him in and as she did felt a wetness in her crutch. Jason had a key, so she went into the downstairs toilet to investigate. "Dear God, don't let me become incontinent just yet," she thought.

Jason opened the door at exactly the same moment as she realised this was a show. She had experienced it twice before and it had not lead to her waters breaking. In fact she had had to have this done medically at the hospital both times (apparently she had a very strong lining,) so she was not too bothered. She went to meet Jason, who had just put the kettle on. As she passed the kitchen table the piece of A4 paper, with the start of her list, fluttered to the floor, face down.

Oliver's Branch

Six.

Jill followed Jason into the kitchen. She noticed the dark terracotta tiles needed a good wash. It was strange, she had exactly the same tiles at Paparooni, but somehow they always looked shinier than these. She sat on a stool next to the worktop, waiting for him to speak. It was still comfortable to maintain a silence when they were together but she wondered why he had come round. Nowadays there was usually a reason.
"Well most of the paperwork is finalised and you've signed almost everything. The only thing we need to do now is sign the papers from Angelina on Crete. Then we just wait for your house to sell, you pay me off and it's all done."

Jill thought this was a little glib. Whatever happened over the next few months she knew things would never be 'all done'. Jason did not mention the other piece of paperwork which they still had to sign and so Jill let this pass. "I had an e-mail from her yesterday. They should be here early next week. She really is a Godsend isn't she?"

Angelina was the agent who they had bought the house from and who, for the past two years, had kept everything running smoothly and paying the bills. It had turned into an easy friendship between the three of them. They met up with her for a meal, whenever they were on Crete.

"That's fine then" Jason said, helping himself to a digestive. "Actually there's something else I wanted to talk to you about."

Jill braced herself. His tone sounded serious and philosophical, this meant something profound was on the way. At this point in time the last thing she needed, was to have to think too deeply about anything. She looked at his long, slim body amazed, as always, that he could eat anything he liked and never put on an ounce. She was completely the opposite, looking at a cream cake could add a couple of pounds to her not-so-slender frame. At least while she was pregnant she had an excuse for carrying the extra weight. How she was dreading what her body would look like after the birth. She awaited Jason's next words with trepidation, then they both heard a key turn in the front door. A voice called out, "Hi mum." The moment was lost as Nick strode into the room.

In obligatory jeans and T-shirt with a good tan and slight stubble, she found it hard to associate this young man with the little boy she had known. He had had big, blue eyes and a effervescent excitement for life's daily experiences. Everything had been so new and exciting

to him. Yet now, somehow, he seemed to have been beaten down by life, even though he was still only 21. Somehow the enthusiasm and shine had gone out of his eyes. They appeared hooded and somehow secretive. She worried constantly about him and felt responsible for him, in a way only a mother can understand. She hoped the future would be kind to him and he would find the happiness he deserved. A commitment to something, or somebody, or both. "Just what I need, a nice cup of char. Hi Jason, how's it going?"

It had taken Nick some time to come to terms with the fact that (a.) his mother was pregnant and (b.) he was going to have a half-brother 21 years younger than himself. After the revelations of Boxing Day he had made a point of not 'popping in' as regularly as he had in the past, conversations between them had become stilted and formal. Jill had sent text after text which were not answered and had cried herself to sleep on a regular basis. Too much was going on and too many balls were being juggled. It felt as if she had dropped one of the important ones, namely her relationship with her son.

Nick was talking about going into the army and had been busy training as well as trying to quit smoking. He left home at eighteen to set up home with his then girlfriend. He stayed on in his flat when the relationship fizzled out. Jill was fine with this. She had left home to train as a teacher when she was eighteen, and before that had been at boarding school, so to her this was the normal progression of things. Grace was still at home then, so the space left by his absence had not been so bad. When they had disagreed on Boxing Day however, and he had stormed out, Jill felt almost as though she was grieving over the loss. It had been mid-March before they had their first real conversation. Jill arranged to meet him on his birthday and as he knew this might be a financially lucrative meeting, he had agreed.

They met in a local pub and talked politely about life in general over a bar snack. Only after the meal did Jill feel that it was time to talk about the present situation. She started by asking him if he was aware that she was off work with PTSD. Because he was close to his sister they kept in touch and he obviously talked to her. He therefore knew about, and understood, the whole situation. He expressed the view that all people in authority were bastards. Then he asked her what she was going to do. Grabbing the moment, she explained that she had no idea, and felt too hurt and angry to do anything about it. She had talked to her manager who had agreed, because of the pregnancy and the work situation, a sick note was the best way to

proceed, at least initially. At this point Nick had looked at her now quite swollen belly, and asked how the pregnancy was going.

"Apart from the back pain everything seems to be going to plan. Do you want to talk about how you feel about it or not?"

Nick had looked at her and smiled then replied, "Actually Mum, I'm OK about it. I've had plenty of time to think and, although I don't agree totally with your plan, I think moving to Crete is a brilliant idea. Think of all those free holidays I can have. I know I was angry at first, but I've known from the age of seven that when we left home you were going back to live in Greece. It's not something you threw at me, or a whim you had. I'm still not sure about this baby thing, and I admit I don't understand it, but as you've always said to Grace and me – as long as you are happy, that's the main thing. So I guess the same applies."

Jill remembered biting her lip and holding back the honest reply. The honest reply was she wasn't happy with any of this situation; she was miserable and cried all the time. The honest reply was she should have had an abortion and just got on with the life she had. She did not want this baby. The honest reply was she was scared stiff about going to live on Crete without Jason and she wanted everything to be different. Instead she looked at him and said, "Everything will work out fine. You know however far apart we are, you can always call. If there's ever a problem I'll be there as soon as I can. You know how much I love you. So can we be friends again?" Nick had smiled, moved round to her side of the table, and given her a hug. "I've missed you Mum," was all he'd said, a glimmer of a sparkle in his blue eyes. It was enough.

Nudging herself back to the present she saw that he and Jason were talking animatedly about some football game or other. She shifted on the stool; the back ache didn't seem to be easing today. If anything it was getting worse. She decided if it wasn't any better tomorrow she would make another doctor's appointment.

Nick helped himself to a handful of biscuits and stopped talking long enough for her to join the conversation, or at least change the subject.

"How's the non-smoking going, son?" she asked. She had given up as soon as she knew she was pregnant with Oliver but she had no doubt she would start again once the baby was born. The year before she fell pregnant with Nick, she had been for acupuncture to quit. She had walked away from the one-hour treatment feeling healthier

and cleaner than she had felt for years. All that day she craved healthy food and drank gallons of water. She had felt instinctively she would never have another filthy, foul-smelling, health-destroying cigarette as long as she lived. Unfortunately this euphoric state only lasted until the following morning when she woke up gasping for cigarette. She talked to her then husband about it, because the hour had cost £75.00, which was a lot of money. In the end she decided she would give up for 2 weeks and see how it went. With the help of nicotine gum and an inhaler, that reminded her of a tampon, she had actually quit for 7 years before starting again. This meant both her children were born nicotine free. She had not had a cigarette since she found out she was pregnant with Oliver and a sudden urge to light up was quickly quashed. This new life she was carrying deserved a nicotine-free beginning and it was one thing she would be able to give him.

Nick had given up for just over two months now and was extolling the virtues of being a non-smoker, as he chomped on his fifth digestive biscuit. Jill pulled herself back to the present wondering why she was having so many memories about the past. She congratulated him as he walked off to go and use the internet. She watched him close the conservatory door then turned back to look at Jason, who was pouring another cup of tea, draining the pot. The day seemed to have been dominated by memories and cups of tea. She needed to hear what Jason was about to say, before the interruption, so she broke the silence. "OK. So what did you want to talk about?" Just as she finished the sentence an agonising spasm shook her whole body and she felt a rush of water pouring between her legs, forming a large puddle on the tiles. Looking down on it her first thought was that she wouldn't be washing the floor, at least not in the foreseeable future.

Seven.

Jason turned round as she gasped, he had a look of real concern on his face. "What's the matter? Is it your back getting worse?" he asked.

Jill looked at the puddle which was beginning to spread across the floor and then back at him. She felt totally numb, yet totally drained, as though she had been through the labour already and was now just waiting for that glorious 'after birth cup of tea'. (Was she getting totally addicted to tea?) She also felt as if she was losing something, a part of herself which she would never have again. She began sobbing noisily and slumped with her head on her arms against the work surface.

Jason felt powerless and was totally lost for words. The whole situation was about to play itself out and, although he was to be a major player, he wanted to be anywhere but where he was at this moment. He put an arm around her but she was oblivious of his presence and continued to cry, silently now. He went out and fetched the mop, thinking how banal a gesture this was, but not having the faintest idea what else he could do. When he came back into the kitchen Jill was wiping her eyes and sitting up. She looked at him and smiled. He wanted to go over to her and take her in his arms, but was afraid she would push him away, as she had done so many times over the last few months. Instead he systematically mopped the floor until he was satisfied it was clean and non-slippery. He returned the mop to the utility room, racking his brains for the right thing to say.

Jill got slowly up from the stool, wiping her eyes. She went and splashed cold water on her face and then dried it. She didn't want Nick to see her in this state. He was still on the internet, oblivious to the drama which was beginning to unfold. She went and opened the conservatory door and as she peeped in, Nick looked up and smiled. Mustering up all her strength and attempting to act as normally as possible she said, "I'm just going to go and freshen up, son. Will you still be here in another half hour or so?" Nick glanced up briefly before replying,
"Yeah I guess so. I'm just looking up some stuff about fitness on the army website. I really have to take this getting-fit far more seriously." He then looked back at the screen and was immediately transported into cyberspace once more. Jill left quietly and made her way slowly up to the bathroom. She wondered if Jason would still be there when she came down. She hoped very much he would.

Ruth Manning

In the bathroom she looked in the mirror at her drawn and tear-stained face, glad that Nick had been oblivious of her present emotional state. She undressed and put the offending, soggy smock in the laundry basket. She wasn't going to risk a bath so turned on the shower and carefully stepped in. She turned the power on full and stood totally still, letting the heat and the water wash over her. So, this was it then. The beginning. The end. The time she had been dreading. The time she had so desperately wanted to come. The moment from which her life would never be the same again. A time where she wanted to stand still yet knew she had no choice but to move on. A time for new life, discovery, joy, hope... and loss. How could she possibly deal with all of this over the ensuing hours, along with the physical pain? She felt frightened and bewildered. She needed to feel strong and sure. A memory of something her mother used to say wafted into her mind, along with the aroma of shower gel. "Whatever happens to you in your life Jill, this is an old adage I think will give you strength. 'Look backwards with gratitude, look upwards with confidence and look forward with hope.' I've found it has helped me through some of life's more demanding moments."

Jill wondered what her mother would say about her present 'life demanding moment' and was glad she was not around to witness it. Her mother had been a great one for 'adages' and it was a joke she now shared with her children, often quoting something she remembered from her youth. Her mother had helped her learn the poem 'If' by Rudyard Kipling when she was only 10 years old. She ran through it, as she began to wash her hair. She mentally stopped at the last 4 lines of the third verse.

'If you can force your heart and nerve and sinew
To serve your turn long after they are gone,
And so hold on when there is nothing in you
Except the Will which says to them: "Hold on"'

She wondered if she could do it. Could she be strong emotionally, mentally and physically through the next few hours, days, weeks, months, years? She wasn't at all sure she could, but at that moment she felt a sudden surge of confidence, as if the 'old Jill' was trying to find her way back in. She smiled inwardly and began to rinse the out the shampoo. When she felt her hair squeak with cleanliness she moved both her hands to the large bump which had already changed her life and was imminently going to change it still more, in ways she knew she could not yet even imagine."Well Oliver, this will be the last shower you ever take with me. I'm going to miss our chats and singing together, more than you will ever know. Good luck little

one, here's to a not too traumatic next few hours and lets hope we get it over with reasonably quickly. You need to know, whatever happens, I love you now and I always will."

Jill had gotten into the habit of talking out loud in the shower to her unborn son. On one level it was true she did not want this child, but on another, infinitely deeper one, she had been unable to have him aborted. Instead she developed the habit over the months of talking to him, privately and intimately. She had told him everything she thought he needed to know about herself and her life. She had sung him her favourite songs from the 70s and 80s and hoped somehow, intrinsically, this closeness and understanding would somehow be with him, to guide him, in the future. She stepped out of the shower and gently towelled herself dry. While she was brushing her hair back out of her eyes (God, it was a mess, why hadn't she had it cut?) she made a resolution to herself. Looking straight into her own eyes in her reflection she said out loud, "You can do this Jill. You can hold on."

With these words echoing in the stillness of the moments resolution, she went to look for some reasonable clothes and check her hospital bag.

Downstairs Jason was getting jittery. He wanted to go upstairs to check she was OK but felt he might be intruding in some way. A distance had grown between them and he was painfully aware the next few hours would increase it, maybe even to the point of no return. He could hear the shower running and gathered she was getting herself ready for the impending ordeal. They had agreed he would be present at the birth and had talked about the implications of this. Although he had his own 3 children, now all grown up and seemingly settled, he had not attended any of their births. This would be an entirely new experience for him and he had no idea what to expect.

He did not hear Nick walk into the kitchen and was suddenly aware he was talking. "Jason, is mum still upstairs? I think I'll be making a move soon. Are you OK?"
Noticing Jason was looking pale and preoccupied, Nick wondered, not for the first time, how this 'baby thing' as he called it, was going to pan out.

Jason nudged himself back into the present and was unsure if he should tell Jill's son his mother's waters had broken. This seemed a dilemma he was not sure he wanted to deal with. Was it down to him, or should he leave it to Jill? If he didn't say anything and Nick

left before she came down, would he feel he had been sidetracked and not 'kept in the loop', as he was often heard to say. If he did tell him, would Jill feel her position had been usurped? Luckily he was saved from having to make any decision as Jill walked in through the door.

"Mum, I'm off. I'll pop in again over the next few days just to say Hi."
"Actually, son, if you've got a minute there's something I need to say. I don't want you going away thinking I've kept you in the dark, so you need to know I'll be going into labour quite soon, my waters have broken."

Nick looked at her as if she had just landed from another planet and was green with little feelers sticking out of her head. Although he had accepted the situation, he had somehow managed to put the final scenario, the birth, on the back burner. Now suddenly the wheels were in motion and it really was going to happen. Had it been anyone else's mum, he might have found it zany and quirky, but this was *his* mum and he found it totally bizarre. He tried to behave nonchalantly and hide the sheer amazement he was feeling deep in his gut.

"You're kidding, right? I thought you had a few more weeks to go. Oh my God, it's really happening then. Is there anything I can do?"

Jill looked at him and was filled with pride. Somehow they would all get through this and things would be OK.

"No, son. Jason is going to come to the hospital with me and he'll keep you informed. Don't worry, everything is going to be fine, there haven't been any problems up to now. Just keep your fingers crossed and I'll see you soon. Hopefully I'll be quite a few pounds lighter!"

With this she gave him a big hug and kiss and looked up into his concerned eyes. She could see he was unsure how to react and she wanted to make light of the situation. He grinned at her half-hearted attempt at a joke.

"OK then, Mum. Shall I let Grace know or will you? Will it be OK if I come up to the hospital to visit you when it's over, though?"
"I'll text Grace a bit later. There's absolutely nothing she can do, so I won't worry her yet. Of course you can come up to the hospital, but I'd wait until Jason lets you know Oliver has arrived, and then come and meet him. How does that sound?"

Oliver's Branch

"OK, I guess. Well just take care, and keep me in the loop."

With that he waved to Jason, gave his mum another kiss and made his way out of the house. They all knew there was nothing else to say. Jill watched him go with a lump in her throat, but felt the chink crack, allowing just a little more confidence and optimism to enter her soul. She turned to Jason and took his hand. "Hold on" she said to herself. "You can do this. Just hold on."

Eight.

As the door slammed, (Nick had never learnt how to close anything quietly), a silence descended over the room like a thin mist, enveloping them both. They stood for a few moments looking at each other and for Jill the old yearning, the too-often-wished wish of things returning to how they had once been, raised its ugly head. She shook it off, knowing it was childish. Jason had become someone else, almost a stranger. She felt he may well rebuff any attempt at even partial reconciliation. She said nothing and went to lie on the settee.

Jason looked at her, wishing with all his heart they could start again. He had never loved or laughed with anyone the way he had with her, but he was sure she felt nothing for him any more. Whatever they had shared had been more fragile than either of them would have ever thought possible. Now it was shattered, like a delicate glass ornament. Their joint hopes and dreams broken by the awful, unnecessary argument. There was no taking back any of the insults or cruel words they had hurled at each other. They had passed the point of no return. All that mattered now was Oliver and afterwards, well the story would play itself out. Jill would never attempt any kind of reconciliation. If she did, he knew he would want to build bridges and maybe they could have a second chance. He had to admit, to himself at least, that he still loved her, but there would be no future for the three of them, Jill had made this fact totally clear and he was unwilling to be rejected again, if he tried to heal the rift. It had all been too painful, he would not, could not, go there again. For now, at least, he knew he must be calm and supportive. He too, said nothing. Instead he went to make another pot of tea.

Jill broke the silence. "You came over to talk about something, what was it, Jason?"

In the kitchen Jason pursed his lips. This was not the time for the discussion he had hoped to have. Pouring the water into the pot he called back. "Oh, it can wait. I think there are more pressing issues at the moment. Shall I put some sugar in this tea, to boost your energy levels?"

"No thanks, to be honest I'm all tea'd out but I know what you could do. There's an unopened tin of peaches in the fridge, will you open it for me?"

Oliver's Branch

Peaches had been a feature of both her previous pregnancies. With her son they had been a craving during most of the nine months she carried him. With her daughter during the final 3 months. Before that she had eaten yoghurt with bean sprouts until it had come out of her ears... This, her third pregnancy had seen the craving for peaches return. She had eaten them at every given moment, with gusto. Maybe this accounted for the fact that she was twelve pounds over her ideal weight, or so the doctor had implied. She nestled down into the cushions as Jason handed her the full tin, with a spoon balancing precariously on the top. He sat down on the edge of the settee, putting his tea on the table nearby.

"Well, here we go then. Somehow it all seems slightly unreal. How do you want to handle the next few hours? Shall I stay and we'll just play it by ear, or do you want a bit of space?"

She desperately wanted to beg him to stay, but was unwilling to put any pressure on him, instead she replied, "Thanks all the same but I think I'll opt for the second choice. I need just a little more time to gather up all the resources I can muster. How about I give you a call as soon as the contractions start in earnest?"
Looking rejected and sad Jason could only respond, "OK then. I need to go and sort out a few things at home, so I'll do that and come back as soon as you call." He gave her a small kiss on the cheek, finished his tea and got up to leave.
"You know Jason things will be OK. Somehow, it's all going to pan out and one day we'll all look back on this and laugh" Jill said, briefly catching hold of his hand.
"I hope so, Jill," he said looking down at her, "I really do."
Then he disengaged himself, walked into the hall and let himself quietly out.

As the door closed, Jill shut her eyes. The silence of the house encircled her. Within it sounds and memories entwined themselves, the past whispered and laughed to her. She saw the large Welsh dresser, full of cards, welcoming Nick into the world. She saw herself gorged with milk sitting on this very settee, feeding him and imaging how his life would be. She knew now, nothing ever turned out for your children the way you imagined or hoped it would, or in your own life come to that. The sounds of laughter and children's footsteps running up and down the stairs intermingled with the later raucous teenage parties and the music she never understood the appeal of. All good memories though. Strange how time cheated you and manipulated the past.

Ruth Manning

She thought about her ex-husband and how they had become strangers under one roof. There had been no violent rows, only a silence, which became a cloak, weighing down on them both and consuming their energy. The children had accepted their decision to divorce and had opted to stay with her; all three of them still saw him quite regularly.

The memory of her first meeting with Jason fluttered through her thoughts. A summer's evening at a party, in a restaurant by the sea. The awful, garish, yellow shirt he had been wearing, with nude Hawaiian dancers printed on it. The way she had ducked under his arm to get to the bar for a drink. The all-night conversation and the laughter they had shared. The immediate knowledge, unspoken but shared by both of them; this encounter was special. How rugged and strong he had looked. She remembered Sunday mornings with the papers strewn all over the bed. The love-making and their conversations, which never seemed to peter out. How happy they had been right up to the pregnancy.

Her backache was getting worse and there were muscles seemingly pulling on her swollen belly. Her body was beginning to take over and she knew there was no point in trying to fight it. The knowledge of the pain and the contractions she was soon to face rose to the surface. Strange, she thought, how after each baby you forget what an ordeal you've had-until the next time. Then the memory returns with a vividness and clarity that takes your breath away. She crossed her fingers and made a silent wish for things to be straightforward and quick.

Deciding she was getting positively maudlin she struggled clumsily off the settee and made her way to the CD player to put on a track from one of her favourite albums. There had been many occasions when the words to this song seemed so appropriate. A broken relationship in her teens. Her daughter's last day at primary school, when she had cried and cried because she didn't want to grow up. The sudden and unexpected death of her father. Jason walking out after 'the big argument'. *Yes,* she thought, *everybody hurts sometimes*, and she had a feeling this time was going to hurt far more than she could ever imagine. "Hold on," she whispered to herself. "Hold on."

Oliver's Branch

Nine.

The following 3 hours seemed to pass in a haze. She must have dozed off for a while, because when she opened her eyes it was pitch black outside. The pain in her back immediately returned and she groaned quietly. There had been no phone calls and no visits. All around everything felt very still. She decided to make herself a small snack and manoeuvred herself around to get up. As she did so her whole body was racked with a powerful clamp-like spasm. She breathed through the pain, relaxing as much as she could. As the contraction subsided she sat perfectly still, waiting for normality to return.

Normality. There would never be normality again, at least not as she had known it. Was she being 'a stupid cow who had lost track of reality'? One of her 'so called 'friends' from work had said this to her some months ago, when she had explained her situation on the phone.

"You cannot be serious, Jill. You've got two grown-up kids already, why not just abort this one and put it down to a bad experience?"

Jill had slammed down the receiver and with it her desire to try and talk to anyone about her situation ever again. It was then that the walls had slowly begun to enclose and isolate her from anyone who tried to get close. Like concrete and mortar she had single-handedly started to build her very own fortress. It was also when she started to push Jason away. She realised this and knew it would take a long time to dismantle the wall, brick by brick, if she ever could. The idea of having an abortion haunted the early months of her pregnancy yet, somehow, the more people advised this quick and painless solution, the more she wanted to experience pain and punish herself, like a slow Chinese torture; a rat slowly gnawing into her very soul to escape the heat of the bowl it was trapped under. On so many levels her emotions and hormones mixed into what felt like a debilitating concoction of lethargy and panic.

Another contraction brought her down to earth and as it subsided she knew she must go and get her things together for the hospital. Looking round her bedroom, full of memories of the last twenty years, photos of her children at different ages, the tapestry on the wall given to her by her ex-mother-in-law for her wedding day, the kidney shaped dressing table she had lovingly restored, she felt as if she was saying goodbye to it all. Life would never be the same after today. She would never be the same. She let out a long sigh, picked

up her holdall and walked slowly back downstairs. Dropping the bag in the hall she returned to the living room. Seeing the present Astrid had left for Oliver she picked it up and put it in the bag then returned to the living room again. She wouldn't call Jason yet, not until a regular and close pattern of pain had established itself.

For the next few hours Jill busied herself with mundane things. She did the washing, tidied the kitchen, fed the animals and let Dyson out, finally she dusted the lounge. Although hindered by the contractions, it was only in the third hour things really began to move. They were coming every six minutes now and she was sticky with sweat. She picked up the phone and called Jason, who promised to be round in 'fifteen minutes, tops'.

When the door opened Jill felt an immense sense of relief. She wasn't alone any more and Jason would be with her now, at least until after the birth. He followed her into the living room. She let Dyson in, feeling guilty, he wouldn't get a walk today, then she sat down again as another contraction took hold.

Jason came and sat down next to her. "My God in heaven. That's been the longest four hours of my life," he said, taking her hand. Jill didn't pull it away. "How I didn't come over earlier I have no idea. Anyway, how are things and what do you want me to do?"
"I think a hot drink and a short wait will be all that's needed, the contractions are stronger now and more difficult to manage. I've brought my stuff down so we can leave as soon as ..."
Jill didn't finish her sentence as the next contraction doubled her up. It seemed to last forever and left her panting and weak.

 She clenched Jason's hand, feeling it was as if they were strangers meeting on a train, but this had been no brief encounter. She turned to him about to explain her mixed emotions and tell him how much she still loved him, but hesitated, and the moment was lost.
"On second thoughts, let's just go. At least they can settle me in and I can lie on a bed. I am a geriatric mother you know." She knew she was trying to take charge of the situation and felt another brick being cemented into the invisible wall between them. *Come on confidence,* she thought. *I will stay strong. I can do this alone, I know I can.*

"OK sweetheart." The endearment had slipped from his lips before he could stop it. He wanted to take her in his arms and hold her close, but he didn't. Instead he continued, "Are you sure about this, all the plans and everything? I know we've gone through it so many

times, what about the instructions for the midwife. Do you still want me to give them to her?"

Without looking at him she replied, slowly and with a confidence she did not feel, "Yes I'm sure. There is no going back now, is there? Did you manage to get everything done at your house? I think I went into 'nest building' syndrome and I've cleaned everything in sight. Come on then let's get there. I think I'll feel safer at the hospital, just in case anything goes wrong."

She walked into the hall and out of the front door, looking back once. It was as if she was saying goodbye to an old friend who she would never see again. A past life and another world. Jason bent down and picked up the small hospital bag, then followed her out, closing the door quietly behind him.

The journey was short, silent and uneventful. Arriving in the car at the maternity entrance, Jill felt another sharp contraction. She sat perfectly still, breathing deeply, gripping Jason's hand tightly. He sat quietly next to her. So close and yet so far away. He felt completely helpless and didn't know what to do or say. When the pain past he disentangled his hand from hers and went around the side of the car to help her out. They walked, close together, to the entrance. Looking for all the world like any other couple. Older than most they may be, but they were just another two people having a baby, just the same.

Inside the entrance Jason found a wheel and chair for Jill to sit in. "Better safe than sorry" he said, and winked. She couldn't help but grin and obediently placed her somewhat cumbersome frame into the chair. For all her exterior bravado she actually felt old, tired, lost and in pain.

Arriving at the ward she was allocated a room and all the tests were carried out. She was introduced to her midwife for the 'duration'. She was a German woman named Heidi. Large and big-breasted with a double chin and a large mole on her cheek sporting two wispy hairs, she would certainly take no nonsense from her patients. Jill saw her having a long discussion with Jason and frowning, but she nodded her head as understandingly as he carried on talking. Looking around the sterile room Jill thought how everything seemed to have become far more technical and computerised over the last nineteen years. She was unsure what most of the machines and monitors were for. She was informed all was well and she was 6 centimetres dilated. Things were moving fast and her contractions were becoming more intense. She remembered gratefully accepting the gas and air offered to her, sucking on it greedily as the pains became more acute. She remembered Jason talking to her, holding

her hand and wiping her hair out of her eyes. Heidi seemed to want to 'bond' with her and kept telling her how important *their* relationship was for the well-being of her child. How following her 'instructions' was crucial for a problem-free birth. Jill wanted to tell her she didn't give a shit about bonding with her, but frankly couldn't be bothered. At the same time she sensed some undercurrents of disapproval, which, on one level made her feel like a young child who was being reprimanded. On another level however, she felt a sense of detachment and pity for this officious young woman. She remembered telling Jason to shut his mouth, (well a few expletives meaning roughly the same thing), and if he knew so much, why didn't he have the bloody baby? The gas and air numbed her brain and the pain made her want to push. Only Frau Heidi's command, "You vill not push yet, you must hold on.." registered. So she held on (now this *was* a new meaning to the phrase.) She held on until she thought she would burst and sucked on the gas and air as if her very life depended on it.

She felt Heidi part her legs to a point where she thought her hips would crack and then the midwife's breath on her groin. What was this woman doing? Then came the loud command...
"You are voolly dilated. Now you must push."
Jill pushed. She pushed for all the hurt and humiliation and anger, for all the frustration, isolation and fear, and for all the yesterdays and tomorrows of her life.
She heard from far off a primeval scream coming from somewhere deep within her very being. Suddenly a sense of floating and being free surged through her with the intensity and light of a vision. The pressure and pain stopped and dispersed into the sterility and harsh brightness of the clinical, machine-dominated room. It was then she heard the newly born infant's cry.

She tried to sit up, to see Oliver. Her very being needed to hold her son, put him to her breast, feed him and protect him.

Heidi pushed her back forcefully. Jill noticed that her arms were very hairy and covered in small, brown moles."It is verree important now zat you lie down pleeze. I must bring zee avta birth."

Oliver was being wiped, checked over, and swaddled and Jason came back into focus. There were tears in his eyes and he was physically shaking.
"My God, sweetheart, you were amazing. That was amazing. He's absolutely perfect." He looked deeply into her eyes for a long time. *I will always love you and I am so sorry you made this choice. I wish*

Oliver's Branch

you everything you want for yourself and I hope your dreams come true. Take care; I will always love you, he thought, but didn't say. Then, without a word, he kissed her on the cheek, moved away and left the room. Oliver was wheeled out behind him.

Heidi appeared to have dealt with the 'afta birth' and Jill felt herself being wiped down and washed.

"Vood you like tea?" she asked somewhat coldly. Jill nodded and resisted the temptation to reply "Ya-vole."
Heidi bustled from the room and suddenly it was empty. She was alone. Even the machines around her were silent. An auxiliary brought her a cup of insipid tea, but it still tasted good, the 'best cup of tea in the world', even if it was about the eighth cup within the last twelve hours. She lay her head back on the pillow and put her free hand on her hollow, empty belly. It was over; well almost over.

For the next twenty minutes she was left in peace and then the door opened. Jason walked in and went to her bedside. He put a piece of paper next to her empty cup and looked at her uncertainly.

"The papers arrived today. That was what I wanted to talk to you about. Just sign on the dotted line, if you're sure you can live with your decision. We can still work this out if you want to. I still love you, you know that."

Jill took the pen he offered her. Hold on? Let go? How she wanted to hold on but now it was time to let go. This is what she had been preparing herself for over the last nine months and now it was time. She placed the nib on the dotted line…As she did so she looked at the legally binding document in front of her. She was giving up her son and making Jason his full-time, paternal guardian. She would have no rights and no part in her son's future. She would never see him again. She would never hold him close, be there when he teethed or when he lost his first tooth. She would never see him take his first step, or hear him say his first word. She would never see him smile. She was going away and leaving him far, far behind. She felt like an empty vessel, a used-up surrogate, a ship adrift on a becalmed sea.

Minutes passed. Jason stood waiting patiently. He didn't speak; there was nothing left to say. Jill picked up the pen, with tears blotting the page, she signed away any future rights she would ever have, of being Oliver's mother.

"Let go," she whispered to herself, hoping one day she could.

Ruth Manning

"Look upwards with Confidence"

Ten.

Jason left, after informing her Nick was on his way. She made a mental note to phone Grace when she arrived on the ward. Because of her age she knew she would be staying until the doctor checked her out in the morning. Then, if her uterus had gone down she would be free to leave.

A stout porter with a froggy grin came into the room. His skin was pale with a lardy quality and he smelt of cigarettes. He was very cheerful and started congratulating 'the proud mum'. *If only he knew,* she thought, *how ashamed I actually am.* She said nothing and he continued to talk. Apparently there had been a major accident on the A21 earlier, which was why he had been so long in coming down to pick her up. A&E was in chaos. Jill said it didn't matter and hoped there were no fatalities. It appeared there weren't. As they went up in the lift he lent on the wall and looked at her.

"A boy or a girl?" Mr Froggy asked.
"A boy." She replied
"How much did he weigh?"
"Um, I'm not sure." No one had bothered to tell her any details about her son and she felt stupid and ignorant.
"Oh, right..." said Mr Froggy, in a somewhat off-hand way, as he pushed her out of the lift and into the ward.

There were 10 beds, 9 of them filled. Some of the mothers had family around them coo-cooing the latest arrival, some were asleep, others listening to MP3 players or iPods. The thing Jill noticed most was they all looked *so young!*
Jill knew Nick would pop in and wondered what the other mothers would make of her situation. Notably, there was no husband or partner close by and her only male visitor was in his early twenties! She wished she had booked a private room but it was too late now. She got unsteadily off the trolley and onto the freshly made bed. She was glad there had been no stitches this time and things had gone so smoothly. In fact of the three deliveries this one had been the most uneventful physically, although mentally it had been by far the most traumatic. Mr Froggy said his goodbyes and left. Jill got up and drew the curtain around the bed, blocking out all the prying eyes. She got back on the bed, with difficulty. Why were hospital beds always so high? She rang the bell to attract a nurse. As usual there seemed to be about six of them at the workstation, so she hoped the

wait would be short. Sure enough the curtain drew back and a young blonde-haired nurse in a purple uniform came in. Her name tag read 'Tracy Evans' which was pinned lopsidedly on her breast pocket. Even uniforms had changed and were more informal with no sign of the crisp white starched hats.

"Hello Mrs Slater. I was just coming to see how you were. We have had instructions from your partner, Mr Simms, and are aware of your situation. In case you're interested, everything is fine with the baby and he will be going home with his father in the morning." For the second time in just a few hours she felt like a small child being reprimanded. "Oh thank you," she managed to reply. "Do you think I could have a phone? There are a few calls I need to make."

"I'm sure there are," she said, in what to Jill sounded a very supercilious tone. "I'll get you one right away. Is there anything else you want?"

Jill rummaged in the holdall and produced a small soft teddy she had bought a few days before, unable to resist its sad, brown eyes and the embroidered name "Oliver" across his fluffy chest. She also took out the package from Astrid. "Could you give these to the baby please?" she asked handing them to Tracy.

"I'll put them for collection by his father tomorrow," she replied coldly and exited, leaving the curtain wide open.

The phone arrived within the hour and Jill phoned Grace. She was not sure how the conversation would go, but it had to be done. Grace answered on the third ring and not knowing who it was, this number would not register on her mobile, sounded very formal.

"Hi sweetheart how you doing?" Jill asked.
"Oh fine. Short of money, knackered from the job and behind on an assignment. Otherwise everything's going well. What about you? I don't recognise the number."

"Well, I'm fine too. Sore, but fine. Oliver was born about a few hours ago. No problems and he is apparently perfect. All fingers and toes present, or so I'm told. I have to stay the night but will be out in the morning, all being well. Jason is keeping an eye on Oliver and will be taking him to Neptune Road tomorrow. That's it."

There was a brief silence. Grace had found it impossible to believe her mum was giving up her half-brother and had told her so. In the end though she had accepted the decision her mum had made, and

realised it wasn't down to her to moralise about it. This was her mother's life, not hers. Jill remembered saying to her; "Things have a way of working themselves out, 'what will be will be'. (Another well used adage.) No one knows what the future holds, so please let me do it my way, however much it hurts or however stupid you may think I am."

"Oh! OK." She said bringing Jill back to the present, "I'll talk to Jason tomorrow. It's a bit late now. I'm glad you're OK. Will you get in touch, with all the gory details, tomorrow? You must be so tired."

"Of course I will. Sleep tight sweetheart. Talk to you soon. Love you so much."
"Me too, mum. Night night."
As she put the receiver down she saw Nick pulling back the curtain, which she had drawn again when the phone arrived. It had felt like a rebellious gesture at the time.
"Hi, Mum. I've looked in on Oliver. He's got blonde hair. That's so weird, we were both so dark. Anyway, he's fine. He's taken a bottle and looks all cosy and new. Are you OK? Well done by the way, old gal!"
He gave her a hug and unceremoniously dropped a puzzle book and some grapes on the table.

All this was too much information for Jill. It made everything real and all she wanted to do was compartmentalise it and try to move on. Yet the thought of having a blonde child somehow pleased her. She wondered if he would have blue eyes. She hugged Nick, thanked him for the gifts and then listened to his latest exploits and news. It was as if he too was putting his half-brother into some sort of perspective and coming to terms with it in his own way. She doubted they would ever be close, but hoped he would keep in touch with Jason and the rest of the family. God knows what they really thought about the whole situation. Jason had told her a bit about the responses to him raising another son, alone, at the age of fifty two, but now it was a reality and she was not sure if Jason really understood the enormity of it.

Nick babbled on for a while and then said he had to go as there was a really good film on TV he wanted to catch. Then he was going to have an early night. He gave her a big kiss on the cheek, said he would see her soon and left. Jill had probably said no more than a dozen words throughout the whole visit, and Nick seemed to have treated the birth more like a minor operation than the major event she felt it had been. She pondered, not for the first time, the

resilience and self-absorption of youth. Not just Nick. All young people appeared to have this attribute. She wondered if she had been the same and concluded she most certainly had.

The clock on the wall read 11.45. Nick's early nights usually spanned out into early mornings, she hoped he would enjoy the film. As for her, there was nothing left to do. She made her way wearily and slowly to the bathroom and had a hot shower. As soon as she felt better she promised herself she would have her hair cut. Feeling slightly more human, she made her way back to bed. Her curtains were open again. She drew them round like a magical cloak, making her invisible to the outside world. She curled up under the sheets and turned onto her stomach. It was the first time she had been able to do this for months. Pushing both hands under the pillow, she nestled down and settled into an exhausted and deep sleep.

Eleven.

As usual, life on the ward seemed to start at an unearthly hour. By six O'clock she was wide awake. Her curtains had been drawn back again, obviously while she slept and a nurse, not Tracy but Mandy this time, had already taken her blood pressure, checked her uterus level, which apparently was virtually back where it should be and then disappeared. No doubt back to the workstation to discuss something meaningful with the other nurses, like sex or love or lust or their last date (they all looked so incredibly young.)

Jill knew there was no point in trying to go back to sleep. She left the curtain open and looked around the ward. Somehow this gesture made her feel stronger and more confident. She would never see any of these people again and now she had to start making plans for the rest of her life. Anyway, they all looked totally absorbed in their maternal duties or were just holding their carefully wrapped bundles of joy close, looking lovingly at their tiny faces.

The thought of Oliver and how he was doing was constantly at the forefront of her mind but she tried to push it aside and concentrate on her plan of action. She wondered what had happened to the list she had started at home and decided this was as good a time as any to start another one. Delving into her overnight holdall she pulled out a small notebook and a pen. Originally the book had been for thoughts and feelings throughout the pregnancy. It had been given to her by her old school friend, when she had heard the news.
"It's going to be a hard time for you, I know, but you've always enjoyed keeping a diary, so I thought this would be useful." Sarah had handed her a beautifully leather-bound journal which had been made to look like something Jane Austen would probably have written in. Jill had loved it straight-away and promised she would use it. As the months had gone by, however, she had found it harder and harder to put her feelings onto paper. They were too mosaic, too transient, too unpredictable. Most of all they were too hurtful and too real. Somehow the journal had been abandoned and exiled to a shelf in the kitchen, to gather dust. She had picked it up a few days earlier and decided to take it to the hospital, just in case.

Sarah was a nurse and had been a midwife. She lived in Wood Green with her husband and dog. Both her children had also left home, but Sarah, like Astrid felt only complete liberation. She and Jill had known each other for over thirty five years. Where Jill had been the flighty, often wild and rebellious young woman, Sarah was the calm, responsible and grounded one. Although Jill had calmed down over

the years, she was amazed at how strong and resilient her friend had become. In their school days it was Jill who led the way (usually into trouble) now she turned to Sarah for support and wisdom. Thinking of her friend, she opened the journal to a fresh page and wrote:
1) Phone Sarah as soon as I'm home
2) Get plastic storage boxes and tissue
3) Phone the property management bloke
4) Get hair cut and coloured
5) Throw away all maternity clothes
6) Phone the estate agent re. selling the house
7) Talk to June about the cats
8) Talk to Grace
9) Think about resigning from the job.

She paused, thinking of Brightey and Aspro. She had decided there was no way they could go with her to Crete. Firstly it was too hot and secondly they were too old. When June had 'popped in' yesterday (was it really only yesterday?) a plan had come to Jill. Maybe, just maybe, June would have them. They spent most of their days in her garden anyway and seemed to be OK with Archy. June often fed them and when she was gardening they lazed around watching her work. She decided it was worth talking to her neighbour about it.

"Anything to eat?" A gruff voice butted into her thoughts. An auxiliary, who looked about fifteen and had buck teeth, was standing over her bed, encroaching on her personal space. Jill moved slightly and shook her head.
"No thanks, I think I'll wait a bit."
The auxiliary made a sort of 'hmmph' noise and darted off to the next bed. The clock on the wall said nearly eight o clock. Jill had never been a breakfast person and during the last few months had not been a morning person either. Having no work to get up for she often stayed in bed till around ten, reading a good book, or sometimes a magazine. She put the journal back in her bag and went to take a shower. Wash away the shame? Purge the guilt? Drown the sorrow? she wondered, as she walked slowly down the ward. She decided, after very little hesitation, it was all three.

Amazingly there was no one else in the shower room. She noticed a bidet in the corner and went over to it. Nick had come out 'punching' and had ripped her. She had had internal stitches and been very sore. The young mum in the next bed had suggested she used the bidet and then a hair dryer instead of a towel. This had proved a godsend and became a joke on the ward. Whenever they heard the

dryer going behind the closed curtains someone would say "Oh! Jill's having another blow job!"
She wasn't nearly as sore now but used the bidet just the same, then hopped into the shower. The water was hot and powerful and she felt invigorated by it. For the first time in a long while she felt something resembling normality. As she towelled herself down she could not help but notice the saggy skin around her belly. "Exercise" she said out loud. She would add this to the list.

Back in the ward it looked as if one of the doctors was doing an early round. She recognised him. He had been the doctor who had discharged her after she had given birth to Grace. Mr Chichargee, or something like that, was a small man, with long tapering fingers, which she seemed to remember had been freezing cold when he examined her. Half-rimmed glasses balanced precariously on his nose. She doubted he would recognise her. At that moment he moved round to the side of her bed. The nurse, (Trudy this time,) pulled the curtains round them.
"Well, Mrs Slater, lets have a look at you." He glanced at the notes Trudy handed him.
"All straightforward then, considering your age. How do you feel?"
"Actually I feel fine. Much better than I thought I would." Mr C asked her to lie back and pull up her nightie. She was glad she had put sensible knickers on after her shower. He asked her to remove them. Somehow even though she had been pummelled and prodded so much over the last nine months, she still felt embarrassed exposing herself.

After a very brief internal examination and cold hands prodding her stomach in search of the uterus level, she was declared fit for discharge. As he walked briskly away to another bed, Jill breathed a sigh of relief.

This is it, she thought. This is the first day of the rest of my life.

Having dressed and signed out at the nurses' workstation, she realised she would have to take a taxi home. No one would be around at this hour to give her a lift. Anyway she wanted to cherish the feeling of being totally anonymous and faceless to all around her. Walking out of the hospital she switched on her mobile. She had 4 text messages. One from Grace asking her to call. One from Sarah who wondered where she was as she wasn't picking up the phone at home. One from Astrid asking her to call and finally one from Jason. He explained he would be taking Oliver home at about midday and that all was well. Saying it would be fine if she rang him at any

time. Ending with congratulations and well done, with four kisses tagged on. She dialled up a taxi, then walked to towards the exit, to wait. Every sinew in her body was pulling her back, to go and just take a look at her new son. Somehow, she managed to resist, knowing it would only make the whole situation worse. Her hormones were in turmoil and her very core ached to hold Oliver, but taking a deep breath, she pushed open the doors and listened to them close behind her.

It was an amazingly clear day, quite warm with blue sky. She saw this as a good omen for Oliver. His first day in the world was going to be a good one. She hoped all his days would be blessed. It seemed strange to think he would never know her and consequently never miss her. The empty space in her womb was the only thing left acknowledging his development and recent departure. Yet she hadn't cried in the hospital. She wondered if this was a good sign or if she was in shock and the enormity of it all would hit her later. She hoped it was the first. Now there was a great amount to do. It was time to summon up some of the old, assertive, business-like, optimistic Jill. It was time to find the person who had all but disappeared just lately. Looking up at the cloudless sky, she waited patiently for her taxi to arrive.

Some ten minutes later the pip of a horn brought her back to the present, as a Ford Mondeo pulled up. She got in and gave the cab driver her address. He was a young man, possibly Bulgarian or Rumanian. It was obvious he was not going to engage her in small talk. He set the sat-nav then entered the line of commuter traffic. Ten silent minutes later she was outside her front door. Alone again, she took out her front-door key, opened the door and walked slowly in.

Twelve.

The house was, of course, just as she had left it. The silence hung in the empty spaces, occupying every nook and cranny, like a thick fog; even the dog had not appeared to notice she was home. This was going to be the hardest part. This was the moment between two worlds, past and future. This was the moment which would shape all other moments, for the rest of her life. She retrieved her journal, dropped her bag by the stairs, and went through to the kitchen, opening the conservatory door to let out a now very excited Dyson. He jumped up and nuzzled her, wagging his tail manically. She wondered if all Labradors wagged their tails in a clockwise direction, or if this was a trait peculiar only to him. She hugged him, glad of the physical contact. He wriggled free and disappeared into the garden.

In the kitchen she put on the kettle to make a strong black coffee. She wasn't sure she would ever drink tea again after yesterday. While she waited for the water to boil she opened the journal and turned to the list. She decided there was no chronological order and so scribbled out the numbers down the side. She was just about to pick up the phone and call Sarah when it began to ring.
"Hello," she said half-heartedly into the mouthpiece.
"Mrs Slater, hi, it's Nathan from Properties to Go. I wondered if you could possibly come down for a chat in the near future."
Nathan, with his neat little silver Porsche Boxter and smart suits. Financially too rich, too young. Emotionally poor, too late.
"OK, fine. I'm actually free later on today, so I can come to the office, if that's good for you?"
"Yes, absolutely fine. Look forward to seeing you. I'm in the office all day."

Jill hung up and made a coffee, let Dyson in and sat down. Well one thing on the list had dealt with itself. She dunked the last digestive into the cup – breakfast. Then she went upstairs, cleaned her teeth and decided to go straight into town and find out what her officious little agent wanted.

Having parked in the phenomenally expensive multi-storey car park, she walked to the office. Now was the time to be who she used to be and use her wits to ward off any difficulties the agent was going to present. Some more of the old Jill forced itself into her psyche. "Here we go," she muttered to herself then pushed open the estate agent's door.

Oliver's Branch

In the office a sense of doom seemed to hang in the air. She walked over to Nathan's desk and sat down, waiting for him to finish his phone call. When he hung up she was straight in. The new, or was it the old, Jill?

"So what's the problem then, Nathan?"

Ten minutes later having explained the possible crash in the housing market, the imminent recession and all other impending doom he concluded; "So I'm afraid in order to sell your house we will have to reduce it by at least £25,000." There was not a hint of emotion or care for the impact this would have. He looked at her dismissively then glanced at his mobile phone. It felt as if he was willing it to ring. Any distraction to enable him to terminate the meeting. As far as he was concerned the news had been imparted. His job was done. End of.

This was not good, Jill thought. Five months earlier at the start of the sale, she had cut the asking price by the same amount, hoping for a quick sale. This would put the initial estimated price down by £50,000. With present financial commitments it was not viable.

"Tell you what, Nathan, let me think about this and get back to you. OK?"

He nodded his agreement and she stood up, looked him square in the eye, then walked out without a backward glance. She hoped Oliver wouldn't grow up to be such an arrogant, shallow human being.

The next thing she decided to tackle frightened her. She would be sailing into uncharted territory. Maybe she was grasping at straws but it was either: a) renting out her home and maybe getting a mortgage, moving on and starting again; or b) existing, for the next five years, in the same dull, unappealing life with no direction or real meaning, hoping house prices would rise. She had given up Oliver. She needed to start again.

She felt no inclination to look round the shops but stopped off at one of the cheap shops and picked up six large plastic containers and a big packet of tissue paper then went straight back home. With a determination to 'get the ball rolling' she picked up the phone and rang William Slowstern. After two rings a deep voice at the other end asked,

"William Slowstern, property management, can I help you?"

"Ah yes, hello. I was given your name by a friend. I wondered if you could spare the time to explain the principle of renting out my property?"

Jill could hear pages turning and rolled her eyes at the thought of maybe a week or two week wait for an appointment. She needed to do things, not just sit around and twiddle her thumbs.

"As it happens I'm free this afternoon at fourteen hundred hours. If this is convenient I will come up to you. This will give me an opportunity to peruse the property."

"Perfect!" Jill replied, wondering if he had a moustache and a monocle. "I'll stay in. I look forward to meeting you." She gave him her address and full name plus details of where the house was situated.

"Know the area well. See you in a few hours, Mrs Slater. Goodbye." With this Mr Slowstern hung up. Jill stood holding the receiver, imagining the man she had just spoken to. As she put it down she clicked her heels together and saluted. "Yes sir," she muttered under her breath.

Mission accomplished she suddenly felt immensely weak and exhausted. She should not have attempted to do so much so soon after her ordeal. She had just had a baby, for heavens sake. A wave of nausea swept over her and she sat down at the table. She wanted to cry curl up in bed, surrendering herself to sleep, escaping the terrible emptiness she felt both physically and mentally, but she knew this was a bad idea. She picked up the journal and crossed out numbers 2, 3 and 6. She couldn't call Sarah yet, she felt too emotional and realised she must wait until she felt stronger. How different from her arrival home after both Nick and Grace's births. All the calls and visitors, laughs and congratulatory hugs. The house had been a hive of activity, the welsh dresser bedecked in congratulatory cards. Soft toys, baby-grows, blankets and other gifts scattered everywhere, along with the wrapping paper. Her then husband had helped with all the chores and watched over them, the proud dad. Jill's mother and father had been there too. Yes, they had been real family occasions. This time no one was even aware of her child's birth, except her own children and obviously Jason's family. She glanced at the clock. It was midday already. Oliver would be going home. She wrapped her arms tightly round her body, needing to feel some kind of physical contact, even if it was only her own. This was the nearest she would get to being held, for a long time.

When Jason had moved out, finally, in April, they had hugged and agreed their friendship would survive. Their relationship had shifted, but not completely disintegrated. He would, he promised, keep her updated on the baby's progress, if she wanted to know, of course. She hadn't been sure how or what she would feel, so they arranged she would make the first call after the birth. They would take things from there. She had to admit, she missed Jason, mainly because there was a large gap in her life where their relationship had been. After the quarrel, things had been on rocky ground but

surprisingly had improved once the decision had been made that Jason would take over the upbringing of their baby. She was adamant, once it was all over, she would want no because contact with Jason or the child ever again. "You are the one who wanted this little bastard, so you can bloody well have him," she had shouted. She cringed at the memory and knew just how wrong she had been. A red mist had engulfed her and the hurtful words once spoken could never be retracted. Now she felt totally different. She hoped with all her heart day she could meet Oliver one day. She had given up all her rights to her son, now she could only pray it was not forever. For now everything was too painful to dwell on. She was emotionally bereaved and physically spent. Until everything was in some sort of perspective and her friends and family accepted the choices she had made, she was unable, or was it unwilling, to form any kind of relationship with her son. She felt guilty and selfish and totally confused.

"Enough," she murmured to herself. "Move on. Be confident. Get your life in order. Function. Astrid was right. Stop beating yourself up and get on with life." Only the silence listened to her self-remonstrations. Suddenly aware of how hungry she was hastily prepared herself a sandwich a cup of coffee. So far she had managed done nothing but feel sorry for herself, when everything was down to her and the decisions she had made. She gave Dyson a stroke and with a deep sigh, looked again at the list, adding number ten. *Start packing the boxes.*

Having busied herself washing up the plate and mug she dried them and put them away. They looked so pathetic sitting there on the draining board, alone. She was wiping down the surfaces when the doorbell rang. Wiping her hands and throwing the tea towel over her shoulder, she went to answer it. An exceedingly short, clean shaven and somewhat rotund middle aged man, stood on the step.
"Good afternoon. Mrs Slater, I presume? I'm a little early. Allow me to introduce myself ma'am, I'm William Slowstern."

Ruth Manning

Thirteen.

So much for impressions, Jill thought to herself. She'd been so wrong it was laughable. This man's physical presence and his telephone persona were completely at odds with each other.

"Do come in, Mr Slowstern," she said and motioned to the living room.
"William, please," he said, then followed her in. He waited for her to sit down at the table, before following suit. Jill couldn't help but think how many different moments had played themselves out at this table. Family meals, family birthdays, Christmas dinners and long, protracted conversations. It had seen its fare share of arguments, laughter and tears. It was a part of the family, their lives together engrained in its wooden frame. Jill wondered if there would be another momentous, life-changing revelation to add to all of these in the next hour or so.

William was very relaxed and organised. The first part of the process was a look around the house. Jill explained about her house on Crete and her desire to live there as soon as possible, but nothing more. Would he be surprised to know only yesterday she had given birth to her son? She wasn't sure. He seemed the kind of cool, controlled man who was not easily fazed.

After the tour William informed her there would be no problem renting the property out. The main thing was to decide how much mortgage she would need. Next they would look for a reliable mortgage-to-let company willing to proceed. He explained about interest rates and the fact that they may be high, but if they sorted things out the rent would pay the monthly charge. He went on to say he would want total autonomy over the management of the property. He would be in charge of the tenants, the house and the finances. She would be able to go to Crete and 'enjoy life' while he did all the work... for a 10% monthly charge based on the rental, of course. He showed her numerous pieces of paper explaining how the agency ran, many of which she would have to sign if she decided to proceed.

It was mind boggling. Jill knew if she made the decision to do this, there was no going back. She asked various questions and hoped she sounded business-like and financially astute. Inwardly she felt totally confused and bewildered. She needed time to decide and wanted to talk to Astrid about all the implications. She wanted to talk to Jason too. He was far more money-minded than she was and had often accused her of being too generous with her money,

especially to her children. She knew she wouldn't contact him though. She was on her own.

Two hours later with the tabletop covered in official-looking papers and scribbled calculations, William took his leave of her. They had agreed she would think things through and contact him with a decision, when she had made one. They shook hands and she was surprised at how firm and brisk his handshake was. As she closed the door behind him she felt oddly elated. This could be the way forward. If things worked out she would be able to walk away, into the sunshine, never looking back. That was the theory anyway.

"Yeah right, Jill," she said to the empty house. "Get real. This isn't some soppy romantic B movie where everything happened just the way it should, with more sugary coating than a sugared almond. This is real life." She realised this was *her* real life. Her recent past certainly was not a 'happily ever after' scenario. Still, there was a lot to think about. She sent a text to Astrid; "Plenty of chocolate up for grabs. Any chance you can come over for half an hour?"
She decided not to mention Oliver's birth until they were face to face. It was too enormous an event to belittle by some crass text statement like... "and hey Oliver's arrived..."
Within minutes her mobile chirped a received message.
"No probs babe. I'm almost finished here. Be round in about 20 mins. Put the kettle on."

Jill sorted the papers and did as she had been asked. True to her word Astrid was on the door step exactly twenty minutes later. Jill wondered if she would notice the lack of the bump, but as she was still in a smock thought she would not be scrutinised too closely. True to form, Astrid wafted past her and sat at the table, waiting expectantly for the promised tea and chocolate. Jill dunked a bag in a cup. She still couldn't face a cup herself, then putting cup and chocolate in front of her friend, she sat down.

"You look tired babe. All dark under the eyes as if you've been up all..."
Astrid stopped, gaped and quickly got up. She moved round the table and put her hand where the bump should have been.
"Oh my God! Oh my God! He was early then? Are you OK? How was it? Is he with you or did you really go through with it? Why on earth didn't you let me know?" She put three cubes of chocolate in her mouth as if she knew she needed to stop asking questions, but couldn't.
Jill looked at her and felt strangely serene. She was going to tell her the whole story and when she finished, she would lock the memory

away, somewhere deep within her heart. Suddenly she knew exactly what she was going to do. She would use her friend as a sounding board, but the ultimate decision, she knew, had already been reached.

For almost an hour she talked through Oliver's birth. How great Jason had been. How the midwife had tried to bond with her, in a Germanic sort of way, but with an air of disdain, as if she was only following protocol. She explained how reasonably easy it had gone but also how incredibly hard it had been not to take Oliver in her arms, and just love him. She described the froggy porter and the three nurses who had dealt with her. She laughed at them all having names ending in y. Where had all the good old fashioned names like Elizabeth, Anne and Victoria gone? She described coming home, her mixture of emotions and the hormonal overload she was feeling.

Astrid listened in stunned silence, but Jill hadn't finished. Although she was emotionally drained, she had a need to continue but there was something she had to do first. As she leaned back in her chair, taking a moment to internalise things, she wrapped the memory of the experience, and her loss of Oliver, in an imaginary piece of white satin. She placed this precious gift in an equally imaginary intricate box with gold trimmings. She locked the box carefully with a large gold key and placed this invisible talisman next to her heart. Only then was she able to move on to her visit from William Slowstern. She recounted all the information and implications of the rental idea and explained the facts and figures she had on the scribbled pages in front of her.

She had never known her friend to be so quiet. When she finished the ensuing silence was palpable. Jill waited, worn out from the effort of talking for so long. At last Astrid spoke.
"Are you sure this is the right thing to do. What happens if you have second thoughts about Oliver? What happens if this Slowstern bloke can't get lodgers? What are you going to do if or when you do go? You don't have many friends out there and it's going to be so lonely and isolated for you."

Jill considered carefully, before replying. "I have to go. I can't possibly stay here and go on as if nothing ever happened. I hate the job now anyway and there is nothing, absolutely nothing to stop me. Nick and Grace have their own lives. I'll only be four hours away by plane. I need to do this, because if I don't, I will just sink back into the life I had before but without the colour and the joy of the

tapestry the kids and I wove together. Clean page. Clean slate. New friends. I can do this Astrid. I can and I will."

They talked for another hour about how much she would need to do. No more was said about the birth of Oliver and Jill was grateful to her friend for being both diplomatic and sensitive, not one of her most obvious traits most of the time. Astrid said she would help in any way she could and hey, what a great place it would be for her to go during the summer. Jill was not so sure she would be entertaining much, especially at first, but she let it ride.

It was dark when she said goodbye to her friend at the door. She promised to keep her up-to-date with everything, and then she went back to the living room. She added number eleven to the list.

    11)   Call Mr S tomorrow and agree to rental of home.

With that she closed the journal and drew all the curtains. She was going to have a hot bath, watch a DVD, have a glass of wine and then go to bed.

Fourteen.

After a restless and tearful night filled with images of the previous one plus an emptiness she could hardly endure, Jill awoke to a drab, grey day. Looking out of the window she felt as if her emotions were being reflected by the weather. If she wasn't careful she was afraid she would sink back into the depression and self pity, which she knew had driven Jason away. At the same time the realization of what she had done was beginning to dawn on her. She had given Oliver, her son, away. She had signed his life over to his father and with it her maternal rights and part of her very being. How callous and selfish was she? Most of her friends had been amazed at her decision and all had expressed their concerns. Apart from the postnatal depression they all agreed she was bound to experience, they all seemed to believe she would never get over her decision and the guilt would destroy her. She would be emotionally fragile and unstable before the birth, and none of them could even begin to imagine how she would cope afterwards. Pessimism, doom and gloom were all around her, but her resolve to prove them wrong was emerging like a small butterfly from its cocoon. She got out of bed and headed for the bathroom. She was sore and stiff and very alone, but she knew she had to stop wallowing in this quagmire of recrimination and feelings of loss. It was time to moving forward.

The bath lifted her spirits. The scales told her she was 12 pounds lighter. The mirror told her to make a hair appointment. She dressed in jeans and a fleece and went downstairs to start a new day.

Deciding to eat later, she made a large mug of strong black coffee, let Dyson out into the garden, then went and sat in the conservatory. Picking up the phone she dialled Mr Slowstern's number. He answered on the second ring. She told him her decision. He made an appointment for her to go to the office at 3 O'clock the same day. She then phoned Sarah on her mobile. Like most people, her friend was at work and said she would ring in the evening. Jill did not mention Oliver. She picked up her journal and crossed out number 11 on the list, along with number 1. Next she phoned her local hairdresser, a lovely woman called Zoe, and made an appointment for later in the morning. Jill was pleased to be getting organised, she crossed out number 4. At this rate the list would be completed in no time and with the appointments to fill her day, she felt a sense of purpose. It was just after ten when she left the house. She had seen to Dyson and the cats, washed her mug and placed it on the draining board. Again she thought how lonely and isolated it looked, mirroring how she felt. She turned back, picked it up, and returned it to its rightful

place, with all the other mugs. If only she could become a part of something so easily, a mug among countless other mugs, sitting comfortably on a shelf with a real purpose in life. Raising her eyebrows at her stupidity and sentimentality (over a mug, for God's sake,) she walked out of the house into the greyness of the morning.

Zoe was surprised to see Jill, minus the bump. She had called in a few weeks before, to drop off a book she knew Zoe would enjoy. They had often talked about books in the days when Jill had appointments on a regular basis, and discovered they had the same taste in literature, although Zoe had read very few classical books. Jill had taken in a copy of Hardy's 'Far from the Madding Crowd,' knowing she would enjoy it. Zoey had commented on the obvious pregnancy, but Jill had offered very little information, apart from the approximate 'due' date.

"Hello, Jill," Zoe said warmly, as she walked in. She was ten minutes early. "Looks as though you've had the baby then. I hope everything went well?" Jill said it had all been fine, but did not elaborate. Zoe asked the usual questions, boy or girl? His weight? Hair colour and so on. Jill answered them all, making up Oliver's weight. After a while, Zoe realised Jill was not going to have an animated discussion about the baby. Seeing Jill to a chair, having washed and conditioned her hair (which had obviously not had any attention for at least six months) they discussed the cut and colour. Having never been very enthusiastic about how her hair looked, as long as it was reasonably short and manageable, Jill opted for 'her usual.' They chatted idly about the Hardy book and several films, as Zoe snipped and clipped and snipped some more. Once the colour was on, Jill was ready for some peace and quiet. She picked up a magazine and started to read. Her hairdresser went off happily to another customer and left her in peace. There was a good feature on how to de-clutter your life called 'Out with the old.' It was practical and unsentimental advice, suggesting absolutely anything you haven't touched, looked at, or worn for over six months should be weeded out. It went on to give examples of individuals who had followed the advice and become minimalist. They were all, apparently, totally liberated and amazed at their new sense of freedom and self-worth. "I used to spend two hours a week dusting; now it takes me ten minutes," one satisfied interviewee had exclaimed. Jill could almost hear other supporters raising their hands and chanting "Praise the Lord". She had always been a hoarder and a sentimentalist. Thinking of all the packing ahead of her, she wondered how much would end up at charity shops, in the bin or outside the garage, with a 'Help Yourself' sign. She had de-cluttered part of the conservatory and living room in March. Some bits and pieces went to the charity

shops, but a large percentage went outside her garage door. After a few days of doing this, and noticing everything always disappeared, she had started doing it on a regular basis. A small group of elderly regulars now stopped for a chat and to see what was being parted with this time. It had become quite a sociable meeting area. On dry days this informal gathering chatted and laughed, some even brought flasks of coffee and stools to sit on. Jill thought it was wonderful. Her waste had brought companionship and laughter to some very lonely people.

Zoe returned after the allotted forty minutes and washed her hair again, then used a conditioner reserved for those most in need. After a quick blow dry and a little tussling, Jill found herself looking at a different person. Somehow, this simple act of giving up a few hours of her time into the competent hands of Zoe had transformed her. She looked, not only younger but fresher and brighter. Her hair was no longer dull and lifeless but radiant and really *shiny*. Delightedly she paid the £58.00 and bought some of the Virtual conditioner for another £22.00. "Worth every penny," she had been assured. She thanked Zoe and left, promising her she would never, ever neglect her hair again.

Leaving the shop with a bounce in her step, she was amazed at what a tonic it had been. Somehow she felt more her old, confident self and things seemed to be settling into some kind of order. She spent the next couple of hours trawling all the clothes shops in the town centre, spending far too much money. She allowed for about another half-stone weight loss and bought clothes to fit accordingly. She stopped and had a cappuccino and a Danish pastry before looking at, and purchasing, some really nice shoes. Unlike Astrid she was not chic, she could not wear high heels due to an ankle injury some years before, but she knew what she liked and usually looked smart, as if she took care over her appearance. OK, so the last eight or nine months had seen standards dropping, in fact seen her turn into a total scruff, but all that was behind her. She was going to make something of the rest of her life. She just wasn't sure yet what the 'something' would be.

It was just after 3.00pm when she entered Mr Slowstern's office. It was very organised and modern. A secretary was filing away a manila folder as she entered and she smiled at Jill. "Can I help you?" she enquired politely. She was in her late thirties or early forties, trim with a good complexion and very green eyes. Jill explained about the appointment with Mr S. "I'll just go and get him

Oliver's Branch

for you" she said, and strode purposefully over to a staircase leading up to a mezzanine above.

"William, Mrs Slater here to see you."
"Thanks." The dapper man looked over the railings. "Would you like a coffee, I'm just making one?"
Jill declined and was led over to a large desk at the back of the room, by the secretary.
"He'll be right down. At home he always allows me to make him his drinks, but here he refuses to let anyone do it. Very strange." She laughed and went back to the filing cabinet.
Mr S came down the stairs with a large mug which had the words "The Big one" written on it in large letters.
"Sorry if I kept you waiting. I hope my wife has taken care of you?"
Jill was surprised to discover this smart, attractive woman was his wife. She would have imagined a much stockier, dowdier partner, but she said nothing. Being judgemental hardly something she had the right to be, now, or ever again.

Within ten minutes she was totally immersed in the information being imparted to her. It was over two hours later before Mr S sat back in his chair and stretched his hands up behind his head.
"That's about all there is to know. The processes, time scale and lease date are all only estimated, but I've been in the business a long time. It's very rare I get things too far wrong. I also think, with the present climate and mortgage débâcle, I will have no difficulty renting out your property."

There had been a lot to take in but because William (she felt this was more apt now, having disclosed most aspects of her financial life and some aspects of her private affairs,) had been so clear and straightforward she felt she understood the process. If she signed the property management agreement and was successful in getting a mortgage there was no going back. It was daunting, yet at the same time it was liberating. They had looked up mortgage brokers on the web and sent a couple of applications, just to get a feel of the market. William reckoned it could all be 'done and dusted' by the end of July. So, in about 10 weeks.

Jill could not believe anything could be so straightforward, but she trusted this man and wanted to believe it was possible. He had made her feel more optimistic than she had felt for months and months, though she was also completely overwhelmed by the enormity of it. If this all worked out, she could be leaving for Crete in August. Her home would no longer be her home but someone else's house. The rent would probably just about cover the mortgage, (depending on

how much she wanted the mortgage to be). He would receive 10% of the rental, a month. She would have to set up a new bank account for the house. Once tenants were found he would deal with any problems or difficulties.

"And you're free to go and start your new life in .... Where is it, Greece?"
"Crete" she had replied, and although there was an underlying sense of panic, it was counteracted by an underlying optimism. This could work. She would not have much money to live on, but she could sort out her debts, pay Jason back his share of Paparooni and leave.

She looked into his eyes and knew he would not rip her off. Picking up her pen she turned to the last page and signed the lease agreement.

They talked for another forty minutes. She gave him her mobile and home telephone numbers again and they arranged he would call her, when he heard from the mortgage companies they had selected.

It was almost six when she walked out feeling stronger and more positive than she had for a very long time.

Oliver's Branch

Fifteen.

Returning home with a portion of cod and chips from the best *chippy* in town, she was greeted by the now almost bearable silence. She would get used to this lack of noise and company she told herself, she had to. The life ahead held very few encounters of camaraderie or long discussions into the early hours. Jason had been a good talker too. It was very rare he was at a loss for words. Often the facts he came out with amazed her. He seemed to know so much about a vast number of things.

After quickly feeding the animals she unwrapped her meal, put it on a plate and sat down to eat. Feeling hungry she managed to finish the whole lot, even the vast portion of chips. It was the first time she had eaten with such gusto in a long time. Washing her plate and fork she returned them to their rightful place. A sudden urge to ring Jason and find out about Oliver surged through her in an almost primal way. Instead, she picked up the phone and rang Sarah, in Essex.

Luckily she was home and answered on the third ring.
"I was just about to call," she said after Jill had identified herself. "How are things? Bet you're getting uncomfortable now. Is the heartburn still as bad?"
"Actually," replied Jill, bracing herself for her friend's reaction, "I had Oliver yesterday. Everything was fine. He went home with Jason today."
"You went through with it then?" (a kind of sigh registered from the other end of the line.) "You gave him away? God, I really thought you would have second thoughts and keep him. I know I'm not a particularly maternal person but you so loved the time you spent with Grace and Nick, I thought you may weaken. No judgement though, Jill, just a comment. It's totally your choice, and you know I'll always be there for you."
Jill told her about the events of the previous night and also the meetings with her estate agent and the leasing agent . Sarah was a good listener and waited until Jill said, "And that's about it. I have to get on with life. I think I'm just going to resign from my job, a month before I leave for Crete."
"Amazing. Shouldn't you still be in bed recuperating? I don't know if you're truly brave or just plain stupid! You do sound a bit more like your old self though. Maybe the thought of giving birth, then giving the baby away, was affecting you more than you thought. Anyway, you know if there's anything I can do, I'll come down straight away."
Jill would have dearly loved to tell her she could come down tomorrow if she wanted to, the loneliness would at least be averted

for a few days if she did. Instead she answered, "No it's fine. I need to get my head around things and I'm not ready to talk about the birth or loss or anything, yet. If the re-mortgage goes ahead, maybe you could come down for a few days then. I'm totally exhausted and empty Sarah, I need time to recharge my batteries and try and get my head around everything." She asked about Sarah's family. They all appeared to be well. Sarah loved her job and so explained her latest projects at the doctor's surgery, where she was chief nurse/manager. They talked about life in general for a while, until Sarah explained she had to go as the fish pie smelt slightly charred. They said their goodbyes and Sarah promised to phone again soon.

It was still early and the night seemed to stretch before her like a vast ocean of nothingness. Again she quashed the urge to phone Jason. She knew she would sooner or later, either a phone call or maybe even a letter, but it was the *when* she was battling with. It was far too early, she needed to have some firm plan before she talked to him. The desire to see Oliver and hold him was almost unbearable. She needed to do something. Looking at the plastic boxes she had brought in from the car earlier, she picked them up and carried them upstairs. "Get packing," she said to the silent space all around her.

The rest of the evening was a mixture of memories and cold-hearted sorting. She could not bring herself to throw away all her children's paraphernalia from over the years. She left their memory boxes intact. She hoped one day, in the future, they would go through them and relive earlier moments and times from their childhood. She understood the excitement and selfishness of youth; they were too busy living to start reminiscing. She on the other hand seemed to be doing exactly the opposite and desperately hoped the future would hold more about living in the present than in the past. Only time would tell.

By the time the night had drawn in, there were two large black sacks for charity, three big boxes for 'the garage club,' (as she had nicknamed the group who frequented her garage door, more and more,) plus five nearly-completed plastic boxes. She had labelled them so she would be able to identify the contents at a later date. It seemed weird to imagine, the next time she looked in them, she would be on Crete.

Getting up, a little stiffly, she went downstairs and made a hot chocolate. She remembered to take a pill from the box her doctor had prescribed. She must take 1 every night for the next two weeks, to dry up her milk. Again she marvelled that this time yesterday things

were just beginning. Suddenly a deep and utter exhaustion overcame her. Leaving the half empty cup on the table (who would know?) she went to bed. Within minutes she was in a deep and, thankfully, dreamless sleep.

In the corners of every room, ghosts and memories huddled silently together.

Sixteen.

The next seven weeks would take Jill on a roller coaster of a ride. One which once started could not be stopped. Although every night was still haunted by feelings of guilt, loss and the selfishness of her actions, she was unable to change the course of events which carried her along in their wake. She seemed to be programmed to carry out the often complex and baffling tasks she was set and then, mentally ticking off another box, move on to the next.

Although Oliver and the memories of the night he was born still managed to invade her now purposeful, propelled and somewhat obsessive life, in many ways the whole experience seemed like some long-ago ordeal she had managed to compartmentalise and, to a degree, control. She wanted desperately to contact Jason and ask how things were going with their son, but he did not contact her and as the days rolled into weeks it became a matter of personal resolve. She would not interfere. If Jason wanted to contact her then it was his decision. Somehow she began to see a bigger picture and look at the years ahead as flowers which would, ultimately, open themselves to the sun. The present was a transient thing she would pass through and her new life would bring with it new hope. As long as she kept believing this she could propel herself ever forward. The jigsaw puzzle of official documents and new bank accounts, along with the continual signing of forms and other papers, began to form a picture with straight edges and less misplaced pieces.

The first thing to fall into place was the future well-being of her cats. There was no way they would survive the life on Crete. Being white they were very susceptible to the sun. For years Jill had always put blue sun block on their ears during the summer months. Most cats on Crete are feral and hers would never survive the kind of fights she had seen during the spring months, when the toms were rampant and the females fertile. She therefore gathered up enough courage to visit June and ask if there was any way she would adopt them. Archy was proving a problem. He was growing into a very confident male who enjoyed 'nights on the tiles' and was not at all the type of feline who wanted to sit on anyone's lap, purring and being petted. He reminded Jill of a cat in a Bacardi advert, who went on the razzle and clubbing every night, then spent the following day sleeping it off in hung-over isolation, before repeating it all again the next night. On the positive side though, he had befriended Brightey and Aspro. He could often be seen sitting on the adjoining wall, watching over them. Jill had asked June outright about the idea.

"Actually dear," June had said, "I was going to suggest the same thing, you just beat me to it. If we start getting your two used to coming over to me to be fed, now, it will make it a lot easier, when you leave, for me to keep them and take care of them. It would mean you locking the cat flap and I would start putting out their food, initially leaving it nearer to your house, but moving the plate nearer to mine each day. They would soon know which side their bread was buttered on, so to speak. It would be far less traumatic for them I'm sure. What do you think?"

For Jill this was the perfect solution and one which helped to strengthen her resolve to move on. The idea of losing them was painful. They had been part of her children's lives for many years. Parting with them was like letting go of one more element of her past. At the same time it was an act which was to make her stronger, more determined, and able to let go.

They discussed the details and agreed they would start the plan of action the following day. On the evening of their last night with Jill, she purposely spent a lot of time fussing them and explaining the situation to them. They looked up at her, supremely ignorant of how their lives were about to change, and purred happily. The following day, a sunny and bright one with crisp blue skies, Jill sealed the flap with mastic then watched as they sauntered off into the garden, ignorant of the changes which were about to take place. Jill cried quietly as she watched them sniffing in June's flowers. She felt an enormous sense of loss. It was something she would come to experience more and more over the coming months. When she looked back on the feelings she was experiencing, as she stood looking out at them, she realised it was almost a dry run for the coming endings and ultimate goodbyes.

June handled the whole thing expertly. She fussed them both and had long talks with them in the garden. Slowly the bowl was moved evening by evening, further away from Jill and their home. They still considered Jill's garden their territory, but Archy was slowly accepted into their lives. On many occasions over the ensuing weeks Jill watched them as they looked in at her from the balcony. Yet there was no malice or anger in their stance or in their eyes. They accepted the situation and seemed to have adjusted to it without so much as a backward glance.
If only, I could be like them, Jill had thought. *Their lives are so simple and yet somehow serene.*

June was a rock in other ways too during these weeks of change, loss and confusion. The Garage Club would often see her approaching with a plate of tuna sandwiches and some orange juice in a big glass jug. There was now an old table and chairs permanently outside the garage door and the group had taken on a social life of its own. It had given them a group identity which also seemed evoke a sense of purpose and well-being. The group had also become great friends with Jill and one day asked her if they could help her clear out the garage. There was no room for a car in this garage. It held 22 years of detritus, memories and junk. 22 years worth of items Jill was sure would someday be useful. Tools and car cleaning materials, old light shades and boxes of things she had brought over from her father's house when she had cleared away his and her mother's lives, after they had both died, within a year of each other. Jill had agreed and the table and chairs now formed the backdrop and communal meeting area of the chaotic garage, with the door pulled open. This also meant the house was accessible by a side door which led into the utility room and from there into the kitchen. On impulse Jill had told them to use the kitchen whenever they wanted to and over the following weeks the house became the centre of hustle and bustle. It appeared to be coming alive again, as if it had been waiting to be needed and appreciated. The group never imposed or tried to take over, but somehow they managed to guide Jill through most days and at the same time order appeared to be restored.

The garage was an ongoing project where Jill would input information about what she really wanted to keep and what 'could go'. Little did she realise, in the early days, just how much of a lifeline she had thrown to this small group of lonely people.

John, a retired car mechanic, appeared to organise the rest of them in a calm and gentle way. He was sixty-eight and as fit as a fiddle. His wife was in an old people's home, suffering from severe dementia and he visited her every day. It had been John who had seen the chance of 'making a few bob' out of Jill's discarded possessions. One day, while they were going through a large box of books which Jill had not looked at since she was at university, he said to her; "You know, Jill, we could have a little second-hand stall and garage-sale on the go and maybe get a bit of cash for this lot. There are things in here I can clean up and I know the others will do the same. Lotty found a whole load of soft toys and dolls in one bag. She reckons she could clean them up real nice, and Fred says there are some pictures and frames well worth renovating. What do you think?"

Oliver's Branch

Jill immediately agreed, mainly because the twinkle and mischievousness in John's eyes was infectious. "What a great idea, John, if it's what you want to do. There's so much else to think about. As long as I've sorted what I'm taking there's no problem at all in you doing whatever you like with the rest. I would have chucked it outside the garage and that would have been that if you lot hadn't shown up. No, do whatever you like. We'll just sort and package up the things I'm taking and then it's all yours."

John went off to tell Lotty and Fred her decision. Lotty, 73, was a retired nurse, who was exceedingly proud of her collection of dolls and miniatures. She had lived in sheltered accommodation, just up the road, for the last five years, since her husband had died. She loved reading and sewing and making needlepoint pictures of her doll collection. Her walls were covered in them, all professionally framed and never sporting even one speck of dust. Although Jill didn't know it, Lotty was working on one of Brightey and Aspro, from a photo she had taken of them one day as they lay on the wall together. It was to be a parting gift to Jill. Lotty was also a computer enthusiast and all her designs for the pictures were done on the computer. Another of her talents was she was a dab hand at finding virtually anything anyone asked her for on the WWW. In fact she was the person who had found Jill a very reliable removable firm, which specialised in moves from England through Europe and over to Crete. They were also very reasonable.

Fred, the oldest member of the group, was 79 and walked with the aid of a walking stick. There was a big sticker wrapped round it which read; 'Older, Wiser, SLOWER!' He wore large, horn-rimmed spectacles and a threadbare, green corduroy jacket with leather patches sewn on the elbows. He had been a postman in the Midlands and only moved south when he retired. "I want to die near the sea with the sound of the waves in my ears and a pint in my hand..." He had said this to Jill, not long after they first met. Jill hoped with all her heart his wish would be granted, she had a soft spot for Fred. He was like the granddad she never had.

The other two regular members of the group were Millie and Tom, a brother and sister, who had lived in the same house all their lives and worked in the local convent school. Both of them were in their late sixties, Tom was a year younger than Millie. He had been the groundsman at the convent and she the school matron. They were as alike as chalk and cheese. Tom was wiry and tall, with thinning grey hair and an infectious laugh. He loved talking about coins and stamps and sometimes from the kitchen Jill would hear Millie tut and say, "Do shut up Tom. If you've told us about your bloody Penny Black collection once, you've told us about it a hundred times."

All the same they were very close and added a certain element of banter to the group.
Millie was a short, dumpy woman with a shock of pure white hair which she wore in an almost boyish cut. She had small round glasses, perched on the edge of her nose in a precarious fashion, and she wore flowing skirts and gypsy shawls in vivid colours, which usually clashed. Her skin was peachy and clear and she was forever extolling the virtues of Ponds Cold Cream.

Other people would come and go during the day, but these were the main nucleus of the 'club' No one was allowed to come and just 'help themselves'. Once the group had started to sell repaired or renovated items, the free-for-all had stopped. In its place there was a feeling of busy industry and a buzz of purpose which it was impossible to miss. Jill was quite happy to have these people in her life, it filled part of the emptiness. Slowly, quietly, they worked their magic on her and she began to feel cared for and loved. By the time she was due to leave they had become like family and she knew she would miss them all. They had learnt about Oliver, her job and 'Paparooni' while chatting over the weeks. None of them had passed judgement. In fact they just accepted her for who and what she was and welcomed her into their hearts.

Each of them, in their own way, filled a gap which she had not even realised existed. Each of them, almost symbiotically, enthused her with not only hope but also with a sense of commitment and purpose.

The birth of this group, small in number, yet huge in spirit, was something Jill was extremely proud to be a part of. She wished she had helped form years ago. They gave an air of community to an otherwise very self-centred road, where there was very little shared. Where the size of your conservatory far outweighed any care or consideration for the well-being of your neighbours.

The group spent many hours discussing how else they could help Jill. She would often arrive home to find a shepherd's pie or toad-in-the-hole, carefully wrapped and sitting on her doorstep. Although they probably didn't realise it, they had also helped her deal with the depression she so often felt, while preparing a meal for one. She started buying cakes and scones and making sure there was always something for them to snack on.

All in all, the Garage Club was a cathartic miracle which entered her life when it was at its most barren. It watered her soul, bringing

Oliver's Branch

sunshine and new growth. More importantly though, these wonderful people gave Jill a sense of purpose, enabling any self indulgence or pity she felt for herself to decrease and wither in the shadows.

Seventeen.

During these seven weeks, the apparent ease of getting a mortgage and the house ready for rental, all went amazingly smoothly. William Slowstern proved to be an efficient and patient organiser. He helped Jill over the various hurdles of lease agreements, insurance arrangements, financial minefields and the abundance of paperwork. It never failed to amaze her, as she plodded through each tome of conditions and legal jargon, how little difference modern technology seemed to make to these sorts of transactions. Maybe Santa had noticed the difference, (even he had an e-mail address, so spent less time opening envelopes,) but, she thought ruefully, she had not. Most correspondence still had to be transferred to hard copy for general perusal and signing.

Nonetheless, by the last week in June, she awaited a cheque for the re-mortgage and all her new 'Rental Account' details. During this time, apart from her neighbour June, The Garage Club (as they called themselves,) and Astrid, she saw very few people. Upon the completion of the mortgage agreement she decided it was time to remedy this. Arriving home after the last visit to William prior to the letting of her home, she picked up the phone and called Sarah.

As luck would have it she was on a half-day and was home. It was an ironic fact that, after years of dutifully working without much enthusiasm in her job, her new roll gave her a completely different outlook on life and the work ethos. Her children had all left home prior to Jill's and Sarah now enthused about how rewarding she found her job. This was almost like a total roll reversal. It was always Jill who was totally devoted and enthusiastic about her teaching roll. Then, as she changed direction, she became disenchanted with the bureaucracy and constant need to justify her existence. Database records and managerial assessment of achieved targets, objectives which must be met before some deadline or other, hours on the computer instead of with children. Jill had found herself questioning more and more the system she felt was losing sight of its main aim, education. Sarah, on the other hand, had settled into a job she actually enjoyed getting up for. Over the years they had both agreed this was the one true test of the work ethic. Jill remembered saying when her children were quite young and she seemed to never have a moment of time for herself: "What's so strange though Sarah, is however tired I am, however little sleep

Oliver's Branch

I've had, I still look forward to getting up and going to work. If I ever feel differently I will know it's time for change."

"That's as maybe, Jill, but you always have been a bit of an idealist. As far as I'm concerned it's a job, I get paid and we live comfortably. Maybe one day I'll enjoy something more than this, but at the moment bringing up the kids and a good standard of living is my main priority."

Sarah had always been the practical and responsible one in their friendship. During their years together at school it was antics Jill suggested which brought them detentions or lines. It was Jill who had taken them on their first smoking expedition in the school woods. With 2 Woodbines from a machine in the local village, they had set off, Sarah berating the fact it was a stupid thing to do and Jill arguing it was a bit of fun. The upshot of this particular jaunt had been a particularly stiff punishment. They had arrived back at their dormitory without detection, green round the gills, and sunk onto their respective beds (made with hospital corners and as regimental as a soldier's). Sarah had spent a long time groaning, Jill had been remarkably quiet, until with a sudden surge of nausea she jumped up and duly threw up in 3 plastic tooth mugs then all over the sink. While she was making a half-hearted attempt to clean this up, one of the nuns had walked in to check dormitory tidiness. The ensuing punishment saw them put in separate dormitories for the rest of term and spending every spare moment for four days writing 2,000 lines. *Smoking is ignorant and dangerous. I will never smoke again.*

Jill was suddenly jolted back into the present as the call was connected."Hiya, Sarah, it must be my turn to phone. Thought I'd just catch up with you and any news."

"Mmm, that sounds ominous, you must want something. Just kidding. Was thinking about you earlier. I'm sorry if I've seemed a bit aloof or standoffish, I'm still trying to get my head around you giving away your baby. You've always been a generous soul, but I still think this is beyond the realms of all understanding. Any way, I'll get used to it. Come on then, what's happening in your somewhat bizarre, but always interesting life?"

Jill did not respond to her friend's feelings about Oliver, instead she filled her in on the progress of the house, and the packing details for her move.
"The one thing I'm waiting on now is a call from the removals company 'Alaxis Ltd'. They have been and assessed the amount of stuff I'm taking and are sending boxes sometime next week. As soon

as they have a date I'll let you know. The property bloke reckons he could have the house rented out from the first of August, so things are moving quite rapidly."

"God, I didn't think you'd be leaving quite so quickly," Sarah exclaimed, with genuine surprise in her voice. "What about Dyson, have you done all the passport and injection stuff for him? You are taking him, aren't you?"

"Yep, on both counts" Jill replied, with an element of pride. "Everything is sorted and I've found a company who specialise in transporting pets by plane. It's called Pets Go2, very original I thought. Anyway as soon as I have some flight options I liaise with them and Dyson and I fly out together. It's really expensive but Grace is adamant Dyson has to stay with me. He'll be company once I'm there. I'm going to be quite lonely, I think."

"You have been busy. You sound much better though. What about all the union stuff? Are you going to do anything about the way they treated you, or just put it down to experience and shelve it?"

"I'm giving in my notice at the end of the month. My sick note lasts another month but I want to leave with everything completed. I will always feel angry and hurt at the way I was treated, but the powers-that-be can just go take a hike now and get on with their pathetic, self-centred, sanctimonious lives. I'm going to get on with mine. I do feel much better and have completely stopped taking the antidepressants, although I still cry quite a lot. In short I'm putting it down to experience and shelving it."

There was a moment's silence on the other end of the phone before Sarah continued, "Right, Well done. You've really taken your future by the hand and started the journey into this new life of yours. You have to tell me a bit about Oliver, though. If we pretend it never happened there will always be a wall between us, we've been friends far too long to allow such a thing to happen. Is he well and how's Jason doing?"

"Actually I have no idea. You would think in a town as small as this one I would have heard something on the grapevine, but I haven't. I still have to pay Jason back his share of 'Paparooni', but I'm doing all of the paperwork through his solicitor. As things stand I may well never see either of them again."
"And how do you feel about that, honestly?"

Oliver's Branch

"I don't." Jill responded, a little too quickly. "I will have to I know, but for the moment I've sort of put it all away neatly in a box and locked it away. Maybe sometime in the future I will have the courage to open the box and discover how I truly feel, but for now there is too much to do going on to try and deal with it. Some nights I lie in this barren, quiet, empty shell of a house, which seems to mirror my own persona, and think I should at least talk to Jason. At other times I want to just leave the whole experience floating in the ether, an intangible, unfathomable, emotional juxtaposition of right and wrong."

"God, that's all a bit deep, you always were good with words. Anyway look. I've got an idea. I'm due some annual leave. We're almost into July. What about I come and stay for a long weekend and help you with some of the packing? We haven't had a good talk for ages. Life, work and family seem to have gotten in the way. So, what do you think?"

Jill smiled to herself. "That would be great. You'll get to meet TGC then as well. It's ages since I've been out and I've lost quite a bit of weight, so it would be a welcome distraction."

"So now I'm a welcome distraction, that's new. OK, I'll book a few days for the second weekend in July and come down. Maybe by then you'll have a moving date. What's TGC by the way?"

"Now there's another story, I haven't mentioned them have I? You'll see when you come. Ring me up to confirm and we'll catch up when you arrive."

They said their goodbyes and Jill hung up. Dyson was sitting quietly at her feet. She went and fetched his lead from the utility room. As soon as he saw it he went into a frenzied run around the table. When he eventually stopped, Jill leashed him and they walked out into the sunshine. For the first time in a long while there was a spring in her step. Maybe everything would work out all right, after all, and she should stop worrying. She found herself singing the Bob Marley song to herself and smiled.

Eighteen.

Outside TGC were all busy and absorbed in their work. There appeared to be a whole table of tools and pumps and a jigsaw, all gleaming and clean, some in their original boxes. Pictures and photographs were adorned by freshly lacquered frames and there were crisp white table tablecloths and ornaments, artistically arranged. John was at the back of the garage sanding down some antique planes, which Jill remembered her father using when she was a child. She said "Hi" to everyone and then walked over to John. The planes were in fact almost all renovated and looked somehow elegant and dignified. She picked one up and admired the contours and beautiful renovation work John had obviously taken so much love and care over.

"They look wonderful, John. Do you know I remember my dad using these."
"Why don't you keep them then?" he responded. "From the photos I've seen of that house of yours they would fit in very well with the rustic feel of it. They're wonderfully made. German, look there's the mark, and they must be at least 50 years old. Don't make tools like this any more."

Jill imagined them adorning a shelf in Paparooni and smiled. "Know what, John, I think I will. I can pay you for all the work you've put into them to make them look so pristine and yet retain their authenticity."
"Wouldn't hear of it, luv. I'll put them in the utility room for you to pack." So saying he wandered off to talk to a 'customer' who was eyeing up the jigsaw.

Jill stayed a few more minutes and looked at the tablecloths Lotty had so lovingly laundered and ironed then told Millie about the arrival time of the boxes. Millie was responsible for finding the firm on the internet at the beginning of June. Apparently Alaxis meant *change* in Greek, and Alaxis Ltd. was an Anglo/Cretan company which dealt primarily in moves to Greece and Crete. Jill was impressed by their professionalism and had thanked Millie for finding them.
"That's alright, dear. You know how I enjoy these little challenges, they keep me young."
She looked at Millie, who was now completely engrossed in organising the table decorations. Giving them a perfunctory wave, she set off with Dyson for a romp on the beach.

Oliver's Branch

Ten minutes later Dyson was gallivanting in the waves, wagging his tail wildly, with what could only be described as a 'doggy smile' on his face. For an old boy he was remarkably fit.

Jill took off her shoes and socks and waded slowly along the shore, the pebbles digging into the soles of her feet and crunching beneath her. So far it had been a productive day, she was feeling excited about actually taking this enormous step, or was she? Although it was something she had always said she would do, she had come to realise having a dream and actually making it a reality, were two very different things.

The dream had allowed her to cope with the monotony and daily 'ordinariness' of life. At the approach of spring, when the children were small, she would look out of the kitchen window, while she washed or peeled or cleaned and think of the future. A future which, when her children were grown and living their own lives, would give her sea, sunshine and new friends. A place her children could bring their own families to and bask in the brilliance of it all. A place they would grow to love and call home.

The reality was something totally, totally different. Firstly, she never imagined she would be going while Nick and Grace were both so young. Neither of them were settled or had found their true way yet. She felt an immense guilt about this. She also felt a sense of isolation. Yes, her friends thought she was either totally mental or extremely brave, she wasn't sure she was either. It was almost as if life was running away with her and she was not involved in the script. There was no other way, as surely as the waves crashed on the beach and ebbed away, her life was being swept on some vast tidal wave, towards a new existence. There appeared to be nothing she could do to stop it. Her old life was being eroded, like the stones beneath her feet, and although she wished she had the courage to enjoy the ride, she felt bereft, helpless, weak and very scared.

She wondered if it really was too late to admit she was taking the wrong path. Suddenly, more than anything else she wanted to talk to Jason and claim back her son. *Her son.* A sudden yearning and almost primeval need passed through her whole body. All she wanted to do was to hold Oliver while Jason stood with his hand on her shoulder, smiling adoringly down on them both. She took out her mobile to call Jason. She wanted to turn back the time, to abate the waves of destruction she was bringing upon herself. She dialled the number and waited for a connexion and at exactly the same moment Dyson hurtled along the shore and jumped up at her. With an

almighty crash she fell into the sea... and her mobile fell into the waves.

It was as though she was awakened from a dream, was falling out of bed, awaking with a start. She had opened the box, where had she found the key? So very nearly she had lost sight of reality and lived within another dream. A 'happily ever after' dream, the type you experienced while watching slushy, romantic, Hollywood films, on a bleak Sunday afternoon. She sat where she had tumbled and grabbed her phone from the sea. It looked totally 'drowned' and totally dead, in as much as a mobile phone could be dead that is. Slowly she got up, pushing Dyson and his amorous face-slurping licks away. The only part of her still relatively dry was her hair. She wondered what people would make of her, as she squelched slowly home. She put Dyson back on his lead and together they dripped their way up the beach, through the local park and towards home. As she did so she replaced the lid on the box close to her heart, which she had so nearly allowed to change the direction of her life. She locked it firmly and stored the key in a recess of her mind. There it must stay until her life, and her emotions, were more stable. Oliver would never be hers, she had signed away any rights to any involvement in his life. *How could she have done such a cold and heartless thing?* She shook her head and moaned out loud. Dyson turned and looked up at her quizzically. She increased her stride and walked on, looking around her for something to distract her attention. The swans were sitting on the island in the pond, surrounded by four cygnets. Swans mated for life. It was an idyllic family scene... No that wouldn't work. She looked up the path and saw an old lady hobbling painfully towards her, using a Zimmer frame to assist her. Jill wondered if her life had been a happy one. If she felt fulfilled and content with her past. Jill walked towards a bench and sat down. An old newspaper was wedged between the slats, she pulled it out. The sun was quite strong now and she was merely damp, as opposed to sopping. She opened the paper randomly and found herself looking at a small section labelled 'A moment of reflection...' followed by, 'Allow yourself a few moments to meander through the experiences of your life'.

The piece was about snakes shedding their skins. Apparently, they did this without any sentimentality for the old skin, and appeared to glide forward in the fresh skin ready for new adventures. It stated the old skin was useless and uncomfortable, there was no further use for it, no life left within it.

Jill could relate to this. She felt in the same situation, living in a worn out skin which made her feel wrinkled, dry and useless. Yet she had the opportunity to shed this skin and move forward with optimism and purpose. Behind her all her mistakes, wrong choices and negativity would lie in a discarded pile... She liked the analogy.

The article went on to question if you were as wise as the snake. It looked at the many roles you may have taken over the years, how metaphorically, you started each new role with a fresh and vibrant new skin. The piece suggested you sit quietly, for a while, and meander through your life, marking out points where you had 'shed a skin' and moved forward.

Jill eased herself down a little on the bench and closed her eyes. She tilted her head back. The sun gently caressed her face. Closing her eyes she began the slow slither through green grass, to explore each stage of her life and each skin. Dyson made himself comfortable at her feet, put his head on his front paws, closed his eyes and went to sleep. No doubt to dream of burying bones or chasing rabbits.

Nineteen.

Awakening with a start, still sitting on the park bench, clutching the newspaper, Jill looked at her watch. She had been asleep for 40 minutes. She smiled to herself, thinking this was her *40 winks*. She stood up slowly and ruffled Dyson's neck. He wagged his tail and got to his feet. Together they walked on towards the house. *How strange*, she thought. *I am already thinking of it as a house, not our home. I wonder if I will ever feel the same way about Paparooni. Will it ever feel like my home? Will the kids consider it their home?* As yet there was no way of knowing.

Arriving at her front door she realised TGC had dispersed and she was alone. As she opened the door a sheet of paper fell from the letter box onto the mat. She picked it up. A scrawled note from William Slowstern explained he had come round with some news. Apparently he tried to phone both her home and mobile numbers, *to no avail*. He asked her to *kindly contact me as soon as you have perused this*. How quaint she thought, as she let Dyson off the lead and went to the phone. On the second ring William answered.

"Hello William, it's Jill Slater here, do you have some news for me?"
"Oh yes... Hello. Hello. I most certainly have, my dear girl. I've just had an e-mail from the mortgage company. Everything is approved and the papers will be with you by the end of this week. A cheque should be in your account by Monday. Such good news, don't you think?"
Jill smiled, she could imagine him straightening his bow tie and pulling on his braces. A habit she had become all too familiar with over the last few months.
"That's fantastic; I really didn't think it would be so quick. Thank you so much for all your help. I don't know what I'd have done without you."
"All part of the service, dear girl. Think nothing of it. No doubt you will keep me informed of your situation and when you are leaving? I will be putting your house up for rental as soon as you give me the date the house will be vacant. The sooner the better you know, the market is very buoyant at present. Strike while the iron's hot etcetera, etcetera, don't you know."
"Oh, OK William. I'll see what I can do. Once I have a date from the movers I'll be in a better position to finalise my move and book a flight. Of course I'll keep in touch. Thank you again." William said his goodbyes and Jill hung up. She walked over and turned on the computer. Dyson nuzzled her hand and wagged his tail, signalling he

Oliver's Branch

wanted to go out. She opened the French windows and he dived past her after an unsuspecting blackbird. Back at the computer she had some incoming messages. 3 appeared on the screen. One from Grace, who asked if she would phone as she had no credit. Apparently she was *totally broke*. One was from William, confirming the mortgage details. The last from Angelina, explaining all the house papers were on their way. They should be with her by the end of the week. She sent a swift reply to Angelina, thanking her. She phoned Grace, who was having an 'amazing time'. Apparently she had a new job in a very arty nightclub where she was hoping to work over the summer. She had a new house sorted with 3 lads for her second year and was almost ready to move in. She was not happy about although being there on her own for 2 months. She thought this was a bit daunting, but felt sure it would be fine. "Anyway what about you mum, how's everything going? Are you feeling OK in yourself after ... well you know...after your experience. And, how's Dyson?"

Jill was just about to reply when Grace gave her apologies. She had to go. She was due to meet a friend and she wasn't ready. With that explanation, she threw lots of kisses down the phone, and hung up. Jill had said precisely three words, "Bye then sweetheart.." Still, she felt happy knowing things were going well and suspected it wouldn't not be long before Grace contacted her again. Jill had a feeling that finances would be on the agenda, and was rarely wrong on this subject.

It was now mid afternoon. She had not exactly made any more headway with the packing. So, for the next 3 hours, she worked her way from the top floor to the middle floor of the house. She stuffed black bags with surplus possessions and clothes. As always this was not an easy task, everything held some memory or other, but she had to downsize. The boxes were due to arrive at 11.00am the following day. All around her was the echo of emptiness. Only memories shuffled from room to room like dark clouds before a storm, following her and nudging at her emotions. Time after time she pushed them away, trying to focus on the task, as opposed to the feeling of loss and separation which kept inching their way into her subconscious. The small locked box, close to her heart, felt heavy and threatening. Jill opened her daughter's long abandoned jewellery box, which played the Blue Danube, while a ballerina pivoted precariously on her podium. It felt as if at any moment it would disintegrate and become nothing more than s heap of dust in her hands. Jill couldn't help but make a comparison between her imaginary box and this discarded trinket. She put the jewellery box in the Oxfam bag, sat back on her haunches and then lifted it out again, deciding to take it with her. Memories of the day Grace had received it flooded back. It was her sixth birthday and her granddad

had given it to her. Inside, in his handwriting, was an inscription. *Happy Birthday Poppet. Enjoy every day, life is what you make it. All my love Grangy Xxx* There was a small velvet bag in there too. In it was a beautiful gold star pendant with tiny pearls adorning each point, with one larger one in the centre. Grace had been so proud of it, she still wore it from time to time. Now though, the box was empty, the house was empty, Jill's heart was empty, her life was empty. Suddenly the primal need to hold her baby in her arms, produced an almost physical spasm of pain, fuelled by regret. Putting the box in the 'to pack' pile she began to sob loudly and uncontrollably. There was no one around to hear her, let alone comfort her........The silence crept away, leaving her alone with her misery.

Jill cried until there were no more tears to cry, then dragged the Oxfam bag downstairs.
This will NOT DO, you stupid woman. Pull yourself together and get on with it, she thought to herself as she to placed the bag next to the other four, in the corner of the hall. *New skin, dreams come true, new life, all that stuff - if you go on like this it'll never happen. Things will get better, you know they will.* Walking into the living room she saw Dyson sitting patiently outside the door. It was just after six and he was a stickler for routine. He should have been fed ten minutes ago. He gave her a scowl as she opened the door, then sauntered in and sat down waiting for his bowl to appear. Jill prepared his food and placed the bowl on the floor in front of him. With a brief wag of his tail he wolfed the food down. Seeing him eat reminded her that she had not eaten for hours. She half heartedly set about preparing a meal of eggs on toast. She was just about to crack an egg when the doorbell rang. She put down the egg and walked to the front door, wondering who could be visiting at this time. Opening the door, she got the shock of her life.

"My God! What the hell are you doing here?" she exclaimed to her caller, who stood on the doorstep, a bottle of red wine in one hand and a suitcase in the other, with an enormous grin on her face.

"Great welcome Petal.." she said, dragging her suitcase over the step and putting it down next to the Oxfam bags. "Thought I'd surprise you, you sounded a bit down on the phone. As luck would have it, my job-share wants to go away for a few days next week, so she asked if she could work my shifts this week and I'll do hers next. Jumped at it. As my old mum used to say - No time like the present." They hugged each other and headed to the kitchen to find a corkscrew. "I thought the bloody car was going to pack up and die on me during

the journey. I've been meaning to have it serviced for months, but I think it may have something terminal, so I've kept putting it off," Sarah called after her and laughed.

Suddenly things didn't seem as bleak as they had such a short time ago. She wasn't alone; she had some good friends and two great kids. They may not always be physically present, but they were always with her. Her memories would never fade. They would be a constant reminder of all the good times and good people who were an integral part of her life. No more regrets, no more being scared. She made a mental note of this feeling of resolve and smiled inwardly.

Memories, freed from their confinement of hurt and regret, cascaded from every room and floated freely through the house once more, in an invisible yet crystal rainbow waterfall.

"Let's open that bottle of wine then shall we?" she said "and what about a takeaway?" Suddenly eggs on toast seemed rather suburban and dull.

Twenty.

The two friends talked well into the night. Jill was amazed how cathartic it was. Up until now people had hedged around Oliver, and his birth. She was sure it was mainly because they didn't want to pry, but talking to Sarah, and reliving the whole experience, somehow put it into perspective. Sarah did have problems coming to terms with the fact Jill had 'given away' her son but she was very practical and had always been a realist.

"You know, I'm not sure I could have done what you've done. I suppose it surprised me when you went through with it. Of the two of us you have always been far more maternal and 'mumsy' than me. I mean I love my kids and would fight to the death for them, but I'm also quite happy to see them all living their own lives, and giving me my space and my life back. I know you are always there for them, but once they've gone, it's as if you put your life on hold for the past twenty-odd years, and now you're getting it back. To have given up your baby though, takes some getting my head around. Do you have any regrets, honestly?"

Jill looked at her friend and the tears came. "Of course I do. It's as if a part of me is missing and I feel completely at a loss as to what to do. Grace and Nick haven't spoken to me about it, although Nick came to the hospital. Apparently Oliver has blond hair. Astrid is too absorbed in her new-found career status to take on an emotional wreck like me, and Jason hasn't phoned. In my heart I know Oliver will be better off with Jason and his family. With me he would grow up in a strange world with a very small family. I have two other children and that's it. I have no other living blood relatives at all. I regret things going wrong between Jason and me. I regret getting pregnant. I regret being swept along with Jason's dream of bringing our child up together in the sun, but most of all I hate the loss of my new son. I cannot believe I will not be there for him. God, he's going to grow up believing I gave him away without a backward glance, and that just isn't true."

Sarah poured another glass of wine and munched on a poppadom. "OK, so here's the thing. The way I see it, you allow this depression and guilt thing to win and whatever you do, wherever you go, you will never be happy again. Or - and this is the crux of the matter - you let it go and you move on. God, the thought of you in your lovely house on Crete makes me green with envy. You know what a sun-worshipper I am? OK, so it's not exactly how you planned it. When does anything ever work out the way we plan it? When my oldest boy

Oliver's Branch

was born, I remember holding him in my arms and mapping out his life. He would be bright and keen, do well at school, go on to university and get a profession. He would go about his life as a contented and rounded human being. So what's he doing now at 25? Working in a small Italian restaurant and humping his employer. She's six years his senior, with 3 kids of her own. But hey, you know what? He's as happy as Larry, that's all that really counts. Just one example, believe me. I've had my fair share of downs as well as ups. You don't know the half of it. So what's it going to be, Petal, choice one, misery and heartbreak turning you into a bitter and twisted old woman, or, a new start and take it one day at a time. Build up a new life and look back without the regret of not having given it a go? You don't know how lucky you are having the option to change your life."

Jill reflected on this, and her mother's old adage came to mind "Look backwards with gratitude." Yet before she replied she knew the answer. She had probably known it all along, but it took someone else to put things in perspective for her. That's exactly what her friend had done.
"OK. Here's the deal. Promise you will come out and visit me as soon as you can and I'll have something to work towards. I know I will be lonely at first, but if I don't try it, as you say, I'll regret it for the rest of my life. I think the choice has already been made for me, or maybe the powers that be have decided my fate. But thanks, talking to you and getting everything off my chest puts everything into a new and clearer perspective. You really are great you know."

After a few more glasses of wine the conversation shifted to Sarah's life. Jill was suddenly made aware how selfish and self-centred she must seem. Sarah begrudgingly explained to her that her marriage was not all it once was. Somehow she and Dennis had started living very different lives. They had been on holiday separately this year for the first time and it was liberating. Peter was involved in the local fight against the Car Parking Zone initiative, which looked as if it would destroy all the local small businesses, as well as make it virtually impossible to park outside your own front door. Then, and if you did get a permit, costing a small fortune, you still weren't guaranteed a space. On top of this another government initiative, to put microchips in all the residential dustbins and measure your waste, plus litter attendants on the streets to snoop in your bins, became the next fight for the group (who called themselves Residents Against Big Brother. Apparently it was very Orwellian.) Most meetings were held at the local pub and as there were about 4 or 5 times a week, when Sarah didn't see her husband from one day to the next.

Jill asked her if she was thinking of getting a divorce. Sarah said after 28 years together she wasn't at all sure she wanted to be on her own, she was certain it was just a phase and they had worked through problems before. They would work things out, somehow. She told Jill how happy she was at work. She explained her responsibilities and described the people she worked with. They talked about their children and laughed at some of the antics they had got up to in school together, all those years ago. By the time the second bottle of wine was finished, and the Indian takeaway was nothing more than bright coloured stains and crumbs in the containers, it was almost two in the morning. Jill needed to be up bright and early the next morning, in case the boxes arrived before the scheduled time and so they agreed it was time to call it a night.

The bed in the spare room was already made up with fresh sheets (and a very lavish satin throw), so Sarah said goodnight and went to make herself at home. She would be staying four days, so she unpacked her case and put all her clothes in the wardrobe. She had a wash, set her phone alarm for **9.00am** and went to bed.

Upstairs, Jill undressed, cleaned her teeth and crawled into bed (having removed another even more lavish satin throw from her own bed.) It had been a long day, but it had also been an important one. She had reached the crossroads and now she knew the path she was going to take. It would be filled with potholes and there would probably be some wrong turns and dead ends, but there was an ultimate destination to reach. Once she was on Crete, life would continue to throw things at her. She realised there was no way she could predict the future. All the same it was a future which now felt far more hopeful and less desolate. One way or another, things would work out. She had no idea how or what was ahead of her, but for the first time in months she wasn't scared or angry. She turned out the light, and curled up, with a smile on her face.

Twenty one.

It was a good thing they had the chat on the first night, the next four days were a whirlwind of activity. Each night they collapsed into their beds exhausted. Sarah was an absolute gem. She proved to be the most efficient box packer on the planet. She also organised all members of TGC and they had specific tasks allocated to them, which they carried out with relish. She was exceedingly impressed with the goods they were selling, and spent £26.00 on items they convinced her she could not do without. Over a cup of coffee, in one of the few moments of calm, she confided in Jill.
"Why the hell I bought a popcorn maker I have absolutely no idea. I can't stand the bloody stuff."

The boxes arrived at the allotted time along with bubble wrap, tissue paper, brown tape and an ingenious tape dispenser. Black bags were sorted through by TGC and only about a quarter of the items made it to the charity shop, the rest were purloined to sell. Millie bemoaned the 'throw away society' she found herself living in. In her day, there was never any waste. In those days you couldn't afford to buy things on a whim, food was the main priority. She told stories about keeping chickens and feeding them all the bits left-overs. How clothes were repaired and socks darned. She talked about the wood burner. "There was no central heating in our house in those days you know," she had remarked, wagging an arthritic finger. She reminisced about how, as a tiny girl of five or six, she was sent out with her brother, to find wood. Sarah was mesmerised by the tales from the past. There was an atmosphere of optimism and fun in both the house and the garage. The laughter was infectious and flooded in with the warm sunshine.

Jill pulled her weight, but there were a lot of things to do in regard to the house and the flight. She contacted the removals firm to see if a date had been finalised for collection and transportation. It appeared there had been a cancellation towards the end of July (the 23rd to be precise). They wondered if she wanted to take this date. If not, they would be looking at the end of August. Going in late July meant the schedule would be really tight but she decided, if she could get a flight with Dyson on the same plane, she would go for it. She contacted William, who was ecstatic. "My dear girl, that's wonderful news. Someone was in only this morning, looking for exactly your kind of property. They want to move in at the start of August. I'll contact them immediately. May we come and peruse the house if they're interested?" Jill sat down with Millie at the computer and they looked at all possible flights and prices. Millie

really was a whiz on the internet, and they soon had a flight booked and the dog sorted. Arrangements were made through the pet transportation company for a dog box, of the right dimensions, to be available on the 24th of July at Gatwick. The vet was very accommodating too. Dyson was now the proud owner of his very own passport and rabies vaccination certificate. Bank accounts were sorted and all that was left was to pay off Jason for Paparooni, and her ex-husband his share of the house. By the time she waved Sarah off, things were falling into place and the house was three-quarters packed. After a hug and the promise of coming over to Crete as soon as she could, Sarah prepared to leave. John had done an oil change on her car and carried out virtually a full service. "In our day, if you had a car you looked after it as if it was a fine young woman. This poor old thing is more like an ageing aunt nobody loves," he had scolded.
All Jill had to do now was write her resignation and pack the last of the breakable items from the glass cabinet.

A visit from Nick a few days after Sarah left saw Jill's trusty vacuum cleaner, IKEA chair, Pine chest and 3 rugs, going to a new home, or flat, which was actually the case. Having recently helped him move to a new place, following problems with a manic and apparently mentally unstable neighbour at his last place, he was always on the look out for additional 'necessities'."
"Can I have the painting we brought back from Crete when we stayed in Georgeopolis?" he'd asked and Jill had given it to him. They had both laughed about the street painter they bought the painting from, a bloke called Manuel who had a ponytail, came from Scotland and had no teeth; but he did make amazing cosmic scenes with cans of spray paint. Aforementioned painting was duly dispatched to its new home. Jill hoped Nick would always have good memories of all their holidays together. The painting would act as a reminder.

By mid-July everything was in place and a lot of goodbyes had been said. Astrid had called twice but was *so busy* she was unable to come over, and the cats had virtually disappeared into June's garden. It was strange to watch them, tails in the air with jaunty steps, following June and Archy into her flat, without even a backward glance. She wondered how many of her friends and acquaintances would follow suit.

As for Jason's payout and her ex-husband's half of the house, her solicitor dealt with both these matters. All documents were duly

Oliver's Branch

signed over without her having to meet with either one of them. She would have to re-register Paparooni once she was out on Crete, but she talked to Angelina, who contacted the Notary and the solicitor and this was apparently 'no problem', as long as Jason signed and the English solicitor witnessed it. Apart from dealing with her parent's estate after the death of her father, these were the only dealings she had had with solicitors. (She divorced her ex with the help of an on line 'Quick divorce' service,) so all the paperwork and bureaucracy suddenly made her realise she was now living totally in the 'adult world.' She hoped someday she would be able to see a world where she was not constantly having to be so adult. Where simple things were the things that mattered. At the moment though, this world and state of mind, were a long way ahead.

The expected 'financial assistance call' came from Grace as Jill had anticipated and money was transferred into her daughter's account, probably for the last time in the foreseeable future. Jill would be on a tight budget. If the house been sold things would have been a lot easier, but she would consider finances at a later date. She already had a Sterling and a Euro account on Crete and money was duly transferred to await her arrival.

William was true to his word and a lovely young couple with three children came to see the house and snapped it up. It was exactly what they wanted and they even did a deal to keep some of the furniture and all the curtains. They would be moving in on the first of August. A six-month contract all signed, sealed and delivered.

Jill decided it was time to thank TGC for all their help, encouragement and friendship. She purchased 6 butterfly fillet steaks from her local butcher and invited them all to dinner, before the rest of the kitchen was boxed away. She spent a day preparing all sorts of treats, and wrapping up individualised presents she hoped they would like. The table was duly laid and at seven-thirty on the 20th of July they all arrived in their Sunday best. Jill, in jeans and a T shirt made a quick dash upstairs and changed, to rise to the occasion.

When they sat down to eat, Lotty remarked on the tablecloth. It was one Jill's mother had made as a young girl. It was adorned with butterflies and bluebirds flying in and out of wild flowers. The needlework and detail were exquisite. Jill explained how her mother had always enjoyed sewing. As she got older she made numerous samplers to ease her arthritis. Lotty produced a small package and handed it to Jill. "I hope you like this," she said handing it over. "I

hope it will remind you of all the good memories and make you smile."

Inside the package was a beautiful jewellery bag decorated with scenes of the local area. Fishing boats, the pier and seasonal flowers, including one of a spring bed of daffodils, Jill's favourite flower were all interwoven in the design. Inside was a beautifully embroidered picture of Jill's two white cats. Lotty proudly explained, "I found a program on the web which transfers photo images onto fabric, and it was free to download. I'm going to miss you, sweetheart. We've decided to keep TGC going. Fred has a big garage and he doesn't use it now. He lost his licence when the glaucoma got so bad he failed his eye test. We've told all our customers and a lot of them are going to bring unwanted knick-knacks, tools and whatever else they would usually discard. We are going to renovate whatever needs renovating and then sell it on, giving them a 25% cut of whatever we make. Should be quite lucrative if all your *junk* is anything to go by. Lets hope the tax-man doesn't catch up with us..."

Once the meal was well under way, John pulled his napkin from under his chin and stood up, glass in hand. "Well, my young adventurer, here's to you. May you find joy and peace and a future full of sun, may you always be as loved as you are now. You have no idea what you have given us. A purpose and companionship. We all hope you will find the same." He produced a shoe box covered in gold paper that looked vaguely familiar. "This is from me to you. I hope you like it." Almost reverently Jill took the box. The lid was wrapped separately, so once she had undone the gold ribbon (which again looked very familiar) she was able to lift the lid with ease. Inside was one of her father's planes, the largest. It was absolutely pristine and looked as if it had just been purchased. The other 4, which had already been packed, had looked good, but not as perfect as this one. "Once you find a place for them all my hope is you think about me from time to time." He sat back down, pushed his napkin back under his collar and started to eat with renewed vigour.

"John, it's amazing. Thank you so much. You know I'll never forget any of you. I only wish we'd all met sooner. Think of the fun we could have had." She walked round the table and kissed him, he hugged her back. She thought of her dad and how proud he would have been, and how chuffed about the care John had put into making the planes like new.

After a small silence during which the fillet steak was devoured with gusto, it was Fred's turn. Remaining seated he put a small flat package on the table. "We all talked long and hard about what we were giving you and it's relevance to you. At first I felt a bit of a

chump because I couldn't think of anything I thought you would want. Then, behind a shelf I found this and just knew it was right. He handed the gift to her. It was wrapped in silver paper with a silver bow. She opened it carefully. It felt as if glass was involved. Inside was a picture of a young child raising her hands in prayer. She had blue eyes, dark brown hair and a little button nose. The last time Jill remembered seeing this must have been about eight years ago. It had been a present from her own mother. She said it reminded her of Grace. It was in a boot sale and "I just couldn't resist it," she'd said, proudly handing it to Jill. Grace had been mortified when it took pride of place. "You cannot seriously believe I have ever been that angelic mum. Give me a break. I'm a wild child, my mother's daughter!" With that she had stomped out with it and placed it on a shelf in the garage. "If Granny asks where it is, tell her it's in your bedroom. She can't get up the stairs any more, so she'll never know." That had been the end of the matter. Looking at it now it was difficult to relate it to her daughter's photos from university. In most of these she was half dressed and half cut. She seemed to pose on a regular basis, pouting seductively at other young men or women or making funny faces. Yet there was something in the picture both alluring and captivating. Somehow her mum was there and so was the tiny young child Jill had nurtured and set free. It was perfect. Things were getting emotional now. She wondered if they knew about her gifts for them.

"Fred, it's perfect. I haven't seen this in years and the frame is superb. It really will be treasured. Thank you so much."

"I found the card your mum gave you with it. I made a special envelope and it's attached to the back." Jill turned the picture over and took the card out of the gold paper envelope. It was a picture of a young girl standing in a field of daisies. *Dear one and only,* she read, *so like Grace, but oh so like you. Where have the years gone? All my love, your old mum xxx* Suddenly the gift and the past fused into one and Jill comprehended perfectly what the gift meant, on two levels. Her mother was saying how she missed the past and Fred was showing her how she was now in the same situation. Like mother, like daughter. How she loved these people and their wisdom. Millie's gift was more down to earth. "I wanted you to have all the necessary stationary and equipment to enable you to keep in touch with us. We all chipped in on this one, hopefully it will encourage you to write to us." She handed over a large beach bag. The last time Jill had seen it, it was covered in cobwebs and looked scruffy and tired. A brief memory of Grace, running onto the beach in Crete about 14 years before, swinging it to and fro in her small brown hand and laughing into the sun flashed through her mind. Somehow Millie had weaved her magic and now it was a beautiful fresh-cream colour with a large rose motif and brand new bamboo handles. The

inside had been expertly lined with plastic. The contents included a pack of writeable CD's ("you can put photos on those too," Millie had explained.) 2 packets of A4 white paper ("For all those letters you're going to write.") 2 sets of ink cartridges for Jill's somewhat temperamental printer/scanner (Just in case they haven't got them out there.") Lastly a USB memory stick ("Remember to back up anything important.")

Again Jill was overwhelmed and gave Millie a big hug. "Of course I'll keep in touch with you all, you are my family." She sat down, unable to think of anything else to say.

Dishes were cleared away and they all chatted amicably over cheese and biscuits. Looking around at the little group, Jill felt a pang of regret about leaving them and wished TGC had been part of her life for years instead of just months. Finally Tom stood up and everyone stopped talking.

"I found this among your father's stuff. There's a note in it with your mum's writing which says he brought it over with him from Germany, just before the war. The leather needed a lot of TLC, but I hope you use it." He handed over a beautifully blackened leather wallet. Last time Jill saw it there was mildew all over it and the edges were frayed. Jill opened it up and there was the note in her mothers flowing script. *Your dad's when he was a young man. Circa 1947.* She was used to these small scraps of history. During her retirement, her mother had labelled everything which didn't move then cross-referenced each item in a catalogue. It had made disposing of her possessions a very arduous and emotional task. She slipped the note back in the wallet. A piece of white paper jutted from another compartment and she took it out. She found herself looking at a cheque made out to her for £1,943.76.

"Whatever is this?" she asked, her hand shaking slightly.

"Well, we know things are going to be tight for you and from the very start of TGC we agreed all the profits would go to you. We have something more than money between us and it's all down to you. Thank you, Jill, from all of us from the bottom of our hearts."

"I will only accept this on one condition," she said when she had recovered slightly. "I want you to put it back into your account, or better still set up a TGC account, and then promise me you will use this money to come and visit me, all of you, sometime in the future."

There was a lot of tutting and shaking of heads but eventually she convinced them she wouldn't have it any other way. She turned their argument back on them, in order to convince them. "All the money in the world is not as important to me as you six amazing people."

Oliver's Branch

By now it was half-past eleven and everyone was tired. Jill agreed to leave the washing-up until the morning and then they would all 'muck in'.

She stood at the front door hugging each of them in turn and as they trundled off down the road she called after them, "Sweet dreams all of you and thank you for an unforgettable evening."
"Thanks," called back Millie. "Same to you sweetheart, same to you." Their laughter could still be heard, long after they all disappeared round the corner.

It was only as she closed the front door she noticed her six, carefully wrapped parcels by the stairs. Another day, she thought, and after turning out the lights she went up to bed. The past few hours had made her realise beyond a doubt; she was indeed loved.

Twenty two.

The following couple of days proved to be even more manic, but by the night of the twenty second, apart from boxes stacked high in every room, the house looked empty. She arranged with Nick that they would go for an Italian meal after the boxes were loaded. The house was going to be lonely and with no equipment there was very little she could do. The following day she would be leaving with Dyson at the crack of dawn to catch the plane to Crete.

The morning of the twenty-third was bright and sunny. A 40-ton container arrived promptly at **10.00am**. There were 4 movers and the manager, who dealt with the paperwork and itemisation of everything loaded into the container. He was a nice young man from Australia, who had been working with the company for 6 years. He was very efficient and obviously knew the ropes. He explained to Jill how the loading was executed and also her role. In general it was obvious what was to go, but there were items they may take which were meant to stay, unless they were instructed otherwise.. She subsequently walked round with the loaders and Ted, the manager, explaining exactly what was to go. In the garden shed and garage everything for loading was placed in front of them. TGC had made light work of stripping out anything surplus and their garage, 10 minutes away in Mountside Road, already looked like a thriving little cottage industry. They decided they would give the money to allocated charities and so there would be no red-tape about profits, VAT or anything else.

As soon as the tour was finished the loaders set to work and suddenly Jill was a spectator. It was a strange and disturbing situation and one she hoped she would never experience again. She was watching the last 23 years of her life disappear through her front-door. The stress and emotion were almost debilitating. She busied herself making endless cups of tea and just hovering in the background.

During one of the tea breaks, (about the fifth, and it still wasn't lunch time), Ted asked her if she was feeling OK.
"You probably know moving house is one of the most stressful experiences and when you are going to another country there is even more pressure. Don't worry if you get flustered, we've seen it all before. Only last week we loaded a retired couple's worldly possessions up in Hull, for relocation to Turkey, and it took me twenty minutes to get the wife out of the container. She insisted she was going to travel in the back, to look after all her treasures.

Oliver's Branch

Jill didn't quite see herself doing anything quite so drastic but the story didn't exactly fill her with confidence. She had watched her fare-share of relocation programmes and sympathised with people whose items were damaged or lost for weeks on end, or worst of all sank on a container ship. She could only hope none of these things would happen to her stuff.

Nick phoned at lunchtime, asking if there was anything he could do. There wasn't, so they arranged to meet up in town at 8.00 that evening. The plan was to go and see Mama Mia followed by an Italian meal. She worried about him, hoping his apparent lack of concern about her imminent departure was genuine. His father still lived locally, and she was sure if Nick needed anything he could turn to him for help.

June came round with some tuna and mayo sandwiches, apologising for not having visited recently. Her mother, in Bath, had been quite poorly, so she had been up there for the last 10 days. Her husband, James, held the fort. The cats were now quite settled in.
"It's so lovely when Aspro jumps on my knee and sits purring contentedly for hours, while I stroke her. Very therapeutic."
Jill smiled and said she thought it was great they were settling in so well. She marvelled at Aspro sitting "contentedly purring" on June's knee. In thirteen years that cat had never so much as sat near to her let alone on her knee. It's true what people say, she thought, you never own a cat, the cat owns you. Dogs were a much better option, as far as she could see.

Throughout all the weeks of turmoil, Dyson was exceptionally quiet. Most of the time he sat out in the garden with a gloomy expression on his face. On moving day he was positively morose and wouldn't even accept the dog biscuit Jill offered him. He skulked off with his tail between his legs and sat on the lawn. When Grace phoned to see how things were going, Jill expressed her concern.
"I'm sure he'll be OK Mum. He probably misses me and knows he's going somewhere new. I hope he doesn't have that fear-of-flying thing. Maybe you can dose him up with anti-travel-sickness tablets, or something?"
Jill didn't think this was such a good idea. Anyway, how could he have a fear about something he couldn't possibly conceptualise, he had never been on a plane before.
She explained to her daughter about the complete chaos and general level of mayhem, but how, apart from this things were going fine. Grace seemed happy and buoyant. Everything was going well with her new job. She had recently broken up from university for the

summer, but in the second half of the term, had taken a photography option. She enjoyed it so much she was going to take it next year, instead of journalism.
"I've definitely found my *fortia*, Mum..... or something like that. I love it and my tutor says I'm one of the best in the group. Anyway sorry, got to go I'm meeting up with friends this afternoon and I've got to get ready. Love you loads, stroke Dyson from me too."
Jill wondered if they would ever finish a conversation again on a different note. She would have liked to have told her *'fortia'* meant *fire* in Greek, but the line had already gone dead. Anyway it seemed quite apt that her daughter had found a *fire* for something. It was almost more expressive than a strength. She walked out into the garden, just missing one of the loaders, who was bubble wrapping a candle stand, a leaving present from her penultimate job. Dyson looked up half-heartedly but managed a slight wag of his tail.
"We're going to be OK, old boy, you and I, and you'll love your new garden." She offered him a biscuit again. This time he took and munched slowly, then he turned his back on her and went back to sleep.

By 3 o'clock everything was loaded, including her beloved Beach Buggy. She would be able to use this around the village and local area. Ted brought the inventory for her to check plus the Visa machine to authorise a payment. After she signed it she had a sudden thought.
"With all this rush Ted, we haven't really talked about the delivery date..."
"My God, you're right. I'll ring you on your mobile as soon as I know. The minimum is 10 days, but it could be slightly more. Is it OK if I contact you when the freight has arrived on Crete?"
Jill replied this would be fine, secretly imagining up to 2 weeks without any possessions at all. She wondered how she was going to manage. She did not mention her concerns to Ted though, merely responded, "Thank you so much for an excellent job, not only were you an efficient team, but you also understand the emotional implications of a move like this. I found you all remarkably understanding yet professional."
After completing the Visa transaction they shook hands. The crew all said goodbye and wished her luck. Ted got into his incredibly expensive 4X4. Jill knew it was expensive; Jeremy Clarkson recently reviewed the same model on 'Top Gear'. He concluded *it was a snip at only £68,000.*
Ted drove away, waving through the window as he set off down the road. The crew all said their good-byes, climbed up into the cab and within minutes were out of sight. The first part of the move was

complete. Jill watched as all her worldly possessions disappeared out of sight. In one way she felt bereft and isolated and yet another part of her felt incredibly liberated. Her belongings and materialistic shackles were extracted from the equation. For a while at least, her only responsibility were the clothes in her case, all the necessary paperwork for travelling, and of course Dyson.

Home, minus Materialistic possessions, minus the past equals *House, plus* a new start, plus the future (and one geriatric dog.)

Walking back into the now virtually empty house, she looked around. For the first time in over 20 years she realised how big the living room was, devoid of furniture and the flotsam and jetsam of a family life. She gazed into the large mirror on the wall, which only 6 weeks ago had reflected the image of a defeated and sad middle-aged woman, and was surprised at the person staring back at her. She looked somehow younger and more radiant. There was a new confidence and demeanour, which had been missing in the lacklustre face during the awful weeks before the birth of Oliver, and during the debacle of her own professional demise. There was a long way to go before things would seem, even slightly, 'back to normal', but smiling at herself she said out loud;

"OK, Jill, this is it. 'Look upwards with confidence'. The next part of my journey is about to begin. I can do this." It suddenly seemed very apt; she would soon be 30,000 feet up in the air.

By 7.30 she was ready to pick Nick up. Tonight was the last time she would drive her little Peugeot 206. Tomorrow her local garage mechanic would collect it and put it on sale. She had known him for over 20 years, so didn't think he would rip her off. He was to send a cheque to her PO Box when it was sold. (She had set up the PO Box when she was last in Crete with Jason.)

Before going to pick Nick up, she went round to John's house with the parcels she had omitted to give TGC on the night of the meal. John was in and answered the door on the second ring.

"Hello! I was hoping to see you before you left. We all wondered what time your car was ordered for. We wanted to ask if we could come and wave you off?"

"That's a lovely thought John, but to be perfectly honest I would like to just slip away with no extra goodbyes. You know I'll contact you as soon as I arrive. I'll write as soon as there's anything to write about, I promise. I actually came to drop these off for you and the others. I was going to give them to you all at the meal, but in all the excitement and after I'd opened all the fantastic things you gave me, it totally slipped my mind. They're nothing nearly as amazing as the presents you gave me, but they're from my heart."

Ruth Manning

John had taken the carrier bag and given her a big hug.
"Thanks from us all, my dear. You know we didn't expect anything. You've already given us more than we ever imagined possible. Friendship, a hobby and a little business to keep our minds active. Would you like to come in and have a cup of tea?"
Jill explained she was on her way to pick up her son and was already running a bit late. "Let the others know I wanted to leave without any fuss, won't you? I know it's going to be incredibly hard leaving as it is, any added emotion and I'd probably never go. Give them all a big kiss from me. Good luck in your new enterprise. Have fun."
With that she had given him a kiss on the cheek and walked back to her car. John stood at the door and watched her drive away, waving as she did so.
"All the very best, my brave lass, here's to seeing you again, one day very soon." Then he had gone back inside, shut the door, picked up his mug of tea and sat down to watch the second part of an Inspector Morse episode on the TV.

The film, Mama Mia, was just what she needed. A touch of Greece with lots of songs and dancing. They both came out laughing and made their way to the local Italian restaurant. Over a wonderful meal, Jill had had Putanesca, Nick a pizza; they talked about the following day.
"Do you want me to stay the night, Mum?" he asked. Jill thought about this for a moment before replying. "No, son. Thanks for the offer, but I want you to remember how the house was when it was home, now it's just an empty shell. It seems somehow sad, lonely and neglected."
"What about tomorrow then, shall I come by to see you off?"
This time she replied without hesitation. "Nope. I want us to say our goodbyes tonight, then the next time you hear from me, it will be from Greece. You gave the dog a good walk and a cuddle when you were over a few days ago. You know how I hate goodbyes and it isn't really goodbye for us, just separation for a while." Nick nodded. "I thought you'd say that, so I brought this with me. It's just a thought, to wish you a safe journey and good luck in your new home." He passed her a flat package, wrapped in paper she recognized from the stationary drawer. In it was a small wooden gate which opened to expose a row of hooks. There was a picture of Nick and his sister, taken on his 21st birthday, in a small frame mounted on the gate. Jill held back the tears and bit her lip. "I know what you're like with keys, Mum. You even managed to loose the fob with that whistle thing on that was meant to locate your keys for you. Maybe this will alleviate the blind panic you go into, at least twice a week, when you

think you've lost them." He gave her a hug and a sloppy kiss on the cheek.
"Yuck, you are a vile creature!" she laughed, wiping her face with her napkin. "Thank you so much, sweetheart, I know exactly where I'll hang it in the kitchen."
They finished their meal and walked slowly back to the car. It was a lovely evening with a clear sky and warm breeze. Jill felt as if she was going to break into small pieces and shatter in a small pile of pent-up emotion and loss at her son's feet. Instead she kept the banter light and cheery. The drive back to his flat was interspersed with laughter as they recounted various memories of the last 20 years. It was only as they arrived at his flat Nick became serious.
"It goes without saying how much I'm going to miss you Mum. I haven't always said it, but thanks for everything you've done for me. I really will come out to see you as soon as I can." He gave her a hug and she held him close, unable to speak for fear of crying. She wanted this to be a positive goodbye and she didn't want to turn into an emotional, blubbering wreck. Taking a deep breath she held him at arm's length and looked into his vivid blue eyes. "Take care, son. I know everything is going to work out for you. There's nothing to thank me for though, my love for you is unconditional and nothing will change that. Now go on, off you go. I'll phone you from our new home and we'll keep in touch. It was a great evening, thanks." They hugged again and Nick got out of the car and walked up to his front door. She watched him put in the key, open it, turn round and blow her a kiss, then the door slowly closed and he was gone. Jill drove in silence to the beach. She parked up and walked towards the shore where she sat down. Looking out at the full moon reflecting on calm sea, she once again felt the overwhelming sense of loss, which seemed to accompany every stage of this journey towards a new life. She felt torn with guilt, as if she was deserting everything and everyone who had been an integral part of her life. Yet there was no going back now. The treasure box in her heart remained firmly locked as she opened her heart up and took in the silence of the night. She clasped her knees between her arms and sobbed quietly. Her salt tears and the sea drowning her in a wave of grief and emotion.

"See you soon, son," she whispered. "I love you so much."
It was time to go.

Arriving home, she found Dyson lying on the empty carpet, looking desolate and confused. He wagged his tail half-heartedly but didn't move. Jill went and gave him a rub on his soft, velvety muzzle. "Just you and me now, old fella, it'll be OK." She knew the last part of the statement was more for her own benefit than the dog's, but it in no

way comforted her. The house was empty and she took one final wander around. She paused in each room, where a thousand memories, good and bad, flooded back. There was an eerie silence, as if everything had already left and she would be the last to go. Rats abandoning ship, survivors in dinghies paddling away as fast as they could, flotsam and jetsam following in their wake; but unlike the captain she vowed she would not go down with the ship. She would come away from this in one piece, proud and ready to move on. She closed each door behind her as she went. Back in the living room she laid out the sleeping bags and one pillow on the floor. The dog immediately took his place on half the covered area. Undressing slowly, she curled up beside him with her arm around his strong warm neck. In an empty house, with an empty heart she lay very still, waiting for sleep to claim her.

Oliver's Branch

Twenty three.

Jill awoke at 5am the following morning to rain and grey skies. *Nothing new there then for the end of July*, she thought to herself. She wrapped the sleeping bags and pillow in a tight roll, then went upstairs and quickly showered. Back in the living room, after feeding the dog, she made a quick cup of tea on the gas hob then sat on the floor, with both hands curled around the mug. Everything was packed, her ticket, passport and Dyson's papers were all checked and in her travelling bag. It was an early start. The mug had a slogan on the side, *World's Best Dad* . It depicted a rotund man, relaxing in his chair, watching TV, remote in one hand and mug in the other. For the last few years it had been used as a measure for the dog's dry food. She smiled, hoping the motto would turn out to be true. From here on in, the children's father would probably find the onus on him, to solve many of the problems which, until now, he had been virtually unaware of. Nick, in particular, would be living close by and she was sure their relationship would strengthen. She washed the mug up and put it on the drainer, the last thing she would ever wash up in this house. What had been the last thing she had dried up? She couldn't remember. As she looked around she heard the words *last time, last time...* echo through the house, bouncing off the walls. She hoped she would not hear or think these words on a regular basis, for the remaining few hours of her time in England. She dressed quickly and was just putting her arms into the sleeves of a fleece, when the door bell rang. She put Dyson on his lead and opened the door. It was 5.30 and the hired car was waiting outside, the engine still running. Although she had insisted no one came to see her off she still looked up and down the road, feeling a sense of total isolation. There was nobody around and the whole neighbourhood was silent.

The driver said a cheery "Good morning, Mrs Slater" and informed her his name was Mike. He picked up the large case and holdall and deftly put them in the boot. Jill closed the door behind her and followed. *The last time, the last time.....*Dyson followed her to the back of the car. He was no longer able to get into any vehicle, and needed assistance. Jill put his front paws on the back floor, lifted his rump and hoisted him in with her right shoulder. He sat down moodily and gave both humans a sulky stare. Jill brushed the dusting of hair from her arms and shoulder, cursing herself for wearing a black fleece. Dyson moulted all the time, she should have known better.

Mike opened the passenger door for her, she sat down and did up her seat belt. Dyson gave a deep sigh from the back and sat down too.

Her door closed and Mike moved round to the driver's seat, nimbly hopped in, closed the door and the car moved slowly away.
She watched with a feeling of abject terror and despair, as all the familiar houses, gardens and street lights disappeared out of sight. Surely this was no way to feel at the beginning of a new beginning, and the fulfilment of a life long dream?

Last time, last time, last time....... whispered the windscreen wipers as the car turned out of the road and made its way towards the A21.

Mike was what her mother would have called a 'congenial sort of chap'. With grey hair and brown eyes, laughter lines creasing the side of his eyes and bushy brows shading them above gold-rimmed glasses, he was a gentle looking man. Within half an hour she knew most of his life story. Born and raised in the Midlands, a merchant seaman most of his life, married to Dorothy, with 3 grown-up sons. He had come down south for the climate. His youngest son had whooping cough as a youngster and the doctor advised a complete change of environment. "They said those kind of things in those days did doctors, and without questioning, we just upped sticks and move down to Eastbourne. Turned out all right though. Mark was soon right as rain and Dot loved the climate and the greenery. Bit different from Leicester, with its grey streets and deserted cloth mills. Only thing I really miss about the place, to this day, is a good bacon bap and a pint of Ruddles!"

They passed the post-box where only a few days ago she had posted her resignation. She smiled and hoped to some degree she had caused some discomfort and administration difficulties, although she knew she probably hadn't.
She was happy for Mike to rumble on. She looked out of the window and was reminded of one of her favourite poem, "Naming of Parts." It is about a young soldier listening to his sergeant belting out the parts of a rifle, and how to use it, while he looks at the japonica blossoming out of the window. He sees a totally different world from the one portrayed by the acts of war. Jill looked out at the luscious green fields and the massive oak trees, which were flashing past on the verges of the A21 and thought, "Today we have breaking of hearts." She smiled at Mike, looking totally enraptured by his autobiographical monologue and said nothing. It was still raining outside and she knew she would remember this journey for the rest of her life, because it was the last time she would leave England. There was no 2 weeks of sunshine, followed by the imminent return to the same old routine, the same job, the same comfort zone of a life,

Oliver's Branch

cruising along at a steady speed with the odd pitfall or hole in the road. This one would be a roller coaster with no turning back.
It seemed like no time at all before they were entering the Southern terminal where the Departures sign over the doors was dripping from the heavy rain. "Here we are then, luv" Mike said, "we've arrived." Jill wondered at what stage in the journey she had become 'luv' as opposed to Mrs Slater. It amazed her how she had been able to travel the 90-odd miles without muttering more than maybe a dozen words. She never needed to talk about herself once. In a way it had been a blessing and she was grateful to him. Dyson had slept the whole way. He was reluctant to leave the warm spot he had made for himself. She handed over the agreed sum for the trip, and went round the back to coax her travelling companion out. Bags were duly loaded on a trolley and Mike bid her a good journey. It was all arranged for her to be met at the departure entrance at 7.00am and as it was only 6.50. She sat on her case and gave Dyson a good rub. Suave business men and glossy, well-manicured women gave her and the dog a wide berth, possibly to avoid the fur generated by this show of affection. Jill was unaware of the spurious looks and supercilious glances. It was only when a tall, gangly man stood beside her and started to talk to the dog, she was once again aware of her surroundings.

"Hello, old chap, you must be Dyson." The dog lifted a paw and put on his most pathetic face. "Hi, I'm Timothy, from the pet transport company, Pets Go2. We've spoken a lot on the phone but it's good to meet, in the 'fur' as it were." Jill was not quite sure what he was referring to until she saw that Jason had a halo of fluffy fur all around him and still more wafting in spirals above the ground. She realised Timothy had made a joke and gave a small smile. All efficiency and light, the young man continued. "Right, well if you follow me we'll go to the packing and loading area to check the crate is a comfortable fit. Jill laughed this time, though only to herself. The so-called crate had been made to measure, was padded and had cost her £279.99 (including VAT). Quite some *crate*. She said nothing but followed Timothy, *do call me Tim it's so much quicker,* to the loading area. He walked ahead pushing her trolley and talking to someone on his mobile phone. She had expected some kind of banter about how comfortable pet travel was and she needn't worry about a thing, but none was forthcoming. The only thing she gleaned from the journey, was Tim obviously had a good night out with Debs the night before."We must do it again babes, and soon." He would give her a ring later, he said, when he was less busy. "God, Debs, it can be so stressful being sensitive to clients' feelings with this kind of work, but hey you know me, always in tune, babe.... Know what I mean."

Arriving at the loading area, Tim pointed out a large box which looked more like a coffin than a *deluxe canine carrier,* the only difference being large air-vents in the sides. "Well, here you are, Dyson. Home for the next few hours. Let's get you settled in and comfortable." Jill bent down and hugged the dog, whispering as she did so, "I'm sorry, bubs, but I'll be waiting for you at the other end." As she stood up, Tim deftly scooped the unsuspecting animal up, plonked him in the box, checked that he would be well protected and closed the lid. "Perfect fit!" he remarked, brushing himself down. "Nothing to worry about, he will get a walk and some water before he's loaded. The only difference between your flight and his is he won't get an in-flight film." Jill looked at the closed crate and felt as if she was losing yet another important part of her life. "Well, Dyson," she said to the depersonalised piece of wood, "that's the last time we'll have a hug in this country, seen you soon. Callo taxeedee." She tapped the lid of the crate and turned to Tim, who was back on his mobile. He obviously realised that his sensitivity level was somewhat lacking and hung up in mid sentence. "Right then, Mrs Slater, all I need now are Dyson's passport and papers and you can leave him in our capable hands." Jill dutifully handed everything over, secretly wondering if 'Debs' thought he had capable hands too. After he had checked all documentation he shook her hand and pointed her in the direction of departures. "You have a good trip now, and don't worry about a thing. Bye-ee!" and he was gone, no doubt to talk to Debs about some more pressing matter than the welfare of her much loved and faithful companion. He would probably go into detail with her what he would do with his 'capable hands' during their next date.

By the time she reached check-in it was nearly eight o'clock and she was exactly on schedule. Everything was checked and her luggage rolled away from her on the conveyor belt. The Generation Game came into her head..... "2 wonderful children, a handful of good friends, the grave of her parents, her home (now merely a house/bricks and mortar) memories, the cats, her car, Dyson, one large suitcase and holdall. Last moments......"Congratulations Mrs Slater, you will be taking all these away with you today from the Regeneration, Repatriation Game!" Jill walked slowly towards departures hoping avidly she would, at some time in the near future, feel regenerated and alive. All she felt at that moment was bereft and empty. Far more a loser than a winner.

Eventually arriving in the departure lounge, after the strict security checks and additional questions, she was lucky enough to find a

seat. It was 8.45 and no doubt she would soon be making her way to the departure gate, for another 2 hour wait. The gate number was not displayed yet, so she sat quietly looking at the assortment of people around her. She had no inclination to look around the shops, there was nothing she needed. The Disney shop was already bustling with young children grabbing the hand of a reluctant parent, explaining why they really, really had to have an Eeyore iPod holder or, if not, a Tigger mobile phone holder. "Pleeeese daddy pleeese, everyone at school's got one..." "I need to keep my phone dust free and scratch proof, that's just the perfect way. Pleeese mummy pleeeeeese..." In the years when her children were growing up, they were happy to get a key ring or a photo frame, Jill thought. Come to think of it, back then mobile phones and iPods were things of the future, not total necessities. She turned away, so as to repress any further memories of family holidays, in a time which now seemed as far away as The Hundred Acre Wood or Never Never Land.

Suddenly feeling totally exhausted she made a decision. She walked across to Boots and bought a packet of herbal sleeping tablets, a tin of mixed fruit pastilles, dusted in sugar (like the ones her dad had always had in the car when she was a child), a bottle of chilled water and some wax ear plugs. She made her way back to her still vacant seat. Undoing the packet of sleeping tablets, she took out 2 from their foil jackets and swilled them down with the chilled 'Original Alpine fresh' water. It was time to go into the void. Hopefully within the next couple of hours the tablets would kick in and she would be able to sleep the whole way, arriving at her destination fresh, optimistic and ready for the hundreds of 'First times' she was about to encounter.

The neon sign announced her flight would be boarding at Gate 61 and was on schedule. She made her way directly there. She was informed it would be a lovely flight. The weather was clearing and on Crete they were experiencing perfect summer sunshine.

She moved into the waiting area, which to her looked more like a holding pen. Lots of small children were racing around jittery parents, screeching with excitement and delight. She was aware of the buzz of conversation all around her and could not help but register the fact that the last real words she had uttered had been to her son, almost eleven hours ago, if you dismissed her various conversations with the dog, of course. She hoped the rest of her life would not be spent with only Dyson to talk to on a personal level. Much as she loved him, intellectual discussion or book debates, weren't among his greatest virtues.

Ruth Manning

The tablets were beginning to take effect. It seemed as if only a few minutes had passed and passengers were being called to board the airline. She obediently joined the queue, to which her allocated seat number belonged, and shuffled slowly along to the open flight door. A smiling young female flight-attendant, you didn't call them hostesses any more apparently, it was politically incorrect, pointed her in the direction of her seat. She sat down gratefully in the window seat she had been allocated and looked out of the window. This would be the *first time* she ever left England for the *last time*. She smiled to herself, blew an invisible kiss to Dyson, who was hopefully settled in the cargo hold, having been dealt with in a 'sensitive way' by Tim, and probably Debs too, and prepared herself for sleep. "Callo tazeedee, filos moo," she whispered under her breath. "Have a good journey, my friend." Fastening her seat belt she wondered at the metaphorical implications of the journey she was now embarking on. Was she in for a bumpy ride or a hassle free and enjoyable future? Only time would tell. She felt the plane speeding along the runway and then shuddered with sheer joy and amazement, something she always felt when flying, at the sudden uplift and feeling of thrust, power and weightlessness, as the giant bird rose into the sky.

My *one and only* take off, my first and my last journey between the old and the new she thought. Putting the wax earplugs in her ears, she settled back, to sleep.

Part 2

Crete

Ruth Manning

"Look upwards with confidence"

Twenty four.

Jill slept through the whole flight. She had specifically not ordered a meal and so she was left alone by the flight attendants. She slept deeply and dreamlessly, sinking into a chasm of total obliteration. She only awoke when the seatbelt warning started pinging. Sitting up groggily she looked out of the window to a crystal, clear shimmering sea and an azure blue sky, with not a cloud in sight. At that precise moment it was as if she had travelled to a completely different planet and she found it almost impossible to believe only a few hours ago she had been listening to the bleak and rhythmic message of a car's windscreen wipers. The fear and the dread were replaced by an exhilarating excitement and a sense of 'coming home.'

Once the plane had landed and the doors had opened there was the usual jostle to get out as quickly as possible. Jill had always found it strange how on outward-bound journeys, most passengers impatiently herded together to enter the plane as quickly as possible then, on arrival, repeated the exercise to exit it. As far as she could see there was absolutely no logic to this at all, as the following procedures were always the same. Once out of the plane at Chania airport you would be crammed into a steaming hot bus, (in which the air conditioning had probably broken down), like sardines, then a 3-minute trip to arrivals and passport control. The faster you exited the plane the more time you spent playing sardines with all the other 'eager beavers'. Cursing the fact your deodorant was in no way going to give you another 5 minutes 'freshness' let alone the 24 hours as promised in the adverts, you would try and hide the sweat marks spreading under your arm-pits. When the last passenger was ensconced in the remaining 1 cubic foot of space, the doors would seal you in this putrid, hermetically sealed piece of tin and you would move on to the immigration check. Again those in the inner, by now completely oxygen-free areas of the bus, would push to get off first, this time through sheer self-survival instincts A virtual stampede usually ensued. Arriving at customs control would be little better for these 'eager beavers', who would now be hot, smelly, wet, dishevelled and experiencing severe anger management problems; only to be met by Greek customs officials, a rule unto themselves. With very little enthusiasm and struggling to look at your passport while holding an iced coffee in one hand and your ID in the other, a uniformed official, with sunglasses and dark Mediterranean skin,

would grunt something, without even glancing up, then move you on. For the next 10 minutes to a possible hour you would be forced to stand around, watching the little digital screen, if it was working, to be directed to baggage claim. Oddly enough you would still be with all the other passengers you had tried so hard to 'beat', whether you had been first, or last, off the plane. When eventually the luggage was unloaded and a conveyor number allocated there would be another mad dash to be there first, followed by the inevitable wait and sheer exasperation because your luggage did not, miraculously, appear on the conveyor belt first.

Jill stood up and exited the plane *last*, and suddenly the word took on a less ominous meaning. It didn't matter at all any more. First or last were all the same.

Having gone through virtually the exact procedure as outlined above, she was delighted when she arrived unruffled and relaxed at the baggage conveyor and the first case and holdall to emerge together were hers. She graciously excused herself to an extremely overweight woman, who looked as if she had been dragged through a hedge backwards, and moved forward to extract her luggage from the belt. As she left she heard the woman say to her extremely harassed husband, whose shirt literally clung to his ample and very hairy chest, "Well, wouldn't you know. That's the woman who kept us all waiting on the bus by being the last one to get on. Some people have no idea how to behave, do they, dear?" Jill merely smiled and headed towards Avis car rentals.

Having secured a hatchback which would accommodate all her luggage as well as Dyson, a surprisingly painless operation which she had set up online, she was pointed to the Customs cargo import yard, where Dyson was waiting. She needed to ask for Tasos to hand over the papers. If anything was going to go wrong, she was sure this would be where it would happen. In the various relocation TV programmes she had watched, along with the tales of woe regarding freight disasters, people coming to 'live the dream' in Greece to suddenly and inexplicably find Greek bureaucracy sometimes threw not one, but 100 spanners into the works. She had seen women in floods of tears when they discovered that Tiddles had accidentally been shipped to Algeria by mistake, or a couple whose beloved Jock, a cairn terrier, had somehow been claimed by a young couple from Ilford. They had apparently been in too much of a hurry to check the exclusive model carrying case and had left just a few minutes before. It appeared Jock's owners did not want the three – year - old miniature pink poodle they were being offered by a Greek official, even though he assured them that according to the paperwork this

was definitely Jock and not Trixiebell, as it said on the mutt's gem-studded, golden name tag.

As luck would have it Tasos was waiting at the imported-live cargo doors when she walked up. Asking, in Greek, if Tasos was there as she was picking up her dog, he had given her a big, toothless grin, waved the paperwork aside and taken her straight to Dyson. He had already been for a walk and had some water. He looked remarkably unscathed considering his experience. He wagged his tail enthusiastically and jumped up to welcome her. The bright sunlight highlighted a handful of fur, as it wafted into the air, but the white short sleeved shirt Jill was wearing was completely unaffected. She thanked Tasos and gave him €10 for his help. Tasos walked over with Dyson to put him into the back of the hatchback. Jill was amazed to see that the dog needed virtually no assistance in jumping in; she thanked Tasos again and left.

Suddenly she was alone once more and about to confront a demon. Parking up in a lay-by exiting the airport, she psyched herself up to deal with this all too-well-known and feared phenomenon. *Driving on Crete.* Loud noises, the sound of brakes, bikers appearing from nowhere and the ever-dreaded taxi drivers and tourists in hire cars. Jill had to come to terms with driving on Greek roads with all the above, as well as the most perplexing phenomenon of all, Greek drivers. Up until this point Jason had always done the driving. She heard his voice as clearly as if he was sitting beside her. "One day sweetheart, you are going to have to overcome this fear of driving. Especially when we come to live here."
"I will, you know I will, just give me a bit of time to adjust." she had just smiled and manically clutched her seat. Now the time had arrived, there could be no adjustment period. It was make or break and she was trembling from head to toe. She knew the journey to the village like the back of her hand, but even so she sat frozen in her seat, her hands clutching the steering wheel, her knuckles white from the pressure. *Well I guess it really is going to be a white knuckle ride,* she thought to herself and acknowledged her pun. She breathed deeply, checked the mirrors and indicated to move out onto the road. For what seemed like hours she felt as if she was in suspended animation, waiting for the screech of tyres, the buckling of metal, the blasting of horns. Instead she found herself travelling down the main road at a quite respectable 40 kilometres an hour behind a pick-up. The two goats in the back looked at her unperturbed. Wish I was a goat, Jill thought, and then decided she probably didn't. Her destination was probably far preferable today to theirs.

As the journey progressed she found herself becoming more and more relaxed, apart from her constant mantra of 'keep to the right, keep to the right'. She approached the National Highway without so much as a scratch and turned off some ten minutes later still unscathed and actually enjoying herself. Unlike all previous journeys, she was unable to appreciate the beautiful views of Souda Bay and the surrounding mountains, as she had in the past, but she felt this was a small price to pay for re-establishing herself as part of the independent driving community.

After negotiating the tricky turning off the slip road onto the Omalos road, she knew she was almost home. Suddenly she found herself singing the lyrics to an old Bob Marley song. *Don't you worry about a thing, cos every little thing going be all right now....* she sang, tapping the steering wheel to the imaginary beat. Dyson took it all lying down and seemed totally relaxed. Things really were looking up. She found herself reflecting on the fact that all the upheaval and worry, prior to her departure, seemed far less daunting in the brilliant sunshine, with her destination in sight.

Swinging a right, (very jauntily she thought...) to the village of Alikianos and crossing the bridge leading to her village, she saw colourful signs advertising bouzouki evenings. She hoped she would be able to get to at least one during the summer. Another turn and she was in totally familiar territory. Everything appeared exactly the same as when she was last there, over a year ago. A good thing too she thought. She had not come for the fast pace and materialistic malaise of her past life, she was here come simplicity of life and basic values. She hoped she would be able to encompass them in reality in the way she always had, in her dreams.

Rounding a corner she saw her house, just as she remembered it. Pulling the wire netting away from the entrance, she parked the car in the carport, dragged the netting back again and secured it. *The first thing I must do is get a gate,* she noted to herself. Dyson would love the freedom of the orchard, but she needed peace of mind that it would be secure. She left Dyson in the car, for a few more moments, just so she could check the rest of the perimeter. Everything seemed secure. At the far end of the orchard was a large, cleared area, also surrounded by fencing and a large rickety but secure gate. She and Jason had not decided what they would do with this area but at the moment this was not her top priority. She walked back through the orange trees and opened the boot door for Dyson. Without further ado he leapt out and was gone. Jill followed him into the orchard where he was sniffing happily at every tree and post. Deeming it

safe to leave him to explore, she dug out the house keys and walked down the steps to the kitchen door. The house was built on two levels, a basement with a large kitchen, small living room, (the snug as she and Jason had named it), shower and toilet plus a large storeroom. Upstairs was a through living room, a single and a double bedroom, both quite small, plus another shower and loo. Everything was sparkling clean, thanks to the efforts of her agent Angelina. She arranged for it to be cleaned the week before Jill arrived.

Jill walked around the balcony on the upper level, opened all the shutters then went down the steps leading from the front door, round to the back of the house. Dyson was still in 'sniff' mode.

She had no outside furniture; in fact she had absolutely no furniture at all, for inside or out. She possessed a single-ringed Primus camping gas stove, 2 mugs, 2 plates, a hotchpotch of cutlery and a garlic press. That was it. She sat down at the top of the basement steps and breathed in deeply. She couldn't remember the last time she had felt so totally free of the shackles of materialism or the stresses of the recent past. She knew she would have to deal with personal, emotional and practical issues in the future, but for just those few moments she felt euphorically liberated. She looked out at the orange trees, *her orange trees..* The 30 Merrilies were now devoid of fruit but the 10 Valencias dripping with luscious ripe golden orbs. She felt totally at peace.

I'm home she thought to herself. *Welcome home, Jill.* As Dyson came and nuzzled up to her and she hugged his warm furry body, she felt confident things really were going to *work out just fine.*

Oliver's Branch

Twenty five.

She had no idea how long she had been sitting there just soaking up the sun and the silence (apart from the cicadas chirping in the trees) but suddenly she heard some one calling her name over the fence; it was Eleni her next-door neighbour.

During the past few years, when she and Jason had come to visit and stay for a few days, they had come to know their elderly neighbours well and their hospitality and joie de vie were infectious. Eleni was 72 but didn't look a day over 65. Her hair, although pure white, was thick and luxurious and she wore it in a haphazard knot on her head, often held in place by a kebab stick. Her skin was smooth and clear, with only a trace of lines around her mouth and laughter lines around her inquisitive brown eyes. She had no facial hair, moulds, warts or other embellishments which seemed common in many of the other Yaya's (grandmothers) Jill had met or knew. Her husband, Mitsou, also in his seventies, although he had no birth certificate and so was, theoretically, of indeterminate years, was a large bear of a man with a full head of grey hair and a moustache any Greek would be proud of. He was dark skinned and weather-worn but had a presence about him. Jason had joked Mitsou made him feel he you should stand to attention. He was very traditional with set beliefs on how life should be lived. Once, when they had been visiting and had been invited over for a meal (one of many; Eleni was a marvellous cook) he had turned to Jason and said, "If you do not eat meat *you will die...*" in such a forceful almost aggressive manner. Jason immediately picked up another large chunk of lamb, and bit into it with conviction. Later Jill had joked with him, "You certainly looked a bit *sheepish* when he told you his adage on the importance of meat, Ha ha..." "Actually it was lamb," Jason had replied, laughing, "....and absolutely amazing it was too."

Jill went over to the fence. Eleni and Mitsou spoke no English, although their three daughters spoke it very well, consequently all conversations with her neighbours were in Greek. Jill was by no means fluent, but she could get by on the basics. It often frustrated her when she could not express opinions or sentiments or talk to people on a deeper level. She was determined to master the language in the years to come. "So you have returned, Gilleena" Eleni said, "...but where is Yaysen, is he in the garden?" Jill spent some time explaining that 'Yaysen' would not be coming to live with her. It was just her and the dog. Things had not gone well and they had decided to go their separate ways. (Literally she had said taken different roads, but Eleni understood.) For the older Greek women, divorce or

separation were completely incomprehensible, but Eleni had made it plain to Jill, long ago, that she was aware Northern Europeans did not lead their lives in the same way, and she accepted this.
She asked Jill how long she was staying and Jill explained this was her home now, she had left England forever. "Then it is time to eat," Eleni said without further ado and beckoned Jill round to their house. Jill found a piece of rope and tied Jason up outside the door, placing a tin bowl she had found in the orchard some while ago beside him, filled with fresh water. Although there appeared to be a slight shift in the way the Greeks now treated their animals, it is well known they can be cruel and callous with dogs and cats. Jill was not going to take the risk of Dyson getting out, especially at this early stage, he could easily be shot.

As Jill approached the back door, Mitsou came out from the orange orchard he maintained, along with a vegetable patch, chicken run and various other pens containing goats and sheep. He had the largest cabbage in his arms Jill had ever seen and she wondered if they would eat it all or use it for fodder as well. Passing it to Eleni he swept Jill up in an exuberant hug and boomed out, "Welcome back, my girl," as he returned her to terra firma. The three of them went inside where Eleni deftly laid another place at the table and Mitsou and Jill sat down. Eleni immediately produced plate after plate of food. Along with traditional Greek salad and greens there were small fish, octopus and sardines, potatoes, tsatsiki and big chunks of bread. Mitsou poured them each a glass of his home-made wine and they all helped themselves to the various dishes.

During the meal Mitsou asked Jill what her plans were. She explained to him, in faltering Greek, her imminent needs, hoping she wasn't making too many mistakes. Because she had no furniture until the container arrived in August, she would make do with the air bed she and Jason had used on their previous stays. There were 2 sleeping bags plus a pillow, so she would be fine, initially. She asked how she would go about getting a car, as she did not want to have the rental car for more than 2 weeks. Also if there were any problems with the plumbing or lighting she wondered if they would be able to point her in the right direction. Mitsou explained how she must take photographs of herself to the police station to obtain a residence permit before buying a car. He promised to take her to look at some. He had a cousin, who had a friend whose brother owned a very good garage, and *he was an honest man*. He also had relatives, linked to friends, with various businesses in the area. They would be able to deal with any domestic problems she might encounter. The next 2 hours passed in a flash and the wine flowed freely. By the end

Oliver's Branch

of the proceedings Jill was feeling satiated and relaxed and thanked them for all their help and hospitality. Exchanging the three kisses on the cheeks, so much a part of the Greek tradition, she waved goodbye and went back to her new home. Eleni had given her some scraps and a bone for Dyson. He who crunched the whole lot up in about four minutes.

It was about 4.00 pm and suddenly all the excitement, travelling and change swept over Jill. She felt totally exhausted. Opening the basement door, she went in, closely followed by Dyson. She blew up the air bed, laid out the sleeping bags and pillow, then, without even taking off her clothes, although she did manage to kick off her sandals, she collapsed onto the makeshift bed. She was asleep within minutes. She was so soundly asleep she didn't even feel Dyson creep onto the sleeping bag, nudge her over slightly and settle down beside her, his head resting on half the pillow.

When she awoke it was dark outside and she delved into her bag for her mobile to see what time it was. Pulling it out she realised she hadn't even switched it back on when she left the plane. She did so and was grateful to see it was fully charged, she didn't fancy trying to find an adaptor just yet, although she knew there was one in her case. Several beeps told her she had 4 missed calls and 4 text messages. It was nearly 11.00pm Greek time, 9.00pm back in England. She had slept solidly for 7 hours. Although she was hungry, she knew she could manage until morning. Then she would go into Alikianos and stock up on basics. She wasn't at all sure that Dyson felt the same. He was still lying outstretched on the makeshift bed watching her. She felt incredibly guilty, she had nothing to give him. "Come on bubs, let's get you outside for you to do your thing." She switched on the outdoor light and Dyson followed her falteringly up the steps which were tiled. He slipped around initially, but soon found his footing. "Get used to it ol' boy, this is the only way in or out for you." Jill gave him a helping nudge and he wandered off into the orchard. Following him up to look at the moon, which hung like a silver orb surrounded by stars, in a crystal black sky, she nearly fell over a large plastic bag at the top of the steps. Leaving Dyson to his ablutions, she picked it up carefully and carried it back inside. The contents turned out to be a container filled with stuffed vine leaves, some large butter beans in lemon and oil, a wedge of crispy bread and a litre of wine. Obviously Eleni was not going to allow her to starve to death. There was another large bag which contained a generous helping of bones and some pasta in tomato sauce. This she assumed was for the dog. She reflected how, in all her years in England, not one neighbour had ever shown her the

same hospitality, thoughtfulness or kindness. She was deeply touched.

Dyson had obviously heard the rustling of bags and came jauntily down the steps, without any hesitation this time. Wherever food was involved he was a master of acquired skills; he sat down in front of Jill, expectantly.

Jill put the bones and pasta on a plate then took the rest of the food and sat on the bed. Pouring herself a large tumbler of wine, the only glass she possessed, she tucked in, imbibing on the wine as she ate. She completely finished the lot and the bottle was half empty, when Dyson came and sprawled on the bed. She had no entertainment and wanted to let the food digest before she went back to sleep, so she took out the torch she had brought with her and found the book she was reading. That way she could just switch off the torch when she wanted to sleep, without having to get off the bed to turn out the light. Nudging Dyson across the bed, she curled up and started to read. It was then she remembered her mobile and was amazed she had not immediately looked at the messages or found out who had been calling.

She went first to the missed calls. Two from Sarah, one from Astrid and one from Grace. No messages had been left. The texts backed these up.
Hiya mum. Hope you arrived OK. No news is good news so YOU say! You would be freaking out if I hadn't let you know I'd arrived safely somewhere when I went away. Text me. Love you G XXX MWAH"
From Sarah - H*ey, know you're probably exhausted but if there are any probs, give me a call. Miss you already.*
From Astrid - *Well babes the new life starts here! Hope it's everything you wish for. Don't you DARE forget me. Xxxxxxxxxx*
The fourth message was from Nick. *Hey Ma! Haven't heard from you so guess all is good. Get in touch as soon as X*

She wrote one reply to them all. *So sorry! Very hectic, lots of things to do! Will ring tomorrow, sometime after 6 your time. Flight fine, slept. Dyson fine and seems totally at home here. As am I. Take care. Loads a love. Me XXX* She pressed send to several, clicked on their numbers and sent it off. It was strange, she reflected, how in England she was never without her mobile. If she didn't get a text from someone at least once an hour, she felt bereft, yet today it had literally been, for her at least, out of sight out of mind. This was a very strange concept. She did not for one minute believe she would feel this way in a few days, when things returned to some kind of

normality. What amazed her most was the fact that all the things which had seemed so vast, so insurmountable and so overwhelming had somehow been pushed to the back of her mind. A saying her mother had often quoted came to mind, *Better to have loved and lost than never have loved at all...* With her children and friends there was an unconditional love which scaled the heights of mundane reality, but what about Oliver? This was the first time the bejewelled box had been nudged for a few days. He was always in her subconscious yet the actual implications of her decision to 'give him up,' 'let Jason bring him up,' (he would do it so much better than she would) 'abandon him,' 'give him the chance of a normal life' 'free herself from the responsibility of motherhood,' 'selfishly put herself first,' and many, many more such thoughts, only now came into focus again. Yes, *Better to have loved and lost...* but, *Never to have loved and lost...* was something totally different. Oh yes, she could love from afar, feel guilt and derision, longing and maternal love, but the bridges had been burnt. There really was nothing she could do. She had made her choice and now she either lived with it, or let it erode into her psyche and destroy whatever this new life had to offer. Nobody on Crete had any idea about this most complex of all secrets. Hopefully they never would. She tried to imagine what Jason was doing now and from nowhere the smell of newborn babies and the softness of newborn skin, crept into the air around her. Dyson cuddled into her side and brought her back into the present. There would be time enough to put all her emotional meanderings into some kind of perspective but this was not it. Setting her alarm for eight, she switched off the torch and snuggled into the warm, totally comatose body, of her travelling companion and future co-inhibitor. "Well, Dyson, this is it. You and I within this world......" Minutes later the veil of sleep had encompassed her once again. She slept an uninterrupted sleep, until her alarm woke her, the following morning.

Twenty six.

Jill awoke to bright sunshine and the sound of things being moved around under the pergola, at the top of the steps. She dressed quickly and with Dyson not far behind, went to see what the noise was all about. She was greeted by Mitsou who was in the process of arranging a white plastic table and four chairs. "Ah Gilleena, good morning. Did you sleep well?" Jill told him she had slept like a log. She actually said "I slept like a tree," as she didn't know the word for log, but he seemed to get the gist of this and nodded, knowingly. He explained this was old furniture which had been sitting in the shed for a while. He hoped it would help out until her things arrived from England. Just then Eleni came round the corner, with a large flask of coffee, fresh bread and a plate with cheese and hard boiled eggs on it. "Here you are, breakfast. Good eating." She placed the fayre on the table and was gone before Jill could thank her. Mitsou explained it was a name day. His wife had to get food ready, as they were having a table in the evening. He insisted she came. It was time to meet some of her neighbours, as well as say hello to his family. She thanked him for the table and chairs. It would be so much more relaxing than sitting on the steps. Then, with a wave and "See you later," he was gone.

Jill sat down to eat. The village was peaceful, apart from the occasional cockerel crowing, dogs barking to each other across the valley and the odd passing pick-up. It was a beautiful day. Jill felt invigorated, ready for the hours ahead. After breakfast, she washed up and then sat outside to make a list of all the most important tasks she had to do.

First on the list was to go shopping. She wrote a list of essentials she knew she would need, as well as dog food for Dyson. Following this were the more complicated issues:
Go to police station about residence permit.
Talk to Mitsou about buying a car.
Find out who could make a secure (cheap) gate for the carport.
Check PO Box in Alikianos for mail.
Phone Angelina about landline installation, plus payment for cleaning.
Find out where to buy a TV/satellite?

She stopped and looked out over the orchard. It had been quite neglected since her last visit and there was a carpet of thick weeds all the way to the end. Jill had never been a keen gardener and although she wanted to learn how to maintain the orange trees, she

was also a realist; there was no way she would be able to do all the pruning, strimming and clearing, which so obviously would need doing over the next few months. Finances may be tight, but she needed help.

Ask Mitsou about a gardener?

She hoped before too long she would have made few more contacts. She didn't want to rely on Mitsou and Eleni for everything, they both had their own lives to lead, and so did she. Wonderful as they were, Jill knew she had to maintain an element of independence and stand on her own two feet. She threw a few scraps down for Dyson, then securing him on his lead with some extra rope, she hastily cleaned her teeth, splashed her face and, picking up her keys, went round to the car. Although she had on a fresh T shirt and shorts she felt grubby, she made a mental note to have a shower in the imminent future.

*

The next two weeks were manic, in a sunny, warm, totally disorganised sort of way. She soon became aware that lists could never be followed and there was going to be no chronological adherence to plans either. All the same, things were sorted and ticked off in a haphazard way.

The first thing to be dealt with was the carport gate. Mitsou had talked to one of the locals who was a welder and asked him if he would have time to measure up, make and fit a gate for her. He had explained about the dog, who needed a bit more freedom around the orchard. Arriving back from her shopping expedition in Alikianos, she was greeted by a burly Greek with a loud voice, mischievous eyes and a head of thick, grey wavy hair. He was sitting on the step playfully cuffing Dyson (although the exuberance with which he was doing this, looked to Jill as if Dyson could end up with concussion.) He stood up and offered Jill his massive, work-stained hand, introducing himself in his deep, resounding voice. His name was Lefteris and he had already measured the area for gates, he just needed to know what sort of gates she wanted. The options were varied and so were the prices. For an automatic, sliding, wrought iron gate she was looking at between 3 or 4 thousand Euros. For two wooden, manually operated gates it was about 1,500. For manual, wrought iron (with attractive swirls to match the balcony of the house) maybe 2,000. All of these were way out of Jill's budget. She explained she just wanted something simple, but secure, which would keep the dog in. She drew an example, a metal frame with cross bars and then some kind of metal fencing to fill in the gaps. A number of the orchards had these. Lefteris immediately understood.

"Ah, I understand. This is no problem" he said, in Greek, as he spoke no English. "I will have these made and fitted within two days. With fitting it will be three hundred Euro. Is that OK?" Jill said it was absolutely perfect, secretly wondering if he actually meant weeks, knowing the Greek reputation for speed.

He insisted on helping her with the various bags and boxes she had in the boot of the hatchback and gratefully accepted a cold beer, which she dug out of one of the Inka bags; Inka being the largest chain of supermarkets on the island. She apologised, because the beer was slightly warm and explained. She didn't have a fridge because it was somewhere between England and Crete, with all her other possessions. He laughed and swilled from the can, quickly emptying it. Wiping the froth from his moustache he said his goodbyes and was gone.

Unfastening Dyson she went down into the kitchen and started unpacking all the bags. Because she had no fridge she had thought carefully about what to buy. She ended up with a great many cans and packets and very little fresh produce. All the same she felt she had enough to keep her going for the following week, at least. She also managed to find a suitable dog food and dried biscuits for Dyson. As she unpacked these he cocked his ears and waited expectantly. She put a couple of dried biscuits in the tin bowl she was using for his meals, until his own, heavy duty dish arrived. She had also bought an orange/lemon squeezer, as a number of trees had rich, juicy Valencias hanging from their branches. It was well past harvesting, but they looked delicious. She went into the orchard and picked three, which she then squeezed, filling a half litre water bottle with the juice. She poured herself a glass, and went to sit under the pagoda. It was nearly lunchtime, but she felt she had achieved sufficient for one day. She had been told by Angelina last year, "If you get at least one thing done every day you were doing well." She had already done two. Such a different philosophy from the past, when at times she had felt like a hamster spinning round on its wheel, with too much to do and too little time to do it in.

Her silence was shattered by a head poking over the wall, followed by a lot of Greek, which was excited, fast and shrill! Within minutes the gate opened and Irini was giving her an enormous hug, smothering her in kisses. Irini was her neighbour from across the road. An effervescent woman in her mid-seventies. She lived alone as both of her sons were married and lived in Heraklion and Athens. On every visit Jason and Jill had made, Irini miraculously appeared with words of wisdom, and an energy which at times wore Jill out.

Oliver's Branch

Irini adored Jason and her enthusiasm to greet him once led to her thumping him on the back, to such an extent she almost winded him. After the initial greetings she looked around for him and not seeing the object of her affections asked Jill where he was. She explained, as best she could, they were no longer together. After her initial disappointment she exclaimed, "Never mind, he will come." Jill doubted it but said nothing. Irini stayed for an orange juice and some Greek biscuits then with another big hug she made her exit. Dyson had initially stood on the steps looking at her but when she said she was afraid of big dogs, he was put inside. Jill wondered who was the most afraid, but left Dyson indoors for the duration.

The days flew by, only the nights were long and often daunting. She did not have a lot to do and although Dyson was warm and comforting, she missed being able to talk to friends and family. She longed for the furniture to arrive, so she could start unpacking. She had brought a good selection of books with her and so most nights she would eat something (usually supplied by Eleni, but Irini also started dropping-off food.) Then she would wash, change, send a few text messages and afterwards snuggle down to read and go to sleep early, usually with the help of a couple of glasses of Mitsou's home made wine. She managed to get a great deal done in the orchard though, and it wasn't long before she was rewarded for her efforts. Eventually, she knew she would need help, but initially there was enough pruning and weeding to keep her occupied. She decided to keep notes of all the things which made her laugh, eventually she would make a newsletter for her children and a few friends. She knew Sarah and Astrid would enjoy it and could imagine TGC all sitting together reading it out loud, so she started a book of notes, entitling it 'Thoughts from Crete'."

Lefteris was as good as his word and arrived to fit the gate, as promised, on the third day. He came round in his maxi and after unloading it asked his 16-year-old son, Vassili, to give him a hand unloading the other item, which was roped into the van. An old, battered but useable fridge.
"It's very old," he said "but it still works and will be OK until yours arrives." Jill was more than grateful as it meant she could buy some fresh produce, cheese and milk. It had been impossible before as it was very hot, even in the kitchen, which was partially below ground.

Once the gate was fitted, Dyson was able to have the run of the orchard and took to lying under a fig tree at the back of the orchard, overlooking the piece of land which belonged to the house and which Jill had no idea what she was going to do with. She thought, maybe in the future, if she could get it rotovated, she would learn how to

grow her own vegetables. Jason had expressed enthusiasm regarding a vegetable patch and so many other things. She often missed him, not only because there was so much outside they had planned to do together, but because he was meant to have been a part of this 'new life'. Instead he was thousands of miles away doing God knows what, bringing up their child. She found herself thinking about Oliver. How he would have loved the freedom Greek children seemed to enjoy, how she would delight in his growing up. She knew these were idle daydreams, but they nudged to the forefront of her mind more and more frequently.

She had still not contacted Jason. She promised herself she would, but somehow there never seemed to be the right moment. Anyway she wondered, what on earth would she say? "Hi Jason, thought I'd just ring and see how you and Oliver are doing and let you know things are going OK." Yeah, right. How crass and feeble she would sound, and what if Jason didn't want to speak to her and hung up?

Maybe when she was more organised and unpacked, she would sit down and write him a letter. Maybe...............

Oliver's Branch

Twenty seven.

A phone call from Ted at the start of the first week in August informed her that the freight was due in Souda on the 15th of the month, later than expected, due to a strike in England. There was no paperwork to do, as this had all been completed by the removal firm. He asked if it would be OK to give the driver her number, so he could phone her with an estimated time of arrival, as well as for directions to the village. "Absolutely fine, Ted" she'd said, feeling the excitement well up inside her. At last she would have furniture, bedding, kitchen paraphernalia, as well as all the things which would make Paparooni into her home.

She managed to sort out her residence permit without any problems and Mitsou took her to look at cars. It was quite amazing on the island, second-hand cars were almost as expensive as new ones. In the end she settled on a little silver Peugeot 206. With the back seats down there was plenty of room for Dyson, and it was quite big enough for her. It also reminded her of the one she had left in England. Jason would have disapproved as, with his long legs, it would have been very cramped for him; he would have preferred some fuel-guzzling 4X4, but Jason had his beloved Mondeo back in England, so it made no difference.

All the paperwork and car tax were sorted out with relative efficiency and a great many official stamps. Her insurance broker, who Angelina introduced her when she bought the house, sorted the house insurance and he was the epitome of efficiency. The rental company agreed to come and take the rented vehicle back, and on the 14th of August she became the proud owner of her new 'little' car.

The first thing she did was put the back seats down and took Dyson for a romp along her favourite beach. She and Jason first come to this beach with some English friends they made when they started coming to Crete. Jill had not been in touch with them yet, but promised herself, when she was more settled she would take a trip up to their lovely little house in the mountains, near Kolimbari. The beach was about 20 minutes away from Paparooni. August was the height of season and there were thousands of maniacal drivers in hire cars on the roads, which made driving a somewhat harrowing experience.

The beauty about this beach was so few people used it, and those who did were mainly Greek. Consequently it was reasonably quiet and there was always somewhere to lay your towel. No lively club

music, no leery 18 to 30 groups getting drunk at a bar, no fat families from Newcastle, wearing virtually nothing and radiating a puce burn, constantly complaining about how "bluddy 'ot it is..." None of these or other exceedingly annoying tourist antics, just peace and a beautiful, crystal blue sea. It was a sea which also had its own specific moods. Some days there were massive waves which pummelled you about, leaving you feeling battered and sometimes even bruised. Jill had called this "Gods very own wave machine." Then at other times it was as calm as a mill pond, glistening azure blue, shimmering, with diamonds on the surface. On this day it was the latter. She let Dyson off the lead and watched him leap straight into the water. He always loved the beach and it was a while since he had been this free. Jill joined him and they played ball for a while, then after a good soaking, they went back onto the sand. Dyson rolled over and over, ecstatically, until he looked more like a sand sculpture than a dog.

They walked together the full length of the beach, watching young children playing and laughing and generally whiled away a good 3 hours.

Returning home she found a pan of food on the table and a bottle of wine. The pot contained goat stew with potatoes, carrots and courgettes. There was a large lump of fresh Greek bread in a paper bag next to it. Jill took it inside and put it on the Primus to heat up, fed Dyson and settled down for a quiet night. The following day was going to be a busy one and she wanted to be relaxed and refreshed, ready to deal with it.

After washing her plate she snuggled down on the floor with Dyson and within minutes was fast asleep.

*

Awaking at 8.00 the following morning she was amazed how rested and alive she felt. It must have been the sea air and the long walk, she thought to herself and went into the kitchen to boil up some eggs, from Irini, for breakfast. Looking out at the orchard with the sun already shining down on the trees and making the orange-tree leaves an incandescent green, she suddenly realised things were beginning to fall into place. She actually felt content. It was a complete revelation. Everything was starting to improve a hundred times faster than she ever imagined they could or would. Once the house was sorted she and Dyson would go to the beach every day. Before long she would be tanned and sun bronzed. Surely that was what it was all about anyway? No more grey, loathsome days, just

sunshine, blue seas and some wonderful new friends. Suddenly she realised she really was home....at last.

The phone interrupted her thoughts. A voice at the other end, having established he was indeed talking to Mrs Slater, informed her it was Rod from 'Alaxis' to confirm the container's arrival. She would be the first drop off. He and 'the team' would be with her in about an hour. She felt a surge of excitement but managed to control her emotions long enough to give him directions to the village. "I'm afraid there are quite a few twists and turns, I hope it won't be too much of a problem" she said, proud of her ability to think about any possible pitfalls they may experience.
"Don't reckon it'll be so bad," replied Rod. "You're not in the mountains or totally off the beaten track and at least all the roads are tarmac. You wouldn't believe some of the obscure places we have to deliver to. At times I think we should get danger money. By the way, can we park close to the house or will there be a lot of walking involved?"
"No problems there, you can park right outside, the road is wide enough for cars to pass and access to the house is easy." This was it. She really was taking up residence. Rod said goodbye and she wished the team a safe journey. As soon as she hung up she dashed to the loo to relieve herself, the excitement was obviously all too much. Afterwards she went into the orchard, grabbed Dyson and gave a holler of joy. Eleni looked over the fence and inquired if everything was all right.

"Absolutely great, my furniture will be arriving in an hour. Then I will be able to make my house into my home," Jill replied, laughing.(She actually said, my home is coming soon, but it was the best she could do.) Eleni understood, never the less.
"Then I must go and make some cakes for them" she said, and was gone before Jill could say another word. It was just after 9.00 and for the next hour she busied herself in the kitchen. She put plastic bottles of fresh water in the fridge. The water from the mountains was totally pure and crispy cold. She found biscuits and crisps and put them in bowls and afterwards did a quick sweep with the broom in every room, just to keep busy. She had just finished and sat down with a cold orange juice (squeezed by her own fair hand, from her own trees in the orchard), when Irini came through the gate.
"Hello. You look very happy, that is good. In life as long as you have your health, enough food and oil, and wood for a fire in the winter, you should be happy." Irini held out a plastic bag. Inside were 2 litres of olive oil and a loaf of bread. "These are for you. Enjoy. And why are you looking so pleased with yourself?"

Ruth Manning

Jill explained the imminent arrival of the container and as soon as she heard the news, Irini was out of the gate. "Then I will go and make some cakes" she called and was gone. Jill envisaged a table heaving with home-made cakes and pastries and wondered what else might be produced before the day was out. The whole village would no doubt know Jill's news within the hour. Irini would tell the baker and the baker would tell all her customers, who in turn would tell their neighbours and friends.

Irini's exit was followed 5 minutes later by the arrival of the container. She jumped up and went to the gate, tying Dyson up on the way. The driver turned off the engine and jumped out of the cab. 3 more athletic looking young men did the same, from the passenger side. The driver was by far the smallest and thinnest, with a mop of ginger hair and freckles. He looked about 30 and had the broadest and most endearing smile Jill had ever seen. His teeth were very white and even, Jill thought he had missed his path in life. He should be in one of those toothpaste ads, where a star-like glint is added at the end, with a kind of a 'ting' sound. Rod didn't need any kind of computer enhancement, his teeth really were that shiny!

"Hello, Mrs Slater" he said, proffering a freckled hand. "I'm Rod and this is the crew. Chalky (a six foot something, very brown Adonis with blond hair and deep green eyes,) Andy (an equally-tall African, with a mop of frizzy hair and buck teeth, but arms like Popeye's main adversary Pluto,) and last but not least Angus, who comes from Southend but is.........." "OK, Rod, lets not get into that one now, I'm sure Mrs Slater doesn't want to hear your slovenly humour," butted in Angus, who really should have been standing in for Arnie Schwarzenegger as a stunt double. Well, Arnie in his younger days anyway. Angus was all rippling muscle, sun tan, six pack and very short shorts. It didn't take much imagination to work out why he was nicknamed Angus. "Actually my real name's Cedric, so I suppose any other name is an improvement..... Hi." He shook Jill's hand and nudged Rod, almost sending him flying.

Jill welcomed them all and asked them to please call her by her first name. "There's masses of cold water, orange juice and biscuits in the kitchen, but if you want anything else, please just ask. I've got a feeling you may be inundated with Greek cakes in a short while, but until then help yourself, as and when you are hungry or thirsty."

They thanked her and within minutes were all gulping down litres of cold water; it was already 37 degrees and getting hotter. Then they opened the container, put down the ramp and without further ado

Oliver's Branch

started to unpack Jill's material possessions. Her Beach Buggy was the first thing to be unloaded. It was so good to see it again Jill almost hugged it. Everything was there. No fatal accidents or loss. (*Eat your heart out Place in the Sun, she muttered to herself. I'm OK, Jack.*) She started the buggy up and drove it round the side to the carport, where she parked it next to her shiny new car. As she walked back round the corner, to direct all the boxes to their allocated areas, Irini was positioning one of her borrowed white plastic chairs, and a soft cushion she had brought with her, right outside the trailer. Obviously she was going to take an inventory of everything Jill had brought with her. "Jill, bring me some water. The cakes will be out of the oven in about 30 minutes, until then I have come to help."

During the following hour the crew worked non-stop (with Irini overseeing proceedings). Jill directed boxes and furniture according to the colour-coded labels she had devised when she first started packing up in England. Irini remained planted to the spot, commenting on various items of furniture, asking Jill where she had bought them, and how much they cost. She demanded a constant supply of cold water but did leave for a short while, to return home, take the cakes out and be back in her chair in the space of about 3 minutes.

At eleven o'clock they all stopped for a break. The cakes were demolished; the water and orange juice finished and conversation flowed, congenially. All 4 of the crew lived on the island and told Jill she would never regret the move. None of them had any intention of returning. Angus was married with 3 children, all of whom were bilingual. Rod was getting married to a Greek woman as soon as they had found somewhere to buy and the other 2 had families back in England, but were divorced. Irini watched them all chattering, as she duly ate her way through a whole pack of chocolate digestive biscuits.

They were interrupted by the arrival of Lefteris and Sophia, who were carrying large trays of chips, cheese pies, salad and bread, which they placed on the now-erected kitchen table. Eleni passed over a pot of fish soup and another tray of sweet cakes, covered in honey and still hot, but explained she couldn't come and 'help.' She was going round to look after her latest grandchild while her daughter went shopping. Jill had breathed a sigh of relief. Things were getting very crowded and she was concerned the crew would be unable to do another stroke of work if they ate all the food on the table. Luckily they all agreed they would complete the unpacking before eating another thing, and the unloading was resumed.

Ruth Manning

Irini reinstated herself on the plastic chair, having bolstered it up with another cushion to make herself more comfortable. Sophia started inspecting all the furniture and then busied herself unpacking a box of cutlery and other kitchen equipment. Lefteris had stood at the gate with a frappé in one hand and a cigarette in the other, directing the 4 men to all 4 corners of the house. It was at this point Jill gave up any hope of the colour coding having any further impact. She virtually accepted she was no longer involved in the unloading process at all. She topped up all the water bottles and squeezed more oranges instead.....

Another break was taken at midday, and Jill expressed her concern to the men about her Greek neighbours' interference. She hoped it wasn't causing them any problems. "Don't worry about it," Rod had assured her. "This is totally normal, in fact I would be worried if there weren't locals *helping.*" He raised his fingers and put speech marks around the word helping. "The Greeks are an inquisitive lot" he continued, "and at least it shows you're getting to know people."

By 3.30 everything Jill had brought with her was off the container and after another round of drinks, cakes, cheese pies and nibbles of all the culinary fayre, they were ready to leave. All the paperwork was signed and the inventory accepted, then, with much shaking of hands and patting on backs, the team left with a wave and thumbs up, wishing her all the luck in the world.

Jill, Lefteris, Sophia and Irini were joined by Eleni and Mitsou shortly after. Mitsou produced 3 litres of his wine, Sophia heated the soup on the Primus and everyone sat down for a hearty meal. Two hours, with most of the food eaten and all the wine imbibed, everyone dispersed to their respective homes, explaining they had things to do and they didn't want to impose. They knew Jill had a great deal to do.

Suddenly there was peace. After another hour of clearing away, Jill decided the most important thing on her agenda was sleep. There was no way she could possibly start on any of the unpacking; she was emotionally and physically exhausted. Manoeuvring between the hundreds of boxes,184 to be exact, plus the paraphernalia, she retrieved her sleeping bag and made her way to the downstairs bedroom. Angus had kindly put up all three beds, but this was where she was going to sleep, at least in the near future. She sank down onto the soft mattress, glad she was no longer at floor level. With Dyson making himself comfortable on his own bed, Jill was asleep,

Oliver's Branch

before her body fully sunk into the wonderful orthopaedic mattress
and her head hit the glorious feather pillow.

Ruth Manning

Twenty eight.

The following 2 weeks were a bustle of activity. Jobs she couldn't do, such as putting up curtain rails and drilling holes for pictures, were undertaken by Lefteris. All the unpacking and sorting, Jill did alone. In some ways it was a difficult task. When she had put away all the family photo albums she had been unable to open any of them, frightened of how the memories would affect her. She wondered when she would feel strong enough to walk down memory lane and accept memories with joy, a cathartic part of the healing process. When would she really be able to look back and smile, then move on?

Getting the house organised was all consuming. Jill needed a home again. Somewhere her children would feel comfortable in and accept as a place to come back to, and where she felt safe and settled.. She was left alone by most of the village, although Irini and Eleni still constantly dropped in with gifts of food or to insist on her sitting down for a coffee and a chat. She discovered she could fend off these advances in most cases by saying she was working. Work was the backbone of the society and as Mitsou said one day, "You have to work or you go *mad.*"

In between unpacking, placing and sorting she also managed to arrange for a new, 32 inch, flat-screen TV to be installed. She had decided she would stick with terrestrial channels but somehow an Arabic satellite was offered as part of the package and as there was an English BBC Prime channel thrown in, she had taken the whole thing, lock, stock and barrel. This meant the evenings now involved getting to know what was available, out of the possible 1,000 plus channels. After much channel-hopping she eventually surmised she would probably only be watching about 6 channels, all of them on the Arabic satellite, and these were culturally so different. The Arabic adverts made her smile and seemed to involve using Dettol in all shapes and forms or drinking tea. BBC Prime lasted about 4 days, after which it literally disappeared. The man in the shop explained to her, when she went to find out why she could no longer get it, that they had shut down the satellite. Something to do with costings and the recession apparently. Terrestrial was fuzzy and muffled, which Lefteris said was the norm in the village because of the surrounding mountains. She was happy enough though with the films constantly broadcast on the Arabic channels. These were all in English, and she soon learnt to ignore the subtitles.

There were also various phone calls from England. Sarah who was a sun worshipper turning green with envy at Jill's daily jaunts to the

Oliver's Branch

beach, with hints at a visit. Jill got the feeling things were not quite all they seemed with her, she seemed pessimistic and deflated by the economic climate and life in general. Usually she was buoyant and upbeat about life, always the optimist, but her calls seemed to be tinged with a hint of regret and pessimism. She seemed less upbeat about life than she had been in the past. "There are times when I wonder what the hell this is all about, Jill. Things seem hollow and pointless and totally devoid of colour. Yes that's how I would describe my life. Black and white with not a rainbow in sight." Jill had never heard this kind of negativity from her friend before. There was little news which didn't involve doom and gloom relating to the latest recession, credit crunch or property debacle. Doom and gloom. Jill felt she must dumb down her joy and enthusiasm for her new life, and usually listened to other peoples news, rather than talking about her own.

Things were going well for Grace, who was bubbly and enjoying each new day. Nick was having preliminary trials for the army and John had phoned with all the news from The Garage Club. Everyone was well and the business was thriving, the recession made their recycled items both popular and sought after by those with little spare cash. They wanted to hear all her news. She asked John what he thought of her doing a monthly letter about her life, and this was met with enthusiasm. He seemed to have become a spokesman for the group and Jill always enjoyed their chats. She mentioned the garden and how much work it was and John sympathised. Apparently he had owned a house with a large garden for many years and he knew it was a full time job. "It used to take up all my spare time, my wife wasn't keen on doing the work in the vegetable patch, but she loved the results. Actually there are times now when I really miss my garden," he had said, "Somehow a window box isn't quite the same."

Astrid phoned once and was very offhand. Apparently her job description seemed to dictate a great amount of work, on top of her already hefty workload. She was not a happy bunny. "They get 120% out of me as it is" she had berated. "Now the bastards seem to be going for my blood too, from my god damn jugular!"

The days flew by and although Jill unloaded box after box, she was amazed at how much stuff she had actually brought. Some mornings when she got up, she could almost swear the boxes were duplicating themselves overnight, amoebas and binary fission came to mind! Things she was certain she had unpacked the day before appeared to still be packed in their tissue paper and/or bubble wrap, nestling happily in their cardboard containers.

Ruth Manning

The weather was glorious, day after day of crystal blue skies and bright sunshine. It was exceedingly hot outside and the house seemed to be soaking up the heat. Part of the reason for this, she had been advised by one of the Greek men who ran the cigarette and newspaper shop, was because she needed the roof painting white. This would apparently reflect the sun. She had absolutely no idea how to go about such an operation and had stated this fact to him. Like magic he had told her he knew 'just the man for the job.' He would send him over to see her the next time he was in the village. The same day, while Jill was working out which cutlery to use and which to store, there was a tap on the kitchen door and a voice called out, in good English, "Hello.... Is there anyone here?" A tall, well built man of about 40, as brown as a berry with hazel eyes and a glossy moustache, stood in the doorway. He would certainly never have hair loss problems, a thick mop of blue black hair covered his head and cascaded down his back in a well tended pony tail, which any female would be pleased with. "Yes, I'm behind the box by the table" she called, struggling to manoeuvre around all the boxes and stand up.

"I hope I'm not interrupting, but Costas in the village said you wanted your roof painting. I'm Stelios. I hope I didn't scare you." His English was impeccable although there was just a hint of Greek, which was very appealing and sexy. No way could this great-looking man with the resonant, deep, husky voice and the physique and looks of a Greek god possibly frighten anyone. He might stir other emotions, Jill thought to herself, but fear certainly wasn't one of them.

"Not at all" she said, trying to pull her somewhat dishevelled hair out of her eyes. "I'm really glad to see you. I'm Jill."

"I know" he replied as they shook hands. He had enormous hands. "Costas told me. Anyway, if you would like me to do the job it'll cost you 10 Euros for the white wash and another 10 for the work. It will take me about two hours and I will bring all the materials with me, in my maxi." He pointed to his pick up truck, which seemed to have hit quite a number of inanimate objects and was covered in dents, rust and dirt. The bumper appeared to be held on with string, which was then tied round the exhaust, presumably to maintain its position 6 inches off the road. Both wing mirrors were hanging off and there didn't appear to be a rear view mirror at all.

"That sounds great. Will it really make a difference though? It sounds very cheap for something which is apparently so effective."

"Ah. I will let you into a little secret" he said, tapping the side of his nose with his index and middle finger. "There is a very expensive waterproof paint which will last for three years and which many

Oliver's Branch

foreigners buy, but the locals all use a mixture of ground marble and whitewash and they do their roofs every spring. I can use the more expensive one if you would prefer?"

Ever conscious of her financial position (no more burning plastic or running up vast amounts on store cards for this particular woman,) she enquired how much it would cost to have the more expensive paint, thinking it may pan out as more economical over three years. "To cover your roof would cost about 300 Euros. As I said the marble mix would cost about 10 Euros a year, plus labour."

Jill quickly did the maths and decided 30 years with the cheaper stuff seemed a far better deal. "Well, I guess at least for a while, I'll go with the cheaper option" she said and laughed.

"Very wise choice. All the Greeks use it, the foreigners who buy the more expensive stuff are actually being ripped off, but they don't seem to mind. OK, if we're agreed, would tomorrow, very early, be OK? Next year you should paint it in May. Because it is summer now, it will have to be done very early in the morning, before it is too hot from the sun. Will it be all right if I come round at about six?"

"Um, that would be fine. Shall I give you the money for the paint now?" she said, grabbing her purse from the kitchen table.

"No, tomorrow will be fine, when I have finished. I will not disturb you when I arrive, but will let you know when I have finished. Now I must go, I have other work to do, Goodbye." He then walked to his car without a backward glance.

The following day he was as good as his word and he had completed the job by quarter past eight. Jill had just made a pot of strong coffee and he had sat and dunked a large croissant he accepted from her, into the mug. She paid him the amount he had quoted the previous day and was now the proud owner of a freshly whitewashed roof.

"Where did you learn to speak such good English?" she asked him, taking a sip of her coffee.

"Ah. It is a long story. For many years I was on the boats and after I spent four years in England, working for a haulage firm. I spent most of my life travelling, but now I have come home. Anyway if you have any jobs let me know. I work for myself and am what I think you call *a handy man.* " Jill was sure he was, in more ways than one. He wrote his phone number down and she assured him she would call if there were other jobs she needed doing. If there weren't she would just have to invent them, she thought to herself, smiling inwardly like a naughty school girl. She watched him climb into his jalopy and disappear up the road in a cloud of smoke and clanging of loose metal.

During the ensuing weeks she was able to find various jobs which needed doing and was thrilled when he offered to help out with the

138

orchard. "My family have a number of olive and orange orchards. I grew up helping my father in them. You need a lot of clearing and tidying up done to bring your trees back to good health." Jill agreed it would be very helpful and he became a regular visitor. He would do an hour here and there and always had time to answer her questions regarding life on Crete. They became firm friends and although it appeared he had never been married there was no question of any kind of romantic attachment.

"I do not *do* the ladies," he had said to her one day, raising an eyebrow. "I have many men friends and we go out in Chania to have a good time." Jill suddenly realised why there was a twinkle in his eye. Stelios was gay. In actual fact it was an ideal friendship from which they both benefited. It wasn't long before the orchard was looking spick and span and even though she worried he undercharged her, it meant he had at least one supply of regular income. She also discovered he liked his wine and on numerous occasions he had arrived slightly the worse for wear. When she heard him singing in the orchard or sitting down for his umpteenth cigarette she just left him to it. Usually though he was a hard worker and an asset to have around.

So with his help and with Lefteris and Mitsou overseeing every development, by the end of the month things were beginning to look incredibly organised and Jill could say, quite categorically, Paparooni was no longer just a house. At last.......... it was beginning to feel like her home.

Oliver's Branch

Twenty nine.

With things going so well Jill decided it was time to go into Chania and get to grips with her banking. The very thought of it made her go weak at the knees. It was crazy in the centre of Chania, with motorbikes whizzing in and out of cars, drivers indicating but usually doing exactly the opposite to what they were supposed to do, pedestrians completely ignoring all traffic and randomly crossing as and when they felt like it and buses, well they were a law unto themselves. Everyone seemed to be on their mobile phones and at least half of the drivers were also drinking coffee and smoking at the same time. All the same she ventured out and apart from two near crashes, one near pedestrian injury (luckily avoided by veering down a one way street... in the wrong direction,) she and the car emerged intact. More than could be said about her nerves, which were in shreds. The bank was simple and the clerk was very impressed with her Greek. She carried out the whole transaction in Greek and it was only as she was leaving the clerk said to her, in English, "Your Greek is very good for an Englishwoman. You have a nice day now."

Arriving back to the relative calm of the village, she parked the car and was just going inside for a well-earned coffee, when she heard the dulcet tones of Irini from across the road.

"Jill, Jill you must come now. It is important, you must come here." Jill obediently crossed the road and went around to her neighbour's back door. Irini had scuttled off like an excited rabbit and was nowhere in sight. Jill drew back the fly screen and went into the kitchen.

"Look, look." Irini accosted her and dragged her by the arm into the living room. "You have a visitor."

Jill actually thought she said, "you have an outdoor line," but in the next few seconds learnt the word for visitor. There sitting at the table, which was positively sagging under plates of cakes and Irini's culinary delights, sat ...... Sarah. Her friend looked as if she was in shock or even mildly traumatised. Upon seeing Jill she jumped up and raced towards her. "Thank God you're here. If I have to eat another thing I'll burst. Christ it's good to see you."

With obvious relief, she had given Jill the biggest bear-hug imaginable.

Jill was absolutely speechless, which was a good thing because she would never have been heard over Irini's excited screeches and laughter. "I found her outside your house. She was lost and she speaks no Greek, but it did not take long to understand she has come to see *you*. Why didn't you tell me you were expecting a visitor

Ruth Manning

or that you have a friend? I think she has come from England. Poor dear she looks so tired and worried. I have given her some food and a glass of wine. You are a bad woman, allowing a guest to come to see you when you are not here."

Sarah did indeed look bemused, but Jill thought it could better be described as shell-shocked, though she didn't say so. Instead she thanked her neighbour, and guided Sarah out of the house, across the road and onto a chair underneath the pagoda, without saying a word. It was only when she had sat down opposite her friend that she spoke.

"Sarah, What in God's name are you doing here and why didn't you let me know you were coming?"
"I thought it would be a nice surprise for you. I arranged to have a month off and then booked a one way ticket with Easyjet. It just seemed like a good idea. I caught a taxi from the airport and it all went amazingly well. At least until he dropped me off outside the house and I realised you were out. Then I was kidnapped by Irini, and have been force-fed for the last hour and a half. I actually feel physically sick."

Trying to take in the fact that her best friend was sitting opposite her, and almost lost for words, she went over and gave her another hug. "Well, it's great to see you and I'm sorry about the 'Irini experience,' still you've survived that so you can survive anything. Welcome to my home." With that she opened the kitchen door and picked a large jug of cold water out of the fridge. She brought it and two glasses back up the steps and poured them each a glass.

"So, tell me what this is all about? Great though it is to see you, I have never rated spontaneity as one of your attributes. Is everything OK?"

Sarah took a large slug of ice-cold water and swallowed it. She looked as if she was trying to find the words to explain, but somehow couldn't. Then sighing heavily she looked at Jill and said "OK, I spent the entire flight working out a speech to give you. One that would explain my present state of mind but leave out the parts which, on a need-to-know basis, I didn't think you needed to know. Somehow though it all sounds incredibly contrived, so, in my new spontaneous persona I'll just come straight out with it. I've left Dennis."

Oliver's Branch

Apart from the noises of the village, the crowing cockerels, the barking dogs and the passing of a lone pickup there was an audible silence as Jill tried to take in this revelation. Of all the people she knew, Sarah's marriage had always seemed like a rock amidst the tumultuous seas of other people's continually ebbing and flowing relationships. Now suddenly it had disappeared and Sarah was wallowing around in the ocean of uncertainty, along with all the other mere mortals, who seemed to be constantly bobbing around trying to make sense of life, love and relationships. Suddenly Sarah was '*not waving, but drowning.*'

"Actually, that's not strictly true. Dennis and I are giving each other a bit of space to decide what we actually want to do. If I had stayed in England everyone would have been offering me help and advice and I don't want it. I want to talk about things when I'm ready and I want to decide where I'm going, but I want to do it with you, because of all my friends I know you will be the least judgemental. God, Jill, I just want to see the rainbows again."

"OK, so that's exactly what you'll do. It's great to see you and as long as you're happy sharing my life for a while you're welcome to stay for as long as you like. When you're ready to talk, then you talk, until then, as far as I'm concerned you're on holiday. The sun is shining, it's a beautiful day and you have escaped the clutches of Irini, hopefully without food poisoning. How about you take your case upstairs and unpack, it's the room opposite the stairs. I'll make us some lunch and then we'll go to the beach. How does that sound?"

Sarah expressed thanks and agreement and went upstairs to the spare bedroom. Luckily the bed was already made up. Jill had felt it was wrong to have sad, denuded beds with all the blankets folded neatly and the pillows stark of any cases. It reminded her of the end of each term when she had been at boarding school. They had to clear their dormitories and leave only the blankets and pillows under the threadbare candlewick bedspreads. "Now girls, remember coffin beds should look neat and tidy with NO bumps or creases." She could still hear Matron barking out the orders as she moved from room to room amidst the hustle and bustle of end of term activities. Thus, the seed had been planted. Jill had always made up empty beds, throughout the whole of her adult life because she certainly wasn't having any *coffin beds* in her home, ever.

Jill prepared salad and cheese with hunks of fresh Greek bread and Sarah had come down, already in a new summer sun dress with bikini straps poking over the back. They enjoyed a pleasant meal, catching up on Sarah's news and the state of affairs in England, skimming along the surface of reality. They both knew at some point

they would plummet to the murky depths, but, for the moment at least, they would enjoy the day.

Armed for the beach (Sarah with her new zany, multi-coloured beach towel, matching new beach pillow, new novel to read, new flip-flops and new factor 8 bottle of suntan lotion, plus of course her new,very swish beach bag,) they set off for a swim. Jill couldn't help but smile. Her best friend may have developed a new sense of spontaneity but she had also prepared well for her visit.

The sea was ultra calm and there were only a few other people along the 5 kilometre expanse of beach. Jill suggested her friend take off her bikini, so as not to get strap marks, but Sarah drew the line at this. "I'm not a naturist and never will be. Anyway without the marks how will I know I have a tan?" She looked quizzically at Jill and then did a double take as she realised her friend was lying on her back , relaxed and still glistening with sea water from her initial dip, as naked as the day she was born.

They didn't talk much, just enjoyed the sun, sea and sand until after a couple of hours Jill suggested they make a move. "It's fine for you," Sarah groaned, trying to eke another hour out of their stay. "You're as brown as a berry. I'm lily white. It's so gorgeous here, can't we stay another hour?"
"You'll be coming to the beach every day and you'll soon colour up. Anyway, two hours is quite enough for your first day, you don't want to burn." Sarah reluctantly packed away all her paraphernalia and followed Jill back to the car.

Arriving back at Paparooni round about five, they discovered a large plate on the table covered with a cloth. On closer examination it turned out to be a rich stew surrounded by potatoes, courgettes and carrots. While they were trying to work out if it was goat or lamb Eleni called over the fence. "Irini told me you have a friend staying and today I made rabbit stew. I thought you would enjoy some, and this is from Mitsou to welcome your guest." She handed over a litre and a half of Mitsou's wine (in a plastic lemonade bottle) and Jill introduced her to Sarah, explaining they had been friends since school. "Welcome Zarra" she said. "Enjoy your meal. Good appetite." She then disappeared back into her kitchen, the wind chimes above her door, letting out a cacophony of tinkles as she shut it.

The rabbit was delicious and Mitsou's wine, as always, far too drinkable. For the rest of the evening they sat and talked about everyday events and Jill explained about life in the village and the

Oliver's Branch

people, who were already having an impact on her life. She told her friend about the idea of sending a monthly newsletter to her children and to friends in England who might be interested and asked what she thought about the idea.

"You absolutely have to" Sarah had replied. "And make sure I'm at the top of the list. By the time I leave here it will all make sense and I would love to hear how things are going."

They talked about the past and their days at boarding school together. Sarah laughed when Jill told her about her habit of always leaving beds made up, because of her loathing of 'coffin beds...'
"My God," Sarah laughed, "It was a Spartan existence wasn't it? Five articles on your dressing table, no posters and definitely *no radios.* Do you remember how we used to listen to Radio Caroline, snuggled under the covers, and the ingenious hiding places we found to hide the radios?"

It was a pleasant evening but by just gone ten Sarah was ready for bed and after a quick shower disappeared upstairs to sleep. Jill sat outside in the warmth of the evening, looking across at the orange trees. In a few months they would once again be bearing fruit. She knew her friend would open up and discuss her marital problems, when she was ready, and she wondered if she too, would soon be ready to face her own demons.

As she lay in bed waiting for sleep to envelope her she metaphorically looked at the small bejewelled box, lying close to her heart, then, for the first time since she had locked it away, she retrieved the key. She was sure soon, very soon, she was going to have to open this most personal emotional casket up and come to terms with the questions, feelings and pain, which needed so desperately to be set free

Thirty.

Over the following week life took on a gentle rhythm into which Sarah fitted comfortably. She took long walks with Dyson and explored the surrounding area. She helped with the gardening and put Jill to shame with both her knowledge and enthusiasm for flora and fauna. They ate outside at lunchtimes and most evenings, and the locals began to accept her and talk to her as if she were an old friend. Nothing was said about her personal problems, until one evening, returning from a meal with Lefteras and Sofia, she broached the subject of her marriage.

"You know, Jill, watching those two together and seeing the way they look at each other makes me realise how hollow and pointless my own marriage is. Dennis is so self-absorbed and utterly egotistical, I sometimes wonder if he actually realises we are married. Maybe he thinks I'm just some sort of live in au pair or maid or whatever. I can't remember the last time we even talked. I need to decide what I'm going to do. Should I make him face the reality of the present situation, that is to say, we are in a loveless, barren relationship going absolutely nowhere; or do I try and pull back some of the substance of how our marriage used to be? I mean, he must know something is slightly adrift by the mere fact that I upped and left without any explanation. I just told him I needed a break! He didn't even ask what I wanted a break from, just looked up from his newspaper and said he thought that was a great idea. There's no one else, at least I don't think there is, in fact I think he's more in love with his golf clubs than he is with any other human being. Oh God... Tell me to shut up, I know I'm rabbiting on."

Jill waited a few moments in case her friend had anything to add. She knew Dennis to be rather blinkered and unaware at times, almost other-worldly, existing in what seemed to her to be a parallel universe, or on Mars maybe, but she had always seen Sarah's marriage as solid and dependable. At times she had felt inadequate and personally lacking in social or relationship skills when compared with Sarah. During her divorce Sarah had been both supportive and caring, but there had never been any sign of even a ripple of dissatisfaction or doubt from her. She thought back to Sarah's last visit, in England, and remembered her saying she would never divorce because she was afraid of being alone in her latter years.

"O Sarah, I don't know what to say that can possibly help you. My track record with men is so bad it's not even worth listening to any advice or opinion I could give you, if I could give you one that is, but I don't think I can. I guess it all comes down to what you want for

Oliver's Branch

yourself or how you see your future, what you would like your future
to be. Only you can really decide the direction you want to take and
what options you have."
"You know you're right and I've been thinking along the same lines.
This is my life and I have to make the choices. Can I tell you what I
think? The peace here and the long walks with the dog have helped
me to put things into some kind of simplified perspective. Before I
came here everything seemed so complicated and involved and
somehow I had lost sight of myself. Being here has helped me to
clarify things, almost as if I've detached myself from my existence
and can look at what I have from a far more objective and realistic
viewpoint. Watching the old man go by every day on his donkey,
passing with a wave and a smile, somehow makes far more sense to
me than what colour scheme I need in the refurbished kitchen at
home." She looked over at Jill, wondering if she had anything to say,
but Jill merely nodded her head and looked at her expectantly,
allowing her to continue.

"OK, then here it is. The life of Sarah by Sarah, in a nutshell...All
my life I have put other people before myself. Even at school, you
were the dominant one and I just followed. Don't get me wrong. You
weren't a bully or anything like that, it was me. I was subservient
and always eager to please, anything for a quiet life. Later, while I
was training, I stayed pretty much the same and just sort of
wandered through life. I enjoyed the work, after all nursing is all
about helping people, but I was never one to set the world on fire,
that was your job. I was, 'steady' and 'reliable,' you were wild and
chaotic and in so many ways that was great. I could watch you
making all the mistakes and feel smug in my well-ordered and calm
life. Then I met Dennis. Solid, reliable Dennis. Secretary of the
Conservative club in Wood Green, a keen cricketer and golfer, a civil
servant up in the city. Yep, I met him, was 'courted' by him , got
engaged to him and married him; all within a year. Tell me when
I'm boring you, I know I'm rambling and you know all of this
anyway."
"You're not rambling at all. It's good to hear it all from your
perspective. Carry on please." She poured them both a glass of wine
and put some crisps into a bowl.
"OK then. So there I was twenty-two and married, while you were
about to gad off around Europe, with no specific aim or agenda, by
the way. Thing was, I didn't envy you. In fact I felt sorry for you
because you seemed so restless and insecure, while I, on the other
hand, was now settled in a lovely little home with a good job, devoted
husband and provider and, metaphorically speaking, knitting booties
for my first child, even though I wasn't even pregnant yet. Yep, I
thought I had it all, while all you had was the pack on your back and

146

Ruth Manning

some hair-raising adventures. Then the kids came along. Dennis and
I had had a year alone, and don't get me wrong, we had had a great
time. Concerts, theatre, meals at classy restaurants, all that stuff.
I'd made friends with the women whose husbands played cricket and
was adept at making urns of tea and plate-loads of cucumber
sandwiches. Life was good. Anyway, I digress. Along came the
tiddlywinks, in quite rapid succession. Four within five years. Of
course we moved to a bigger, better house and I bought all the
children's clothes from Marks or Debenhams or any other top of the
range store I fancied. We had money, status and a family. I was
living the dream, while you were now ensconced in a remote village
in Greece, picking oranges, loading lorries and God knows what else.
No competition, I had the perfect life." Sarah stopped for a moment
and drank some wine. Jill sat very still and waited, feeling there was
nothing she could say at this point.

"Anyway, life was great. Dennis was well on his way *to the top*, as
they say. I gave up work and was a full-time mum, making play-doh,
keeping a spotless home, making sure the kids were 'learning
through play' and goodness knows what else. I was like an advert for
a perfect parenting magazine and I was totally immersed in all of it.
I was changing, though. Having children made me tougher. I would
seriously have fought to the death to protect them and I was
developing opinions on politics and personal values. Life with Dennis
was ticking along. He would go to work every morning at seven and
return at six most nights, at least in the early days of family life. We
ate together every evening, with the children of course, and we
discussed the events of the day. *Very important social interaction
and an essential part of child development* according to Practical
Parenting, I seem to remember.

We coasted along like that for years. Once the children were all at
school, I took a part-time job, nursing, and juggled all the balls of the
working mother. We were the epitome of respectability and success.
Somewhere along the way you came back to England and after a
couple of years got married. I watched you slobber over Nick as a
young baby and listened to you extol the joys of motherhood,
although I couldn't believe you picked up bits and bobs from charity
shops or boot sales for them, this to me was a complete paradox of
values. Anyway, back to me. Sure you're not bored yet?" Jill assured
her she wasn't.
"It's good to hear you talk about it all and, as I said, to see it from
your perspective!" She poured them both another glass of wine and
refilled the crisp bowl.

Oliver's Branch

"I think things went on very much in this ilk until the children became more independent, that's when in retrospect, I think there was a very subtle shift. Our lives started to change. Dennis stayed up in London for 'drinks with the boys' more and more often. I became involved in the local council and began to dread having to make another sandwich for the bloody cricket club, As the children began to formulate their own lives, I began to change mine and my new life had very little space in it for Dennis. Anyway to cut it short, it was once the children left I realised we were walking separate paths. There was no question of separation, what was the point? I think I've said that to you before. Anyway, I had nowhere to go and no aspiring dreams of change. I was solid, my marriage was solid, if somewhat humdrum. I didn't even recognise or understand the feelings of discontent and dissatisfaction I was feeling were quite normal. I thought I was emotionally unstable or barren or something, so I never talked about how I felt. The little things which had seemed so important, the house, self image, style and lots of other things were no longer paramount. With the children gone I was sitting across the table from an absolute stranger and I was unhappy. I wasn't like you though. I never felt void or lost when the children had gone, I just felt empty and used up, and that's where I am now. There was no specific moment of self evaluation and revelation, no rows, no anger, just complete and utter …Nothing."

To Jill's amazement her friend burst into floods of tears and covered her face with her hands. She had never seen Sarah like this, in fact the last time she had seen her cry was after the death of her father and that was years ago. It stunned her and she was completely at a loss as to how she could provide any comfort. They had never been very physical with each other and although she wanted to go and envelop her best friend in her arms, she was not sure it was the right response and so she refrained from doing so. Instead she responded, "Hardly nothing, Sarah. Look at what you've achieved and how highly you are thought of and respected. Your kids adore you and you have a beautiful home. OK, so now you can work out what you want and add it to the equation. Have you thought of any options or things you want to do, things to make *you* happier?"

"Yes, I have." Sarah replied, wiping away the tears and smiling into the distance, "Oh yes. I have."

Thirty one.

"OK, so here's the deal" Sarah said, taking another sip of wine. "I have to book a return flight and sort everything out, but, if things go according to plan, can I come back here for Christmas? In the New Year I'll be ready to move on?" Jill looked at her friend, totally taken aback. Sort things out and move on, both these concepts seemed so totally out of character, this was not the responsible, stable Sarah she thought she knew. Yet she could almost feel a new strength and resolve emanating from her friend, she still said nothing (her counselling skills were coming back, and Jill was a good listener.) Subsequently she just waited patiently wondering what on earth was coming next.

"I am almost sure I can take a year's sabbatical from my job, especially if it's to work in a specialised medical field. So, that's what I want to do. I have to explain something for you to understand this. While you were away travelling a great many things happened to me, which it seemed pointless to tell you about at the time. One of those is a demon I have to face. You see I had a fifth child, a little girl. She lived for forty minutes but died of cardiac problems in my arms. She was so beautiful, Jill, but she had a really bad cleft palate and harelip. I know if she'd lived, with surgery both could have been corrected, but she didn't live and ever since I have had an interest in the oral surgery and after-care of palate deformities. I donate to a charity called *Smiles* and have done ever since Catherine, that's what I called her, died. Doctors donate their time and skill to spend 3 to 6 months operating on children with clefts and harelips in developing countries and they are always looking for nurses to do the same. So, that's what I want to do..."

She looked over at Jill, who was still trying to assimilate the information her best friend just imparted to her. The fact that she had known nothing of this traumatic experience and not been able to be with her friend during such a trauma, left her feeling bereft and totally at a loss for words. There was a silence hanging over them, and Sarah appeared to be totally exhausted and drained.

Oliver's Branch

"God, Sarah, I am so, so sorry. Sorry for your loss, sorry for my total ignorance and sorry for not being there for you. If only I had known…"

"Nobody knew, apart from Dennis. As far as the rest of the world is concerned I had a stillborn baby and carried on with life as if nothing had happened. Dennis never, ever mentioned her again and neither did I, not to anyone. It's all a long time ago and somehow if I do this, I feel I will be honouring Catherine's memory. I know it may seem extreme, but it makes sense to me."

"So what about your marriage, Dennis, your family, aren't they going to have a say in all of this? It sounds pretty dramatic and life changing."

"Of course I'll tell them, but my mind is made up. If Dennis wants a divorce then so be it, but I'm hoping he will wait until I return and maybe take stock of his life and his priorities. The kids will think I've totally lost it and maybe I will tell them about Catherine, it's time. So what do you think of the idea and about spending Christmas with you?"

"I think it sounds amazing," Jill replied and went over to hug her friend. The tears were shed, decisions reached and Sarah was going to walk along a new path, Jill felt proud and in awe of her friend's resolve. "Of course you can come back for Christmas, I must admit I was dreading spending it on my own. The Greeks see it in a totally different light. It's much lower key; Easter is the big celebration over here. There is nothing I would like more than to share Christmas with you."

"Right then, so we've decided. We can go and book a return flight next week and I'll face my demons when I get home. I really do feel as if an enormous weight has been taken off my shoulders. I know the work involves caring for others but then I think that is an integral part of my personality, and it seems right, in every way. I'm totally exhausted, Jill, do you mind if I go to bed? I think I'll sleep better than I have in a very long time." She gave Jill a kiss on the cheek and got up to leave. "And by the way, thank you for helping me to reach this point. Without you and all the wonderful people I've met here, I don't think I would have had the strength or the conviction to do anything quite so dramatic, but now I have." With that she squeezed Jill's shoulder and smiled at her, before disappearing inside.

Jill sat perfectly still. The warmth of the evening enveloped her like a comforting shawl and the clearness of the sky, with its myriad of twinkling stars, seemingly looking down on her, made her suddenly

150

Ruth Manning

aware of her own deeply-buried feelings and loss. She closed her eyes and allowed her imagination to lead her to the beautiful, locked casket, buried so deeply within her heart. With trembling fingers she put the key in the lock and opened it, expecting there to be a darkness and emptiness which would engulf her. Every nerve in her body was taut as the lid gently opened. Jill held her breath waiting for the pain and the grief to sweep over her. Instead, there was only light. Not ordinary light but a multifaceted and glistening light which radiated through her body. She could physically feel the darkness and the coldness which had enveloped her very psyche for so long, begin to evaporate. In its place was sheer joy and warmth. Very slowly she felt a realisation dawning and was amazed at how reassuring and comforting it was. Oliver was not dead, Jason was not dead, she was not dead. She had been dormant for a while, but now like a flower unfurling its petals in the sun, she felt herself begin awakening to a new-found understanding. She still loved Jason and God how she missed him, she felt fragmented without him. Even more amazing was the realisation that she wanted and needed to be involved in raising their child. She needed to be a part of Oliver's life.

So the box was open at last and Jill felt a peace and understanding fill her with optimism and joy. It was the beginning of another journey, and although she had no idea where it would lead, she felt invigorated and alive. She was ready to make the first tentative steps into her future happiness.

She sat very still in a vacuum of time and allowed the last year to run through her mind. It was like watching the events build up neatly in front of her eyes. The initial elation at the thought of having another child, the crumbling of her relationship with Jason, the trauma over her downward spiralling career, the echoes of her empty home and then the decision to rent it out and leave everything behind, or in fact, to run away, as was clearly her real motive. She had been lucky with the move and with the people who offered her support without ever questioning her, but now she knew she must start a new chapter, one which involved the presence of both her lover and her child. Now she just needed to work out how she could do this. If she was not careful Jason may turn round and tell her to go to hell and leave them both alone, but something inside her knew he still had feelings for her, she just had to awaken him to them.

Oliver's Branch

Quietly, she went inside and turned on the computer. The start of a plan was taking shape and she was afraid if she didn't respond to it, the moment and the feelings would be lost.

The house was very still, even the dog was fast asleep and did not acknowledge her. She suddenly felt exhausted but was determined at least to write down some initial thoughts and experiences while they were still so clear in her mind. She initially felt it was not yet time to write a personal letter to Jason but she also knew she wanted to share her new life with him and with her children.

She opened up a new word document and typed a heading.

"Letter from Crete 1. September 2008"

Then without further hesitation she began to type but somehow she could not concentrate, she suddenly realised how mixed her own feelings were. As if by magic she felt the release of all her pent up emotions from the last few months and realised this letter could wait, there was a far more important letter to write and now she was ready. Deleting the heading, she started to write a letter, from the very core of her being.

Ruth Manning

Thirty two.

Dear Jason

I have no idea where to start with this letter and no idea where I will end up. All I know is I need to write it.

There is so much to tell you about the last few months but somehow that seems glib. I don't want this to be a "newsy letter" I want it to be an explanation and a journey into my own feelings, and how they relate to you and me, and of course to Oliver.

I still can't understand where it all went so wrong. I can only think it was a culmination of factors which somehow weakened not only our love and friendship, but the very underpinning of our whole relationship. In hindsight I was illogical and unbalanced and I can offer no excuses. I know I miss you and my decision to give up Oliver was irrational and stupid, but the mistake has been made.

After Oliver was born a part of me seemed to shut down. It was as if I had put a defence mechanism in place to try and deal with the loss of both of you. I "put you away" somewhere deep in my psyche and was totally unwilling to think about what I was doing. All my life I have pushed people away or put on a front of total independence and uncompromising strength, but you know there is another side to me, one which is painfully insecure. I am a person who seems unable or unwilling to accept support and love. I sometimes feel I'm totally unworthy of any kind of love and actually I don't deserve it, anyway.

The move here without you was immense. I still can't believe I actually did it. Without you here there is still an almost bottomless chasm of doubt and regret. Doubt of my ability to survive here alone and regret because this was our shared dream and you are not here to share it with. Without you to talk through our plans or to help with all

Oliver's Branch

the projects we had discussed everything is so much more complicated and somehow pointless. Don't get me wrong there are still the good day to day things which make me smile and I'm sure the underlying personal issues will be resolved in the long term. Time alone will tell.

As you can imagine, everyone has been brilliant and helped in any way they could but the nights can be lonely and so quiet. I knew at some point I would have to face the true extent of my isolation and my emotions; I think this is the time.

When I returned home from the hospital and you had taken Oliver I decided I would put all of this emotional baggage into a tightly sealed box, close to my heart. I would only open it when I felt strong enough to face up to how and what I wanted to do about everything. Because of the roller-coaster ride of the last few months I have been able to keep busy and pretend to myself everything was fine. Now I realise the time has come to be honest with myself and admit to you everything is not fine. I have made a really serious mistake, in losing both of you I have lost part of myself.

Don't take this the wrong way. I don't expect you to jump on the next plane and arrive on my doorstep to start where we left off. I know there is a great deal of hurt and anger still to be addressed, but I also know we will only be able to do that if we can build bridges and meet each other halfway. I know I have given up all legal rights to our son, but signing a piece of paper makes me no less his mother and I realise now I want, more than anything else, to be a part of his and your life, and for both of you to be a part of mine.

I can almost see you raising your eyebrow now and shaking your head, thinking how like me it is to want my own way and expecting it to be the right way, the only way. You may well have adapted to your new life and want nothing further to do with me and if that's the case I will

understand; but, before you decide, I hope we have a chance to talk. I enclose the house phone number and my Greek mobile number. The PO Box address you already know.

Sarah has been staying with me over the last few weeks and I think her strength and determination to sort out some relationship problems she is having have helped me to unlock the box and at least accept the mistakes I've made. It may be too late but I hope it isn't. We imagined such a bright future together. I can see now it would only be made better by the presence of Oliver and a shared responsibility with you, for his future.

I'm not going to write any more as I will start to have unrealistic hopes and dreams and I don't want to do that. It's up to you to decide how (or if) you want to act on this letter. I promise I will not harass you in any way. The ball's in your court.

Sending you love and greetings from Paparooni.........

Jill X

After printing off the letter and getting it ready to post, Jill felt totally drained. It was a balmy, still evening so after giving the dog a quick run she went to bed.

*

The rest of Sarah's stay went all too quickly. For some reason Jill did not tell her friend about the letter, but she had also started the first Letter from Crete and shown this to Sarah, who laughed out loud at a lot of the anecdotes written in it. "You just have to send me a copy when it's finished," Sarah said laughingly. "Now I know a little bit about the people and places I can relate to it all. God you are so lucky, I really do envy you this life."
"I know. It was a big step but now I'm settled in it feels more like home. I think things are going to work out. I do have reservations though you know."
"Like what?" Sarah asked looking slightly bemused.
"Like being lonely or getting ill and not having any one around. Like the winter when I can't get out and about as much and will probably

155

Oliver's Branch

turn into a couch-potato, watching my limited collection of DVDs all day and night. I don't know, but I guess time will tell." She did not mention Oliver, and neither did Sarah. It was as if her friend understood Jill was working things out in a private and insular way. She was not going interfere.

They had been into Chania and bought Sarah's ticket during the week and all too soon the day of her departure arrived. Jill drove her to the airport and saw her off. There were fewer holidaymakers now, although the season would not officially end until October. If Sarah did come back for Christmas she would have to fly to Athens and then get an Aegean flight to the island.

"Well, I'll see you in a few months then." Sarah hugged her friend and walked up the stairs to the departure lounge. She turned around briefly before she disappeared. "I will be back you know, and I'll keep you up to date with all my news and how things are going. I bet you'll be glad to have a bit of peace and quiet."
"I'm going to really miss you and worry about how things turn out, but as long as you keep in touch I'll be OK. It will seem quiet though but I'm sure I'll be kept occupied and amused. Have a safe journey, *Callo Taxeedee* as the Greeks say." They waved again and Sarah was gone.

The journey home from the airport was relatively uneventful. It was strange entering the house knowing she was on her own again. After tidying up and putting out the wash she had done earlier she decided a quiet afternoon was called for and sat out on the balcony to read a book. She must have dozed off, because she was only vaguely aware of the phone ringing in the kitchen. It took her a few moments to orientate herself before she ran down the steps.

"Hello" she said, somewhat breathlessly and waited for a reply.
"Oh my God thank goodness you're in. I've been trying to get hold of you for hours. I really need your advice and I need it *now*. Have you got time to talk?"
"Hi Astrid! Um yes of course I have, but this is a surprise. I haven't heard from you in ages, I thought you must be on holiday or something. Anyway, yes of course. What can be so important? You sound really stressed."
There was a moments silence on the other end of the line and then Astrid began to sob, surprising Jill with the total unsuppressed pain she could hear in her friends weeping. She waited for her to compose herself, wondering what could have happened, this did not sound like the confident, bubbly, composed Astrid she knew and loved.

156

Ruth Manning

After a minute or so Astrid spoke. "It's the job, Jill. You are just so not going to believe this, they're trying to get rid of me for incompetence, but they're doing it in the most horrible way. I think I told you that they were giving me more and more work and it was getting more and more diverse? Well suddenly I was being sidelined and getting really menial stuff to do. Anyway it got to the point when I just couldn't do it any more, it all seemed so pointless and that's when I went off with stress-related illness. It's been four weeks now and I haven't spoken to anyone, I just cry all the time. Barry is getting totally fed up with me and has even threatened to go and stay with his mother until I straighten myself out. I just don't know what to do and to make it worse Janine has informed me she's pregnant and she's moved to Glasgow, to shack up with the baby's father *Trevor*, a bloody out-of-work actor from Australia who has about as much common sense as a gnat. Christ, how can things have gone so horribly wrong?"

Another outburst of tears followed giving Jill a few moments to think of a response. It all seemed so ironic and she wasn't sure how she could help without sounding patronising. "Astrid, I'm so sorry. I don't know what to say. Have you any thoughts on what you want to do?"
"Oh God, I don't know. I went back and got an extended sick note from the doctor, so I have another month to try and *sort myself out,* but I don't want to be alone and I can't talk to Barry. When he saw me yesterday I tried to explain how unhappy and lonely I was and do you know what he suggested? He said I should get over to you, have a holiday. Some sun might do me good; then he gave me a cheque for £300 and said if I didn't do something soon he would *leave me.* I know Janine has to live her own life, she's twenty-four for God's sake. She was furious when I said I thought she would be better off having an abortion. We haven't spoken since she left. Her last words were to call me a *cold-hearted, callous cow, and not fit to be HER mother, let alone a grandmother.*" With these words she once again started crying uncontrollably.

Jill waited patiently almost unable to take in the bombshell Astrid had just thrown at her. Come to stay with her, here, now. How could this be happening?

When there was once again a lull, she could hear Astrid taking large gulps of air, she said to her, "I think we need to talk about this when you are feeling a little less distraught. How about you make yourself a cup of tea, open a large bar of milk chocolate and then ring me back, then we'll have a really long talk. How does that sound?"

Oliver's Branch

"You're right. It's pointless trying to talk about it now, I know I'm totally irrational. Will it be OK to phone you back at about eight tonight, your time, that's six here isn't it?"

"That sounds great. It'll give me a chance to think about things too. Whatever happens you know I will always be there for you. Talk to you later then, OK?"

"OK, thanks. I'll do exactly as you suggest. Bye for now."

The line went dead. Jill stood with the receiver in her hand wondering what the next few weeks held in store. The quiet life seemed to be turning into anything but.

Ruth Manning

Thirty three.

Jill poured herself glass of the village wine, made locally and tasting of rustic oak and grapes. It was not as good as Mitsou's but a snip at €3.00 for a litre-and-a-half bottle. She went to sit outside. Initially she let her mind remain blank and just enjoyed the ambience of the orchard and the day. It was just gone five o'clock which meant she had three hours to try and get her head round everything that was happening to two people she loved.

Seven months ago her life began to spin out of control, longer if she included the breakdown of her relationship with Jason and her unexpected pregnancy. Now, two of her closest friends were experiencing things on an individual level which in many ways mirrored everything that had been thrown at her. Sarah's breakdown of her marital relationship and her decision to experience another life, without the support or backing of family. Astrid's situation and the downward spiral of her career, leading to depression and loss of self esteem, plus her daughter's unexpected pregnancy. Onlookers had already decided abortion/death of the unborn baby was the logical decision to make, while the baby's own mother had decided on life. Irony seemed an understated word to describe any of this. She wondered if either of her friends had made a connection between their own personal experiences and what she had gone through. The emotional tidal waves both Sarah and Astrid were experiencing were linked to her past, like invisible threads of a cobweb. The only difference being, she had experienced them all, and somehow come out the other side intact if somewhat battered and bruised.

Sarah was laying the foundations of a changed life which may or may not include a husband and seemed resolute and sure of her recent decisions. Now Astrid was to make the same journey. Jill wasn't sure she was the one to help her. When Astrid had expressed her shock at Jill's own decision to have the baby and tried to bully her into emerging from her depression, telling her to "get on with it, this isn't a rehearsal you know."Jill had known she would be unable to take this tack, and indeed didn't want to. She wasn't sure if she was emotionally equipped and strong enough to guide her friend through her crisis. On top of these concerns there was also the timing of it. She had just spent nearly a month with Sarah. Now she was looking forward to returning to life in the village. If Astrid came, all of this would once again be on hold. September was at an end and October would see the beginning of change and cooler weather. How

Oliver's Branch

could Astrid's situation have occurred virtually back to back with Sarah's with no respite or personal freedom? It meant Jill would have no time to recharge her batteries. She wanted to clarify her own thoughts and feelings concerning Oliver and Jason. She knew this was selfish, and she would be there for Astrid if she really did need her help, but she couldn't help but feel slightly put upon, if only for a moment.

She knew without having to ponder the matter, she would not hesitate to accommodate Astrid if she really wanted to come, but Jill wasn't sure this lifestyle was quite what Astrid expected or needed. Her friend was far more *refined*. She enjoyed weekends in Paris, romantic trips to Venice or Rome, she was not a country girl. A 'refined and cultured' life at Paparooni was a dichotomy of ideals. She made a mental note to put this to her friend, before a final decision was reached.

Her thoughts were interrupted by the creaking of the front gate. "Hell Jill," came the always enthusiastic and booming voice of Irini. "I've brought you some eggs and feta cheese, the hens are laying well now." For weeks Irini had been scolding and tutting at her chickens about their apparent laziness and lack of egg production. Grace had given her mother a re-released Penguin classic called 'Keeping chickens and rabbits on scraps' and Jill was hoping next year to have her own chickens. She read a great deal about rearing them and on a number of occasions pointed out to Irini that they usually started laying at about 4 months. Hers were only just reaching laying age. Irini had waved a hand in condescension and merely said "Ah Jill, what does the book know about my chickens? After all, these are Cretan chickens."

Irini closed the gate and sat down opposite Jill fanning herself and looking around. "Your friend has gone then?" she asked, knowing full well she had. "Now you will be able to get on with all the jobs you wanted to do. It is nice having a holiday but if you don't work you *die*." Jill was slightly dubious about this philosophy but did not pursue it, instead she thanked Irini for the eggs and cheese, gave her a fresh glass of orange juice and a small cake, then sat back down. "Actually, Irini, I'm not sure I will be on my own for very long. I have just recieved a call from another friend of mine. She may be coming to stay for a while." Irini looked over her glasses and wagged a finger. "This is no good for you. You will be lonely in the winter if you have so many visitors so soon. Better to stagger their visits and have some time for yourself." Jill agreed with her and said she would wait for her friend's call and see what was decided. They talked affably for another half-an-hour, then the old lady left, saying she

160

Ruth Manning

had to collect some vegetables and have something to eat. She walked away sternly repeating the adage, "Remember, Jill, if you do not work you *die...*" then she was gone. The gate creaked shut in her wake.

Jill went inside and added a note to her Things-to-do list, *remember to oil the gate.* The list seemed to be getting longer by the day, but, she thought to herself, *I have plenty of time to get things how I want them, sigar, sigar(slowly, slowly).* She cleared away the glass and plate then realising it was another hour until Astrid phoned, decided to take Dyson for a walk. Afterwards she would prepare a quick bite to eat.

*

When the phone rang at precisely eight O'clock Jill was ready. Dyson was sprawled outside in the evening breeze. She had eaten a delicious omelette, courtesy of Irini's newly-laying hens..

She usually answered the phone in Greek, but knowing who the caller was she merely said "Hi, Astrid, what exact timing."
"Oh God, Jill, I've been sitting watching the clock since I phoned you. I've made lists and notes and flow charts to try and make sense of it all and it's still the same bloody mess it was before. What the hell am I going to do?"
Jill sensed another weeping attack and so answered quickly, "The first thing you're not going to do is start crying again. This will be costing you a fortune and we have to decide one way or another what your next move will be. You can't wave a wand and make this all magically go away, or go back to how things were before. Putting it into perspective isn't going to happen instantly. OK, so a question. What do you want to do to enable you to get through your current emotional crisis? Just one thing, Astrid, without all the tears. Take a deep breath before you answer." Jill knew she was being hard, but she felt she had to get Astrid to focus and deal with one thing at a time.
"OK, well I've made a list so I'm going to read it to you. Ready?" She took a deep breath and began. "Firstly, I'm going to phone Janine and say I'm sorry for trying to force her to have an abortion and promise I will support her in anyway I can.
Secondly, I'm going to talk to Barry and reassure him I'm going to be fine. He just needs to give me a bit of time, and thirdly," there was another loud intake of breath, "I want to come and stay with you for a while, if that's OK with you? I know I can get my head round all of

161

Oliver's Branch

this, but you've been there and come out on top, I know your strength will help me through the quagmire I feel I'm in and out the other side." There was a silence before she added, "Of course if it's difficult for you I won't come."

"I think you've made the first step in the road to recovery. Of course you can come and stay, but I'm not sure you'll enjoy the rural life and basics of my home. It's not a four-star hotel and it's a quiet and very simple life."
"I know, but I think it's probably exactly what I need. Away from it all, to sort myself out. If you've stuff to do I can always help out. I don't intend to cry my way through each day. This is a positive move forward, not a backward step, honestly."
"OK, let's go for it then. When are you hoping to come?"
"Well, I've looked on the internet and I can get a flight to Chania the day after tomorrow, arriving at 12.45. How is that for you?"
Slightly taken aback by the imminence of the visit Jill hesitated for a moment, before replying, "That sounds fine. You'll have a few things to sort out before you arrive and so you'll be kept busy. Just put everything else on the back burner until you get here. OK?"
"Brilliant, I'll phone you from Gatwick then and see you in Chania. Thank you so, so much."
They talked for a few more minutes and as she hung up Jill hoped this really would be a positive move and not just a total disaster. She poured herself another glass of wine, turned off the kitchen light and went to sit outside and listen to the noises of the night, before retiring to bed to enjoy the solitude of a night alone.

Ruth Manning

Thirty four.

The following day sped by. Having sorted out the bedroom and washed sheets and towels, she spent a few hours in the orchard, tidying up. Stelios was around for most of the day and finished painting the side of the house. Things were beginning to take shape and Stelios was a Godsend.

Irini popped in with a bag of eggs and stayed for a cup of tea. She was very partial to English tea with milk, so different from the mountain tea she was used to. In the evening, Jill was invited round to Mitsou's where she tucked into a beautiful leg of lamb and all the accompanying extras. She explained to them how, in England, lamb was roasted and accompanied by roast potatoes and numerous vegetables, plus mint sauce and gravy. The fact these were served on one plate, all at the same time, surprised them. They couldn't get their heads around the concept of gravy at all. At a Greek meal, you helped yourself to food as and when you felt like it, and meals tended to last a good few hours. At midnight she offered her apologies and went home to bed. She had a busy day ahead of her.

The following morning the weather was beautiful as she left for Chania airport. It was still hot and sunny and the coolness of winter, which she had been warned about by Irini, had not as yet, raised its ugly head. She only needed to wait 20 minutes at arrivals before Astrid emerged. At first Jill didn't recognise her. She had lost a great deal of weight and her usually glossy, coiffured hair looked unkempt and lifeless.

After an initial hug and walk to the car the journey back was quiet. There was an awkwardness Jill couldn't quite put her finger on.

Astrid looked at the views, especially the stunning Souda Bay. In many ways, Jill took the scenery for granted, although not a day went by when she did not marvel at the mountains she could see from her window, or the beautiful crystal blue sea of the Mediterranean. She broke the silence by saying, "Souda Bay is where the ferries come in and go out from on this side of the island, it really is quite stunning from up here isn't it?"
"Absolutely amazing. I hadn't realised it would be such a beautiful island. You know I really am grateful to you for letting me stay; is the beach very far from where you live?"

Oliver's Branch

"Well the nearest beach is Maleme, which is great in September through to May as there's hardly anyone around, but the beach I go to is about 25 minutes away. I wonder if you'll fall in love with it as much as I have."

Jill turned off onto the National Road and concentrated on the other drivers, keeping a special eye on the rental cars.

"Whatever else happens over the next few weeks I'm going to enjoy the climate. It was pouring with rain when I left and I can count the sunny days this summer on my fingers. I really am going to try and be positive you know, but I can't explain the total and utter feeling of uselessness and self-loathing I seemed to have fallen into. It's as if nothing really matters any more. I was so proud of my career. I thought I was doing really well. I can't believe senior management have done everything in their power to get rid of me. Condescending, arrogant bastards. I have absolutely no idea what I'm going to do but I do know I can't go back there, it would feel like crawling into a hole and being totally surrounded by filth. Even my so-called colleagues have told me to *snap out of it and get on with my life*. Can you believe it?"

Jill smiled to herself remembering Astrid's words to her just a few months previously. She wanted to say of course she knew how her friend was feeling having experienced a similar predicament, but she thought it would probably sound patronising, so she kept her thoughts to herself.

"This is something you have to sort out for yourself, Astrid. Of course I'll support you in anyway I can, but you have to decide what you want to do and then act on it. I really hope you recharge your batteries and when eventually you return to England, you feel ready to deal with the situation."

Jill turned into the carport at the back of the house. Astrid gasped. "Oh my God, is this it? Somehow I imagined it being much smaller with other identical houses all around."

Jill retrieved the suitcase from the trunk and led the way round to the steps leading down to the basement kitchen. Inside it was cool and quite dark as it was built below ground. She lugged the case up the internal stairs and showed Astrid her room. "It's not massive but it's big enough to make yourself comfortable in," Jill told her. She went and threw open the French windows and pushed back the external shutters. Outside was a balcony with a small round table and two chairs. Astrid followed her out. A whistle from somewhere in the orchard caught her attention. "Is there someone in the trees?" Astrid asked. "And are those all orange trees? There doesn't appear to be much fruit on most of them."

Jill explained three-quarters of the orange trees were Merrilies and the fruit was picked from late September to March. The other trees,

164

Ruth Manning

with oranges on, were Valencias. These were picked during the summer months. "I've also got a couple of olive trees, two lemon trees, a few mandarin trees and a grapefruit tree, although the grapefruit is only a baby. And yes I think Stelios is working in the vegetable garden, he has been my saviour, friend and odd-job-man over the last few months. Come on, let's go down so you can meet him."

Stelios was indeed working in the vegetable patch which was thriving under his green fingers. He had not used the piece of land at the end of the orchard but rotavated an area in the other corner, among the trees. Tomatoes, peppers and cucumbers were growing in abundance as were watermelons and potatoes. "This is my friend Astrid, Stelios" she said, introducing them. "I told you about her yesterday." Stelios smiled and offered a somewhat soil encrusted hand which Astrid hesitantly shook. "You spoke to him in Greek" she uttered in amazement. "Does he speak any English?"
""I speak a little," he replied. "But I know Jill wants to learn better Greek, so we speak it a lot of the time," he said in English. "I think I understand more English than I can speak." He looked directly at Sarah as he spoke and she barely managed to respond, "Oh, right, that's fine then. It's lovely to meet you."
Stelios returned to his gardening and Jill showed Astrid around the orchard. Afterwards they went to get some orange juice. Astrid went upstairs and changed out of her jeans and long-sleeved top. She definitely wouldn't be needing them again for a while. She unpacked her case and chose a bright sun-dress she bought the week before in the sales, then went and stood on the balcony in her bare feet, looking at the mountains and the surrounding countryside. Already she felt as if all the problems she had experienced were being put into some kind of new perspective. It was so quiet everywhere, apart from the sound of cicadas in the trees and a dog barking in the distance. She knew it was the right decision coming here and she already felt at home. She had never been in a rural Greek village before, but she knew she would enjoy it. Jill would make no demands on her, she was sure, and by the time she returned she hoped she would have the strength to deal with the future. She walked down the steps to find Jill sitting enjoying yoghurt with honey and a glass of orange juice.

"That looks more like it," Jill remarked. "I love the dress. I thought you might like more than just yoghurt. There's fresh bread, a Greek salad and some feta cheese, plus a few boiled eggs downstairs if you want to help yourself. I'm not very hungry, but if you want some, be

165

Oliver's Branch

my guest. I'm afraid I don't do much cooking, but there's always enough food. Most evenings I make something, so you won't starve."
"That would be great, I hardly touched the meal on the plane, it looked too revolting and smelt worse, so yeah, a bit of bread and salad would be much appreciated. I hope you'll let me help with the meals though, I quite enjoy cooking and I'd feel better if I was helping out. How about it?"
Jill said she had no aversion to anyone else cooking as she never saw the joy of spending hours in the kitchen. "If you're not too tired" she went on, "how about a trip to the beach and a swim. It's quite sandy but I've got two sun beds, so you'll be comfortable."

After they had eaten they loaded the sun beds and their beach bags into the car and half an hour later were sitting on the beach, looking out at the blueness of the sea and the sky framed by the mountains of Kastelli and Ravdoucha. The beauty of this beach, apart from the lack of tourists, was the fact you never quite knew what mood the sea would be in. Today, it was as calm as a mill pond but Jill explained how sometimes there were massive waves which tossed you around. "It's great fun" she laughed, "I think you would love it."

After a swim they settled down, each with a book, and made the most of the afternoon sun. It was a quiet time and Astrid allowed herself to immerse her thoughts in the sound of the sea. She could feel the sun warming her skin and bones and for the first time in what seemed like forever, she began to relax and enjoy the experience.

After about 2 hours of quiet companionship, Jill suggested they go home. It was an intense sun and Astrid was very white. Jill explained to her that usually two hours was all she spent sunbathing as there was so much else she should be doing. It felt very déjà vu and she smiled when she thought back to Sarah's first day, when Jill had said basically the same thing. After they had loaded the car and were on the National Road, Jill noticed Astrid was already slightly pink. She was one of those lucky people who went brown almost immediately, but for now she just looked slightly sun-kissed and content.

"I think I could get used to this life you know" Astrid remarked, looking out at Kolimbari Bay. "I know I've got a lot of heart searching to do, and when I first realised I would be here with you, I was slightly concerned I would be in the way. Also the fact that I might hate it. You did make it out to be a peasant lifestyle you were living. It's hardly that though is it? You've even got air con and a big flat-screen TV. Hardly backward if you ask me. Anyway, what do

166

Ruth Manning

you do here for entertainment in the evenings? Or do you go to bed early so you can get up at first light?"

"No, I've always been a bit of a night owl and I usually get up about nine. After that I try and do at least one thing out in the garden plus a bit of tidying up in the house. It's weird though, I never seem to get bored. Although I suppose in winter, when it's dull and raining, there will be times when I get a bit stir crazy. I'll let you know when I've experienced it. Also I've had Sarah here for the past month, so I haven't been on my own. Some of the Greeks I know now are great too, like Stelios and my neighbours. I'm sure you'll meet them in the near future. All Greeks are very curious and in a village everyone knows exactly what everyone else is doing. You can do whatever you want, whatever you feel the most comfortable with. I'm also going to start writing a monthly 'Letter from Crete' so I will probably do a bit of it each day. It's mainly for Nick and Grace, but Sarah made me promise to keep her up to date on day by day happenings, so I'll see how it goes."

Back at the house they rinsed through their swimming paraphernalia and spent a comfortable hour together in the kitchen, then sat down to eat the fajitas they had prepared. After a few glasses of wine and some friendly banter, Astrid said she was going to go to bed as it had been a long day. Jill was left with Dyson and her thoughts for company.

It was half-past-ten. Usually she would read a book or watch TV, but tonight she decided to start the monthly newsletter she kept talking about. She started the computer. Opening a new Word document she saw the saved letter wrote to Jason just a few days ago. It would not have arrived yet, but subconsciously she crossed her fingers and whispered to the evening stars, "Please get in touch, Jason, I'm ready to work things out and I need you." Then she started on her first sentence of her first 'Letter from Crete.'

Oliver's Branch

Thirty five.

She was awoken at half past eight the following morning by sounds of activity coming from the kitchen. Before she went to sleep the night before, having written two pages of the first newsletter, she found herself worrying about Astrid. Things could pan out one of two ways, she thought. Either a) Astrid was not quite as depressed as she had made out and would utilise her time on the island having a holiday. She would recharge her batteries before returning to England, re-establishing herself in her job and accepting her daughter's decision, supporting her as best she could. Or, b) Astrid was indeed clinically depressed and would be unable to face the complications of her present predicament. She may break down and shatter into small pieces. Jill hoped desperately it would be the former. As she entered the kitchen all the signs pointed to this being true. Astrid was washed and dressed, not moping about in her dressing gown and looking dishevelled, in the way Jill herself had for so many months. The table was laid and coffee was brewing. As she walked in, Astrid cracked eggs into a pan and pushed the bread down in the toaster. So far so good thought Jill. She greeted her friend with a cheery, "Good morning you, this all looks very industrious. Don't forget you're on holiday though, I don't want you going back even more worn out than you are now."

Her friend eyed her mischievously and laughed. "Actually, I decided last night exactly how I want to go about the next few weeks. Let me run it past you and see what you think." Jill nodded. "OK, this is how I see it. There are fundamental decisions I have to make and I want you to listen to me and guide me, but to make those decisions I have to recharged and positive about things, in a way I haven't done for months. So, here's the deal. For the first week I don't want to talk about any of it. I'm on holiday, the sun is shining and I want to go swimming, eat good food and meet your friends. In other words there will be no self-indulgence, self-pity or melancholy. Anyway, with this glorious sunshine and the peace of it all, except for the bloody cockerels at God knows what hour, I'm already finding it hard to relate to the gloom and the depression of England. So, complete escapism for a week. I've turned my mobile off and I won't talk to anyone back home. It's just you and me..." without pausing she went on, ".....and you have to promise me something too; if you hear me crying at nights or wandering about, you mustn't come and try to console me or see what's wrong. During this week I will write down all my thoughts and feelings and then, hopefully, you can be there to support me in whatever decisions I make. Is it agreed?" She looked questioningly over to Jill, who nodded again and took a swig of the hot, aromatic coffee, which had been placed before her. She

168

Ruth Manning

suggested they move up and eat under the pergola, which they did.
Once they were settled and enjoying the early sun, Astrid continued
explaining her plan of action.

"I've thrown away my pills and I sent Barry a text last night saying I
would be in touch when I had some idea about what I was going to
do. One thing I do know though, the way I've been with him can't go
on and I really do love him. We've been together forever, I've never
been with any one else. We were childhood sweethearts you know?"
Jill just smiled. "Anyway everything seems so far away and so
abstract from here, I know whatever problems I have are not
insurmountable. I have a really good life and I'm to blame for
making it so hard. I need to understand it all and put things in a
different perspective."

At that precise moment an old woman, perhaps in her late seventies,
dressed in black with a wrinkled, weather-worn face, walked past
the house with an enormous sack of mountain greens on her back.
She was bent almost double, but seeing the two women she gave an
enormous toothless grin and called over "Hello, Jill. Today is a day of
work and preparing for a festival. I have all my family coming and I
must work hard. That is good, for if you do not work hard ... you
die." Then, with a hearty wave of her stick, she was gone.

"That's Katerina," Jill explained. "She has only recently recovered
from a fall in which she broke her hip. After masses of surgery, and
new hip she was in bed for months .Sofia spent the winter months
looking after her. Now she's back on her feet and just look at her.
There are so many things here which make me feel humble and
inadequate. One of those small miracles just walked past."
"Exactly. You see, this is precisely what I need. A complete break
from the stupidity and speed of twenty-first century life in Northern
Europe. I already feel as if the sun is warming me through to my
very core. Does that sound stupid?"
"Not at all," Jill laughed. "This is a different world. Priorities are
different and people's needs are based around family and harvesting.
Materialism is beginning to creep in with the younger generation
but the older people seem to be content just to accept the fruits of
their labour and support each other. Irini, my neighbour, once said
to me, *As long as you have your family, good health, bread, oil, food
and wine with wood cut for the winter, there is nothing else you
need.* You know it seems a good way to live. I never hear any
mention of broadband, iPods, fast cars, expensive clothes or the need
for fancy home-furnishings. I think we've lost sight of what is truly
important. Being here makes me appreciate the simple things."

Oliver's Branch

"Well, here we go then. Let's enjoy." Astrid picked up the plates and mugs from the table and went back down into the kitchen. Jill sat perfectly still and looked out into the orchard savouring the moment. Dyson came and nuzzled up to her, then contentedly plonked himself on her bare toes, resting his chin on his paws. It was very early in the morning to take it all in, but she felt she had a rough gist of how things were going to be, at least initially. It was a far better beginning than she ever imagined.

For the rest of the morning Jill busied herself in the orchard while Astrid took a sun-bed onto the balcony, smothered herself in factor 8 and nestled down with a book. Stelios arrived at just gone eleven with a bag containing a loaf of bread, a chunk of feta cheese, 2 tomatoes and a bottle of wine. He laid them out carefully on the table. "I thought we could have a snack together with your new friend, to welcome her to the village. Is she here?"
Jill took off her gardening gloves. She had been pulling ivy from the walls where it obstinately wanted to stay. She wiped the sweat from her forehead and pointed to the balcony where Astrid was oblivious of the world, stretched out in a bikini with an MP3 player plugged into her ears. "What a kind thought, Stelios, hang on I'll go and get her, then I'll fetch up some plates, glasses and knives. Sit down, I won't be a minute."

When Astrid heard about the impromptu 'snack', she put on shorts and a T shirt and joined him at the table. Once all the crockery and cutlery was in place, he cut up the bread, the tomatoes and feta and told the two women to eat. Stelios asked Astrid questions about work and family and how long she was going to stay, while Astrid flirted and laughed, obviously having a good time. Jill smiled to herself thinking of Stelios and his sexual preferences, but he too was enjoying the moment and obviously the company. At the end of the meal he asked Jill if it was convenient for him to do some work in the vegetable patch, it needed watering and clearing. He then ambled off singing to himself, leaving the two women alone, but not before he had kissed Astrid's hand and told her what a pleasure it was meeting her. She, for her part, was totally enamoured by his charm and good looks.
"What a lovely man," she had remarked, "so natural and spontaneous. God, Jill, it's only my first day and already I love it here. I remember how you used to go on about moving to a Greek village and I just couldn't see the appeal, but already I understand what you were looking for. It's so far removed from anything I've ever experienced before. To be honest, I never thought you would do it. In fact I never thought you would leave the baby and I hoped you and Jason would get back together and everything would end up

170

Ruth Manning

Happily Ever After. Life isn't really like that though is it? So, here's to life and an afternoon on the wonderful beach of yours, before I cook you a sumptuous evening meal. I've taken stock of your fridge and pantry and I reckon I can make us a half decent lasagne. How does that sound?"

After clearing up together, they said goodbye to Stelios and headed for the beach. It was a hot and sultry afternoon but with a slight breeze and when they arrived, Jill was thrilled to see the waves lashing and pounding near the shore. Having sorted out their sun beds they both ran down and dived in, to be pummelled and thrashed and knocked over by the frothy white waves. They laughed and pulled each other about, ducked each other under the foam and generally enjoyed 'God's Wave Machine'. To onlookers (if there had been any,) they would have looked a strange sight. Two *not so young any more* women, frolicking about like small children, laughing and gambolling in the waves, seemingly without a care in the world.

Oliver's Branch

Thirty six.

Astrid was true to her word and for the first week there was no
discussion about her job, daughter or husband. She settled in to the
peaceful way of life, meeting Mitsou and Eleni, Lefteris and Sofia
and, of course, Irini, who was especially curious about Jill's visitor.
She came across on a regular basis to drink tea and ask questions.
Jill managed to sidetrack any gossip by keeping her answers vague
and minimal. It was all too easy in the village for gossip to spread
and especially when it concerned the foreigners, who a great many of
the Cretans were sure were 'Trelos' – *MAD*.

There were nights when she was aware of Astrid moving around the
house in the early hours and one night, while she had been writing
the newsletter, she heard her friends muffled weeping, but she was
as good as her word and didn't interfere. In the mornings, Astrid was
as positive and energetic as ever and she took on the role of chief
cook and bottle washer. They went to the beach every afternoon and
Astrid was already turning a beautiful shade of brown.

Jill had checked the post over the last few days of Astrid's first week,
but there was no correspondence from Jason. No text, no phone call,
nothing. She began to wonder if she had indeed burnt all her
bridges. One of the interesting things which had come out of having
her friend around was the fact she had begun to open up and talk
about Oliver. Until Astrid mentioned him on the very first day,
nothing had been said about him. Nick and Grace in their weekly
phone calls never mentioned him and conversations were mainly
about what they were doing. It seemed likely they would try to get
out and see her the following summer, probably in the June, but it
was such a long way away and it was still only speculation. Jill
missed them both incredibly. She still had pangs of guilt about her
absence, but they were both getting on with their lives. As long as
they were happy and healthy she was satisfied. John had been in
touch with all the news from The Garage Club and muted a visit in
the spring was on the cards. Jill wasn't sure if he meant all of them
but decided to let things take their course. All was going well with
the rental of the house, although news about the recession was all
doom and gloom. She even received a call from June who told her
both the cats were now well ensconced in the flat. They didn't miss
her one bit. So as far as settling in, things were going well, even
though neither Sarah or Astrid had been in Jill's initial *settling in*
plan.

Ruth Manning

Her thoughts about Oliver and Jason were another matter entirely. It was amazingly cathartic telling Astrid all the details of the birth. She broke down a couple of times when she explained how immense the space left by both the baby and Jason left in her life, but each time she spoke about them the pain eased a little. She knew in her heart they were both safe and well, she had not given up on a reply from Jason. The newsletter was taking shape and even she found herself laughing at some of the anecdotes she wrote down. She hoped other people would laugh too. She longed to share some of the stories with Jason and wondered if he would appreciate a copy of the newsletter, once it was finished, but put it out of her mind. If he had not reply to a personal letter it was because he wanted to sever all links. If this were the case, there was nothing whatsoever she could do about it.

The second week passed much like the first and the days fell into a regular pattern. Astrid seemed totally content, although sometimes a little on the quiet side. Jill decided to just go with the flow. When or if her friend wanted to talk she would and she had proved a good listener. Somehow, each time Jill talked about Oliver she became more optimistic about the outcome. Something inside her kept whispering, *It's going to be fine, just hold on.* She was used to *holding on,* at so many levels, so she decided she would do just that.

It was during Astrid's third week that a noticeable shift took place. Astrid went out most mornings, borrowing the beach buggy, and she returned around lunchtime. She was vague about what she was up to and all Jill could make out was it was something to do with the Internet café, personal stuff her friend was sorting out. She didn't ask for any further information, feeling sure she would be given any relevant details when Astrid was good and ready. She enjoyed having some time to herself and although it was extremely hot she started painting the railings around the house. Having the mornings free meant she was able to get on with this without too much interruption. Of course Irini still popped in most days and she was able to sit down with Eleni, who would give her helpful hints about Greek cooking, but on the whole the village was quiet. Stelios had gone to the mainland to visit family and friends and was due back at the beginning of November and Lefteris and Sofia had friends staying from Athens, so they were out and about a great deal more than usual.

The afternoons were still spent at the beach and Astrid continued to prepare delicious evening meals. They would sit outside all evening and after the meal chatted about their lives and families. At the end

Oliver's Branch

of the third week, during one of these conversations, Astrid surprised Jill by saying, "Anyway, Jill. I've sorted everything out. It was all so easy once I was able to distance myself from the problem and be objective. Is it really only 3 weeks since I arrived in such a mess? I was like a shattered piece of glass, all sharp edges and shards of decimated, irreparable, fractured particles. God that's a bit profound for me, sorry, but you know what I mean."

Jill nodded. She had been a similar broken entity and she liked the analogy. "Looking back at the whole work situation," Astrid continued, "the stress and upset, the total inability to function or drag my self-esteem out of the gutter, I can't believe I allowed it to get me down in the way it did. I'd seen it happen to you and I remember how offhand and unsympathetic I was. I'm so sorry about being so insensitive, Jill. So here's the plan, well three plans actually......"

Just at that moment the phone started to ring in the kitchen. "Sorry, Astrid, do you mind if I answer it? I think it's probably Grace, I haven't heard from her this week and she sent a text earlier saying she would call." Astrid sent her off with a wave of her hand. It was dark and cool in the kitchen. Jill picked up the receiver. "Hello 82150. Is that you sweetheart?"

There was a moment's silence and then an all-too-long unheard voice replied. There was humour in his tone and she could imagine the smile causing dimples as the sides of his mouth.

"Well that was an unexpected greeting. Jill, it's me, Jason. Can you talk?"

For a moment she was unable to move, then she pulled up a kitchen chair and sat down heavily. Her heart was beating too fast and too loudly and she drew in a deep breath before replying. After nearly 5 months she wondered what her first words would be.

"Yes, quite well actually, I've had quite a long time to improve my ability to communicate." *What a banal and stupid comment* she thought, raising her eyebrows and slapping herself, hypothetically. "Jason! My God, this is so unexpected. How are you?"

"Everything's fine. I got your letter a week or so ago and I've read and reread it over and over. You know what a bad letter writer I am, so I'm ringing because I need to ask you a question and I want you to be totally honest, OK?"

"OK" she replied, unable to think of anything else to say. The surprise and shock of hearing his voice leaving her physically weak. She had no idea what he was going to ask and an element of fear made her feel dizzy and disorientated.

"Right. So here's the question. Are you serious about building bridges and wanting to see us both?"

174

Ruth Manning

"More than anything else in the world," Jill answered without a moment's hesitation. She waited for a reply.

"Right then. Here is what I suggest. We'll keep in touch and I'll tell you all the news from this end and you can tell me all the goings-on in the village. No promises, no plans, just talking to each other. We'll see where it leads us. How does it sound to you?"

"I think it's a great suggestion and a start to the bridge-building I so hoped we could do. Yes, it sounds hopeful and it will be great talking to you again."

"You too, but not now. I want to get my head around all of this and besides it's Oliver's bath time. Don't ask any questions now. I'll call you in a few days. Would it be best if I text first so you are expecting the call?"

"Sounds like a plan. I'm not sure I can talk much more at the moment anyway. I'm all weak and overcome. What a pathetic individual I can be."

"No, it's fine. OK, I'll be in touch, and Jill..."

"Yes?" she asked, wondering how the conversation would end.

"*Oneera glika. Callee nichta.*" She smiled and repeated the Greek words. Then Jason hung up the phone. She sat absolutely still for a few moments, feeling both elated and deflated. There was so much more to say and she desperately needed to know more about Oliver. The longing and aching need returned and engulfed her whole body, but he had promised to phone again. Maybe then she would be able to talk to the only person who would really understand her regrets and fears. Maybe they would build and cross the bridges together, re-uniting on the other side.

Suddenly she remembered Astrid had been on the point of some sort of revelation. She decided she could contain her excitement and find out what exactly her friends plans were.

She went and sat down again under the pergola. Astrid was just pouring them both another glass of wine. "How's Grace doing then?" she asked. Jill, being unable to reveal her true emotional roller coaster of emotions mumbled, "Oh, She's fine. Broke as always, but fine. Anyway, where were we? You were just about to tell me your plans. I'm all ears."

Astrid took a sip of wine and carried on from where she had left off. "So there are three plans, all interrelated but all standing alone, if you get what I mean? You may have noticed my absence during the last week?" She looked at Jill inquiringly.

"Mmm, it's been duly noted and I realised you needed space and time to get your head around everything. Anyway, go on, it sounds quite exciting."

Oliver's Branch

"Well I've been in touch with my Union. They feel I have a strong case for bullying and breach of contract, but it will be a long and bitter fight. If I remember you were involved in something quite similar and you walked away from it with your head held high. So, I decided I would do the same. As soon as I had made the decision, the rest was easy. I contacted my line manager and explained to him I wanted to look into the possibilities of redundancy. God, Jill, I could almost see him rubbing his hands together in glee. The department is in a severe financial predicament. I bet he was already weighing up what the other suckers could be coerced into doing. Making them take on more work just to keep their jobs. Anyway he took it to the MD and I received an e-mail the other day offering me a more than generous package, plus an exemplary reference. So, I accepted and will not be returning to the job......*ever*. End of plan one."

Jill looked at her friend who was smiling from ear to ear. She wondered if she would or should have had the strength to follow a similar path, but she dismissed the thought almost as quickly as it had formed. She had made her choices and her life was moving on. "What are your plans then, for your future and work?" she asked. Astrid shuffled forward in her seat.

"Let's just say this led on to plan two. Barry and I have had a long talk, several actually. We discovered how unhappy and concerned we both were at how distant and self-absorbed we'd become. Anyway, Barry's mum is getting on and she wants him to go into the family's furniture restoring business, which has been in the family for 3 generations. He grew up helping both his father and grandfather with the work and has a real talent and eye for detail. I was totally unaware of his interest and he said he hadn't pursued it because we needed the money for the house and family. With the redundancy money he will take over and develop the business, while I take on all promotions and advertising. There are so many opportunities now, with the net and everything. It's going to be brilliant."

"Well, I've learnt something new. I never even knew there was a restoration business in the family, let alone that Barry had the necessary talent and interest in it. Are you sure this is really what you want though? Will it be enough of a challenge?"

"We've talked about that too and I'm going to go to night classes at the local college, to learn about the process of setting up internet web-pages for the business website. It's something I've wanted to learn for ages, but there never seemed to be enough hours in the day."

Jill nodded again, trying to take it all in. "I assume this leads us on to plan three? OK, sock it to me."

"Plan three was a far trickier one. Barry heard from Janine almost as soon as I left the country. Apparently she was absolutely devastated when the scum-bag boyfriend had ripped her off for three

months rent and then simply disappeared into the ether; *presumably to rejoin the flotsam and jetsam of depravity, from whence he had come.* Those are Barry's words by the way not mine. Anyway Barry worked everything out and Janine is now back home. He explained she was looking at flats just in case I wasn't comfortable with her living at home. He asked me if I thought I could cope with being a grandmother and all the responsibility it would entail for us all as a family, and you know something? Suddenly it was exactly the right thing. Losing Janine was devastating and I realised this is *her* life. I could either be a part of it on her terms or lose her altogether. There was no question, it will be great to have her back and be there for her throughout the rest of the pregnancy. What an idiot I was trying to get her to have an abortion. I really can be a hard, hostile bitch, you know?"

Jill thought back to the early days of her own pregnancy, when only Sarah accepted her decision and stood by her without judging. Astrid seemed to have forgotten how she went down exactly the same road with Jill as she later took with her own daughter. Her matter of fact approach to 'the problem' rang in Jill's ears, because, once she had realised the baby was going to be born, Astrid had been very matter of fact. She told Jill to *stop beating herself up, because although things were in a dreadful mess, they would get better and one day. She would look back and it would be just a distant memory.*

It seemed ironic how easily and almost seamlessly Astrid seemed to have work things out. Both she and Sarah arrived with problems they initially thought were insurmountable, yet somehow the magic and simplicity of Jill's small world had enabled them both to work things through remarkably quickly; and yet she was still nowhere near a solution to her own pain and despair, almost six months on.

Astrid interrupted her thoughts... "Oh and by the way, I'm going to cut my visit short. I've managed to rearrange my flight and I'm meeting Barry in Athens. We're going to have a romantic week together before we travel back. I'll be leaving on Monday. It goes without saying, Jill, you have been a life saver; without you and this incredible place I think I would have just sunk into total apathy and despair. Everything would have fallen apart. I will never be able to thank you enough. Is there any way I can repay you?"

Jill decided to lighten the tone of the evening. She was tired and emotionally drained. Now she knew Astrid was well on the way to a much happier time in her life, Jill needed space and peace. It was time for bed. "There's nothing to repay me for, friendship is about

Oliver's Branch

support and love, not about favours. I tell you what though, if you promise to send me a regular supply of tea bags, we'll call it quits."
"It's a deal. If it's OK with you I'm going up to bed, it's been an exhausting time and tomorrow I need to pack for Athens." She gave Jill a hug and disappeared upstairs.

Jill turned off the outside lights and called Dyson who had spent the evening chewing on a large bone under the fig tree. They went inside together and after clearing up and giving him a quick cuddle, she went upstairs to bed. As she nestled down in the crisp white sheets she whispered Jason's last words to her before he had hung up. Words they said so often to each other in the past, before they snuggled down together to sleep "Oneera gleeka - callee nichta." *Sweet dreams - good night.*"

Somehow she knew there would be no demons tonight and any dreams would indeed be sweet.

Ruth Manning

Thirty seven.

Astrid was incredibly organised and was packed and tidied up by lunchtime. "I've only kept out my beach-wear stuff and a change of clothes for tomorrow," she said. "That way there will be no rushing around. I thought we could go to the beach for the last time this afternoon, then have an evening meal in that lovely taverna in Alikianos, my treat."

There was a certain chill in the air for the first time and although the sea was still crystal, azure blue they didn't swim for long. Wisps of cloud could be seen in the blue sky and as they were leaving Paparooni, Mitsou had called out to them, "Good day, ladies, you are off to the beach?" They laughed and said yes, it was Astrid's last day. "Well, enjoy, I feel from tomorrow we may see winter, it is in the air." With these words of wisdom he disappeared with a hoe over his shoulder, singing in a deep bass voice. Instead of swimming they walked the length of the beach, gathering pure white, marble pebbles as they went. Jill had an idea for a leaving present for Astrid, but wanted it to be a surprise the following day. They found a beautiful, perfect seahorse, fossilised on the shore, and after about an hour they staggered back to their sunbeds, laden down with armfuls of stones.

"They really are lovely Jill, but what in heavens name do you want with all of these and why did you keep examining them as if you were looking for faults or something?"
Putting all the stones into a heavy-duty plastic bag, apart from two which she secreted in her beach bag, Jill laughed. "I don't know. I just find them fascinating. I'm going to use most of them in the tops of my potted plants, some I may place 'artistically in a glass bowl.' Oh, I have no idea really, I just love them."
"Me too. I'm going to take a couple of them home just to remind me of this beautiful beach." Astrid said. Opening her palm she revealed two perfect, glistening white orbs.
"Good idea but I hope the curse of taking stones from the beach doesn't happen here the same way as it apparently does in England."
"What curse is that?" Astrid queried.
"Well I'm not sure it's really a curse but I was once told if I took a stone from the local beach, it meant I was always destined to return. I guess here though it would be more of a blessing than a threat."
"I'm definitely taking two then, because I really want to come here again in the future." Astrid placed them in her bag. As they left, Jill could see her saying a silent goodbye to the beautiful landscape and sea.

Oliver's Branch

Arriving home they decided to shower then sit around and enjoy the late afternoon sunshine, before going to the local taverna. They talked about how quickly the days had passed and Astrid remarked on some of the wonderful people she had met and how Greek hospitality was so spontaneous and such fun. They did not talk about Astrid's plans but Jill felt this was a good time to mention her phone call from Jason.
"You know the other day, when I cut you short about your plans, to answer the phone?" Jill asked. "When Grace had called?" Astrid had nodded. "Yes, well actually, it wasn't Grace... It was Jason. I couldn't get my head around it at the time, but I didn't want you to leave without knowing he's been in touch."

Astrid looked at her incredulously, almost lost for words. There was a moment's pause, the silence filled only by a large black beetle buzzing through the orchard. "My God. Was it a positive call or is there something wrong he thought you should know about?"
"It was a good call, I think. He was responding to a letter I wrote to him a few weeks ago." Jill produced the letter from her bag and passed it over. Astrid read it, twice, then looked up.
"Are you sure about this, Jill, is it really what you want? I know we haven't talked much about Oliver but I got the impression you wanted to do this by yourself." She waved her hands theatrically around the orchard, "Did he phone to say he wanted to patch things up and everything would be OK. Fairy tale endings, and all that stuff?"
"Give me a bit of credit please! I know there can be no *Happily Ever Afters*, life isn't like that, but I think there could be, *Better Than Things are now,* for the 3 of us. Maybe, just maybe, I will be able to be a small part of Oliver's and l Jason's lives. He said he would like to build bridges too and we've agreed he will get in touch so we can talk. It's a start at least. Everything is so up in the air, I need to ground them somehow. I don't want Oliver to grow up thinking I just abandoned him."
"Well I wish you everything you wish yourself Jill and far, far more. Just keep in touch and don't forget to send me a copy of the newsletter. I can't offer advice or judgement; I've ruined too many things with my big mouth throughout my life by doing that. So, unless you want to talk about it, maybe we should wait and see what happens. There's no earthly point in ifs, buts or maybes at this point is there?"

"No, there isn't and I'll keep you in the loop, as they say. As for the letter from Crete, I'm going to have to get my finger out. I'd like to be able to enclose the first one with Christmas cards for friends and

180

Ruth Manning

family, so you may get one before next year. You will let me know how things go for you though, won't you?"

Astrid said she would and after finishing the wine they had poured, they went into Alikianos, for a traditional Greek meal.

*

The place was crowded and a number of Greek families were at tables with between 10 and 20 people gathered round. The waiter showed them to a small table on the outskirts of the lively groups and said, in perfect English, "I hope this will be all right. There is to be a bouzouki band tonight and there was a large wedding earlier today in the mountains. We are very busy."

They both assured him they were fine and he handed over the menus. "We have some specials tonight, would you like me to tell you what they are?" They both nodded and he continued. "We have wild boar in tomato sauce, rabbit in traditional tomato sauce and local goat cooked in mountain herbs and rich tomato sauce." With this information duly imparted, he went to fetch the iced water and glasses.

"Apparently tomato sauce is the order of the day then," Jill laughed. "Actually I quite fancy the wild boar, I've had it here before and it's delicious." The waiter returned with the water and glasses and they were about to order, when Jill heard her name being called out from the other side of the courtyard. The restaurant had a large outdoor eating area with a full vine canopy and beautiful, subtle lighting. It was a little breezier than earlier in the week but they both brought cardigans to compensate for this. Looking round, Jill saw Lefteris waving madly at them. "Come here, come here. You must join us. Come. Come." He was pushing through the crowded tables. Small children were running in and out screaming and laughing, and waiters, with trays packed with steaming meals held high above their shoulders, were artfully dodging them. He arrived at the table just as the waiter was placing the water down. He spoke in an excited and raised voice with the waiter who nodded and slapped him on the back. The upshot was, within minutes they found themselves being dragged across to a large table with about 15 people sat around it. The waiter added another table, after clearing a space, and they found themselves surrounded by friendly faces. Sofia kissed them both and welcomed them. She explained that their friends from Athens were returning home in the morning, and so they were having a meal with them and other family members.

Oliver's Branch

The waiter stood by patiently while introductions, kisses and handshaking were exchanged, then, with his order pad in hand he asked Jill and Atsrid if they were ready to order. Apparently though, this was not to be. "They will eat with us." Lefteris said, giving the waiter a friendly if rather exuberant push, which almost sent him reeling into the musicians stand, such was his force. "We have many things and if you want anything else you must ask. You are our guests."

The waiter took his leave and after the two women sat down, Sofia pointed out various plates on the table. "The oval plates are the taverna specials" she said. "Stella, who owns this place is a wonderful cook and makes some very special dishes. See, there is wild boar in tomato sauce and rabbit too. Her sauces are famous throughout the valley...Eat, please eat."

The table was heaving under the number of dishes filled with various meats and vegetables, as well as Greek salads, tsatsiki, hummus, olives, baskets full of fresh bread and far more besides. The wine was flowing and once the band started to play, the atmosphere was electric. Laughter, back-slapping and a general overall feeling of celebration and happiness filled the air.

Both the women whiled away a delightful few hours and ate far more than either of them thought possible and medically would have dieticians positively swooning with apoplexy... but eventually they felt they had to excuse themselves. Jill explained to them about Astrid's early morning flight.

"You cannot go before you have danced with us though," Lefteris said and without further ado he was up and making his way over to the lead bouzouki player. He shouted something to him, paid some money and returned, with a large grin on his handsome, expressive face. "They will play for us after the next table has danced. I have dedicated the dance to you, Astrid, along with our friends, wishing you all a safe journey home and a swift return."

Astrid was a little dubious and whispered, "I have no idea how to do Greek dancing Jill, I'll just watch."
"No you won't, they would see it as a total insult. Just follow the children; they do the basic steps without any of the frills attached." Astrid meekly followed the rest of the table and joined hands with Sofia on her left and Jill on her right. Within minutes she was well into the steps, following the moves of a tiny girl, no older than five, who was dancing opposite her. Jill watched her friend swaying confidently to the music, her feet keeping up with the basic steps of the dance. She looked brown and confident, her hair shiny and sleek and there was a twinkle in her eyes. Crete had once again worked its

182

Ruth Manning

magic on another of her friends. Jill prayed she too, would be touched with some of the same magic, in the very near future.

They arrived home at just after one in the morning. They needed to be at the airport for eight, so hugging each other, they said goodnight. "What a perfect end to something which has been so amazing. Thank you so much Jill, for everything."
Jill looked into her friends eyes and smiled. "Good night Astrid. Somehow I think it's more the place and the people here you should thank, not me."

With that they retired to their rooms, exhausted but satiated and happy.

Oliver's Branch

Thirty eight.

Jill awoke early to the sound of rain beating down on the carport roof. Mitsou was right, this certainly would not be a beach day. They had agreed they would both get up at 6.30 and leave just after seven. Jill's clock showed it was just after six. She had something to do and this was the only time she would have, before Astrid's imminent departure. She retrieved the two white stones she had put in her beach bag, found super glue, an indelible marker and a small box then sat down with it all, at the kitchen table. The box contained tiny diamond-like gems in ascending sizes. They once belonged to her father and she could remember, as a small child, how intrigued she had been by them. She remembered spending hours arranging them on his work bench in complete awe. She could not imagine what he used them for and asked him. "Ah Jill. These are magic gems. When I make little boxes or jewellery caskets I always try and put one in each. It brings the owner luck. Have a look at the jewellery box I made for you, when you were born. See if you can find one." Later, Jill picked up the ornate, padded box with its domed top and examined it closely. At first she found no sign at all, but on closer examination she discovered one of the larger gems, in the top left inside corner. It formed the middle of a tiny, decorative silver daisy, embossed in the lining. From then on it became a 'trade mark' of so many of his little gifts and was their secret sign.

She lifted up one of the stones and assessed the size of the hole in the middle of it. She thought most of the pebbles would have some defect, but this was not the case. Finding just two took her quite a while. She picked out a gem which looked as if it would sit snugly in the hole, then put a tiny drip of super-glue in the hollow. Carefully, with tweezers, she placed the glinting crystal in the hole. It fitted perfectly and looked as if it had always been there. She repeated the operation, this time picking a slightly larger gem, again it fitted exactly. She left them to dry for a few minutes, while she put on the kettle, let Dyson out and collected a small velvet tie-string purse from her bedroom. It was deep crimson and had belonged to her mother. Sure the gems were well set, she then wrote on the back of the first stone, *Happiness* and on the second *Friendship*, in a neat italic hand. She blew on them until the ink was dry and then deposited them in the small purse. Mission accomplished she placed the purse in her handbag and made a fresh pot of strong, aromatic coffee. Then she went upstairs to get washed and dressed. She was just pouring herself a coffee when she heard the distinctive clumping of a suitcase being dragged down the front steps and wheeled to the

Ruth Manning

carport. A few moments later Astrid came down into the kitchen looking fresh, if slightly damp, ready for the journey ahead.

"Phew, I don't remember my case being so heavy when I arrived. I've put it by the car. The coffee smells wonderful." Jill put the toast she had just made on the table, plus a pot of her own, home-made marmalade, and a large mug of coffee. They ate in silence listening to the rain beating down outside.

After clearing up and a final walk around the house, to make sure Astrid hadn't left anything behind, they headed to the car. The rain was torrential. Heading out of the carport, Jill had to stop to let Michalis, the 90 year old donkey man, go slowly by, shouting and cursing at the poor beast in his shrill voice. The two women looked on in amazement. The old man was sheltered by an enormous, brightly coloured beach umbrella with the words *Life's a beach and then we die!* printed in bold colours across the back. The donkey could just see the road ahead but the only sign of its rider was a pair of legs, the rest of him was totally enveloped by the umbrella.

"Well, there's something I never thought I'd see," said Astrid, just before they turned onto the main road out of the village, which was like a deep running river. This in itself was a complete change from the dusty, dry roads of the past six months but what made it all the more surreal were the oranges floating and bobbing on the surface, cascading down the road in the torrent. "... or that" she added, watching the oranges continue their journey, towards the next village.

The roads were a nightmare but they managed to arrive in good time for check-in and the airport was all but empty. After checking-in Astrid was ready to go. Jill fumbled around in her bag and brought out the scarlet purse. "Here's a small leaving gift. Maybe in the years to come you will be able to add more. Take care and have a great time in Athens. Give Barry my love. I hope the weather improves over the next few days, or drowned rats come to mind."

Astrid pulled open the strings and shook the two stones into her palm. She looked at them carefully, the little gems twinkling in the halogen lights overhead. After reading the two words, she turned to Jill with tears in her eyes. "What a great leaving present and yes, you can guarantee I will be adding to them as often as I can. Thank you so much, I'm going to miss you and this beautiful island so much. I'm actually quite pleased it's raining, it sort of fits my mood." They said their goodbyes and Astrid disappeared up the flight of

Oliver's Branch

stairs to the departure lounge. Jill walked slowly back to the car and arrived home before the village clock struck nine o'clock.

Once again the house was very still and the village completely devoid of people or activity. Even the two kafeneions had closed their doors and lights were twinkling inside.

Jill tidied up and then felt at a loss as to what to do next. She decided, even though it was another month until she sent Christmas cards, she would continue with the 'Letter from Crete.' So far she had explained the visits of her two friends and some of the happenings in the village, but she hoped to have enough to fill it. She somehow couldn't imagine what would be noteworthy over the next month if this was how winter presented itself. She had just started to write up about Michalis and his umbrella, when there was a knock on the door. Outside, Irini stood waiting patiently with a supermarket carrier bag over her head and a plate in her hand.

Jill opened the door. Irini shook herself off like a big old dog and took the carrier bag off her head. "It's raining" she said, as she walked down the steps and lowered herself into a chair. "I have brought you some crepes. They have ham, cheese and bacon in them. I made them myself."
Jill thanked her and put the produce in the fridge, knowing Dyson would enjoy them later. She reminded herself to keep a check on how much of Irini's culinary delights she gave him, he was putting on weight.
"Thank you so much, now I won't have to cook today," she lied.
"Would you like a cup of tea?" Irini accepted and Jill busied herself, putting some sticky cakes on a plate and making the tea. Then she sat down next to Irini and asked, "Any news?"
"It's raining" Irini said again. "It is winter now and already I feel ill, my back is hurting." With this she put on a pitiful expression and held both her hands at the base of her spine. Jill asked if there was anything she could do and miraculously Irini produced a bottle from her pocket. "This is made with stinging nettles and is very good for back pain." Jill had the brief memory of the old woman chasing Jason around the orchard to whip him with a giant handful of nettles, a distant recollection, a lifetime ago.
"Do you want me to rub it in your back?" Jill asked tentatively. Before she finished the sentence Irini was standing in front of her, skirt hitched over her head, enormous knickers covering her equally enormous backside. Jill applied the lotion to a cacophony of "Ooohs" and "Ahs" emitting from her neighbour. When she finished applying it and massaging it in, she stopped and was just putting the lid on

186

Ruth Manning

the bottle as Irini gestured at her back again. "More, more. It is very good. It feels better already."
Half an hour later Jill said her arms were getting tired and Irini, begrudgingly, pulled down her skirt. She stayed another half hour explaining to Jill the problems experienced by locals in surrounding villages, who were being burgled on a regular basis. "It is the foreigners who come to pick the olives. There is no work this year; the olives are small and very late. They have no money for bread and so they steal."
Jill was aware of this problem and assured her neighbour she would make sure to lock up the house securely, whenever she went out. Finishing her second cup of tea, the old woman said her goodbyes and hobbled painfully up the stairs, through the gate and across to her own house.

Jill smiled and went to write up this little incident in the newsletter. The rain had abated but not stopped and it was getting darker by the minute. The beautiful mountains were hidden by a foreboding covering of thick black cloud. It was cold in the house. This was the first time Jill had felt cold here since she and Jason visited the winter before. Luckily there was a half-full tank of diesel for the central heating and she switched it on. The radiators gurgled and clunked, it felt a bit like being in a submarine 1,000 feet under the sea, but within half-an-hour, after Jill had bled all the radiators the house was cosy and warm. There was a large open fire in the upstairs living room, but she needed to get some more wood. The last occupier left some but it would only last a few days with the big fire. She made a note to ask Lefteris or Stelios where she could get some, the following day.

Having heated herself an ample portion of chicken wings she decided she would call it a day. It was nearly six in the evening and she would watch whatever was on TV, or if there was nothing worth her while, she would find a DVD, and watch that instead.

TV offered her a rerun of *So you think you can dance*, *Knight Rider*, *Bay Watch* or *The X files*, not exactly what she felt like watching, so instead she opted for a DVD and chose *Ghost*, which she loved. Cuddled down on the settee munching chicken wings and singing away to 'Unchained Melody,' which always made her feel slushy. When her mobile informed her she had an incoming text message she was jolted out of her romantic indulgence. Communication had been somewhat sluggish for a while so she had no idea who it was.......

187

Oliver's Branch

The text was from Jason.... *"Hey Jill, will it b ok if I ring u tomoz about 2 ur time? Got the day off so it would be good 2 tlk?! Jason x"* She sat reading and rereading the message, the pit of her stomach felt hollow, but she also felt euphoric. Jason had thought it through and he wanted to talk. She was unsure which way the conversation would go; it was after all almost 5 months since she last saw him. She could still remember him standing at her bedside waiting for her to sign Oliver over to him. *"We can still work this out if you want to. I still love you, you know that."* But she had signed without acknowledging him and he had left without another word.

"That would be great. I'm really looking forward to it," she sent back, then after sitting quietly for a few moments, she turned the DVD back on and rewound to the start of the melody. She sang along all the way through to the end, without skipping a word or a beat.

Thirty nine.

Jill awoke at almost half-past-ten the following morning. Dyson was whacking a kitchen cupboard with his tail and barking half-heartedly. She could vaguely hear a male voice outside calling her name. She dressed quickly, calling out to wait a minute. When she opened the kitchen door, Stelios was standing outside. Dyson dashed past him into the orchard. It was no longer raining and there was a watery sun trying to shine through. "Good morning, Jill, how are you?"

Gathering her thoughts she replied she was fine though obviously she had overslept. "It is of no importance. This is your life, you do as you please, but with all the rain last night, I thought you may need my help. It was cold and I see you have very little wood. I can help you." He sat down under the pergola and lit a cigarette. Jill put the kettle on and then went to join him.

"I sometimes think you Cretans can read my thoughts. I was going to ask either you or Lefteris how I went about buying wood, and here you are.."

"So help is at hand. I have a friend who will sell you a ton of *dry* wood for €120. This is a good price and will at least start you off for the winter. I have also been asked to help grub out a very large orange orchard with a mini digger. The owner will pay me with the wood. He has no fire, I have no fire, but I think I will be able to do it in 2 days. He would pay me €30 a day. I estimate there will be at least another ton, ton and a half of wood. I will sell you this for my wages, €60. Then you will have enough wood for the winter. What do you think?"

Still not completely awake Jill looked at him a little vacantly. "Go and make coffee and then I will explain it all to you again." Stelios laughed and sat back in his chair. Jill went and made a pot of steaming hot coffee and took it back up with cups and a plate of biscuits. Once she was settled he repeated the whole scenario. Although Jill was having to budget to keep within her means she knew this was a good deal. She had talked to other people who had bought wood locally and they paid as much as €160 a ton. The maths was simple enough even for her somewhat befuddled brain. She told him she thought this would be great and would there be delivery dates. She would need to get the money from the bank. Here every transaction appeared to be paid with cash.

He explained the orange wood could not be cut until the trees dried out a little, but it was not expected to rain again for about a week. His friend could deliver tomorrow and he would fetch the orange

Oliver's Branch

wood at the end of the week. It was a done deal. It also meant Jill would have to get some cash out, but she decided to wait until after Jason called, to do this.

She sat with Stelios in a comfortable silence, while they relaxed, drank their coffee and smoked. Cigarettes were cheap here and there were none of the stringent EU laws in place about non-smoking areas, or if there were, Jill had seen little evidence of them. The Greeks in the villages totally ignored them.

Stelios broke the silence. "It is also a good time to fertilise your trees. We use something called *Leeplasma*, which is €30 a bag. I think one bag will be enough for all your trees. Shall I bring some over and do them for you?"

Jill felt incredibly naïve and stupid. She would have been so lost without this lovely man's guidance. She wondered how she could repay him, especially as he constantly refused money when she offered it.

"That would be great, thanks so much, but you must let me pay you."

"Pah." he snorted, "I enjoy your company, I do not want your money." He drained his cup and got up to leave. "Thank you for the coffee. I will see you tomorrow then at about 9.00 am with my friend and the wood. Maybe you could clear an area under the trees for it? We will stack it under the balcony together." With these words he jumped over the wall, climbed into his car, and drove off. Jill had no idea how you stacked wood and looking at the area he had pointed out to clear, decided she would do this later in the day. She wasn't in the mood quite yet. (Subconsciously she wished Jason was here to do it. He was very fit and enjoyed manual work... she pushed the thought to the back of her mind.)

By the time she finished breakfast it was just before eleven. After tidying away, Jill sat down to make a list of things she had neglected over the last 7 weeks due to the upheaval and unexpected company.

She had been very lax with communication to her children and friends and decided to catch up with some of them early in the evening. OTE, the Greek telephone company, was expensive and unreliable. Maybe when she was more settled she would look into other options, but at the moment it was better than nothing.

The house was already looking dusty and uncared for, so she jotted down , 'do domestic stuff.' She hated housework, but in her new life she had no choice but to take responsibility or become slovenly and lazy. She knew this was not as an option. Then, raising her eyebrows, she suddenly realised it was pointless just writing it

down, action was needed. Rooting out all her cleaning materials plus mop and bucket she went upstairs and starting at the front door, dusted and wiped anything which didn't move, every surface and sill, every ornament, every shelf. She cleaned the windows and the shutters, cleared the cobwebs with her feather duster, amazed to find it could be adjusted. (She brought it with her from England, but this was the first time she had ever used it...) Then, finally, she mopped the floor. She had worked without a break for nearly two hours, when she heard the village clock strike one and was amazed at how much she had accomplished. Everywhere looked clean and shiny. She vowed to do the cleaning on a weekly basis from now on - *yeah, right!*

There was just over an hour to kill before Jason phoned. She wasn't hungry, her stomach was a mass of butterflies, so she pottered around putting away all the cleaning paraphernalia then took her book onto the balcony and sat down to wait and listen.

The sun had warmed everywhere up and it was calm and restful. Her mind meandered down memory lane and she allowed herself to remember all the good times she and Jason had shared. They loved the Battle Proms, air shows, theatre visits, cinema, and meals out. All the things couples enjoy doing together. He always had the ability to make her laugh and their conversation never seemed to dry up. They both worked hard and played hard for over six years, before things begun to crumble and fall apart. How she wished she could turn back time and respond to everything in a totally different way.

The phone rang, interrupting her thoughts. Suddenly her heart was beating so fast she thought her whole chest cavity would explode. She took a deep breath, stood up and went in to answer the call.

*

"Hello," she said nervously, "Jason, is it you?"
There were a few strange gurgling noises and then an infant-like chuckle on the end of the phone. She knew immediately, without being told, it was Oliver. "Hello, my little boy.." she heard herself whispering as if in the distance. "You sound very happy. I bet your dad's tickling you to make you laugh like that."
"He certainly is..." came the familiar voice she knew so well. "Oliver, that voice on the other end of this phone is your mum. Say hello."
More chuckling followed and Jill was at a complete loss for words. Tears were streaming down her face and yet instinctively she knew

Oliver's Branch

things were going to be all right. Jason had introduced her to her son and the call was filled with laughter and expectation. "Hi Jill, well what do you think? Your first talk with your son and he understood every word."

He then went on to describe Oliver to her and tell her all about his progress. He was blond with blue green eyes and a turned up nose. "Just like yours" Jason said. He was proving to be a very easy baby and slept all through the night from a very early age. Jason's family spoilt him rotten and Jason had managed to hire a wonderful young girl to cover the times he was not around. He answered all Jill's questions. Had there been any problems in the early stages? Was he starting to crawl? Could he eat with a spoon? The list went on and on. All the while she was conjuring up images of her other two children, trying to form a mental picture of what he might be able to do at 5 months and what was impossible. She had forgotten so much about babyhood and its many stages. She was sure teething came later, so she didn't ask about it. Jason answered everything without any hesitation, sounding like the proudest father ever. After about twenty minutes in this vein, Jason changed tack.

"Anyway, I promise I'll put some photos in the post today, how about you tell me some of the news about life in the village. Is Irini driving you mad yet and how's my mate Lefteris? What have you been up to and are you settling in?"

Jill filled him in on some of the news. The arrival of the furniture, visits from Sarah and Astrid, what a Godsend Stelios was. She told him about the summer and how winter was fast approaching. How she was getting some wood for the fire the following day. She asked him the best way to light the fire, about the immersion heater, which was incredibly efficient as the water was always piping hot. He listened and answered all her questions. They laughed about her lack of practical understanding and basic survival instincts.

They talked about Jason's other family and Jill told him all the news from Nick and Grace. She was surprised to learn Grace had kept in regular contact with Jason. She knew all about Oliver and if she spent Christmas in the town she would be visiting them. She had never said a word about any of this to Jill.

It was over an hour later when Jason wound the dialogue down. "Anyway, Jill, this is my mobile and I dread to think what it's costing me. I'll try and work out one of those cheaper packages for phoning abroad, that is, if you want me to phone again."

"Of course I do. We've so much to catch up with and there's so much I want to say. I haven't even started to explain myself and my actions. I really do want to put things right, Jason. I can always phone you too, would that be OK?"

Ruth Manning

"As long as it's not one of your garbled late-night calls after one too many glasses of wine, it'd be fine. Don't forget I know you too well! Anyway, I'm taking Oliver for a long walk now. It's dull and grey but not raining. I was thinking of getting him a dog, but I've decided to wait until he's older, what do you think?"

Jill was immensely touched. He had asked her opinion and somehow it felt as if a brick was crumbling out of the invisible wall which had grown between them. In fact a number of bricks seemed to have shifted and the foundations felt as if they may be less secure. Maybe there was a chance for them all, just maybe.

"I agree with you," she replied "and I'll text before I ring. If I phone about seven in the evening, your time, will you be able to talk?"

"Make it eight and we have a deal. Oliver will be bathed and in bed by then, so I'm often at quite a loose end." They said their goodbyes and Jason tickled Oliver again making him chuckle into the receiver. "Goodnight, my little boy. Sweet dreams" she whispered and then with one final goodbye to Jason, they both hung up.

Oliver's Branch

Forty.

Jill managed to get through the rest of the day in a daze. She went into Alikianos for some money from the cash-point. She took Dyson for a walk and she then cleared the area in the orchard Stelios had pointed out, for the wood.

She was invited over to Mitsou's home for a meal, but declined, saying she was very tired and wanted to have an early night. After preparing herself a pizza, she shut all the shutters and once the pizza was cooked, took it upstairs, to munch on while she made a few phone calls. Dyson, fed and satiated, was settled down happily on his bed. Outside darkness was closing in.

She rang Nick first, as she had not heard anything from him in a while. He answered but asked if she could phone back later, as he was just going to have a bath. Jill smiled to herself. There was only a shower at the house and so she hadn't luxuriated in a bath for about four months. She would see this first winter through, but, funds permitting would install a bath next year.

Next she rang Grace. She decided not to mention anything about her talk with Jason. She would probably find out anyway. The phone went through to voice-mail. Jill left a brief message, asking if everything was OK and to ring back, any time.

Next on the list was Sarah, but somehow she felt the ball was in Sarah's court and didn't ring her. She knew when her friend was ready and her plans were in place, she would be in touch. If she was coming for Christmas Jill knew she would let her know in plenty of time.

Jill sat for some time thinking about Christmas. How different it was going to be this year. She hoped Sarah didn't change her mind about coming. Spending the festive season alone seemed so sad and so depressing. She made a resolution to put up some decorations and then remembered the pomander balls she used to make at school. All you needed was a fresh orange (no problem there) and lots of cloves, which you pressed into the orange until you had covered it completely. Once the orange was dried out it gave off a lovely fragrance, which Jill always found very Christmassy. She had always given her mother one, at least until she had her own children, after which life became far more demanding and free time was a luxury. She decided she would make some as presents for

194

Eleni, Sofia and Sarah plus a few for around the house. All she needed to do now was find cloves.

She decided to try John next, hoping furtively she'd have a bit more luck. His phone was answered on the fourth ring. There was a lot of laughing and background noise. "Hello, TGC headquarters.." he said, with merriment in his voice.

"Hello, John. It's Jill. Am I calling at an inconvenient time, it sounds quite lively there?"

"Jill! How lovely to hear your voice, we were just talking about you." He went on to explain how TGC now held a monthly end of month knees-up. Since left it appeared more and more people had become involved in the venture. It was now well established as a social base for all the elderly people in the area who were interested in helping in some way. The parties were held at his house as it was 'a tad warmer' than the Garage Club's premises.

"Anyway dear, everyone wants to talk to you. I've got them queuing up here. I'll pass you over and then talk to you afterwards..."

Lotty was first on the line. "Jill. How wonderful of you to phone, tonight of all nights. We have a few more TGC members now and we were just talking about you. We were going to ring you at Christmas to say hello. We are so busy. You wouldn't believe how well we are doing and we are all so much more competent. Before I go on, how are you, love? Are you living your dream, at last?"

Jill told her a little about the last few months, the fact she was happy and settling in and all was well, then steered Lotty back to her news.

"Well, we have been discussing the idea of coming out to see you next year. I know we're all a bit long in the tooth. But we've decided we all want a holiday and we all want to see you. Voila! Combine the two and what do we get? I've been looking on the Easyjet website and the earlier we book, the cheaper it is. Do you know it could work out cheaper getting a return to Crete than it does a return train fare to Glasgow, not that I have any interest at all in going to Glasgow, God forbid. We've done loads of research and we reckon the best time for us weather-wise is about mid-May. We can book in to a small complex, quite near you, with diddy little chalets and it even has a pool. What do you think of the idea?"

Jill was taken aback. She could not believe they all really wanted to travel so far to see her, she felt very honoured. In her mind's eye she saw the five on them in their 'swimwear' lying on sunbeds, guzzling G&T's. She said she thought it was a brilliant idea and of course, they were welcome any time.

"Well then, I will look into the details and let you know what's going on. Give me your e-mail address." Jill explained she didn't have one,

Oliver's Branch

much to Lotty's amazement. "Then I'll just have to use a very outdated land-line telephone, won't I? Now then, I must pass you over. Everyone's prodding me and raising their eyebrows. Goodbye, dear. I'll be in touch."

Millie and Tom shared the receiver and it was quite difficult to follow the three-way conversation. The gist of it seemed to be they were both well and having a marvellous time with all their friends. Both of them were really excited about visiting her. "Can you get Ponds Cold Cream over there by the way?" Millie asked as they were saying their goodbyes. When Jill said she wasn't sure (being an Astral exponent herself, but she didn't say this,) Millie exclaimed, "Well then I will be sure to bring a value-size pot with me."

Frank talked about his constipation problems, once the greetings were over, and the fact he now had glaucoma, but otherwise he was doing fine. "Well, I'll get all the news from the others. I'll tag along with them if I'm still alive. God willing." The phone was then handed back to John.

"So, what do you think of the plan? You know we've all been so busy with TGC we haven't had time to spend our pensions, so we have plenty of money to spare, as well as the money you insisted we keep." He went on to ask how the newsletter was coming and her plans for Christmas. She informed him all was going well and she was hoping Sarah would be with her over Christmas.

"I will make sure we give you a call dear, don't you worry. The old marbles are still all there, even if I'm slowing down a bit. Use a stick now, just so I always get a seat on the bus! Anyway we are all going over to Millie and Tom's on Christmas day, so we're looking forward to it. The shops are ridiculously busy already and I'm fed up with the sound of bloody Christmas music. It's not even December yet. Now I better shut up. I sound like Victor Mildew, or whatever his name is."

After having promised they would keep in touch, John hung up, just as someone in the background could be heard singing the opening bars of "We'll meet again...."

The whole call had really raised her spirits and along with Jason's earlier in the day she felt as if she was, even if only obliquely, at least back in the loop of other people's lives. She decided to spare any further strain on her OTE bill for a while, so sent a text to Nick hoping he was enjoying his bath and all was well, then finished off her now somewhat cold pizza. After a quick shower she cuddled down in bed with a good book.

196

Ruth Manning

Forty one.

Knowing Stelios and his friend were arriving early with the wood,
Jill was up and ready when they arrived at just after 9.00. The maxi
was overflowing with logs and Jill could not envisage using it all up
in one winter. The two men unloaded it and after Manolis had been
paid, drunk a quick raki with a beer chaser and had a good look
round the orchard, he left, with a wave and a smile.

Stelios was true to his word and after unloading the Leeplasma, he
deftly threw large handfuls of it around the base of each tree. When
he had finished he showed Jill how they would stack the logs and
together it took almost an hour to move them, but when it was done
it looked very rural and organised. Jill was pleased with the result
and having played a part in it. Stelios produced a bottle of village
wine and some cheese pies from his maxi and they both sat under
the pergola, chatting about the price of olives, how badly things were
going for Greece and the EU generally, whiling away another hour.
Jill paid Stelios, including a little extra, which he left on the table,
as he jumped into his maxi and disappeared.

Throughout the remainder of the week the weather held. Jill
managed to find packets of cloves in the local supermarket and
whiled away many a happy hour making pomander balls. She hoped
to have about 8 made by Christmas. She also started making
individual, handmade Christmas cards and wrote more of the
newsletter. She felt she would be on task to have everything ready to
post by the end of November, and the gifts completed for her local
friends, the following month.

Stelios was true to his word and arrived with another maxi full of
wood, all beautifully cut and ready for stacking, on the Friday. They
neatly piled all of it on the other side of the door and there wasn't a
spare inch for any more. "This will see you through the winter, but
next year I think you should have a somba upstairs instead of an
open fire. It is far more efficient. We will have a look around in the
spring, if you want to."
Jill would never have thought of anything this practical, but it
immediately made sense. She agreed she would have one fitted next
year. "I will be able to do it for you, without you having to pay the
fortune they ask for fitting. I fitted one in the kafeneion up the road,
and even if I say so myself, I did a very good job. I will be around
next month, but I think there may be some olive picking I must do .
If you need me you have my mobile. I am never far away."

Oliver's Branch

Jill asked him what he would be doing for Christmas and he said staying at home. Home for Stelios was a tiny house, with only one room, in the middle of an orange orchard. Although he had running water and a fire it was very basic, but he explained he was happy there. "It belonged to my grandparents and one day I will maybe extend it and make it more of a home. For now it gives me all I need."

When he left, Jill again marvelled at how content these people were with so few of the modern day comforts. Although the life she was living was far removed from the trappings and ease of life in England, she still had everything she needed to be comfortable. She had about a hundred times more facilities and comforts than Stelios. She was truly grateful.

On the last day of October she found a large brown envelope in her PO box and immediately recognised the writing. She put it on the front seat unopened and only when she was seated under the pergola at home, with a glass of wine, did she venture to open it.

Inside was an envelope containing photographs, a travel guide for Crete and a large plastic bag full of tea bags! A note hastily written said only
"May you always have tea in the morning, a path to follow through the day and love to guide you..."

The photos were of Oliver.

Jill spread them out on the table then picked up one and looked at it closely. Oliver must have been a very new baby in this one; he was lying on a soft, fluffy blanket on the floor, sleeping peacefully. He was wearing a baby-blue romper suite with a large carrot on the front. He was absolutely perfect. She turned it over and saw a date 30th May. He had been just 2 weeks old. He had a mass of golden hair and podgy little hands. Turning some of the other photos over she saw they were all dated and so, looking at them again she played a game, trying to pick them up in the right order. Each picture saw a development she had missed out on. His eyes wide open and smiling into the camera, sitting on Jason's knee pointing at something, sitting up bolstered by pillows looking thoughtful and content. The more she looked at them the more amazed she was at her own stupidity and ignorance at having given away this beautiful child. *Her* beautiful child. She resolved to ask Jason if he would ever consider bringing Oliver over to meet her in the near future. She also knew she needed to talk to him again. With the photos strewn across the table like a mosaic, in a myriad of colours, she sent him a

Ruth Manning

text asking if it would be OK to ring in the evening, at about 8.00 English time. A text came back almost immediately. It would be fine and he was looking forward to it.

Although it wasn't cold, there was a definite chill in the air and so the beach was no longer an option. Still, the end of the third week in October wasn't bad for a final swim, she thought, remembering her final swim with Astrid. Without trips to the beach, there were a few hours in the afternoons when initially she felt at a bit of a loose end. She started to fill them by going for long walks with Dyson, sorting through some of the boxes she had looked through but not unpacked and keeping the house clean. She also began the mammoth task of unpacking all her doll's house furniture and miniatures and setting up house again, albeit on a much smaller scale.

She busied herself, while she was waiting to talk to Jason, by unpacking all the tiny furniture and attic paraphernalia she had built up over the years. As the light was beginning to fade everything was in place and the attic, at least, was restored to its original state. She was amazed at how quickly the time had gone with no interruptions, from Irini, or any one else.

It was just after seven when she finished what she was doing and went down to the kitchen to feed Dyson and make herself a snack. She was wondering what to do to while away the next three hours when she heard a thunk on the kitchen door. She opened it to Irini, leaning heavily on a broom handle with one hand and holding her back with the other. The thunk had been an orange she had lobbed at the door.
"Ooh Ruth, my back hurts so much. Will you give me a rub?"
Jill set about making a cup of tea as the old lady made her way slowly and noisily down the steps. From somewhere she produced the nettle oil and re-enacted the pulling up of her skirt over her head, then stood waiting expectantly, in all her glory. Jill obliged and massaged her back for a good half-hour, but this time it didn't seem to be relieving the pain. She was surprised when, instead of staying for a chat, her neighbour finished her tea and got up to leave. "Tonight, God is not with me. The pain is still there. I am going to go to bed and pray I am better by the morning."
By this point Jill was quite concerned and accompanied the old lady over to her house, helped her into her night dress and put her to bed. She sat with her for another hour, until she was asleep. She was still sighing and moaning but Jill had no idea what else she could do. Quietly shutting the front door, she went back home.

Oliver's Branch

She had been with Irini longer than she thought. It was 9.45pm. She poured herself a glass of wine, gave Dyson some TLC and then felt ready to make the call. She waited until 10.05. The waiting was almost unbearable and interminable. Her fingers were shaking as she punched in the numbers. Jason answered on the third ring.

"Hello! I've been waiting for your call. I presume you've received the photos. So tell me what do you think of *our son*?"

She was taken aback. He said *our son*, not; "my son" not, "the baby" not even just, "Oliver." He said "*our son*."

"I think he's perfect and although I know what you mean by his eyes and nose, I can see a lot of you in him too."

"Phew... Good thing too or I might have suspected the milkman. Being serious though, I want to pre-empt you, Jill. I know this is very early days and we have only talked once, which I don't think constitutes the building of an *entire* bridge, but I want to be totally honest with you. Since we talked I've been trying to put things in perspective. Suddenly my neatly established little domicile and single-parenthood seem a little crass and lacking a vital component.... YOU." Jill was about to interrupt, not wanting him to say anything or make any rash promises at such an early stage, but Jason continued, almost doggedly.

"Don't interrupt me, Jill. I need to say this and see how you feel. Just hang on OK? Right, I'm not going to suggest I up-sticks and take the next flight over to see you, that is totally unrealistic. You know the last thing you could ever describe me as is sentimental. But, and it's a BIG BUT, which depends entirely on you... What do you think of the idea of the two of us coming over next summer, for a visit?"

There was a silence on the line while Jill tried to weigh up her emotions. In one way it was everything she could have hoped or dreamed of, but somewhere deep inside she felt an element of disappointment. Next summer was at least eight or nine months away. Then she realised it was actually a sensible and responsible idea.

"My God, are you serious?" she asked trying to keep any disappointment out of her voice. "I mean, it's such a big step and I'm frightened that once I see him you won't be able to stop me wanting to be involved more, when you're back in England."

"I've thought about it long and hard, Jill. I've talked to my family and done a great deal of soul-searching and I feel it's Oliver's right to know his mother. More than that, I want to get to know you again too. I said something to you when you signed the papers at the hospital, after Oliver was born. Do you remember what it was?"

Jill whispered a quiet "Yes."

Ruth Manning

"Well, I know it's still the case. It was you who had to come to terms with your emotions and your decision and it was you who needed to make the first move. I must admit, I was getting disillusioned and worried when I didn't hear from you. But now I have. So, does it sound like a good idea?"

"It sounds amazing and yes it's more than I could have ever hoped for. What a stupid, selfish, ignorant bitch I've been. I'm so sorry Jason, I'm so sorry." With these words she burst into floods of tears and it was as if the past six months of locked away regret and emptiness were flowing away, like poison being released from her very core.

Jason tried to comfort her but soon realised this was cathartic and essential for Jill's ability to adapt and adjust to a future. A future where she was no longer an island. When she quietened he went on, "You've been without any emotional tie with Oliver too long. No man is an island and you've been suppressing emotions you probably never even knew you had. I think I understand, really I do. We'll take it slowly, Jill, I promise. If we agree to a couple of weeks sometime at the beginning of June, Oliver would be just over a year old by then, which would make things easier. Plus the weather wouldn't be too hot for him."

The irrational and compulsive part of Jill wanted to book a flight and just go back as soon as possible, but she knew in her heart Jason was right. They must take it slowly.

"It sounds brilliant and it will give you time to organise things. I agree completely with the plan and I'm amazed how well you seem to understand my emotions; although I shouldn't be really, you always could read me like a book."

They carried on talking well into the night. Jason told her stories about Oliver's first six months and also a little about work. It seemed the recession was hitting small businesses badly and his boss was concerned about the downward trend. It had been hinted at, more than once to Jason, that if things didn't pick up there may have to be redundancies. Jason was under no illusion about the precarious situation he was in. Jill asked him what he would do if the worst came to the worst.

"Well, I've got the money through from my share of Paparooni, so I wouldn't be completely destitute. By the way, the whole transaction went through amazingly smoothly. You had a good solicitor. Well done."

Jill was glad he had some rainy day funds and said as much. Then, with a yawn, Jason said he had to go, he had work in the morning and still had things to do before he went to bed. They said their good byes and just before he hung up he said to her, "Oneera glika, Agapi moo. Calee nichta."

Oliver's Branch

Before she could reply, the phone went dead. She whispered the words to herself. "Sweet dreams, my love, goodnight." She wrapped her arms around her body and sat very still, feeling wanted and loved in a way she hadn't felt for a long, long time.

Ruth Manning

Forty two.

It was only when she looked at the clock she realised she had been on the phone for over an hour. She decided it was time for bed. She was emotionally exhausted and physically drained. She let Dyson out for his last wander, feeling a cold draught blow in through the door. It was getting much cooler now. It wouldn't be too long before she would be lighting a fire. Dyson must have thought it was cold too as he didn't hesitate when he was called. Usually he would find some reason for just a few more sniffs before coming in. Tonight he came straight in and curled up on his bed.

Jill turned out the lights and went upstairs. She had just bedded down for the night, when her phone began to ring. She had no idea who it could possibly be. Everyone knew Greece was two hours ahead of England and it was gone half eleven, her time. Putting on her dressing gown, she went back downstairs and answered it.

"Jill, where are you? I'm in pain, I need the doctor. Please come NOW!"

It was Irini and she did, indeed sound in distress. Jill assured the distraught woman she would come over as soon as she was dressed, and amidst her neighbour's moans and cries, she hung up. She was across the road within five minutes. The front door was ajar and she went in. Irini's bedroom was off to the left and she could see the old woman lying flat on her back, without any covers on.

The wailing started afresh as she entered and it took some moments before Jill could silence her. After covering her up, she asked what she could do. "I must go to the hospital, now. Sweet Mary, I am going to die! You must take me, Jill. I must go now."
Jill had no idea what to do. She could get little sense out of the wailing woman and did not know how to contact either of Irini's sons. The village was silent. There were no lights on in any of the houses nearby. There was no choice; she would have to drive her to the hospital.

When trying to get her dressed proved a complete impossibility, Jill found a dressing gown and scarf and managed to wrap her up in them. After laying her down again, she went and picked up the car, stopping outside her neighbour's front gate. Once in the house again she found a bag and threw in Irini's wash bag and toothbrush, her purse and mobile phone from the kitchen table and a bible. Jill didn't know the system or what would happen at the hospital, but at

203

Oliver's Branch

least Irini would have a few bits and bobs if she stayed. With a gargantuan effort she managed to get the old woman's large bulk up and out to the parked vehicle, grabbing a blanket as she went. She locked the front door and put the keys in the bag. Once in the car she made her patient as comfortable as she could then started the drive to Mournies.

The twenty-five minute drive was noisy and very unnerving. Apart from the constant prayers to The Virgin Mary, calling out about her imminent demise and constant wailing, which was off-putting to say the least, Jill hated driving in the dark. She hated it enough in England, but here none of the village roads were lit and on the main road lights were intermittent. Eventually though, she arrived at the emergency department and leaving the wailing woman in the car, went in to ask for help. It took all her powers of persuasion to get the receptionist to acknowledge her, but eventually she looked up from the newspaper she was reading and told Jill to find a wheelchair and bring the patient in.

She located a wheelchair, after about five minutes of searching, and managed to place her charge into it in another five. At reception once more she was pointed to some double doors. On passing through them she found herself in a room full of white-coated men and women, eight beds, six of them in use and a general commotion of Greeks dashing between beds, getting glasses of water, cotton wool, cleaning cloths and every other type of health requirement they could lay their hands on. The patients were calling out instructions and Jill soon surmised these busy extras were the relatives of the patients.

A doctor (she assumed it was a doctor) pointed out one of the empty beds and within a few minutes Irini was lying on it. By this time she was wailing even louder than before.

Another doctor arrived remarkably quickly and within five minutes Jill found herself following a porter, towards X-ray. Because he was already pushing one trolley, Jill was directed to push the other, which seemed to have a mind of its own. *Never again,* she thought, as she strained to keep it rolling forward with some vague semblance of a straight line, *never again will I complain about unmanageable supermarket trolleys,* pushing the gurney was twenty times harder.

After what felt like a ten-mile marathon, the porter came to an abrupt halt and Irini was pulled into the X-ray department. Jill sat down to take a breather, while the porter disappeared leaving the

Ruth Manning

other patient, an old man of about eighty, with Jill. He was obviously in pain, but thankfully not nearly as verbal as Irini. She sat there, feeling totally at a loss as to what to do, a stranger in a foreign land. Luckily, she only had to wait about 10 minutes before her neighbour was wheeled out, complete with X-rays and, as if by magic the porter appeared (reeking of tobacco smoke) and wheeled the old man inside. As he did so, he looked at Jill and pointed back down the corridor.

Jill assumed she was meant to go back to the emergency ward and so she set off once again. Irini seemed to get some comfort from the X-ray folder and held it tightly to her chest, mumbling far more quietly than before.

Arriving back at the ward, sweating profusely from the exertion of pushing the trolley, Jill helped her patient back onto the bed. A young woman impeccably turned out in a white uniform arrived within minutes and took the old woman's pulse and blood pressure, as well as a taking blood sample. Then she was gone and Jill wondered what she was supposed to do next. Irini appeared to have gone to sleep so Jill was just about to creep out and have a crafty cigarette. Suddenly her wrist was grabbed in an iron like grip. She looked down to see Irini holding on to her for dear life.

"You mustn't leave me. Here the relatives do all the menial jobs. I would like some water." She pointed at what appeared to be the workstation. It was in fact where all the relatives were obviously going to get the basics which would keep their loved-ones comfortable. She went over to fetch the water and on her return was surprised to see the old woman, who only moments before was seemingly at death's door, chatting animatedly on her mobile phone. As she got closer she realised Irini was cancelling her social calendar, for the next few days at least. It was only when the doctor came to examine her that she grudgingly said her goodbyes and hung up. Jill stood at the end of the bed and waited patiently. When he finished he went up to Jill and in perfect English informed her the patient would be staying in hospital, as there was a serious problem with her kidneys. He asked if she was staying, she said no and suggested they look on her mobile for her sons' contact numbers. She then went and said goodbye, explaining the doctor would contact her sons, and then showed her what she had put in the overnight bag. After a great deal of kissing and thanks, Irini let Jill go. Within minutes she was back in the car and driving home.

Oliver's Branch

It was nearly two in the morning as she climbed upstairs and fell in to bad. Her last conscious thought was, *I wonder if you have dreams when you are in a coma brought on by sheer exhaustion?*

*

After what seemed like a maximum of half an hour's sleep, Jill woke to the ringing of her alarm clock. After the usual morning rituals, letting the dog out, making a fresh jug of coffee, washing and getting changed, anything to put off what she knew was the inevitable, she finally got in the car and headed for the hospital once more. She would have liked to have been able to phone and find out what the news was on her neighbour, but her Greek was not up to it.

She arrived at the hospital, parked the car and made her way to the main reception. After a great many questions, impeded by the fact Jill didn't know Irini's surname, the receptionist eventually located her. Jill was taken to the ward by an elderly gentleman, who appeared to just be passing through.

There was a drip set up at her bedside and a nurse was hovering at the edge of the bed. Jill walked up and asked, in Greek, how the old woman was. The nurse replied in perfect English, "She was operated on in the night. She had, how do you call them? Kidney pebbles. We used a new laser treatment and we believe it was successful. Now she will need rest and care for about a month, if not more. Are you a relative?"

Jill explained she was a just neighbour. After giving her a questioning glance, the nurse left. Jill was pleased to see her name was Dimitra, no Tracy or any other names ending in Y here.

Irini opened her eyes."Ah. I am alive and God is good. I have slept for a few hours. They woke me very early, after the operation and explained it to me. I am a lucky woman, the Virgin has helped me. Now, you must talk to my son, he has something he wishes to ask you." With these words she produced her mobile, dialled up a number, and passed it over. Jill hoped this conversation would explain why neither of her sons were at their mothers bed-side.
"It is my son Panayotis you will speak to." Irini informed her.
"Hello, mama?" answered the husky, male voice.
"Um no, it's her neighbour, Jill."
"Ah, Jill. Good. I have something I would like to talk to you about. I have had a long talk with my mother." He spoke very good English, much to Jill's relief and so she asked him what is was he needed to talk to her about.

206

"We have a problem!" he said. Jill could well imagine why, with a mother like Irini."Neither my brother nor I can come to help my mother for at least a month. Vasili, my brother who lives in Heraklion, is away in the States on business until the second week in December and I cannot leave my job in Athens, even for family illness, without giving a month's notice. This means my mother will have no one to look after her throughout November. I wondered if you would be willing to carry out this job. We will pay you of course. Does €600 for the month sound reasonable?"

Jill was tempted to ask if maybe somebody else in the village would possibly more suitable, but Irini, who obviously knew what was being said, once again grabbed Jill's hand in a vice like grip and was nodding at her with a huge smile on her face. "Erm, is your mother agreeable to this plan?" she said instead.
"Oh yes. It was her idea. She will be able to tell you what duties will need doing. We would be so grateful and I will come as soon as I can."
Jill agreed to talk through her 'duties' with his mother and then she handed the phone back to her. After a few minutes she said something to her son about a gift from heaven, blew him loud resounding kisses and hung up.

Over the next half hour she explained to Jill what would be expected of her. During her stay in hospital, Jill would be expected to bring in food, clean bed clothes and any other little things she may need. The food would be cooked by her good friend, Costulla, who also ran the bakery. It was already arranged. (My, my, she has been busy thought Jill, but kept her mouth shut.) Irini continued. Jill would obviously visit her every day while she was in hospital and bring her home when she was discharged. All she would have to do from then on was keep the house clean, do the washing, light the fire in the evenings and clean it out in the mornings. She would also do the shopping and keep her company in the evenings, if she had nothing to do. Jill's heart sunk, it sounded like a full time job and she wanted to get all her Christmas mail organised, finish the first newsletter and have the house decorated by the beginning of December, (not to mention the pomander balls she wanted to make.) She had a feeling Sarah would be with her around about the third week, so she could put decorating on hold and they could do it together. She also knew she had very little choice and at the end of the day, €600 was €600. Fate had dealt her this hand, for the next month at least and there was nothing she could do about it. She smiled confidently down at the old lady, prised the gnarled hand from her own wrist and said,

Oliver's Branch

"Of course I'll look after you, but you'll have to teach me how to light a fire."

An hour later, after having taken her to the toilet, picked up some light snacks from the cafeteria, straightened out her bed, combed her hair and made a list of things to bring from the house on her next visit, Jill was once again exiting the hospital. Irini's front door keys were now nestled in her bag.

Life on Crete was definitely never dull!

Ruth Manning

Forty three.

So, November became Irini's month. She was discharged from hospital a week after the operation. Jill was given first-aid training in cleaning wounds and changing dressings. In all her life she had never been involved in any form of 'health care' and although she found it hard, she soon became a regular little Florence Nightingale. Her mother, who was a nurse all her life, would have been proud of her she thought, on more than one occasion.

Jill cleaned right through Irini's house during this first week (so as *to cut down the risk of cross infection.)* She also put clean sheets on the bed, polished the windows and generally made the house spick and span, (as her mother would have said.) Irini was delighted when she returned. She hobbled in, leaning heavily on Jill as she went. "Why, it is like new" she remarked, as she glided a finger over the telephone table and checked for any dust Jill might have missed. *At least I won't have to go to the hospital every day anymore*, Jill thought to herself, as she desperately searched for a silver lining to her present predicament.

Life settled into a routine and although it meant Jill had to work around her 'duties,' she was still able to make Christmas cards and continue with the newsletter in the evenings. Irini was in bed (with her light out) by 8.30 each night, and then Jill was free to spend her time as she pleased. She explained the situation to Stelios, and he showed her the art of lighting a fire. He could not believe she had never lit one before. He also brought in all the wood most days and managed to keep Irini amused with stories from the village. She also had a great many visitors. At least three or four times a day one of the old yayas (grandmothers) would come and sit with her, drinking tea (made by Jill) and munching with toothless gums on jellied sweets or soft biscuits, which they usually brought with them.

Costulla did indeed provide food each day. She would beep the horn loudly at midday outside the house and Jill would go and fetch it from her. This she included in her daily bread round and was always in a hurry to move on, to supply bread to her many customers.

Conversations with Jason continued on a regular basis and became more and more comfortable. It was the next best thing to having him close to her physically. Although at times she longed to feel his arms wrap around her and a primal need to cradle her child, she knew she would have to be patient.

Oliver's Branch

Nick was now getting very excited about joining the army and was jogging daily. He was going to spend Christmas with some of his mates and they were hoping to paint the town red.

Grace had organised a stay with one of her new friends from university, who lived in a small village near Warrington, but she had said to Jill in a phone call, "It won't be the same though mum. I just want to spend Christmas with *you*. I want things to be how they used to be."

Jill remembered their last Christmas in England. After all the presents were unwrapped and before Grace headed out partying with a group of her old school friends, she had sat down at the table next to her mother, with tears in her eyes. "I know it's stupid, Mum," she said, "But why can't things stay the same? Christmas has always been a magical time and you've always made it so special. I don't want to grow up. What will I do without a Santa sack and our games of make-believe? It's just not fair..."

Jill went round the table and hugged her. "You know, sweetheart, it's all part of life's rich pattern. Yes, we have had brilliant, magical Christmases, and I hope one day you will be able to enjoy the wonder again with your own children. For now though, you must hold onto the memories and enjoy your Christmas celebrations with new friends. If the worst comes to the worst, just remember the good times, and smile."
"You're right. What is it you say, we all have to move on? It's just you're moving *so far away*. What will I do without you?"
"You'll become independent and fly, just as I always knew you would. I have given you wings and maybe one day Paparooli will become your home and your roots." Jill managed not to cry. Instead she wiped away her daughter's tears, kissed her on the cheek and told her how much she loved her. By the time the door bell rang and she skipped out to the taxi, Grace had put on her glad rags and make up and looked a million dollars, with not a tear in sight.

Returning to the present she said to her daughter, "It's not long now until the summer and hopefully you can spend it with me. I think there will be enough to keep you occupied and it will be a chance to recharge your batteries." She decided it was a good opportunity to tell her about Jason's visit, planned for the June. She was surprised when Grace said, "You lucky thing. I just so want to meet my little brother. I've kept in touch with Jason you know? I've got some great photos of Oliver. Did you know he's blond with eyes like you and a little snub nose just like yours."

Ruth Manning

Jill said she had received some photos too and explained about the phone calls and how well their friendship was going. "Wow, mum. You're such a dark horse. Who knows, maybe you two will get back together and live happily ever after." Jill refrained from saying she thought Grace had been a bit of a 'dark horse' too. She had said nothing about her phone calls and correspondence with Jason up until this exchange of news. Instead, she bit her tongue and repressed any kind of sarcastic retort.

"Anyway, I'll send your card and bits and pieces to your friend Nicole's house." She let out an involuntary snigger, and then continued, "Sorry, can't help thinking of the car advert whenever I say that name."
"Mmm, I can think of worse names ...... your middle name for one," Grace retorted. They laughed together. Jill had always hated her middle name and only under duress, would she say it at all.
"OK, let's not go there. Enjoy the rest of term and keep in touch."
They said their goodbyes and hung up. Jill felt as if another weight was lifted off her shoulders. Another secret had been shared. Everything was as it should be, once more.

Sarah phoned with an arrival date. She had talked with her husband and children and after initial exclamations about her obvious insanity, possibly due to premature dementia or even Alzheimer's, they reluctantly accepted her decision. Dennis said he would 'hold down the fort' and wanted to be given another chance. They agreed they would see how they felt about each other during the separation and hope the adage, *absence makes the heart grow fonder*, was indeed true. Everything was arranged for her sabbatical year at work and a bursary was in place from the medical council, to back her placement and training.
"So everything's been organised. I told the kids about Catherine and even showed them pictures of her, which Dennis took, just before she died. I can't understand why I didn't tell them years ago, it all seems so totally right. Anyway, I'll be arriving on the twelfth of December at 2:20 in the afternoon. I've booked with Easyjet to Athens and then Olympic to Chania. Does that sound OK?"
Jill said it sounded perfect and she would meet her at the airport. No more arriving unannounced and giving her a heart attack.
When Sarah asked if there was any other news, Jill told her about Jason and his planned visit with Oliver, the following June. Sarah was delighted. "So, at last you two are behaving like adults; and about time too. I can't wait to see the photos."

211

Oliver's Branch

When she hung up Jill felt excited and happy. At least now
Christmas would not be such a lonely event. She went over the road
to light Irini's fire. She was humming *The Holly and The Ivy.*

Astrid also got in touch. She and Barry enjoyed a fantastic week in
Athens. It had been like a second honeymoon. "Honestly, Jill..." she
had gushed, "You don't want to know how many times we had *it*
every night..."
"No, I don't!" Jill replied. "Far too much information. Remember, I've
been celibate for what seems like eternity. Anyway I'm glad you had
such a good time."
"Yes, it was amazing. Also, my redundancy is all going through and
Barry and I have started making improvements to the business. His
mum agreed to lend us some money until we are on our feet. Plus,
I'm booked into night classes from January, for the web-page design
course I wanted to do. More important than any of that though is
that Janine is really happy and settled back at home. She's great
and helps out with all the housework and the cooking. She's turned
into quite the Mother Hen. The baby's due mid-April, so I hope it's
not early and born on the first..."

Jill was relieved everything was working out so well. She may be a
cynic about happy endings but both her friends seemed to have come
a long way since she had last seen them. She told Astrid about the
developments with Jason and was pleased when she replied, "Well
now it's your turn for some happiness. Let's hope that island of yours
weaves some magic for you too. You deserve it." She promised to call
on Christmas Day and informed her there was a mystery present for
her, in the post.
"And don't you dare open it until Christmas Day..." she instructed
her.

John called from TGC. "I just wanted to see how things are, before
we are completely overcome by the Christmas rush." It appeared
business was flourishing. He was sure they were all looking and
feeling 15 years younger due to their interest, enjoyment and
involvement in the work. "We've even got a logo now. Lotty made it
up and we've even done a Christmas card, with it on, for all our best
customers."
He filled Jill in on all the news and she told him about Sarah's
arrangements; he was over the moon she would not be alone over the
festive season. "Then only 5 months and we will see you. We're just
waiting for confirmation of booking and then we're all organised. It's
all everyone talks about, when we have a free moment to natter,
that is."

Ruth Manning

Jill didn't mention Oliver or Jason. Although they were aware of the trauma she had been through, they were all very discreet. She knew she would tell them the whole story when she saw them and now she even had some photos, to show off her beautiful child.

All in all, by the time November came to an end, Jill felt as if she had achieved her aims, even with the added responsibility of caring for Irini. She had talked to her friends and family, finished her Christmas cards and the newsletter. She would send them off at the end of the first week in December when she finished writing in them and the envelopes were addressed.

Irini was on the mend and there had been no complications. The doctors congratulated her on her improvement. They said she must have employed a very good carer for her post-operative care. Everything had gone so well, she would be up and about in no time. They were unaware it had all been due to Jill.... and Irini never told them.

Panayotis was due to arrive on the 3rd of December. Jill was taking Irini to the airport to meet him. Jill had been too busy to enjoy the company of her neighbours or Lefteris and his family, but they popped in from time to time and said they quite understood the situation.

The only thing left to do was make the pomander balls and once she was freed of her 'duties' for Irini, she could think of no better way of whiling a way a few relaxing hours.

213

Oliver's Branch

Forty four.

On the 3rd of December Jill drove Irini to the airport to meet
Panayotis, as planned. Parking was easy as there were no tourists
around at this time of the year. The airport was virtually deserted.
Walking to the arrivals gate Irini's eyes lit up when she spotted a
wheelchair for disabled passengers to use. "Ah. I must sit in it....."
she said, and promptly did just that. Up until this point she had
been totally ambulant. Her wounds had healed well and were now
uncovered and totally dry. All the same, Jill made no comment, she
obediently pushed the chair to the allotted area. They waited
together in a comfortable silence, until passengers started emerging
from the plane, and then Irini, spotting her son, began to wave her
handkerchief wildly in the air. "Here Tacky. I am here. Look, your
mother is greeting you. Tacky, Tacky."
A well turned out man in his early forties looked over and waved
shyly. Coming alongside his mother he kissed her on both cheeks
and said in a quiet voice, "Do not strain yourself Mama. It is not
good for you."
Irini proceeded to grasp his hands and kiss them profusely. He just
managed to keep his balance and not land up in her lap as she
enthused, "Ah my son, my son. You are here, now I will be all right.
My sweet boy, my darling, sweet boy."
Jill wasn't too sure what was meant by this remark as Irini had been
perfectly fine beforehand. She decided it best to just keep quiet. "So
you are the Good Samaritan who has cared for my mother. I am
Panayotis, Tacky for short. It is a pleasure to meet you, at last."
They shook hands and the three of them began to move towards the
exit. Tacky replied to all his mother's questions. Yes, it was a good
flight. Yes, ate before he came. No, he was not worn out from the
journey. He asked her if she was using a wheelchair at home. She
replied no, but the journey to the airport was extremely tiring and
she needed to rest.

The journey back was dominated by questions from Irini and upon
their arrival home, Jill said her goodbyes and left them to it. She
had said maybe three words since Tacky's arrival.

Just as she was driving away, he approached the open window and
leant in. "I really can't thank you enough for all your help. I don't
know what I would have done without you." He handed her a plain
white envelope. "Here is the sum we agreed upon, with a little extra.
I am sure it has not been an easy month for you." He gave a knowing
smile, which said it all and continued, "I am hoping my brother and

214

Ruth Manning

his family will arrive tomorrow. We will have a family Christmas, all together."
Jill said good bye and drove into her carport. After letting Dyson out and throwing together a Greek salad, she went and sat under the pergola. She opened the envelope and counted the cash. Tacky had given her €750.

She munched away contentedly. The money would come in very useful, it would pay for the somba, with some left over. She was no longer responsible for Irini's care and more than anything else, she was a free woman once again.

*

By the time Sarah was due, Jill had succeeded in doing everything she had hoped to do. Christmas cards were posted, the pomander balls were finished and dried out quickly on the radiators, she even found some beautiful decorations which she added to them. Even if she said so herself, they looked beautiful, and smelt divine.

Stelios finished picking olives and spent a lot of time tidying up the orchard and the front of the house. "What are you doing at Christmas, Stelios?" Jill asked him one day, as they sat drinking a glass of wine together.
"I think it will be a quiet time. I have family in Piraeus, but I do not want to travel. Christmas here comes and goes in the blink of an eye. I think I will visit everyone at Pascha, Easter is our big celebration, but not now."
"Then you must come and have Christmas lunch with Sarah and me. I am hoping I can get all the things I need to cook a traditional English Christmas dinner. It would be lovely for us both to have more company."
Stelios tried to refuse, but Jill would have none of it and he eventually agreed. With plans made, he went out to fetch some wood and light the fire for her.
"You spoil me, you know. I should be doing that, not you." She said, smiling at him.
"It is the least I can do. For your Christmas present I will light you a very good fire. The fire to beat all fires."

Sarah called to confirm the arrival time of her flight. The days up to it flew by. Jill talked to Jason on numerous occasions, each time feeling their bond strengthening. He promised he would be in touch over Christmas, and was hoping his family would not make all the festivities too exhausting. He had never been one for the hype and

Oliver's Branch

expense of the Festive Season. All in all, Jill felt relaxed and happy.
Life was good.

*

It was a crisp if chilly day, when Jill set off to fetch Sarah from the
airport. Because there was very little traffic, Jill was able to look
over Souda Bay as she ascended along the winding road. It was
exceptionally picturesque, the sea crystal clear and the sky
cloudless. It never failed to take her breath away.

Sarah looked relaxed and very smart. Jill seemed to live in jeans and
a fleece and very rarely had the opportunity, or the inclination, to
dress up.

"Hello you," she said as she gave her friend a hug. "You look really
well and I love the suit."
"I'd have been a lot happier in jeans and a sweater but the whole
family came to see me off, so I thought I better make an effort. Don't
worry everything in the suitcase is far more practical and down to
earth. Anyway, it's great to be back. I've done nothing but talk about
this amazing island and your home since I left. Somehow I don't
think I'll be quite so enamoured with Calcutta."

In the car Sarah continued to explain the posting to her. "I'll be
working with a Doctor Sudru Aziz. He's been amazing and we've
corresponded via e-mail over the last few months. I'm going to be
staying with him and his wife. So as soon as I arrive I'll be getting
straight into the job. He started his career as a plastic surgeon in
California, but found it all so facile and superficial he returned to
India. His wife is a teacher. He met her on the plane flying back to
India. They seem really nice people." Sarah stopped talking and
gazed out at Souda Bay. "God, that view is just so amazing, it's like a
picture postcard. I love this place. Anyway, enough about me, you've
obviously been quite busy. How is your patient? I must admit I never
imagined you being able to provide post-operative care. You never
cease to amaze me."

Jill recounted various stories, revealing some of Irini's 'little foibles'
and they both spent the rest of the journey in fits of laughter.
"The best thing about it is the fact that Tacky gave me €750, which I
intend to spend on Christmas stuff. Don't think you'll just be sitting
around, there's going to be masses to do."
"Just as long as you don't expect me to help you with those clove
orange things. After you'd mentioned it on the phone I had this
sudden flashback. Everyone seemed to pick up the technique really

216

Ruth Manning

quickly at school, except me. I just ended up with a gunky mess of split orange and broken cloves. Matron thought I was just messing around and threatened me with a detention, after I'd desecrated about 4 oranges." Sarah put on an old fashioned, clipped, Queen's English accent and said, *"If you don't apply yourself to the task, my dear girl, I will be forced to give you a detention. You will have to complete a whole pomander ball, which looks like a pomander ball, as opposed to this disgusting abomination! If small Victorian children could make them, then so can you."* I think I just about succeeded, with your help, before she punished me. My mum loved it though and that's all I cared about. Bloody old witch, wasn't she, Matron I mean, not my mum. *"*

They were just turning into the carport as Jill replied. "No, I've finished those anyway! No *arty farty stuff*, I promise. It really is great having you here though, we're going to have a great time."

Oliver's Branch

Forty five.

They did indeed have a wonderful time in the days leading up to
Christmas. After they completed a list of all the food they wanted,
including many traditional English bits and pieces, they went on a
trawl of all the supermarkets and stores, looking for everything. It
proved relatively painless with regards to some items and incredibly
difficult with others. The turkey and rack of lamb they bought
locally. The butcher assured them all the meat was locally farmed.
Bird's Custard, a Christmas pudding, Paxo sausage stuffing mix and
mint sauce were also found relatively easily, if slightly overpriced,
but Jacobs Cream Crackers and pickled walnuts were a completely
different story. Eventually they were directed to a newly-opened
English shop, which imported produce from Tesco, where they
completed their mission. "Bloody *FOUR EUROS* for a small packet
of crackers!" Jill exclaimed. "We ought to buy caviar to put on them
instead of Cheddar cheese."

They also went Christmas shopping in Chania. Jill was clueless as to
what you bought for someone who was going off to work in Calcutta,
but eventually chose a traditional Cretan shawl, woven in bright
colours and as soft as silk. Because there were no real Christmas
trees on the island, and Jill refused to have a fake one, they
decorated a sledge Jill brought from England. Her father made it for
her when she was a very little girl and she knew she would never
part with it. All the wrapped gifts were placed on the seat and it
looked very festive, set off, of course, by two pomander balls, which
glittered in the candle light. There had also been some parcels from
England and these too lay wrapped and waiting. She wondered what
Nick and Grace had sent, but didn't surmise. She was looking
forward to being surprised. Jill also bought gifts for her neighbours,
Lefteris, Stella and Stelios. These were added to the pile.

The days flew by and in the week leading up to Christmas they were
both awoken, one morning, by the sound of tinkling coming from
outside the front door. When Jill opened it she was greeted by about
twenty small children, all happily hitting triangles and shouting
"Happy Christmas." Apparently they collected sweets and cakes
from all the villagers and then there was a big party at the school,
where the produce was demolished. Jill managed to find a family
size bag of Mars bars and they skipped off, delighted with the gift.

Family and friends from Athens also started to arrive in the village.
Every night you could hear the sound of people laughing and singing
in nearby houses. Sarah and Jill were invited over to Mitsou's house

218

Ruth Manning

one evening for a night of songs. When they arrived the enormous table was sagging under plate upon plate of food. Eleni explained that a group of men from around the area joined together, many years ago, to keep the tradition of Cretan music and songs alive. Mitsou was a young man when he joined, but he still went to practices every few months.

Looking around it was easy to see who the singers were. They were all dressed in Cretan national costume, as were various musicians, who were sat around tuning violins and bouzoukis. There were very few women and those present seemed to be busy in the kitchen. Eleni sat the two women down at the far end of the table, close to an enormous open fire place. "You must eat and drink and then eat more. I have spent all week preparing the food, so do not be shy. Mitsou is also roasting a goat on the spit outside, so there is plenty of meat."

It proved to be a magical evening. The singing was sonorous and perfectly executed, the musicians each having a specific part to play. There was a great deal of back-slapping and as the evening progressed and the wine flowed freely, the men started to dance. The women joined in and clapped to the beat, but this was definitely the men's night. The women all helped in clearing plates and producing more and more food.

Both Jill and Sarah had a wonderful time, and when they said their goodbyes, at well after two in the morning, neither of them could walk in a straight line. Luckily they only had to make their way next door. They had both collapsed in their beds exhausted and slightly the worse for wear.

*

Christmas Eve day was beautiful. There was a crystal clear sky and it was relatively mild. The mountains, which rose majestically in the background, were covered in thick snow and glistened in the sunlight.

After breakfast, Jill and Sarah took Dyson out for a long walk. Everyone they passed nodded their heads and wished them "Cronya Polla." - Many years. Dyson ran ahead and disappeared into orange and olive orchards which skirted the sides of the road. When they returned Stella was just coming out of Jill's gate. "I have brought you some gifts and tomorrow Lefteris and I will come to see you. Then, the following day, we will be having a table. You have to come."

Oliver's Branch

On the table was a large box with five or six carrier bags in it. Each one contained cooked meat and vegetable dishes. Completely taken aback she thanked Stella profusely, then on sudden impulse, found herself saying, "You will come and have dinner with us tomorrow then? With all this beautiful food plus what we are cooking we need more than three people. Please come."

"Of course we will come. Because there is only Lefteris and I this year, I will not be fussing in the kitchen. So yes, we would enjoy your company. Thank you."

Jill explained that the meal should be on the table by about two in the afternoon, but to come over any time. Stella went off to tell Lefteris about the invitation. Sarah followed Jill into the kitchen. "Well this certainly is turning out to be a bit of a gathering. Thank God we bought enough food to feed an army. Come on, I think we better start getting organised, we've got a lot to do."

The rest of the day flew by, as they prepared the meat and vegetables, and organised the kitchen so that everything was on hand. By five in the afternoon, with all the food prepared and ready for cooking the following day, and all the washing up done and put away, they were ready.

Sarah sank down on one of the kitchen chairs, running a hand through her hair. "I'm absolutely exhausted, but I think we've done rather well."

Jill sat down next to her, "I agree. Thank goodness we decided to have a quiet night tonight and chill out with a DVD. I've had quite enough excitement for one day. Let's heat up a pizza and take one of those boxes of mince pies upstairs and relax."

They had just finished the pizza and were heating the mince pies, when they heard someone calling them. Opening the door, they saw Stelios walking up the path, with two large bottles of wine in his hands. "I have come to have a drink with my two favourite ladies, to celebrate the coming of Christmas. But first I am going to light your fire for you, as a Christmas gift." He went into the kitchen and placed both bottles on the table, then he brought in some wood and busied himself upstairs. Soon, the crackle of wood and rush of flames could be heard. Jill placed three glasses and a large bowl of crisps on the table, hoping it would be just a quick drink and not a drunken evening.

As things turned out it wasn't until both bottles were empty that Stelios got up to leave. It was almost nine O'clock and they had had a very enjoyable few hours. Stelios was full of knowledgeable, local titbits. He informed them the actual translation of the name of the village, was Bramble Pit. Jill felt this was slightly less romantic

220

than the Greek name. He told them some facts about the valley, and a great deal about the last war, when the Cretans stood their ground against the Germans. He was a good orator and both women were fascinated.

"I could tell you so much more, but maybe another day. Now I must walk home. I am too drunk to drive. I will come to eat about one o'clock tomorrow, yes? I will bring more wine with me." They all wished each other a good night and Jill wished Stelios a safe trip home. With a final wave to them both, he was engulfed by the night.

"So much for the quiet life, Jill. Do you think it's safe to batten down the hatches and watch the DVD now?" Jill was so tired she wasn't sure she could watch a whole film, but agreed to try. "I'll just heat up these mince pies and then we'll give it a go, OK?"
Sarah sat watching her friend as she put them on a plate in the microwave. "This place really is amazing you know. I wonder what everyone is doing right now, in England. This is all so different. People seem to know how to enjoy themselves far more here, don't they?"
Jill was just about to reply when there was a knock on the door. "Oh God, who the hell is it this time?" she exclaimed as she opened it up. Before she took in who was there, a familiar voice was filling the evening silence.

"Hi mum. I told you I wanted to be with you for Christmas!" Grace ran into her mothers arms. Jill was totally speechless. "We've parked the Winnebago on your empty plot, Jason though it was the best place. Come on...here's someone you really, really need to meet." With this she put out her hand and Jill obediently grasped it, feeling like a small child; she allowed her daughter to drag her across the orchard, to meet what was going to be... the best Christmas gift... ever.

"...look forward with hope."

Printed in Great Britain
by Amazon